Dan Fesperman is a reporter for the *Baltimore Sun* and worked in its Berlin bureau during the years of the civil war in former Yugoslavia, as well as in Afghanistan during the recent conflict. *Lie in the Dark* is his first novel and won the CWA John Creasey Award for Best First Crime Novel in 1999. His second novel, *The Small Boat of Great Sorrows*, won the CWA Steel Dagger for Thriller of the Year in 2003 and his new novel, *The Warlord's Son*, will shortly be published by Bantam Press.

Acclaim for *Lie in the Dark*:

'One of the best books I have read for a long time'
Sunday Telegraph

'A quite astonishing first novel which injects the reader into the heart of the darkness which was Sarajevo at the height of the Yugoslav conflict. Reading this book is like being there. If Fesperman had taken me any closer to the action I'd be demanding a flak jacket . . . this is a humane and moving book, a great crime novel. A great novel, period'
Ian Rankin

'A haunting ice-cool novel – *The Third Man* meets *Gorky Park*. Stunning'
Daily Mirror

'A début novel of immense power'
The Times

Acclaim for *The Small Boat of Great Sorrows*:

'Thoroughly recommended . . . Has the tang of someone writing with conviction, compassion and, above all, an understanding of the Balkans'
Observer

'A dark and morally complex novel that won this year's Crime Writers' Association Ian Fleming Steel Dagger – the top award for a thriller'
Daily Telegraph

www.**booksattransworld**.co.uk

Also by Dan Fesperman

THE SMALL BOAT OF GREAT SORROWS
THE WARLORD'S SON

LIE IN THE DARK

Dan Fesperman

PUBLISHED May/04

EDITION NT (01)

PRINT No. 8,850

COVER PTR CW

BLACK SWAN

LIE IN THE DARK
A BLACK SWAN BOOK : 0 552 77268 2

Originally published in Great Britain by No Exit Press

PRINTING HISTORY
No Exit Press edition published 2000
Black Swan edition published 2004

1 3 5 7 9 10 8 6 4 2

Set in 11/12½pt Melior by
Kestrel Data, Exeter, Devon.

Black Swan Books are published by Transworld Publishers,
61–63 Uxbridge Road, London W5 5SA,
a division of The Random House Group Ltd,
in Australia by Random House Australia (Pty) Ltd,
20 Alfred Street, Milsons Point, Sydney, NSW 2061, Australia,
in New Zealand by Random House New Zealand Ltd,
18 Poland Road, Glenfield, Auckland 10, New Zealand
and in South Africa by Random House (Pty) Ltd,
Endulini, 5a Jubilee Road, Parktown 2193, South Africa.

Printed and bound in Great Britain by
Cox & Wyman Ltd, Reading, Berkshire.

Papers used by Transworld Publishers are natural, recyclable
products made from wood grown in sustainable forests.
The manufacturing processes conform to the environmental
regulations of the country of origin.

For Liz

I would like to express my gratitude to some of the many people who helped along the way. Thank-you to Claudia Stillman and Jim Shumaker, for the tools; to Jeff Price, for the opportunity; to Vladimir Jovanovic, Neven Nezemovic, Mustafa Pasha, and Slobodan Kosanovic, for sharing their knowledge; to Muamer Herceglija, Davt Bibic, and Zarko Bulic, for guiding me through Sarajevo's wartime legal system; to Charles Hill of Scotland Yard and Colin Kaiser of the Council of Europe, for insights on the art world's larcenous underbelly; to Milos Vasic and to the fine Lynn H. Nicholas book, *The Rape of Europa*, for historic perspective; to Laura Lippman, William C. Bowie and Patrick McGuire, for valuable advice and support; to Jane Chelius and Juris Jurjevics, for sharp editing and making it all possible; and to my wife, Liz Bowie, and my parents, Bill and Ginny Fesperman, for all of the above and everything in between.

1

He began the day, as always, by counting the grave-diggers out his front window. There were nine this morning, moving through the snow a hundred yards away in the middle of what used to be a children's soccer field. They stopped to light cigarettes, heads bowed like mourners, the shadows of stubble faintly visible on hollowed cheeks. Then they shed their thin coats and moved apart in a ragged line. Backs bent, they began stabbing at the ground with picks and shovels.

They moved slowly at first, working the cold and sleepiness out of creaky joints. But Vlado Petric was in no hurry. He'd watched often enough to know what came next.

Soon brown gashes of mud would take shape at their feet. Then, as the men warmed to their task, the gashes would expand into neat rectangles, and as the rectangles deepened the gravediggers would disappear into the earth. Within an hour only their heads would be visible. Then Vlado would leave his apartment to walk to work through the streets of Sarajevo.

Vlado had come to depend on the gravediggers' punctuality. He knew they liked to finish early, while the snipers and artillery crews of the surrounding hills were still asleep in the mist, groggy from another night in the mud with their plum brandy. By midmorning the gunners would also be stretching muscles and lighting cigarettes. Then they, too, would bend to their work, and from then until nightfall the soccer field would be safe only for the dead.

Vlado wondered sometimes why he still bothered to watch this morning ritual, yet he found its arithmetic irresistible. It was his daily census of the war. As the holes took shape they totted up the day's account like the black beads of an abacus. Large crowds inevitably followed a day of heavy shelling, or one of the sad little hillside offensives that rattled distantly like a broken toy. On one busy morning he'd counted thirty-four men at work, checking twice to make sure as they weaved and crossed, dirt flying as if from a series of small explosions. The vapors rising from their sweat and cigarettes had poured into the sky like the smoke of a small factory.

Lately, however, there had been layoffs and shorter hours. Today's crew of nine rendered a judgement of poor aim and low ammunition on the previous day. In winter the war always lost steam.

One might also call Vlado's interest professional. Sometimes his own workday took shape out on the field, in graves for those claimed not by snipers, explosions, illness, or old age. Vlado was a homicide investigator for the local police, and still gainfully if ponderously employed.

It was an occupation good for a few bitter laughs with friends, amused to find small-time killing still worthy of attention after twenty-one months of war. To them, Vlado's task was that of a plumber fixing leaky toilets in the middle of a flood, an auto mechanic patching tires while the engine burned to a cinder.

Why bother, they would ask. Why not just leave it all until the end of the war. By then all your suspects will be dead anyway.

Invariably he would reply with a muttering chuckle, eyes lowered, in the time-honored humility of all who must answer for making their living from the dead. Then he would allow as how, yes, they were probably right. What a fool he was. Laughs all around. Have another one on me, gentlemen.

So they would drink to his folly, someone's bottle of rancid homebrew passed from hand to hand, and then they would move on to other subjects – soccer, or women, or the war. Always, eventually, the war. But he would linger a moment with his thoughts. No, they were not right at all, he would reassure himself. The same two motivations which had kept him going before the war could still sustain him. Or at least he hoped they could.

One was the small, slender promise that beckons to all homicide detectives – that someday, something worthy and noble would come of his work. For the clever and the persistent, perhaps something larger lurked behind the daily body count. In the way that an epidemiologist knows that a single autopsy can provide the key to a pandemic, Vlado clung to a belief that, now and then, one murder offered a portal to machinations far greater than the pulling of a trigger or the plunging of a blade.

But could this still be true in wartime? And here the doubts threatened to stop him cold, so he hastily moved on to reason number two – the puzzle of motive, diagramming the inner levers and flywheels driving the machinery of rage. Here again, the war had muddled the calculations. Now the mechanisms all seemed increasingly predictable, guided by remote

11

control from the big guns in the hills. Each act shook to their reverberations. Every moment of passion sprang from two years of misery.

Yet Vlado couldn't help but marvel at the enduring popularity of murder. He knew from his history texts what war was supposed to do to people. In Stalingrad they ate rats and burned furniture to stay warm, but they stuck together. Even in London, fat and soft London, suicides dropped and mental health soared. But now he wondered if it hadn't all been some great warm lie of wartime propaganda. Because, if anything, people succumbed more easily now to the passions that had always done them in. And as the siege grumbled on, spurned lovers still shot each other naked and dead, drunks stabbed other drunks for a bottle, and gamblers died as ever for their debts.

The opportunities for such killings had never been richer.

There were weapons everywhere – battered models from Iran and Afghanistan with ammunition clips curling like bananas, sleek Belgian automatics from the tidy gunshops of Switzerland, ancient and hulking old Tommies from God-knows-where, and every cheap Kalashnikov ripoff ever made in the Eastern Bloc. The hills of old Yugoslavia had been overrun at last by the arms of the Warsaw Pact in a way the late, great Tito had never envisioned.

In moments when the war lagged, full employment for these weapons was guaranteed by the smugglers and black marketeers, too numerous to count. They darted about in their own war of attrition, the cheated in vengeful pursuit of the cheating. And with nowhere to run but the deadly noose of the hills, the chase was usually short and decisive.

Even when both of Vlado's reasons for justifying

continued employment faltered, he had a worthy fall-back: The job kept him out of the army. It was no small accomplishment these days, when even young boys in muddy jeans and flannel shirts trooped uphill nightly to the front.

That was the thought that always dragged him from his window on his blackest mornings, out onto the walkway of the dreary block of flats perched above the soccer field.

Had the gravediggers ever paused to gaze back on these mornings, they would have made out the thin shape of a man in his early thirties, draped in dark clothes. Slender to begin with, Vlado had been further narrowed by the diet of wartime until his deep brown eyes were almost spectral in their sockets. A face once quick to smile was now guarded, uncertain. A small crease above the bridge of his nose had deepened and dug in, setting itself up as the new, solemn master of the laugh lines crinkling around his eyes. His black hair was stiff, clipped short and uneven by his own hand with a blunt pair of children's scissors, receding ever more rapidly at the crown and temples. The only holdover from before the war was his voice, flowing out deep and soft, still the comfortable sort of baritone that beckons one into a warm, smoky room of old friends.

Behind him, in the small living room and kitchen, was all that remained of Vlado's prewar world. For more than a year and a half his wife and daughter had been gone, evacuated to Germany. The door to his daughter's room hadn't been opened for weeks, nor had the door to his and his wife's old bedroom. He had gradually drawn his possessions and his existence together, partly because it kept him away from the windows more exposed to sniper and artillery fire, and partly to conserve the precious light and heat from his illegal gas hookups, which burned fitfully and low under dwindling pressure. But it was also his way of burrowing in for the duration, of tending his own weak flame against the forces that could blow it out.

In approaching each day he had developed a keen sense of pace, of constant adjustment. Those who burned too brightly, he knew from watching, never lasted. They were the ones whose passions eventually led them running into free-fire zones, screaming either in madness or in a final outpouring of impotent rage.

But let your flame turn too low, fail to coax it along, and you ended up at the other extreme, spent and empty. You saw them in doorways, or hunched at the back of cafés, greasy-haired, staring vacantly, clothes in tatters. They never stopped retreating, ending up at the bottom of either a bottle or a grave.

Vlado was a Catholic, which meant he was classified as a Croat, something he'd never much thought about nor wanted to until the past two years. The precision of the label was questionable, given his mixed parentage. His father had been Muslim, his mother Catholic. She'd made sure he was baptized, though she'd never been much for church herself. Then she'd spent years dragging him off to religious instruction and holiday mass only to see her efforts go to waste.

Now, one's ethnic background seemed to be the first thing everyone in an official position wanted to know. Your answer could get you killed in some places, promoted in others.

It was easy enough information to find out, listed right there on your identification papers. The ethnic labels were remnants of the various competing empires that had clashed in these hills for centuries. The Ottoman Turks had run the show for a while, bringing

Islam and the sultan's bureaucracy, only to run up against the Austrians, who brought Catholicism, impeccable record keeping, and streets laden with their layer-cake architecture.

From the east there had always been the Russians to worry about, sharing their Eastern Orthodox Christianity and Cyrillic alphabet with the Serbs. Then the Nazis had come along and overwhelmed everyone, linking up just long enough with nationalist Croats, the Ustasha, to lay waste to a few hundred thousand Serbs. Sometimes the Muslims had joined in the killing. Sometimes they'd been among the victims. But all sides were supposedly forgiven under the new mantle of the eventual victor, the postwar communist regime of Marshal Tito. Tito proceeded to hold the fractious sides together for nearly half a century, chiefly by acting as if no one had ever hated each other to begin with. He banished all talk of ethnic nationalism and mistrust, blithely announcing that henceforth brotherhood would prevail.

It almost worked.

But when Tito died, the ethnic zealots rediscovered their voices, and the Serbs crowed the loudest. Tales of past massacres, kept alive through the decades around family tables, emerged shiny and refurbished. The old fears were coaxed out of cellars and attics, renourished by a new diet of ethnic propaganda. Out came the old labels of mistrust. If you were a Croat, that must mean you were Ustasha. Any Serb was a Chetnik. A Muslim? No better than a Turk. When things began to fall apart, they collapsed in a hurry.

The Serbs, holding the bulk of the army, immediately and mercilessly seized the upper hand, and Tito's ultimate failure was now evident in the lines of fire dividing the city. Standing on every surrounding hill were the Serb guns and trenches, and an army determined to squeeze Sarajevo until it became their own. They also held much of the ground within the city on the far bank of the Miljacka River, which curled through the town from east to west like a crooked spine.

Trapped along with Vlado on the north bank, in the old city center, were two hundred thousand people, mostly Muslim, occasionally Croat and very occasionally Serb. But, as with Vlado, the labels were often ambiguous. Mixed marriages accounted for a quarter of the population, which only further enraged the Serbs. Bohemian little Sarajevo, too clever for her own good, was paying the price for years of incestuous pleasure. Now the Serbs seemed bent on leveling the city if they couldn't capture it, taking it apart brick by brick, person by person.

Vlado had gone his entire life without really considering what it meant to be a Catholic, and he saw no reason to start now. He'd stepped into a church only three times in the past twelve years, twice for funerals, and certainly not at all for his marriage, a civil ceremony in which he'd wed the Muslim daughter of a Serb mother.

His only other trip to church had been his most recent, to investigate the murder of a priest found dead in a confessional. A jealous husband had shot the priest after finding a boxful of passionate letters on parish stationery in his wife's closet. The husband had walked into the booth, sat down, fired twice through the latticed partition, then turned the gun on himself. Vlado had felt cheated by the suicide. He'd always wanted to know if there had been any final conversation. He wondered if either side had offered absolution before the gun had passed judgement on both. Both had made adequate penance in the end, by Vlado's way of thinking, never mind what the Church thought.

Had the gravediggers looked Vlado's way on this morning they might also have seen a cup of coffee in his hand. At $20 a pound on a salary of one dollar a month, often paid in cigarettes, it was no small luxury. Such was the state of the local currency and the black market that ruled the city.

He smiled to himself with a slight flush of embarrassment recalling how he'd acquired the coffee the day before. He had begged for it, really. Not overtly, but in an obvious enough way, having learned how to go about such things.

A British journalist had telephoned for an interview and Vlado had gladly set a time. The subject was to be homicide in the city of death, as well as the ever present topic of the local corruption that was eating away at the city from within. It was a topic Vlado was forbidden to discuss, but that was beside the point. He knew as well as anyone that journalists, U.N. people, and other outsiders were always eager to ingratiate themselves with their bags full of booty – coffee, whiskey, cartons of Marlboros, sometimes even sugar. Who knows how generous they might be if you had information they wanted, whether you could supply it or not.

The items a journalist might offer could fetch Deutschemarks, dollars, friends and influence, or even a prostitute for an hour or so. The whores skulking by the gates of the French U.N. garrison could be had for a couple of packs of Marlboros, a price which the U.N. troops found quite reasonable. Some had given up smoking altogether.

The journalist had arrived right on time, a fleshy

17

bundle of bustle and British good cheer, pinkening at the edges from his climb up the stairs, like a soft piece of fruit about to turn bad. He thrust his hand outward in greeting as he fairly shouted, 'Toby Perkins, *Evening Standard*. Pleased to meet you.'

Vlado replied with a grave stare, spooning instant coffee into a steaming cup of water, then stirring the brown crystals with the reverence of an alchemist handling gold dust.

'My last cup,' he announced, holding it toward the reporter. 'Please, take it.' It set just the right tone, Vlado thought. He inwardly congratulated himself, knowing from Toby's thin smile and reddening cheeks that the rest would be easy.

And it was.

Toby immediately set down the mug and ducked toward his satchel, grunting and bending awkwardly from the bulk of an armored flak vest girdling his chest. Just about every outsider wore them, although locals tended to wonder what all the fuss was about. Why go to the trouble when you could still get your head blown off?

When Toby rose, his smile was wide and generous, and he held a one-pound jar of Nescafé. Now he was the millionaire with the shiny coin for the miserable waif. All that was left was to pat the boy on the head. But Vlado had no qualms of pride. He only wondered what else might be clinking around in the big bag.

Vlado first offered the obligatory refusal, down-grading his polished English to singsong cadence to better suit the moment. Play the dumb, stiff local bureaucrat for a while and Toby might give up a little quicker.

'Oh no, it would not be a possibility.'

Toby insisted, as they always did. 'Really. Please. Go

ahead. I've got so many, and, well, I'm leaving Monday anyway.'

Leaving Monday. That always stopped him with these people, whether it was journalists, aid workers, or some Western celebrity seeking a little wartime atmosphere and some publicity. They came and went like tourists, flashing a blue-and-white U.N. card to pass through checkpoints where just about any local would be stopped cold. Or shot. Even if he was a police detective. Only foreigners left town so easily. They boarded U.N. cargo planes, deep-bellied green tubs that lumbered up over the hills and away. Then they no doubt toasted their survival that very night in some warm place where the windows had glass, not flapping sheets of plastic, and where there was electric lighting and plenty of cold beer.

So Vlado felt only the slightest twinge of guilt when he locked the jar of coffee in a desk drawer and announced, 'I am sorry, but my superiors have told me that I really shouldn't talk to you. At least not on this subject. Maybe we can speak a few minutes "off the record," as people in your profession say, but anything more would not be possible.'

Then had come the unpleasant part. Toby had decided to deliver a lecture. 'Yes, that's the spirit, isn't it. Remain silent and preserve the myth.'

'The myth?' Vlado had asked, curious to hear the outside world's latest take on Balkan madness.

'The myth of ethnic peace and harmony among the poor beleagured people of Sarajevo. Of clean government with nothing but noble intent. Yes, you're victims, we all know that. Bloody well can't turn on our televisions without seeing another weeping Sarajevan saying "All you need is love." But whenever the subject of ill-gotten gains and bad players behind the scenes comes up, you go all quiet on us and resort to your ultimate fallback: Blame the Serbs. The Chetniks did it. And they did, didn't they. Threw you out of half the city and three-quarters of your country.

'But you're not exactly saints down here are you, pardon the botched religious metaphor. What about revealing some of your own bad apples for a change? How long do you think this war would go on if some key people in key places suddenly stopped making money off it?'

'You find our hatreds unconvincing, I take it? Perhaps poor old Marx was right, after all, even if he's no longer in fashion. In the West, it's always about money.'

'Because it *is* always about money, or power, or whatever form of wealth you want to name,' Toby said. 'And that's true in the East as well. Why do you think the Serbs grabbed half your country right out of the gate? Not so they could lord it over you lovely people, I can tell you that. It was an economic land grab, plain and simple, dressed up as an ethnic holy crusade. "Save our Serbian brothers. Oh, but while you're at it, take that factory over there, won't you?" I'm not saying there's any shortage of genuine hatred up in those hills. There are enough zealots to keep these armies burning for years. But look at the support systems and the lines of supply. All the bit players that prop it up. Who needs morale when you've got a nice flow of hard currency to keep the officers happy? Take that away and who knows, maybe the whole thing begins to rot from the inside out. Maybe the hatred isn't enough anymore. Maybe you even end up with a ceasefire that lasts long enough for something more than allowing the next shipment of tobacco and liquor to come across the lines. With fifty per cent of the proceeds going to the local constabulary, of course.'

'I think you are oversimplifying a complex situation.'

'Yes, well that's what I'm paid for, isn't it. Take all the nice blurry grays and turn them into black and white for the public to digest before moving on to the horoscopes and the latest from the Royals. But before you dismiss me as just another hack, which is exactly what I am, by the way, let me tell you a little story I picked up down the road in your city of Mostar – then we'll see what you think.'

The last thing Vlado wanted from this blustering little man was an object lesson, but he'd paid for at least that much with the pound of coffee, so Vlado let him ramble on.

'You know the situation in Mostar, right?' Toby said, his face more flushed by the minute. 'Even worse than here, in a way. Croats and Muslims fighting each other tooth and nail down in the streets, shooting at each other from across the river, while the Serbs sit on the mountains to the east and lob shells on the both of them. Like a bored old housewife pouring boiling water onto a couple of fighting alley cats.

'Well, a few weeks ago the local Muslim commander's doing his usual bit for the home side when he starts running low on artillery shells. So he gets on the radio and calls his mate on the next hill to ask for more. "Sorry, lads, we're running low ourselves. Can't spare you a single shot. Arms embargo and all that, you know."

'So who should pipe up on the same frequency, because everybody's using the same old Yugoslav army radios anyway, but our Serb friend up on the mountain. We'll call him Slobo.

'"If it's shells you need, we've got all you'd ever

want," General Slobo says. "And at popular prices."

'"Great," General Mohamad says. '"But what about delivery? The Croats are between you and us."

'"No problem," Slobo says. "My Croat friend, Commander Tomislav, can bring them right to your doorstep for a small commission, say, twenty-five per cent of the ordnance." So they haggle for a while over price, set a time and place for delivery. Then they chat up the U.N. to arrange a temporary "ceasefire" to allow for shipments of "humanitarian aid," and the whole thing goes off without a hitch. The U.N. people spend a whole day patting themselves on the back, then can't understand why things go sour as soon as the last truck leaves. So there you go: enemy number-one arms enemy number-two with the help of enemy number-three, while greasing the palms of God knows how many generals, staff officers, subordinates and checkpoint trolls along the way. And all you people down here want to talk about is hatred, intolerance, and "woe is me." When the topic's corruption, everyone clams up.'

Vlado had no answer for him. Nor did he doubt that Toby's little story had been true. He'd heard much of the same sort of thing around here. So he decided to just sit. Toby would be bored soon enough.

Indeed he was. Sighing, he pulled a business card from his bag.

'If you should ever happen to change your mind, here's my card. You can reach me at room four thirty-four of the Holiday Inn. You know the place, the big yellow dump on the front line with all the shell holes. But it's the only room in town. Who knows, if you decide a week from now to talk, I might even be able to scrounge you a sack of sugar. A little palm greasing for the good guys for a change.'

And it was that parting message, Vlado supposed, that had left him with the bitter aftertaste, a hint of shame that had played at the edge of his thoughts for the rest of the day, like the vivid last image from a waking dream.

But coffee was coffee, and he savored another sip, cradling the cup in both hands for warmth as he gazed toward the soccer field. What was so embarrassing about a little ingenuity, he told himself. He sipped the gritty remains and glanced back outside. The grave-diggers were waist-deep. He had perhaps another half hour before the snipers would be stirring, although he had a feeling it would be another slow day.

Some mornings he killed the extra time by working on his growing army of model soldiers. They lay before him on a small workbench he'd set up in the kitchen, row upon row of dash and color. It was a hobby he'd taken up years ago, partly out of his bookish fascination with military history, only to immediately find it tedious, a headache of minor details. And when impatience turned his work sloppy he'd given it up, packing away dozens of unpainted lead men that he'd bought in an industrious burst of optimism.

Then the war came. His wife and daughter evacuated the city after the first two months of fighting, leaving in a dusty convoy of school buses on a warm May morning. Women, children and old men waved from every window to a forlorn audience of young and middle-aged men, forced by the army to stay behind. Other families spilled from the sides of stuffed panel trucks, their colorful scarves flapping in the breeze that dried their tears.

That evening Vlado climbed to the roof of their four-story apartment block, hauling himself up the fire ladder along with a small folding chair and a bottle

23

of plum brandy. He sat down to watch the nightly bombardment as if it were a summer storm rolling in from the mountains. Distant artillery flashes played against the clouds with the red streams of tracer bullets, and he found himself gauging the range of each impact by counting the seconds before the blast, just as he'd done with his daughter to calm her fear of thunder. For a moment he recalled the fatherly comfort of having the weight of a child in one's lap, resting your chin on the top of the small head, the hair smelling of sunlight, playground sand, and baby shampoo.

He held the brandy bottle, sipping every few minutes, feeling the fire of each swallow ramble down his throat, the level dropping past the halfway mark as the bombardment groped its way around the city.

He was an attentive spectator. Over there was a blast, just by the hospital, yellow and deep, the sound reaching into his stomach. To the southwest, a few spiraling streamers whistled through the sky like crazed birds, headed toward the presidential building. Most everything else was happening off toward the highrise suburbs to the west, or in the hills to the north. Tomorrow there would be more to watch. And the day after that. He could spend the entire war up here.

Then a shell screamed nearby with a sudden moan, and landed with a heaving blast. The compression knocked him from the chair, and as he lay sprawled on his back he listened to glass showering from the windows of the building next door. He lay still for a moment, accounting for himself, attentive for pain, for the ooze and gush of blood. Feeling none, he stood. His face was covered with dust. He still clutched the neck of the brandy bottle in his right hand, but the rest had been shattered by a chunk of shrapnel. He looked shakily across the city, seeing not a soul and hearing nothing but a slight ringing in his ears. Then he turned and descended the ladder as fast as his trembling legs would allow.

The next morning he'd moved into the living room, closing the doors of the two bedrooms and folding open the sofa bed. Then he opened his old footlocker to retrieve his lost battalions of lead men along with the tiny bottles of paint and the thin, delicate brushes. He'd set up a workbench at the end of the small kitchen and welcomed tedium back into his home. That action, he now realized, had begun the slow and careful tending of his own weak flame, a means of nurturing it through the dead hours of winter darkness. By brushing on the gold edge of a tiny belt buckle, or the silver of a saber blade, the yellow of a helmet's plume, he moved through the hours and left them in his wake.

Six days after the rooftop explosion, he'd received word from the Red Cross that his wife and daughter had arrived in Berlin. They were living in an east-side highrise apartment with two other sets of mothers and children from Bosnia. From then on he was linked to them only by the mail that arrived fitfully, when at all, and by a once-a-month phone call that he made with the help of ham radio operators at Sarajevo's Jewish Community Center, one of the few lines of communication to the outside world not controlled by either the government or the international news media.

Now, deep into his second winter alone, most nights found him submerged in a haze of paint fumes and cigarette smoke, squinting in the dim glow of a thin flame of natural gas. The work was slowly blinding him, but it kept him off the roof and away from the bottle.

Vlado's interests ran to the armies of the Napoleonic

Age. He could tell you the trajectory and range of each painted fieldpiece in his model arsenal, or the fighting capabilities of nearly any unit of the era, whether Prussian, Russian or French.

It had occurred to him that perhaps he should think of the hobby as inappropriate now, an exercise in poor taste. He'd never had any illusions about what model soldiers represented. Nor did he doubt that fascination with guns and uniforms had some role in sustaining the war. He'd heard too many tales about refugee boys from country villages, new to the trenches, who were eager to settle old scores the moment they felt the power of a Kalashnikov in their hands.

But just as the men in the hills were no soldiers – an armed mob at best, he told himself – these leaden figures had about as much to do with real war as the drawings in his history books, with their bright arrows colliding mutely on clean, colorful maps.

A week ago he'd lined up twenty Austrian dragoons to spray with a coat of primer, having glued on their heads a few minutes earlier. He should have waited longer for the glue to set, but he'd been in a hurry. The blast of the spray blew off every head, as if by a tiny firing squad. It was a morning's labor gone to waste, but he'd laughed in spite of himself and hustled out the door. Later he'd started to tell some friends about it, then stopped. And when he'd returned home that night he hadn't been able to face them, the men of his toppled platoon, decapitated on his workbench, heads scattered on the floor like shotgun pellets.

This morning he'd waited until too late to get started, but his soldiers would hold until the evening. Their chances of going somewhere were about as good as his. He shrugged on his overcoat and headed out the door.

His office was down by the Miljacka River, just

across a bridge on the far bank, and only a few hundred yards from the frontline. At one time the police head-quarters had been located in the Interior Ministry building in the center of downtown. But early in the war the ministry had formed a new special police force, which promptly booted Vlado's unit out of the building and proceeded to take over nearly every important investigation in town.

Vlado had watched alternately astonished and dis-mayed as Interior's special police force violently rooted out the gangland core of the black market while cannily backing away whenever it scented official involve-ment. As Toby had suggested, it was an open secret that some people in high places with profitable connec-tions would just as soon see the war continue in its slow, plodding march, holding their markets captive a while longer. Yet this open knowledge was of the vaguest sort, names obscured.

Vlado chafed at this implicit demotion, knowing that the secret portals he sought had eased further beyond sight. But his superiors submitted quietly, and his department moved across the river to a newer building in a chockablock section of homes and businesses tucked within a few blocks of the Serb lines. Most of the far bank of the river, in fact, belonged to the Serbs, spreading uphill through the homes and churchyards of Grbavica to the forested rim of the mountaintops, up where the big guns sat.

The main buffer between the police station and the nearest Serb positions was a French U.N. garrison posted a block down river at Skenderia, next to the old speedskating rink from the '84 Olympics. A faded mural of the Olympic mascot, a grinning fox, leered down from a high brick wall, his smile pocked and dented by mortar rounds.

27

The new police building was a squat ugly affair of concrete and brown glass. During Yugoslavia's heyday it had housed a Communist Party youth center. Now about a fourth of the windows were either cracked or blown out, replaced by plywood and sheets of U.N. plastic held down by U.N. tape.

Government buildings were among the few in town with reliable electricity. Three large gasoline-powered generators kept just enough juice flowing to light and refrigerate the crime lab, such as it was. After that there was enough power for a few fluorescent tubes and a scattering of overworked space heaters that glowed like toasters. Every morning lately they were draped with soggy hats and socks. The smell alone was enough to make you want to come in late.

Vlado's walk took nearly half an hour, looping gradually downhill toward the river. When he left his house it began to snow, and by the time he reached the office the snow had turned to rain. It had been a mild winter, not even freezing the ground enough to trouble the gravediggers. Gray slush pooled in shell dimples and on the collapsed roofs of abandoned cars.

By the time Vlado arrived, Damir Begovic was ensconced at the next desk over. He was the city's only other homicide investigator. Before the war there had been a third, Dejan Vasic, a Serb. He was Vlado's friend, a companion for card games and family dinners. Their infant children had played together on weekends, clutching at each other's hair and drooling on each other's toys. They'd once lugged their families out to the Adriatic for a beach holiday, then celebrated their return by building a swing set together. Someday, they said, they'd build their children a treehouse up in a nice spot in the hills, a pretty one with a rope ladder, well hidden from hikers and older kids, but close enough to a good picnic spot to bring their whole families up.

A week or so before the war began, Dejan left town without a word, taking only his family and the service revolver from his desk. Vlado heard later they'd hoped to make it over the hills to Belgrade, but he wondered. Perhaps Dejan was still in the city, farther up the opposite hill, or only a few blocks away, writing murder reports in Grbavica, or in the northwest suburb of Ilizda. Maybe he was in the army, squibbing mortar rounds into the city center. Or he could be dead and rotting in a trench. Perhaps he'd made it to Vienna, or Berlin. Who could say?

Almost everyone still in Sarajevo knew someone like that, usually a Serb, someone who'd vanished without warning on the eve of the fighting, as if privy to a vision of what the city would become.

That left only Damir, likeable enough but seven years younger and, even in wartime, still elbowing happily through a smoky world of cafés and loud music. He was a bit of a rake, really, in his never-ending pursuit of new women, yet forgiveable if only for the childlike joy he took in his pleasures. When Damir had seen Vlado's soldiers he'd gushed like a schoolboy, an exuberant grin spreading across his broad, flat face. He'd hinted impishly that Vlado might even spare him a few, not realizing that Vlado would no sooner divide a unit than an antiques collector would break up a set of chairs. It had been a disastrous evening anyway, with Damir barging into the apartment with a woman in each hand and a bottle in each pocket of his overcoat, arriving to 'cheer up' Vlado with a party. It had taken two hours to usher them out the door, giggling and swaying in a noxious cloud of brandy.

But he was easy enough to work with in his

occasionally overbearing way. Early in the war they'd agreed that each detective would take every other homicide, an arrangement originally intended to keep either from hogging the work back when they wanted to stay as busy as possible. Now Damir seemed bored with death in all its guises, and their routine was all that kept him from slipping into permanent idleness on the job.

This day, like the last several, turned out to be another slow one, with nothing to do but read, gossip, and smoke. To make matters worse, Damir was far from his usual cheery self, sullen and grumbling through every hour. So it was something of a relief when the phone finally rang in the late afternoon.

Damir took the call, listened for a while, scribbled something, mumbled a phrase or two, then hung up and turned to Vlado.

'It seems that a gypsy woman with a grudge and a baby has just hammered her drunken husband to death during his afternoon nap. Her neighbor says the gypsy's ready to confess. I told her we'd have a street officer haul her in. In the meantime, here's where you'll find the dear departed.' He held out a scribbled address. 'All yours.'

'All mine? You took the call.' Vlado was eager for work, but this hardly sounded like the sort of case he'd had in mind.

'I got the last one, remember? Last Wednesday? Card players arguing politics with guns. One dead, one drunk, one arrested. Your turn.'

Vlado frowned and picked up his coat. An hour later and he'd have been out the door, headed for another dinner of beans and rice and a quiet night painting his dragoons and hussars. He mumbled something about the stupidity of taking turns, then cursed the

30

foolhardiness of answering telephones after 3 p.m. He grabbed the address and stalked away.

'Have the gypsy waiting at my desk when I get back,' he called over his shoulder to Damir. 'I want her calmed down and ready to talk. And try not to ask her out before I'm back, although she sounds like your type.'

'Yes, good with hand tools,' Damir answered, offering his first smile of the day.

'And thanks again.'

'My pleasure,' Damir shouted, already easing back in his chair.

2

Vlado headed into the melting slush, bound for the couple's home in what passed for a gypsy quarter, a narrow rack of two-story cinder-block buildings near the top of a steep, exposed hill just north of the city center. The Bosnian army often kept one of its few big guns up there, mostly for nuisance-firing at the Serbs, which prompted plenty of answering nuisance-fire, usually from even bigger guns. But it was only gypsies, the authorities reasoned. In a city where people still liked to talk about the unimportance of ethnic designation, gypsies had always been singled out as the lowest of the low. Their warren of apartments was a nasty place to live, even by wartime standards.

Ten minutes into his walk, a flushed and breathless Damir appeared at his side.

'Change your mind?' Vlado said.

'Needed the walk. Cooped up all day yesterday with nothing but paperwork, then all of this morning with nothing but a hangover. And in between was last night, which I'd just as soon forget altogether. So I'll at least make it up the hill with you. If that doesn't do the trick, I'll even help you write the report. But don't worry. I'll head back in time to have the gypsy woman checked in and ready for interrogation.'

'So, trouble with a woman?' Vlado asked. It was the only sort of trouble he could imagine Damir having.

'I wish. It's my mother and father.'

Damir had moved back in with his parents when the war began to make sure they'd be provided for. Also to avail himself of his mother's cooking. With fresh meat and produce having virtually disappeared, she was one of those resourceful cooks who still managed some variety – pies made of rice, 'French fries' shaped from a corn meal paste, and garden snails, soaked overnight then pan-fried with wild herbs. But the price for a fuller stomach was his mother's temper, vast and explosive, and Vlado figured there must have been another blow up.

'Your mother went off again?'

'Yes. The worst ever. And this time she went for maximum damage, and got it. From my father, at least, and maybe from me, too.'

'Well, give it a few days and it will blow over.'

'Not this time,' Damir said, shaking his head with grim assurance. 'All she did this time was tell me that everything I'd ever believed about my father was a lie.'

Vlado wasn't sure how to respond to that and, based on past experience, Damir wasn't likely to offer anything more until he was ready and willing. So they walked on a few minutes more without a word, until Damir abruptly resumed.

'All these years he's told me what a hero he'd been during the last war. Fighting the Nazis with Tito's Partisans. Hiding in caves and corn fields with the great man himself. Parachuting onto some mountain in the dark. Stories that I've heard a thousand times, and memorized every detail.'

'Then your mother says that he's been making some of it up, right? Which only makes him like every other man in this town over the age of 70. My uncle was the same way. Had us believing he was God's gift to guerilla warfare. And who says your mother's right anyway. She was just angry and saying whatever she could to make it hurt.'

'My father says she's right, that's who. And it wasn't just details she was talking about, or exaggerations. It was everything. The whole damn war. He hid out all right, with the neighbors next door, in their cellar. Looking after their two children. Once he came out to help move some cows – steal them is probably more like it – from the next village. The only gun his family had, he buried, hid it from his own father, and he never dug it up again. When my mother told me all this, he didn't even try to pretend anymore. He confessed just like any other common criminal who knows the evidence is against him. Then he pulled his chair into a corner and did nothing but cry. His face was gray, like he was turning to ashes before our eyes. My father, the great Partisan, nothing but a scared peasant wiping babies' noses in a root cellar.'

Vlado worried that almost any response would seem weak, banal, but he tried anyway.

'Even Tito lied about these things,' he said. 'Now everyone says he was sick in a cave during what was supposed to have been his greatest battle.'

'Yes, but Tito lied about everything. That was his job. This is my father, Vlado, and I'd always been a big enough fool to believe him. One of the reasons I wanted to be a big shot police investigator was so I might have half the adventures he did. When the war started, it's why I almost quit to join the army, figuring it was my biggest chance yet for heroics. And if it hadn't been for my mother crying and throwing a fit about it – and thank God she did – then I would have.

Now, who knows.' He shrugged, kept walking, 'So, here I am. Just taking a walk and doing my job. I'll get over it, though.'

But it was clear that for a while, at least, he wouldn't. Even Damir's customary medicine for a black mood – women and alcohol, taken liberally for one full evening – might be too weak to bring about a quick recovery. Vlado wondered what to say next, if anything. He tried out a few phrases in his head until his thoughts were interrupted by a gunshot, loud and close, echoing from across the river.

Whenever a sniper opened fire in daylight, it flipped a switch on every nervous system within range, especially for anyone standing in an exposed line of fire. Slack jaws tightened, eyes widened, bodies bent and curled, as if trying to melt into the pavement.

One never grew accustomed to it no matter how long the war dragged on, because inevitably someone got caught in the wrong place, fell, blood pooling, and became the twitching center of an empty circle as everyone else scattered. The circle remained empty until the danger passed and an ambulance came. Then the crowds leeched back toward the middle, and the body vanished. The blood remained, for the rain to wash away.

The body in question this time was a man in military uniform, about 30 feet ahead, in an intersection sheltered neither by buildings nor the walls of old cars stacked in protective barriers.

A woman who had just trotted through the area gasped upon reaching the safety of the corner where Vlado and Damir stood.

'I was practically next to him when it happened,' she said, a hand across her mouth, eyes wide. Her makeup was beginning to give way to a burst of perspiration.

35

The right shoulder of her coat was spattered with the man's blood.

'He was just walking,' she said, verging on hysteria. 'Just walking. Like he thought he was any old place, while everyone else was running. He should have known better. How couldn't he have known?'

For a moment it appeared that no one would step in to see if the man was still alive. He wasn't moving, and a semi-circle of blood oozed from beneath him like a scarlet cape thrown gracefully upon the ground. Then a large, well dressed man, smelling strongly of aftershave, shouldered through the crowd and trotted toward the body. He knelt quickly, a gold chain dangling from his neck.

'Stay back! I'll take care of this,' he shouted. People on both sides edged closer to the open area, as if shamed into helping. He gripped the man beneath both arms, grunted, and dragged the body through a smearing path of blood to the sheltered area where Vlado and Damir stood.

'Maybe we need to do something,' Vlado said.

'Better leave this one alone,' Damir muttered. 'The big guy runs one of the gasoline rackets. Must be one of his foot soldiers that got it.'

Reading Vlado's thoughts, Damir said, 'I guess he thought that being a man for all sides meant he was no longer at risk.'

Instead, the gangster's bold stroll through the intersection had violated the siege's unwritten code of conduct. If you showed a sniper respect, running like everyone else, chances are he would give you nothing but a bored glance through his sighting scope. But this fellow had made himself a walking insult, and a shooter, who may have intended to take the afternoon off, had been stirred to action.

For a moment the crowd's attention was diverted by the nearby shouts of a small man who had begun angrily lecturing a U.N. soldier at a sentry post a half-block away.

'You will stand here doing nothing the entire war until they kill us all!' the little man shouted, over and over, his face livid with rage. The plastic sacks in his hands, one filled with rice and the other with bread, swung back and forth like pendulums, as the man spluttered and roared. The soldier, a Jordanian, didn't seem to comprehend the local language, although he couldn't have missed the message. He stared blankly ahead while the man moved closer, dropping one of his bags to point and jab at the soldier's blue helmet.

The sight was arresting enough that at first Vlado paid little attention when Damir began to speak.

'The gypsy case is all yours, Vlado. In fact, the whole rest of the war is yours.'

Damir strolled away. As Vlado turned, he saw to his alarm that Damir was heading straight into the open intersection where the man had just been shot, walking no faster than a shuffling old man, shoulders slumped and head bent, hands in his pockets.

'What are you doing?' Vlado shouted.

Damir stopped only for a moment, looking back with a cold blank anger in his eyes.

'Don't worry Vlado, I will still do my job. I will have the gypsy ready for you, as requested.'

'Screw the work. Take the day off, the whole week. Just get yourself out of the open! Run!'

But Damir resumed his plodding gait, this time answering Vlado over his shoulder. 'In my own good time, Vlado. Not yours or anyone else's.'

The small crowd which had formed to watch the removal of the body now watched Damir with weary fascination. No one other than Vlado shouted or urged him on, conserving those energies for loved ones. Vlado decided to make a run for it, hoping to either tackle Damir or shove him to safety. Before he could move, there was a quick whizzing sound, followed by a loud metallic ping as a bullet struck a yellow traffic sign a few feet behind Damir. Then came the sharp report of the rifle itself, as the sound caught up to the consequences. The traffic sign quivered as if plucked by a hand from the clouds. A fresh hole rimmed in gray joined two others already orange with rust.

Surely the sniper would not miss twice, and Vlado again braced for a run, only to be interrupted by a second shot. It, too, struck the sign, though Damir had continued moving forward. Then came a third shot, and a fourth, with the sign pinging and quivering each time.

The sniper was taking target practice, and with each impact he was tapping out a message, a terse, cynical telegram of his disdain for them all.

Damir, of course, received the signal loud and clear, and as he finally reached the shelter of the opposite corner he turned and shouted to Vlado in a monotone, 'You see, this is our war. Games of chance before a live audience. And when the killing spills into the grandstand, you and me get to sort it out. Maybe someday we can make up our own stories of how heroic it all was.'

Damir kept walking, neither faster nor slower than before. His footsteps were drowned out by the shouts from the U.N. sentry post. The small angry man had still not relented in his harangue of the soldier, who, for all the impassiveness of his face, might as well have been made of lead.

*　　　*　　　*

The gypsy's home was predictable enough, like just about any other overcrowded apartment in the city these days: two rooms, with paint peeling on dingy walls, a garden hose creeping across the walls like a long green snake, carrying gas from an illegal hookup to a makeshift stove and to a second nozzle mounted precariously at eye level, spurting a small jet of flame that provided the only light in the gloom of late afternoon. On the stove was a large pot encrusted with day-old beans. The window glass was gone, taped over with milky, billowing plastic. The bed was pushed into a corner away from the window. A small bassinette sat nearby on the floor. The air was rank from sweat, whiskey, old food, and soiled diapers. And, yes, the smell of blood.

On the bed was the body of a large man sprawled face-down, his head a pulp of gore and matted hair. A hammer lay on the floor nearby, plastered with more of the same mess. Vlado took out his notebook and sat in a small chair to wait for Tomislav Grebo, who in the pared down police department was now both the evidence technician and the medical examiner, although his police work was decidedly secondary to his part-time career as a scrounger and small-time retailer. Grebo was in partnership with his cousin Mycky, who had a knack for coming up with the odds and ends necessary to keep life running in a broken city. Most mornings you'd find them seated behind a card table in the dimness of the drafty old market hall in the city center, peddling plumbing equipment that came in handy for everything from gas hookups to makeshift stoves. They'd recently expanded their operation to a second table, carrying stray cartons of Marlboros or whatever other items they managed to procure.

This meant it always took a few minutes to round up Grebo. Usually someone had to reach him on foot. But within a half hour he breezed into the apartment, rubbing his hands against the cold. He was tall and thin, with an unruly thatch of wavy dark brown hair and a thick mustache drooping above a long, narrow chin.

Grebo looked toward the bed, grimaced, then pulled an Instamatic camera from a bulging coat pocket.

'What's today's special?' Vlado asked, trying to cheer himself out of the funk he'd been in since watching Damir walk away.

'Cigarette lighters. Bics, too. Mycky came up with a whole case, don't ask me how.' He paused, placing his cigarette on a small table, a column of ash hanging over the edge. 'We sold a few and swapped some others for beer – Amstel, not the local shit – and a bag of salt.'

He snapped a photo, the flash popping, then waited for the print to slide from the front of the camera.

'Not a bad morning. He thinks if we're patient we can trade the rest for gasoline.'

'Why would anyone trade gasoline for cigarette lighters?' Vlado asked.

Grebo lowered his camera, frowning. 'Why would anyone trade a blow job for Marlboros?'

'Good point.'

'It all depends on need. Supply and demand. This is gut level capitalism, Vlado. After the war everything will be banks, accountants, and middlemen, so learn the easy stuff while you can.'

Vlado was used to these lectures. It amused him to think of the likes of Grebo as the future of the city's economy. Yet he admitted that the ways of barter and the black market baffled him. He considered his new jar of Nescafé. Perhaps he could trade a little for something to break the monotony of his diet, even if only for some cabbage.

'How much cabbage do you think I could get for a quarter pound of Nescafé?' he asked.

Grebo again lowered his camera, scowling now. 'Jesus, Mary, and God, Vlado,' Grebo said. Like Vlado, Grebo's father was a Muslim, his mother a Catholic, and he had been baptized a Catholic. But like some in Sarajevo, he expressed his religious affiliation mostly through his choice of curse words. 'Only an idiot would trade coffee for cabbage.'

'But you just said . . .'

'That's different. Marlboros for blow jobs, yes. Coffee for cabbage, not even on the same map. It's a matter of comparable worth. I keep telling you, it's supply and demand. You're still thinking like a Communist, a fucking Yugoslav. Coffee's as good as hard currency, save it for something special. Cabbage you can get with army cigarettes, and army cigarettes you can get anywhere.' He glanced furtively around the room, adding in a lowered voice. 'You might even find some here, unless the gypsy's cleared them out.'

Vlado continued to brood about his Nescafé. If not cabbage, then maybe some oranges? It made him tired to think about it. Better just to keep the coffee or he'd only end up feeling cheated.

They stepped around the body as they talked, not once mentioning it. Grebo snapped photos while Vlado jotted a note now and then, plotting out the room's dimensions in case anyone ever asked, which no one ever did. They began talking of food. People in Sarajevo sometimes seemed to talk of nothing else.

'Did you hear about Garovic,' Grebo said. 'Eating again on the U.N.'s tab, and they took him to Club Yez. Again.'

Garovic was Lutva Garovic, their boss. Club Yez was Sarajevo's best restaurant, safe and snug in a deep, brick cellar with a fireplace and a piano player. Every bottle at its bar had the right label, no matter what was really inside, and the kitchen had spices and fresh meat. Deutschemarks only. U.N. people, foreign journalists, and successful smugglers were the only ones who could afford the place, and on any given night they could be found dining together, asking no questions of each other except perhaps whether the special was worth a try.

'His third this month,' Grebo said, disgusted. 'And of course he had to tell me all about it. He was going on and on about this piece of veal. A filet, "Pink as a puckered cunt," he said, the asshole. "And twice as juicy." All you can do is sit there and listen. Tell him what you really think and you'll be up on Zuc shooting at Chetniks by the end of the week.'

'Fat chance. If he fires you he'll have to fill out forms, recruit a replacement, answer questions to higher ups. Aggravation's not his style.'

'You're supposed to say he'd never let me go because I'm indispensable, Vlado. Because the department would fall apart without me.'

'As if that would be a tragedy. Besides, why bother sending you to the front when he can make your life miserable down here.'

'That's for sure, the bastard.'

Two more policemen soon arrived to move the body back to Grebo's lab. As Vlado and Grebo stepped from the apartment a low, deep thud echoed down from the hills to the north.

Grebo waved his right hand toward the sound. 'Speaking of Zuc,' he said. 'Busy as always, the poor bastards.'

By the time Vlado got back to the office, the gypsy woman was waiting at his desk with a policeman, just as Damir had promised, although he was nowhere to be seen.

The woman was short, petite, with delicate features and high cheekbones. She'd obviously spent some time getting ready at her friend's house, and her face was scrubbed and neatly made up, with bright lipstick carefully applied and her hair perfectly combed. She wore a smart brown skirt and tan blouse. After-murder wear, Vlado thought.

The interview went predictably. She said her husband was a brute, always drinking and gambling. He also dodged army conscription, she mentioned, her eyes flashing with a desperate stab at patriotism. Most people assumed that any official of the new government was swept up in the cause for Bosnian nationalism, and Vlado let them think it, finding it sometimes gave him leverage.

The woman continued. Her husband could've worked but never did, always too lazy or drunk. He beat her when he felt like it and yelled at the baby nonstop. They barely had enough to eat. This afternoon he'd slapped her, shaken the baby, then slapped the child as well before stumbling into bed, where he fell into a snoring stupor. She'd seen the hammer, picked it up, walked to the bed. Next thing she knew she was looking down at her sleeping husband, only he wasn't sleeping anymore, and his head looked like a cherry tart. She picked up the baby and strolled to a neighbor's, then dropped off the news along with the baby.

Neighbors would have to be interviewed to check parts of her story, but Vlado didn't doubt it for a moment. He had half a mind to send her back to her son and let the courts sort it out in the morning. But a policeman was waiting in the hallway to take her to jail. Tomorrow judges would be presiding again in their unheated courtrooms with their dim dirty hallways, hoping that the day's trials and hearings would not be interrupted by an explosion. Peacetime procedure marched on.

Vlado sighed, spent a few minutes typing her statement, then asked her to sign it. She read it slowly, hesitated for a moment, then scribbled her name. As Vlado added his signature she asked, 'What will happen to my baby?'

Vlado replied without looking up: 'An orphanage probably, at least for tonight.'

'How long will he be there?'

Had this really not occurred to her until now? Vlado thought back on the times he'd had to tell spouses and friends of murdered loved ones. There were almost always tears and awkward pauses, and he was always tempted to run away, to flee the grief as soon as possible, though instead he had to pay close attention, to check for false grief or lack of surprise. This was worse, somehow. News of death brought finality, an imperative to move on. The news for this woman promised only a long, indefinite slide into despair.

He glanced off to the side, fixing on a clock on a far wall which hadn't worked for months, then slowly turned to meet her stare. Her eyes were filled with tears, but so far none had spilled.

'He'll be there at least until your trial, unless you have family who will take him, of course.' She'd already mentioned she was an orphan.

'No,' she'd said, shaking her head. 'There is only me.'

They both knew that few people would be likely to

44

take on an extra mouth to feed under these conditions. And who, for that matter, would want a gypsy baby.

'When the trial comes, you will be convicted. Your statement assures that. Even without it the evidence would be overwhelming. But if your neighbors can back up your story about your husband, who knows?' He shrugged. 'Perhaps a judge will show restraint. You may be lucky. The sentence could be light.'

'And that would mean?'

'Three years, maybe more. Probably nothing less.'

She said nothing. A single tear had fallen across her right cheek, and she wiped it away. She stared straight ahead, jaws rigid, then gave a small nod. He stood, escorting her to the hallway, where the waiting policeman slept in a folding chair, bundled against the cold. His mouth was agape, exhaling peaceful sighs of vapor into the dark corridor. Vlado jostled him, and in a few moments he and the woman were gone, their footsteps echoing down the stairwell.

Grebo's mass of hair bobbed around the corner.

'Just finishing up,' he said, briskly wiping his hands on a towel, the sharp reek of chemicals accompanying him like a separate presence. 'It looks like twenty-six blows, give or take a few. Quite a bashing for such a little thing. The famous gypsy anger, Exhibit A. Listen, I've got a bottle of some homemade slivovitz for a little after-curfew drink if you can wait a minute or two.'

Vlado sagged with the thought of making conversation. He preferred sleep and silence.

'No thanks,' he answered. 'I'm a little done in. Have one for me, though.'

'That you can count on. See you tomorrow then if there's any action. I'll leave the report on your desk. No surprises, though. The man had enough alcohol in his blood to light a stove.'

There was hardly a sound outside as Vlado stepped toward the doors of the downstairs exit. It was only a few minutes before curfew, so the streets would be empty except for military police and a few prostitutes desperate for one last transaction. If the phones were working when he got home, he would call to see how Damir was doing. It was cloudy, but the rain had stopped. Sniper fire had popped throughout the day like bacon in a skillet, but overall it had been another quiet afternoon, even down by the river. Maybe it would last for the rest of the month.

Then, just before Vlado pushed open the door there was a gunshot – loud, sharp, perhaps only a few blocks away.

Sniper fire at night inspired an altogether different behavior. Nobody scattered unless the Serbs fired off a flare. There were no streetlights, and the darkness encouraged a tame version of defiance and bravado, a little flirting with the local brand of fatalism that Damir had displayed so recklessly that afternoon.

So it was that Vlado's response to the gunshot was to light a cigarette as he stood on the porch, inhaling deeply to brighten the orange pinprick of light.

Here I am, if you're interested, the cigarette said. But I'm betting you're too lazy.

He strolled down the steps and toward the bridge, the streets quiet again except for the rasp of his soles against wet grit. He crossed, gazing at the dimness of the water below, the white flecks of foam and ripples barely visible in the filtered moonlight. He passed under a banner strung across the bridge, as if for a holiday parade, which warned, CAUTION. SNIPER! Turning left off the bridge, he headed another block toward the corner that would take him out of the line of fire, telling himself not to rush, not to panic. Then he asked himself, Who are we fooling here, and he quickened his pace. A dark form lay ahead on the sidewalk.

He stopped.

It was a lump, curled, man-size.

It was a body.

He stooped for a closer look and smelled sweaty wool and something metallic. A widening pool of black liquid oozed toward his feet, warm to the touch, a bit sticky. It seemed to be coming from the head. Vlado reached down to an arm, grasping the wrist to check for a pulse, finding none, but noticing a heavy, expensive watch. Nice cufflinks, too, and the coat had the feel of a rich cashmere. A well dressed man, as far as one could tell in the dark.

He'd probably been killed by the gunshot a few moments ago, doubtless from someone perched in a window across the river, some asshole with a night-scope and nothing better to do. Vlado angrily tossed his cigarette away, watching the small trail of sparks arch through the night as it fell.

For a moment he felt paralyzed. In all these months of war and four years as an investigator, he had never been the one to discover a body. Always he'd been summoned, until this moment. In a matter of hours he had seen one man shot and a second one needlessly risk his life. And now this, a body at his feet with no one else in sight. It was deeply unsettling, but there was also the undeniable hint of a thrill, because for a moment only he and the killer knew. Perhaps the sniper was watching him even now, had listened to Vlado's footsteps and watched the flung cigarette floating end over end, while knowing exactly what terrible knowledge was unfolding down on the corner.

But the sniper had not bargained on the arrival of a professional, someone to whom this would be not just an ordeal but a revelation to learn from, a jittery taste of the odd intimacy between killer and victim.

Vlado straightened and walked around the corner into a sheltered street until he reached the next block. He looked both ways, and to the left he could barely make out a guard in front of the Interior Ministry fifty yards away.

'You,' he shouted, his voice loud but somehow weak at the same time. There was no movement. Was the man dozing? Dead?

Finally the guard turned, shouting back gruffly, 'It is after curfew. You must come here for questioning. Slowly, please.'

Vlado heard the click of a gun's safety.

'I'm a policeman,' he shouted back, feeling the tone of authority return to his voice. 'Detective Inspector Petric. There's a man who's been shot over here by the river. Come and help me. Now.'

The soldier – or was he military police? Hard to tell in the dark, they all carried the same weapons – strolled over at a leisurely pace. But his nonchalance stiffened when Vlado led him into the field of fire by the river, and as they prepared to lift the body he glanced repeatedly toward the wall of darkness on the hillside across the water.

'Help me move him,' Vlado said. 'You take the arms.' Let him rub against that mess of a head, Vlado thought. 'I'll take the legs.'

The guard gasped, and Vlado didn't need to ask why.

Vlado figured they might as well haul the body to the porch of the police building. Grebo could write it up and call the hospital, save the boys at the morgue a few minutes of paperwork. They'd owe him one.

'Why are we crossing the river,' the guard whispered

urgently, sounding alarmed as they moved onto the bridge, the water gurgling below.

'Relax. We're taking him to police headquarters. It's only a few more yards.'

As soon as they reached the porch, the soldier dropped the dead man's arms. He was already worried he'd be missed at his post. He looked down, brushing the front of his uniform and checking for bloodstains, then began to ease away.

'Hold on a minute,' Vlado said. He ordered the young man to fetch Grebo from upstairs.

The porch was sheltered from fire, so Vlado drew out his lighter for a better look.

Good God. Right in the face. A bigger mess than the gypsy's husband. Still, there was something vaguely familiar in what remained of the jawline, in the bulk and shape of the body.

Grebo pushed through the door, followed by the soldier.

'Christ, Vlado. Knew you should have stayed for a drink. How close were you?'

'Not very. I think I heard the shot as I was coming out the door. He was over the river, a block down.'

'And you brought him back here?' A hint of irritation in the voice.

'Figured we might as well handle him, or that you could at least take a look,' Vlado said, feeling stupid now, sheepish.

Grebo shrugged, exhaling through his nose, fumes of plum brandy misting into the night, then pulled a penlight from a shirt pocket and flicked the beam toward the ruined face. Vlado looked away this time, focusing on Grebo, and saw his eyebrows arch in surprise.

'This one's no sniper,' Grebo said, leaning closer, squinting now. 'Whoever did this was close.'

'Close enough to be on the same side of the river?'

'Close enough to be stepping on his toes.'

Vlado let that sink in, then announced what Grebo already knew.

'I guess he's our customer then.'

'Looks that way.'

Now it would be necessary to work, and a mixture of weariness and distaste came over Vlado, though not without a stirring of his slumbering curiosity. His mind shifted into the rote workings of an investigator fresh on a crime scene, and his first thought was a question: Why kill someone in a known sniper zone, unless you wanted it to look like a sniper had done it? That would imply a plan, something more than blind emotion at work, perhaps even something elaborate for a change. It had possibilities, he told himself.

He thought of the guard, who'd already disappeared back to his post without a word and would now have to be questioned, to find out if he'd seen or heard anyone nearby a few minutes earlier. Same thing for the whores at Skenderia, if any had been on duty at this hour. They would have been just across the river from the shooting, skulking next to the sandbagged walls that kept them out of the line of fire but still handy to the French and Egyptian soldiers. Perhaps they'd heard something before or after, though God knows they couldn't have seen a thing in this darkness.

Already he'd made mistakes. He thought with disgust how he and the guard had trampled all over the murder scene, stepping in the blood, then dragging the main piece of evidence down the street and over a bridge. He realized with mild alarm how much he'd let himself begin to slip, despite all his precautions. There was no excuse for it. He made a note to himself to bathe and shave tonight the minute he was home, no matter how cold the water, even if he had to head out in the morning with a load of empty jugs to stand in line for a fresh supply.

For now, he'd have to return with a flashlight to the spot where he'd found the body and search the scene – carefully, though, flicking the light sparingly lest he attract the attention of a real sniper – looking for the pool of blood and whatever else might be around.

But first things first. The victim needed to be identified.

Vlado reached behind the body and pulled out the man's wallet. It seemed full, about seventy D-marks in all, a small fortune these days. There had certainly been no robbery.

'Give me a light,' he said to Grebo, who turned his penlight toward the wallet. The narrow beam landed on the identification photo, that of a brown-eyed man in his mid-to-late forties, coal-black hair. Vlado recognized him at once.

'Esmir Vitas,' he said, without bothering to read the fine print, and his stomach made a small leap.

'Vitas,' Grebo said. 'Sounds familiar.'

'It should. He's chief of the Interior Ministry's special police. Or was.' He looked up at Grebo. 'I'd say he's our customer all right.'

3

'He's not ours,' Lutva Garovic announced the next morning, striding across the office as soon as Vlado arrived.

Garovic was chief of detectives, a bureaucrat whose instincts had never failed him except when it came to actually getting things done. He had survived Tito's death, departmental shakeups, Party purges, the disintegration of Yugoslavia, and the first two years of the war, and he would doubtless still be bossing unimportant people years later no matter who ended up ruling the city. Three decades of meandering in bureaucracy's midstream had taught him that the only way to stay afloat in shifting currents was to swim neither too hard nor too fast. He had mastered the art of treading water, prospering by never aspiring to anything greater than the glory of whoever happened to be issuing his orders. When communism fell out of fashion, he was among the first to stop using Party buzzwords. If it ever made a comeback, he'd quickly learn to say them again.

No realm of state machinery was beyond such talents. Garovic had been a personnel manager at the state-run brewery, an 'intergovernmental liaison' at the municipal waterworks, a midlevel administrator at the Ministry of Housing, and a functionary of vague but supremely self-important duties at the Ministry of Justice. That was the beauty of the state having its fingers in so many enterprises. With the right combination of blandly mediocre qualifications one could work almost anywhere.

A few months after the war began he had materialized one morning in the glass-caged office of the chief of detectives. His predecessor, a gruff but competent Zijad Imamovic, had fought in the defense of the city only to be killed by a mortar shell, blown all over the walls of a building near the front line.

Imamovic had been the only boss Vlado had known in his four years as a homicide investigator. He'd been a deliberate man who counseled professionalism and thoroughness. He'd been determined that each case would be conducted by the book, no matter how insignificant or meaningless it seemed, and he'd drained every last ounce of his budget to send his three investigators off for weeks at a time to pick up the proper training. Vlado had envisioned a future in which he would learn his trade inside out, with no case he couldn't handle. Then the war had come, taking Imamovic and those hopes with it.

It had taken Garovic only a few minutes to settle behind Imamovic's gray metal desk as if he'd never worked anywhere else and, by the time Vlado and Damir had arrived, he'd tacked a picture of his family on the wall, spread a sheaf of case files before him, and was enveloped in a cloud of cigarette smoke. It was as fine an imitation of businesslike efficiency as Vlado had ever seen, and it fooled everyone until at least mid-afternoon.

Garovic was of medium height, with a soft, pale body spreading in the middle like a melting pat of butter.

Lank, black hair was combed straight back over a broad face, and his skin was white and puffy from a lifetime of cabbage, beer and potatoes. He was among the few in Sarajevo who'd managed to gain weight during the war. His eyes, which seemed to blink constantly, were the gray-green of weak broth, and he spoke in the high, crackling voice of a bird used to being heard amid great chattering flocks.

There was nothing Garovic cherished more than the order and tranquillity of business as usual, especially amid the chaos and clutter of war. And in the case of a murdered chief of the Interior Ministry's special police, he sensed the disturbing tug of a whirlpool.

He decided right away to swim for open water.

'Not our jurisdiction, not even close,' he said, shaking his head vigorously as he reached Vlado's desk. 'And just to make sure, I phoned the Interior Ministry an hour before you arrived. They agree, of course.'

His face was flushed, as if he'd just run a race. He stooped across the back of Vlado's desk, his white hands poking through the unruly pile of books and papers. Vlado watched the invasion without expression, leaning back in his chair, arms folded across his chest. Then Garovic found what he'd come for. He held aloft the pale green folder with the report from the night before.

'Vitas, Esmir,' he chirped triumphantly, reading the block lettering. 'An interesting case, no doubt. Who, indeed, would murder the most powerful law enforcement officer in the city? Something to speculate about while you're painting your next regiment, Vlado.'

Damir must have blabbed about the soldiers.

'But now it's officially none of your business. Or mine.'

54

'Whose business is it then? Officially?' Vlado asked, although he knew the answer.

'Interior's special police. Dead or alive, he's their boy.'

The expanding realm of the special police had become an endless source of frustration and fascination for Vlado. At first he had only been annoyed, watching the city's most interesting cases slide across the river to this hybrid at a time when he could have been learning from the experience. It was one part police force, one part army, and a third part secret intelligence service. Some people liked to say a fourth part was the largest – the mafia part, with a complex web spreading to every gang of smugglers and black marketeers in the city, reaching even into the hills of the Serbs. It was hard to say how much of the speculation was true, if any.

Such uncertainty was inevitable in a city that owed its survival to private bands of armed thugs. When the Serbs were poised to rush across the bridges and overrun every main road during the first weeks of fighting, it was the outlaws – thieves, loan sharks, racketeers, and their various enforcers – who had rallied the defense, arming and organizing just enough people to fight off the advancing tanks with little more than pistols and machine guns. Vlado had to hand it to them. They'd fought like tigers, rescuing museums, hospitals, banks, government buildings, and the entire city center. If along the way they'd helped themselves to some of the contents of those buildings, or set up supply networks that filled their own pockets as much as they filled the stomachs of Sarajevans, well, who was going to complain?

But once the Serbs were dug in around the city and it became clear no one was leaving anytime soon, the balance came due for this unorthodox protection racket. The privateers and their roving armies became the de facto local government, and for months they proved far more nimble than the fledgling Bosnian bureaucracy and its brand-new Interior Ministry police. They ruled the streets with an appalling boldness, stopping vehicles to siphon out gasoline, or, if they were feeling lazy, simply taking the vehicles. They stole flak jackets from reporters and aid workers, shanghaied men from cafés and water lines to dig trenches at the front, and stole or arranged U.N. passes as part of a thriving trade in human beings, smuggling friends and customers out of the country. For a price of course. All for a stiff price.

And so, they made money. Lots of Deutschemarks and dollars. They also acquired property, storefront after storefront, but not by spending their riches. Their favorite method was convincing owners at gunpoint to sign over their deeds. Few owners objected for long, especially when offered the chance to stay on as manager at a handsome salary.

As their fiefdoms grew stronger and more numerous, their world inevitably devolved into a fierce war within the war. The struggle for primacy became dazzling for its shifting alliances, for its sharp outbreaks of shooting, but it soon settled into a major standoff between two apparent kings, Enko and Zarko, who eventually worked out an uneasy peace by carving up the biggest rackets between them. Somewhere out on the fringe were the special police, still bickering over jurisdiction with the civil police, the army, the militia and the military police, as if any were really in charge.

In the end it was their swaggering as much as their swag that did them in. Zarko became known for dropping by the presidential building during lulls in the daily shelling, herding his great shifting bulk of muscle and fat down gray aisles of desks, loudly lecturing anyone who would listen, either on the virtues of bodybuilding or the realities of who was really running the country. Him, of course, and don't you forget it.

His audience was usually a meek row of clerks and typists, although the new government's chieftains doubtless also heard through their open doors, gritting their teeth and slowly laying plans for revenge. The U.N. was equally powerless to stop this behavior, but soon adopted the lawlessness as a convenient excuse for not moving aggressively against the Serbs. After all, they argued, what would be worse, a Serb takeover or this petty tyranny of gangsters?

After a little more than a year of this, the aspiring powers of the Bosnian government decided they'd had enough, but it took a few months more before they were ready to strike back. That's when the young police force of the new government's Interior Ministry finally rose to its feet, and Esmir Vitas led the way.

And what better person for the job? As a young scholar he'd won every possible award for duty and honor, yet his classmates had never considered him a snitch or a self-promoter. From university and more top honors he moved into the army, then over to law enforcement, and when the war had begun he'd been the natural choice to head the special police. It was mostly through his doing that the ministry had been able to mount any challenge to the gangs, much less the powerful assault they eventually unleashed. And his strengths were as much evangelical as organizational.

Vlado had overheard him one night as he preached in a café to a tableful of midlevel officers, booming in tones of moral certitude above the noise of a heavy bombardment. The bottles passed around the table as Vitas railed against 'the profiteers and the paper killers, the ones who would have us sitting down here in this bowl of blood forever as long as they can control the markets that are making them rich.'

It now amused Vlado, then shamed him, to realize how much the tirade had sounded like the one delivered two days ago by Toby, the British journalist.

'They may be Muslims, but they are our enemy every bit as much as the Serbs,' Vitas had said. 'Stop them and we stop half of the reason for the siege. Stop them and we save ourselves, both in our own eyes and in the eyes of the world.'

And for a moment Vlado had almost believed it, sitting there enjoying a sip of the bottle that had finally been passed to his table. True or not, it had been a bold moment of inspiration. Dangerous, too, for you never knew who else would be listening in a place like that. Someone in the crowd would almost certainly be reporting the remarks straight back to the gangs. Dangerous people might well take offense at such zeal.

Soon afterward Vitas had backed his words with deeds, drawing upon elements of the army, the military police, and even some of the other gangs that had lost out in the earlier power struggle. He launched a huge assault upon the strongholds of Zarko and Enko, and for two days in October the city shook under self-inflicted fire from mortars, machine guns, and rocket-propelled grenades. State radio crackled out messages for everyone to stay off the streets, as if they'd been safe to begin with, and throughout it all the distant Serb gunners remained oddly quiet. One imagined them watching through their scopes and binoculars with pleasurable bewilderment, seeing their enemy implode with a ferocity long absent from the stalemated fighting in the hills.

Enko was the easier nut to crack. He was killed on the first day, going down in a desperate charge. He left behind a dozen dead hostages, burned like bundled kindling in a basement, hands wired behind their backs.

Zarko took longer. He finally surrendered when his building was surrounded. He couldn't have missed the absurdity of his predicament – surrounded and besieged by an army that was itself surrounded and besieged. So he gave up, strolling into a courtyard of golden chestnut leaves in late afternoon with his top lieutenant, Neven Halilovic, and a handful of others. Four hours later he was dead, shot by the special police while trying to escape. Or so went the official version, but everyone had always wondered, and a thousand different versions sprang up to explain what had really happened. His body was never recovered, no autopsy performed. The following morning the Serb bombardment resumed as if it had never stopped.

Since then, the city had begun to settle, as much as a city could under such circumstances. But no one had ever doubted that the previous beast had survived in some form. It had too many tentacles, and the thinking was that they would regenerate under a new head, even if the head was of a more official nature.

So now Vlado would once again become a spectator of the doings of the special police, like an eavesdropper straining to hear a conversation through the heavy door of a locked room.

He wondered if he would even hear of the investigation again. It would certainly not be good publicity to admit that the city's antigang crusader had been murdered. So perhaps there would be a muted official inquiry that would release muted, official results. The killing would be attributed to, say, a personal disagreement, maybe involving a jealous husband. Women were said to be Vitas's weakness. He was a bachelor, and a man in his position under these conditions had the whole city to choose from.

Or perhaps authorities would invent a tale of Serb cunning and treachery – a gunman slinking through the lines and across the river. God knows it had happened, but it was rare, and usually infiltrators were in the business of spying, not shooting.

Maybe even the official explanation would be true. But Vlado doubted it, mostly because he knew what would have happened if he hadn't found the body. It would have been discovered instead by some poor old woman or wandering boy just after dawn. The hospital's morning crew would have collected it, and out of haste, danger, and the general weariness with death, it would have been deemed a sniper case right away by some overburdened young doctor, or by the chief of the morgue, who was no doctor at all. The conclusion would have been plausible enough, if only due to the location, no questions asked and no autopsy. Even if someone had bothered to question the finding later, he'd be easy enough to silence with the right combination of threats and Deutschemarks. The identity of the victim would have created a bit of a stir, but by then the body would have been tagged, wrapped, and buried deep in the ground, out in another fresh rectangle on the soccer field outside Vlado's window. Case closed.

If this case had been one of those rare portals Vlado was looking for, he'd never be permitted to gaze into it now. His friends, he was beginning to believe, were right. But the job still beat serving in a trench. Now he'd have to wait for the next phone call. Or, rather, for the second call. Damir got the next one. And where was Damir, anyway, Vlado wondered with a vague sense of worry. Vlado hadn't seen him all day. He tried his home, but even his mother and father were out. Or perhaps the line wasn't working, an even stronger possibility.

Vlado pulled a paperback from the pile on his desk and leaned back to read. Something about traveling in Tibet. Within an hour he was dozing, the book splayed across his chest, the backrest of the swivel chair groaning behind him.

Then a cold, flabby hand was on his shoulder, jostling him awake. A high voice croaked in his ear.

'To work, Vlado, to work. I know you're busy with your heavy caseload, but there is real work to be done.'

Garovic again. The green file folder was back in his hand, as if he'd never put it down. He was forcing a smile.

'It seems it's your lucky day, Vlado.' He paused to catch his breath. 'Esmir Vitas is all yours. That's the word straight from the Interior Ministry. And who am I to second guess? It seems they want this to be an independent investigation, all very proper and above-board, et cetera, et cetera. So here, keep the file. But before doing anything else you're to see Kasic at noon, in an hour, at Special Police Headquarters.'

'Juso Kasic?'

'Yes. Acting Chief Kasic.'

'Very efficient.' He fought to temper the excitement in his voice, lest Garovic snatch back the file. 'They might have at least let the chair go cold.'

Garovic refused to rise to the bait.

'Someone has to step in and mind the store,' he said. 'Anyway, if they're going to have a new chief, it might as well be Juso.' He'd spoken with Kasic for the first time five minutes ago and was already calling him by his first name.

'And, Vlado.'

'Yes?'

'This is not some drunken gypsy with a hammer in his head. Don't make trouble for you, or for me. Keep it respectful. The quicker you're through with it, the better. And above all, keep it neat.'

We'll see about that, Vlado thought. He still needed to play it cool around Garovic, lest he set off the man's bureaucratic radar. But he fully intended to run with this until he dropped. The broader and sloppier things got, the better.

So far the case was quite neat. The file folder which Garovic had treated with such grandiose caution had nothing in it but the previous night's reports. Grebo's findings had been standard: Death by high-caliber handgun at close range. No alcohol or drugs in the bloodstream. Vitas's last meal had been about two hours before he was killed – a roast chicken (Grebo must have sighed with envy) and cabbage, a little rice and some coffee. There was nothing to indicate anything other than a straightforward death by shooting. There were no strange marks on the body to indicate a struggle before he was shot. Nor was Vitas armed, unless the killer had taken the weapon. If Vitas had been keeping an appointment, then it apparently wasn't with someone he feared.

When Vlado had gone back to the crime scene he'd found little but the pool of blood. The snow on the sidewalk had melted, so there were no footprints, or none he could find by crawling with his nose pressed close to the wet concrete. No one lived nearby, there were only abandoned office buildings shelled full of holes, gutted and waterlogged. The nearest inhabited place at that hour would have been the Skenderia barracks right across the river, although anyone there would have been unlikely to have seen anything. Still, it would be worth speaking with the duty guard from the night before, and with the usual crowd of prostitutes.

The military policeman who'd helped Vlado move the body had noticed nothing before the shooting, although he'd remembered seeing Vitas leave the building about ten minutes earlier, so he must have come straight from his office. The guard didn't recall hearing the gunshot as such, having heard shots thoughout his posting, which had begun four hours earlier. He'd been more concerned with the cold as it seeped through holes in the soles of his boots, and with an anticipated visit from his girlfriend, who'd never shown up. She was supposed to have brought his dinner, so he'd been left only with his daily ration of Drina cigarettes, one pack, and had fought hunger with deep inhalations. But there had been nobody else on the street after Vitas except for Vlado, and no cars other than the usual U.N. armored vehicles that rumbled by at all hours.

Vitas's wallet had also revealed little – the usual ID cards and a few old receipts, some from well before the war. Vlado glanced fondly at one from a restaurant now closed. He'd gone there once with his wife, a special meal for their fifth wedding anniversary. He thought briefly of the lamb and wild mushrooms, the glasses of red wine, the honeyed pastries for dessert.

In one pants pocket there was only a stubby pencil, in the other a wrinkled and soiled handkerchief. In the shirt pockets, nothing.

As Vlado scanned the report once again, Grebo materialized at his desk.

'Sorry about last night,' Vlado said, looking up. 'Hope you were able to finish your drink in peace.'

'Oh, more or less.'

Grebo was fidgeting, glancing back toward Garovic's office. 'In fact, I'm afraid I was maybe in a bit too much of a hurry to get to the bottle.'

'What do you mean? And what's the matter, Grebo? Still hung over? Actually, what are you doing here at all? Are you meeting Damir on a call?'

'No. It's the Vitas thing. Do you have a minute?' Glancing around again.

'I'd have all day if I didn't have to see Kasic in an hour. What about Vitas?'

Grebo pulled up a chair and sat down, leaning toward Vlado and lowering his voice. 'I goofed. But I think I can fix things. Maybe. If we still have time.'

'What do you mean you goofed. Cause of death?'

'Please. Give me some credit. On that I never goof. A small error of omission, that's all. And if I can't correct it, probably nothing important anyway. It's like this: Whenever I do a body, I go through all the clothes pretty closely. I know you do, too. But, still, things turn up sometimes, and not always in likely places. When we were still doing smugglers it was amazing what you'd find sewn into their coat linings.'

Vlado wondered vaguely where the fruits of the past discoveries had ended up. Probably on Mycky and Grebo's card tables at the market.

'Anyway, I realized this morning I'd forgotten to do Vitas's clothes. They were such a bloody mess last night, and, well . . . that wasn't really the problem, because the clothes of almost everybody I get are a bloody mess. The problem was that I'd rounded up

64

some companionship for drinking after all. And let me tell you, Vlado, she was a lot more interesting to look at than you. So, I suppose I was in a hurry to get away, and I skipped out before checking the clothes.'

'Understandable. And entirely forgivable. What's your point then?'

'My point is that this morning I figured I'd better get down here and take care of it even if I was still hung over. There were a few tests to finish up anyway. And lucky I did, too. The minute I finished, Garovic came down with a requisition form to ship the evidence bag and the whole file over to the Interior Ministry. Anyway, I'd had just enough time to find this.'

He handed Vlado a small scrap of paper. A last name was scribbled on it in shaky pencil, next to a street address in Dobrinja, a precarious edge of the city near the old Olympic Village.

'It was in his right pants pocket,' Grebo said.

'It couldn't have been. I searched his pockets right after making the ID I always do.'

'It was the watch pocket. You know, sometimes there's a smaller pocket just inside the big one. Easy to overlook.'

Vlado frowned. In the dimness of the cigarette lighter he'd missed it. In the old days Imamovic would have wrung his neck for this kind of sloppiness, and he'd have deserved it.

'Well, why didn't you just give it to Garovic, send it over with the bag?'

'That might not have looked so good, would it. Me coming up at the last minute with something we both should have had last night. I know he thinks we've gotten sloppy. And, what the hell, we have. But on a case this big, well, like I said, not too good. So I figured if you still had the file you could slip it in, say that you'd found it. Or log it after the fact. If not . . .' He shrugged.

'I do have the file, in fact. Garovic took it an hour ago but he just brought it back. So don't worry, I'll add it to the record and no one will be the wiser. Though I guess we'd both better be a little more careful from now on.'

Grebo sagged in relief.

'Thanks,' he said. 'I was already imagining myself marching up to Zuc. Anyhow, it's been dusted. The paper, I mean. All the prints belong to Vitas. So it's probably not much anyway.'

Grebo turned to go as Vlado asked, 'How was she, anyway?'

Grebo tilted his head for a moment in puzzlement, then said, 'Oh. Her. Yes, well, not worth the hangover, that's for sure. Probably another reason this case seemed so urgent this morning. Duty suddenly looked a lot more attractive, if you know what I mean.'

Between Grebo and Damir, Vlado had begun to feel like the office eunuch.

Vlado looked at the scrawled address. Dobrinja, a peninsula of Muslim-held territory in a sea of Serb artillery, was anything but a pleasant place to visit. Too many lines of fire. But the phones there almost never worked, so it would have to be checked out in person. He would treat it as a field trip, try to learn something from it.

He started to put the number into the file folder, then wondered whether Kasic might want another glance. He folded the paper and stuffed it in his shirt pocket. No sense in attracting attention to their slackness. Besides, if they really wanted an independent investigation, what did it matter anyway?

'Another number for your black book?' said a voice, startling Vlado into momentary guilt. But it was only

Damir, looking worn out, but grinning, once again the warrior triumphant, back from another successful raid on the young, willing females of Sarajevo.

'Yes, my very fat black book,' Vlado answered with a note of relief. 'You're welcome to it anytime for new contacts.'

'That's all right,' Damir said. 'I've already got the number for the office. And I've no wish to harass your wife in Berlin, and I'm probably the last person in Sarajevo she'd want to hear from anyway. And those are probably your only two numbers, am I right?'

'Close.'

He studied Damir's face carefully, for any hint of a false note, a forced smile. But he truly seemed purged, even renewed. Perhaps the old cure had worked, after all.

'Well, a truly busy day around here for a change, I hear. Sounds like some real excitement last night after I left. Sounds good, unless Garovic decides it's too hot for us and kicks it over to Interior.'

'He already has, but they kicked it back. They've got the U.N. looking over their shoulder and didn't want to seem incestuous. So it's ours after all.'

'Or so you think.'

'You think they'll meddle, you mean.'

'Not obviously. But I'd expect them to put you on a very short leash, offering plenty of "help" whether you like it or not. Tell me, your first appointment wouldn't be with Assistant Chief Juso Kasic, would it?'

Vlado laughed. 'No, it's with the new Acting Chief Juso Kasic.'

Damir arched his eyebrows. 'Impressive,' he said. 'I suspect you'll be seeing a lot of him until this is over. And he'll probably be very generous with offers of "technical assistance" from his various thugs and leg-breakers, if I know those boys. At an official level they'll keep their noses out of it to impress Washington and London and Paris. But if I were you I wouldn't look over my shoulder too much. Might be a shock to see what's lurking in your shadow.'

Vlado then broached a possibility he'd been mulling since Garovic had handed the case file back to him. 'Of course, you could always help watch my back,' he said, gauging Damir's reaction. 'And I know I'll need some help tracking down leads, such as they are. I'll mention it to Kasic, if you'd like. I'd imagine the ministry will want this wrapped up pretty quick.'

'Are you serious?' Damir asked, a trace of puppyish eagerness in his tone. 'Or more to the point, do you think Kasic will go along with it?'

'Can't hurt to ask. Who knows, he may even have to say yes. Feels nice to have some leverage on those guys for a change, doesn't it?'

'Yes, it is nice,' a smiling Damir agreed. 'But remember. It's probably exactly the way Kasic wants you to feel.'

4

For all its power, the Interior Ministry had no heat in its downstairs lobby. Vlado joined seven others who were waiting, bundled in heavy coats and seated on battered vinyl chairs and couches. The brown linoleum floor was a wasteland of cigarette butts and small tumbleweeds of dust. Clouds of cigarette smoke barely masked the stench of urine from a backed up toilet down the hall. The stroking thrum of a generator could be heard from inside a small booth built of plywood and clear sheets of plastic, where a uniformed officer sat, acting as receptionist, taking names and phoning upstairs for authorizations that never seemed to come.

As Vlado waited he considered what he knew of Kasic. He was a man with a reputation for restraint, both in his anger and his goodwill, and this was said to be a product of his history. He had been a young man of impulse and scattered energies, whose sharp remarks and recklessness had stranded him for years in the great bulge of middle bureaucracy. Once he'd passed the age at which up-and-comers generally began to make their mark, plenty of people had written him off.

Then in the early eighties, as the rigid state machinery loosened and adjusted in the wake of Tito's death, Kasic belatedly began to rise, catching up to more fortunate peers and then surpassing them. He moved quickly through the Party ranks under vague titles that seemed to place him as an important man in state security. Those on the outside could never be sure if his ascension was guided by his own power or someone else's, and that seemed to be the way Kasic preferred it.

By the time the Interior Ministry began putting together its new police force he was a natural choice for the hierarchy, and he fell into line behind Vitas as a loyal lieutenant, soon known for his ruthless efficiency.

Like Vitas he had made his name in the October raids, supervising the heavy work in the maneuver that flushed, then trapped Zarko on the second and decisive day. When an errant mortar shell from his unit landed a block north of the mark, killing three old residents of a crumbling flat, he'd flinched, but not for long. '"A small price in the long run," that's what they'll say around here,' he'd concluded on the spot to his subordinates, who'd naturally agreed.

Vlado looked around the lobby at the others, all men. They seemed bored, as if they'd been waiting for hours. Two had dozed off in spite of the cold.

But after only a few minutes the man in the booth rapped on the plywood and waved Vlado upstairs, shouting in a muffled voice, 'Mr Kasic is waiting. Second floor.'

Vlado trotted up the stairs to warm himself, passing security warnings and propaganda posters taped to the walls. BOSNIAN ARMY ON THE BOSNIAN BORDER proclaimed one poster, done up in a nouveau social-realist style. The black silhouette of a grim, angular soldier rose out of jagged black-and-white hills against a purple backdrop, as if he had become part of the very mountains he was defending.

Kasic stood at the top of the steps at an open door in the pose of a tolerant schoolmaster waiting to usher the last pupil into the classroom. His silvery black hair was close cropped at the sides, and as Vlado stepped closer he saw that Kasic's face was a landscape of sharp angles and deep shadows, as lean as an athlete's, reminiscent of the soldier on the poster. Yet it was also still pumped full of vigor and color here in mid-January in this city where everything had grown ashy and pale, as if he'd been working out on a clean gym floor of varnished oak, all bright lights and fuggy heat.

He shook hands, grasping hard with a huge hand. Vlado had noticed him before at joint security meetings and official gatherings, a man whose intensity leaned out at you across desks, dinner tables, and interrogation rooms, giving the impression both of earnestness and of appetite.

The tendency among others was either to pass him off as a toadying yes-man showing off his enthusiasm for superiors or as a man truly wrapped up in his mission. Vlado had never known him well enough to decide.

Kasic led Vlado across an open area of cluttered desks, where men in the dark blue uniforms of the ministry police busily went about whatever it was they did up here. Vlado counted five space heaters, each working at full power. The room was comfortable, even cozy.

They reached a large office with CHIEF OF SPECIAL POLICE on the door. So, he had already moved in, Vlado thought, scanning the walls and desk for signs of Vitas as he settled into a chair. He was mildly angry to find none. He'd hoped to be the first to search Vitas's office, but it was obvious he'd been beaten to the punch.

Kasic slid behind Vitas's old desk, glancing about him for a moment as if still getting his bearings, then leaned forward, clasping his hands before him on a stack of notes. His voice emerged in the deep fullness of a command, although his words were welcoming.

'Now then, Vlado. It is good to see you're on the case. I have done some checking and found you a thorough man and a solid investigator, although I must admit your lack of experience gives me pause. Less than two years as a detective before the war began, and four years total, correct?'

Vlado nodded.

'And I gather you haven't been too busy since the beginning of the war. At least not with this sort of case.'

'Correct.'

'I also gather that your boss, Mr Garovic, while helpful, was not very eager to turn you loose on this. He is, I take it, a somewhat careful man.'

Vlado allowed himself a brief smile. 'That's putting it mildly,' he said.

'Well, I can understand his hesitance. A sensitive matter, this one. And by all rights this should be our case. If it weren't for some special considerations, we'd be handling it, and handling it professionally and well, I have no doubt.'

'Special considerations?'

'The U.N. On some days we can't even take a piss around here anymore without three of them asking if they can come along. We feel we have to prove ourselves every day, then file a report on it in triplicate. If I had my way I'd just as soon tell them to mind their own business – it's not as if they're running the tightest ship themselves. I can't tell you how many times we could have cracked down on the French or the Egyptians, brokering whores and cigarettes, or

72

peddling U.N. passes to smuggle people out of the country at three thousand marks a pop. And we all know they've been licking the boots of the other side throughout the war.

'But for all that, we, or, that is, people far above me, feel that we can turn the corner with them with the right kind of results in this department. And if we turn the corner with them, then maybe we can turn the corner on getting the right kind of help for fighting this war. Bigger guns, antitank weapons – you've heard the laundry list before, and it's not going to be filled anytime soon as long as the arms embargo's still in effect. But in some quarters, at least, there is momentum.'

Kasic paused to light a cigarette, pulling a Marlboro from a pack on his desk. Was this going to be a lecture on the war or would they ever discuss Vitas?

'Which is where this little investigation comes in,' Kasic said, as if reading Vlado's mind. 'Every time they catch the slightest whiff of something dirty blowing from our way, anything to do with corruption, racketeering, profiteering on our side of the fence, it becomes another piece of ammunition for keeping the embargo in place. It's an easy enough sell: "If the Bosnians can't even clean up after themselves, why should we help them make an even bigger mess." We thought we'd proved our point with the raids in October, but the U.N. isn't buying it. Too many loose ends left behind, they say. And they didn't like the way Vitas brought in a few "undesirables" toward the end to help us along. Made all our positive results tainted, they said. We only set up a few has-beens to be the new lords. Still, too much funny money floating around and too many funny ways of earning it, they said. And there's some truth to it. You look at the markets for gasoline, cigarettes, meat, coffee, whatever you want to pick, and it's still in the hands of people just beyond our reach. And I suppose it goes without saying, but I'll say it anyway. None of this conversation is to go beyond these walls. Clear enough?'

'Clear enough.'

Kasic flicked his cigarette at an ashtray.

'But anyone with eyes can see that the problems are still with us. Even if it's not as obvious as before. Too many people are still profiting from the status quo.'

Kasic then leaned forward across the desk, lowering his head, his eyes narrowing in concentration, like a big, sleek dog poking into the burrow of a far smaller animal.

'And frankly, Vlado, although it pains me greatly to say it, Vitas may have been among those who were profiting. At least that's how it looks from what little we've already learned. When we first heard Vitas had been murdered we thought what everyone must have. He made a lot of very powerful enemies in October, and one of them must have retaliated. But now it looks like it may be more complicated, and a lot messier. And as soon as we saw where this was going we called you in. No sense in having the U.N. believe the foxes are trying to guard the henhouse on this one.'

Vlado started to interrupt with a question, because now he had plenty. But Kasic was rolling.

'Besides, I've heard a lot about you,' he said, pointing the cigarette at Vlado's chest. 'Enough to know that you're a good man for this sort of thing. Blunt. Not afraid to step on toes even when it might not be good for you. Probably the very things that scare the daylights out of Garovic, but it's what we need on this one, although I don't suppose you've had a case quite like this one yet, have you?'

'No sir. Not exactly.'

'And it's not as if you've been getting much of a chance for them since we've gone into business. Yes, I know, we've also stolen most of the resources, too. And if Imamovic were still alive he'd have never have allowed this to happen without one hell of a fight. But, frankly, Vlado, and this is not to denigrate your talents or any of your people, our people here are used to dealing with this particular underworld. They've come to know all its little streets and alleys, especially since October, even if we don't have them all quite under control yet. And we do undeniably have the best resources for doing this kind of work.

'Which brings me to my next point. Please, Vlado, use our expertise when you can. Staying independent doesn't mean staying in the dark. Keep me in the dark, yes, fine, as much as you like. But our technical staff is yours for the asking. And I know we have a better lab than your man Grebo's. The same is true of our files. Open to you. Within reason of course, because if your thinking is that you don't really know or trust us yet, the feeling is necessarily mutual at this point.'

Vlado nodded, then decided it was an opportune moment to interrupt. 'As long as we're discussing possible assistance, I'd like to be able to bring Damir Begovic in on the case with me. He's with my department, I trust him, and we work well together.'

Kasic frowned, as if he'd just eaten something disagreeable. Then he sighed, releasing a long, pained breath from his nostrils.

'Probably not the partner I'd choose for you if the choice was up to me. But . . .'

As he paused, Vlado wondered if the meeting was being taped, if perhaps Kasic would replay the whole thing later for some international observer, just to prove he'd been on his best behavior. Whatever the reason, Vlado momentarily got the answer he'd been hoping for.

'Very well, then. Use Begovic as you need him. But sparingly. Keep the major work for yourself. The fewer who have access to your findings, the better. And if you're feeling overwhelmed in tracking people down, or even in getting the information you need, there is, as I said, help that we might be able to offer. I don't know what your interrogation skills are like, but should you happen to hit any brick walls with anyone, we have some of the oldest hands in the city in dealing with that sort of thing.' Vlado knew what that meant, most likely. Big fellows sitting around in brightly lit rooms, sipping coffee while they broke kneecaps and hooked up the electrodes.

'No matter what kind of country we want to have in the future,' Kasic said, 'the old ways sometimes still work best. Don't misunderstand me, Vlado. You're the boss. As I was saying, we want to come clean on this, the quicker the better. That's why when I began to hear certain things this morning about Vitas himself, it became all the more important that we immediately give up our jurisdiction.'

'What sort of things?'

Kasic lowered his head, shaking it slowly, the portrait of a grieving son.

'I'd always heard he was a straight shooter,' Vlado prompted.

'So had I. None straighter, in fact. But maybe with a war on he felt the rules were different, or that they no longer applied.'

'I'm afraid you'll have to be a little more specific.'

'Yes, I suppose you're interrogating now.' Kasic broke into a broad smile. 'In fact as long as you're here you'd probably like to ask me a few things about my own whereabouts last night. I've certainly got motive enough. My promotion was pretty much automatic once Vitas was gone.'

'The thought had occurred to me,' Vlado said, taking care with his tone. 'I'll have to know where you were at the time of the murder and, assuming you have an alibi, where you were when you first heard of it, who told you. Your reaction. Not only from you but from others. And so on.'

Kasic nodded, stubbed out his cigarette. 'Very good. You'll have all of the time you need for those things as soon as this conversation is over. But, in getting back to Vitas . . .'

'His lack of virtue.'

'Yes. The black market, I'm afraid. Nothing fancy. Meat, cigarettes, and liquor, mostly.'

'Marlboros, for example?' Vlado asked, reaching across to Kasic's pack and helping himself to one.

Kasic smiled. He offered Vlado a light and took a cigarette for himself. 'Yes, Marlboros. Drinas, too. And he apparently got in deep enough to get himself killed. It's no real puzzle why, I suppose. Either he was squeezing someone or someone was squeezing him. It came to a head and somebody had to be gotten rid of. It turned out to be Vitas. As for who pulled the trigger, well, we could probably spend the rest of the war tracking that one down if it's like most of these cases. You know how it works.'

'Actually, I'm not sure I do. Our little department seems to have lost touch.'

For the first time Kasic seemed mildly embarrassed. 'Yes. This great dent we've put in your business. And just when you should have been learning the ropes. Well, the way it usually works these days is that when

77

somebody wants to buy a triggerman he gets some soldier who's down from the front for a day or two, someone looking for a few extra Deutschemarks for himself or his family. He's given a gun, a name, and maybe even a location and a time. He does the job, stashes his wad in a mattress somewhere away from a window, or anywhere else it won't be burned or blown to bits, and vanishes back into the mud. That description narrows it down to a few thousand. But if that's indeed what happened, it's not the trigger we're really interested in. It's the one who gave the order, the person who presumably is high enough in the smuggling network to order the killing of the chief of the Interior Ministry's police.'

'You seem to already know a lot about this case.'

'Which is either praise for my men's quick work this morning or a diplomatic way of saying that we're getting a bit ahead of ourselves here. True. And I'm not suggesting at all that you rule out other possibilities. I'm only telling you where our earliest leads are pointing.'

'Then you must have some leads for me.'

'Yes, although only in the broadest sense.'

Kasic pulled open a desk drawer, one that presumably had been filled with Vitas's own work until this morning. He removed four thin file folders and placed them on the desk. 'I'm told these people might be of some help,' he said, tapping the files. 'They've already steered us in a certain direction, as I said.'

'And these people are . . . ?'

'One is a butcher. The other's a production foreman at the cigarette plant. The other two are involved in the supply of black-market whiskey. All four have been doing some undercover work for us. They'd heard things about Vitas before now, but naturally they hardly felt free to pass it along while he was in charge.'

'Word must have traveled fast.'

'In these sorts of networks it usually does. These four gentlemen came forward with their stories before I even reached my desk this morning. Motivated by the thought of bonuses, no doubt. It's yet another way of profiteering, and these people are hardly without their own guilt. In fact, my biggest concern about not having our own people on this is that I'm afraid at times you'll feel like a fish out of water. Our sources aren't exactly the conventional sort, even for undercover people. We can't pay them much to begin with, so most of their wages come from skimming their own profits from the system we're trying to shut down. Which of course puts us in the odd position of having to tolerate it. Let's face it, we're all novices at this game. Before the war half of them were either driving taxis or living in some mountain village, wondering how many eggs they might be able to steal from the neighbor's henhouse. Ask this "butcher" here where to cut a rack of lamb and he'll probably point to the rump. Even the racketeers who had some experience beforehand are operating at a level now they never would have dreamed of, with their own private armies, even now, even after October. But these informers at least know the streets, even if they aren't always what you'd call street smart. A bit rough around the edges you'll likely find.'

'Sounds like they're not much good for anything.'

'I wonder that myself sometimes. But Vitas always figured they were worth it.'

'Maybe because he was using them to tie him into the market.'

'Possibly, and if that's so then any of their information could be suspect. But for the moment it's the only place we have to start. Unless of course you turn up something. Or unless there was something at the scene. But from what I saw of your report earlier, there was little or nothing.'

So he had read the report. 'Yes, precious little.' Vlado thought for a moment of the folded paper in his pocket, with the name and address in Dobrinja, then let the thought pass without comment.

'Yet I must say,' Kasic said, 'even though these people of ours are far from angels, their stories ring true.'

'What makes you say that?'

'What reason would they have for lying? Sure, they might pick up a few D-marks for their troubles, but passing the word on something like this would only seem to make them vulnerable to whoever gave the order.'

'Unless they're in league with whoever gave the order.'

'Maybe. But we've done a pretty good job of vetting these people. And don't think that we haven't ever checked up on them. There are others who do nothing but inform on our informers, just to make sure we're getting a straight story. So I doubt they'd risk their relationship with us by peddling us rubbish. We can put them out of business very quickly. Besides, these four men work in four different places, with three different products, and they live in different parts of town. As far as we know, they've never even spoken to each other. Yet their stories are strikingly similar, at least in the way they pertain to Vitas. And another thing, at their roots, all of these illegal operations are quite simple, whether you're talking about chain of command or chain of supply. Their aims are simple, too: lots of money with as little trouble as possible.

Even when it's tempting to look for complicated solutions and convoluted schemes, the longer you see these people at work the more you realize what a straightforward master greed usually is.

'So I think you can take these men at their word, at least on the big picture. Which might be all you'll get from them anyway. Don't expect much detail. For one thing, it's never been their strength. They're informers, not trained investigators. For another, they can't help but have some fear of whoever's still calling the shots. Killing someone of the rank of an Esmir Vitas tends to have a very bad effect on people's memories. But they're a start, which now is all I have to offer.'

'Even assuming they're telling the truth,' Vlado said, 'is there anyone that high up left in the rackets, anyone still powerful enough to order this murder? In meat, cigarettes and whiskey, I mean. It's hardly the top of the line. Not like gasoline. Or human beings, for that matter.'

Vlado could imagine Grebo cringing through his last remark. Doubtless he'd just betrayed some egregious hole of ignorance on the workings of the black market.

'You'd think so, wouldn't you,' Kasic answered. 'Maybe Vitas thought in his own odd way that he was being ethical by not dealing in the greatest areas of desperation, fuel and freedom. Meat's a luxury, and perishable at that. It's not like you can hoard it as currency. But, cigarettes, let's face it, they're the closest thing some people have to hard currency. It's how we pay our soldiers, or police. Ever since October we've sensed a certain desperation settling into all these markets as supplies have tightened. And if you're already feeling the squeeze and then suddenly the chief of the Interior Ministry's police elbows into your field, well, you can see how someone might see that as a matter of life or death, no matter how powerful Vitas was. But your point is well taken. Our side of the river wouldn't seem to have too many people left with enough clout to order this sort of thing.'

'Then you think the order could have come from across the river. From the Serbs.'

'It's a possibility.'

'Meaning that even if we can identify who gave the order, we may not be able to do anything about it.'

'Like I said. A possibility.' He stubbed out another Marlboro. 'And not a happy one. But it would at least be enough to satisfy the U.N., especially coming from someone outside our department. It might even serve our purpose better. Put more of the blame on the opposite bank of the Miljacka and maybe they'll see our arguments a little more clearly. But this brings me to the most disturbing element of what we know of Vitas. It concerns his possible contacts with the other side.

'Vitas grew up in Grbavica, you know,' Kasic said. 'In fact, you knew him as a boy, didn't you? Although I believe you were better friends with his younger brother.'

Vlado was impressed, wondering how Kasic could have dug up that item on such short notice. Surely Garovic hadn't known. Yet, this was such a small town in so many ways, growing smaller by the day. Fast work nonetheless.

'We went to the same school,' Vlado said. 'But he was eight years ahead of me. And yes, I knew his younger brother well. He was a classmate. Killed just about a year ago.'

'Yes, a mortar shell through the roof. I remember. His whole family. Which left Vitas quite alone, I suppose. His mother was a Serb, you know. His father was a Muslim, although he would have nothing to do with those labels. He was a Yugoslav first and only, he used to say. One can only wonder what he'd be saying now.'

'You knew his father?'

'Somewhat. I met him a few years ago, just before his death. Not long after that his mother died as well.'

'So you think Vitas still had contacts in his old neighborhood.' Vlado asked. 'And if he did, is that so unusual?'

'Not as such. It happens even now. People manage to get news back and forth, along with the gasoline and coffee. Sometimes even the phone connections pop back up for a while. It drives the army crazy when it happens, but there you are. I myself still know people over there. My paternal grandfather was a Serb, though my father and I were both raised as Muslims.'

Meaning, in reality, that he was probably raised neither as Serb nor Muslim nor anything else in particular until it came time to choose sides once the war began. Like nearly everyone else in the city, Kasic had probably thought of himself mostly as a Sarajevan, as set apart from those narrow-thinking rurals of whatever background. So, Kasic had thrown in his lot with the bunch that had pledged to preserve Sarajevo as it was, which happened to be the Muslim government of the new nation of Bosnia. So far he was backing the loser in the war, although neither that nor the Serb flavoring in his background seemed to be hurting his career advancement.

'My house was in Ilidza, you know,' Kasic said.

'I didn't, actually.' It was a suburb now held by the Serbs.

'Yes, and a nice house, too. Big and comfortable. Probably some army commander garrisoned there now, propping his boots on my coffee table while his dog curls up on my bed.'

For a moment Kasic's face had a faraway look, as if he'd looked across the office floor and spotted the booted general lounging at one of the desks.

'But with Vitas,' Kasic resumed, 'I fear he may have had some channels open that were, at best, improper.'

'And at worst?'

'The conduits for illegal activity. Smuggling. Which, if it's true, amounts to little more than providing aid and comfort to the enemy, not to mention considerable profit. The very people he used to rail against so convincingly had perhaps even become his pay-masters. This is not for me to say conclusively, of course. That's for you to discover in your investigation. I only want you to be aware of what is being said.'

'And where does this impression come from?'

'The same place as our other information,' he said, handing over the thin files. 'From these four gentlemen. You'll find the butcher at Markale Market any day of the week. The cigarette man is on shift at the cigarette factory for another . . .' – he paused to check his watch, a massive model favored by the old Yugoslav People's Army – 'for another two and a half hours. So you can catch him there today if you like. The same is true of the two whiskey connections. Their addresses are noted in the file, and all four are expecting a visit.'

He paused, as if about to conclude, then said, 'And now, whenever you're ready, you can question me.'

Vlado was caught off guard. He shifted gears rapidly, wondering if he was being tested. He wasn't ready to question Kasic just yet, and he wasn't going to make a fool of himself trying. He needed to shift control of the conversation.

'Later would be better, actually. But I'd probably start

by asking for a look inside that desk,' Vlado said, glancing at the space beneath Kasic's elbows.

Now Kasic was the one who seemed suddenly at a loss.

'Yes, the desk,' he said. 'I would have waited to move in, but things happen so quickly around here that I thought it best to get right on top of things. His business files, or at least the ones that had nothing to do with this case or with any of these activities, I've kept.'

Vlado started to object, but Kasic raised a hand, tilting his head, and said, 'I know, you'd like to be the judge of that. But you'll simply have to take my word. I know it's not easy, but there are some things in our files too sensitive for anyone but our people to see at present. They have nothing to do with Vitas. They concern other investigations, and I don't want them compromised.'

'Wouldn't it at least be important for context. Perhaps I'd know better where the pieces fit if I can have a better look at the whole range.'

Besides, Vlado was curious, having felt shut out of things for far too long. He could feel himself easing into the rhythm of an investigation, could sense a thrumming in the back of his mind where the workings had been idle for months.

'I believe you'll find all the context you need with those people,' Kasic said, pointing to the thin files in Vlado's hands. 'As for Vitas's other things, I've kept them separate from my own. They're right here.' He pointed to a large cardboard box in the corner of the office, taped shut. Which meant he or someone else had already gone through everything.

'I'll also need access to his apartment. His car, too, if he still had one.'

'Of course.' Kasic reached into the desk again. 'Here are his house keys. His car, I'm afraid, was destroyed a month ago. A direct hit on a building across the street while it was parked out front. And, Vlado, I know Garovic is nervous about all this. About the sensitivity of the case. That's just the way he is. Let me deal with that. You go where you need to go. Ask what you need to ask, and don't worry about stepping on any toes. Mine included.'

Kasic rose from behind his desk, his hand outstretched for a parting shake. As Vlado turned to go, Kasic placed a hand firmly on his shoulder.

'Vlado?'

'Yes.'

'A last word of caution.' Kasic paused. 'There will be people watching you closely on this, and I'm not speaking merely of me and the U.N. Some of them I'm probably not even aware of myself, but suffice it to say that they have the means to influence any and all aspects of your life. They will want results, Vlado, and they will want them quickly. They will not wish to be told of some chain of evidence that drifts off into the hills to points unknown. They will want specifics, name by name.'

Somewhere across town a shell fell to the ground, driving home the point, and Vlado experienced a mixture of fear and exhilaration. Damir was right. No one had a map to lead them through this darkness, and anyone offering to light their way would, by nature, be unreliable.

'So, what are you trying to tell me, exactly?' Vlado asked, as they reached the stairwell.

'To keep your eyes open. To watch your back. And to be aware that now you've taken this case, there can be no turning back. And, that despite all of the help I would like to and, indeed, can offer you, in the most important sense you will be very much on your own.'

'I'm aware,' Vlado answered, trying his best not to sound as timid as he felt. 'And I'm ready.'

'We are all hoping so,' Kasic said. And, with a smile, he turned back toward his office.

5

Vlado's legwork was exactly that. All the police department's cars had been commandeered by the army, and Vlado's own car, a brick-red Yugo, had long ago joined hundreds of other junked vehicles atop a parking deck near his house after a mortar round filled it full of holes and shredded its vital organs.

U.N. trucks had recently begun towing crumpled car bodies from all over the city, victims of every imaginable type of shot and shell. They'd been exploded, ruptured, battered, torn, burned, and perforated. Viewed from a hillside in the middle of town, the collection made a pretty sight, lumped together in a rainbow of color and an occasional glint of chrome, their ruin obscured by the distance, although here and there the burned ones stood out as ugly black smudges, like oversize gum wrappers that had been crumpled and held above a flame.

So, Vlado walked wherever he went, piling up more mileage than he ever had as a foot patrolman. He'd grown used to it, and for all the hazards of extra exposure to gunfire the walking had become something of a comfort. He worked himself into a rhythm on the longer stretches, easing his bleakest thoughts into the open, then pounding them beneath his feet, moving until his mind was blank and he could drift, with an eye out for people running or dodging, and an ear open for the whistling approach of a shell.

Besides, the only people still riding in cars were either U.N. types, foreign journalists, mobsters, officers with the army or government, or anyone else who'd become one of the small moving parts of the war's lumbering machinery. That was an identity Vlado would just as soon do without.

He and Damir had divided up the four contacts provided by Kasic. Damir would handle the two men in the liquor trade. Vlado would take meat and cigarettes.

The only other consideration was making sure he'd be able to reach the Jewish Community Center in time for his monthly call to Jasmina, scheduled as always for 3 p.m. Miss it and you had to wait another thirty days before your next chance.

He decided to head first to the cigarette factory. That meant a long walk out past the western edge of downtown, which would likely be no problem because the day had remained quiet into early afternoon.

From Kasic's office Vlado moved uphill toward Kranjcevica Street, which ran parallel to the river and the so-called Sniper Alley, but was protected by a long row of tall buildings, or, in open areas, by makeshift walls built of wrecked buses, sheet-metal crates, and concrete highway barriers. Some of this stuff wouldn't have stopped even the weakest of bullets, but it blocked the lines of sight of the snipers. Occasionally they fired anyway, perhaps out of boredom, and some stretches of sheet metal were so full of holes they looked like giant cheese graters.

This time of year the route was cloaked in a haze of woodsmoke that poured from the pipes peeping out of plastered-up holes in the sides of buildings. It was yet another way people rigged heating systems, yet another way in which the city was slowly becoming a warren of battered mountain huts, one piled atop another in gray buildings being slowly knocked to pieces.

Every few blocks Vlado passed workers neck-deep in muddy holes. They pulled at the innards of old gas lines or hammered together new pipes, working to keep one or another vital substance flowing to some other corner of town. Some worked for the city. Others were working for themselves or their neighbors, digging up the street to install another illegal gas hookup.

The usual crowd was out strolling. Some toted empty milk containers and jerrycans on small carts, headed to water collection points. Others walked toward the Markale Market at the city center, where most shoppers walked slowly past meager heaps of vegetables – mostly cabbage and potatoes – looking but seldom buying.

Still others, like Vlado, were simply trying to get across town while the going was safe. There were old women in head scarves clutching shawls and tattered bags, wiry men bent against battered canes, and then there were those remarkable young women, still smartly dressed against all odds, with styled hair and touches of lipstick, liner, and rouge.

Weaving through this flow like zephyrs were teenage boys in twos and threes, skittish and glassy-eyed, already as inured to war as if it were a stubborn case of acne. Somehow Vlado could never imagine these boys someday running banks and businesses once the war was over.

Overlaying the procession was the winter bouquet of the siege – a smell of damp and dirty clothes, boiled cabbage, and thawing garbage, locked together by the acrid haze of the woodsmoke.

On several corners would-be merchants had set up shop on the sidewalk, standing at small folding tables or inside abandoned kiosks that before the war had sold candy, magazines and cold drinks, fresh snacks and newspapers. Now you could choose from used paperbacks, stacks of loose cigarettes, a few very old chocolate bars priced well beyond a day's income, and an occasional bottle of beer for about a week's pay.

Almost all the old shops and storefronts were locked and shuttered, although on the south side of the street, less vulnerable to the shells arcing in from across the river, some window displays were still intact. Mannequins wore the same dresses they'd worn two years earlier, gesturing stiffly toward full shelves of clothing stacked behind them in the dust and dimness. In a place surviving on corruption and cunning, it had not yet been deemed permissible to break into these stores, or perhaps criminals figured it simply wasn't worth the trouble.

It was all the more puzzling because the goods of the sidewalk peddlers were far below the quality of what was behind the windows. They were the lowest rung of a black market that had become so meager as to be pitied. Vlado thought of Grebo and Mycky, so triumphant over their acquisition of a few Bic lighters, and wondered how Vitas could have succumbed to such paltry temptations.

Was it possible? Perhaps. Under these kinds of daily circumstances small temptations easily grew larger. When it seemed that the future would never arrive, every day became a sort of judgement day. Every morning seemed a vindication of your behavior the day before, no matter what you'd done, and it soon was evident to all that the innocent fared no better than the guilty. The old rules began to seem almost quaint, in the way that an adult looks back on adolescence and wonders how he ever got so worked up over such trivial matters as exams and weekend dates.

So perhaps Vitas had found some new agenda to operate by, although it didn't fit with anything Vlado had ever known or heard about him.

He remembered the family's gloomy house in Grbavica, the oldest and biggest on the block, standing out like a bunker with its angled shadows and gabled windows. Inside there were lacy curtains, doilies on the couches, a weary sense of never-ending dusting and vacuuming, of pillows that would be puffed and slip-covers smoothed as soon as you left the room. He'd felt nervous about sitting down anywhere, especially when Vitas's mother had come down the long staircase. She was a fluttering, fretful woman, eager to ingratiate herself with the friends of her young sons, attentive yet always seeming to focus on some point just over your right shoulder. She spoke in a delicate, quavering voice, in elaborate sentences that had a way of tailing off before completion, as if her thoughts began evaporating as soon as they bubbled to the surface, and she could never quite catch up to them before they disappeared.

He remembered her particularly from his last week in high school. The Vitas family had invited their youngest son's classmates up to their cabin in the mountains. They barbecued cevapcici over a glowing bed of wood coals, the smell of smoke and the spiced meat delicious on the sharp clean air. Spring blossoms bloomed across the green sloping meadows, with a few strips of snow still lurking in the creases and shadows. They'd all taken a nice walk, crossing grassy fields of buttercups, cutting beneath fragrant strands of balsam, and stepping across clear, rushing streams.

They'd ridden home together in a farm truck, bouncing around tight curves halfway down the mountain before Vlado had remembered he'd left his knapsack behind. He had picked it up the next morning at the Vitas home in the city, sitting gingerly on one of the immaculate couches to stay the requisite amount of time for politeness while Mrs Vitas asked him in an increasingly distracted way about her older son, Esmir, apparently forgetting that Vlado was a classmate of her younger son, Husayn. Esmir, in fact, was by then already off in the army, serving on the Adriatic coast, and already winning glowing reports, as he'd done in every endeavor until now.

Vlado reached the western edge of downtown, working his way behind the highrise apartments along Sniper Alley, also known as Vojvode Radomira Putnika Street, although the new government had already come up with its own, more politically inspiring name for the wide boulevard.

The buildings here had taken some of the heaviest beatings, yet were still virtually filled with residents, unless you counted the apartments facing the river. Most of those were vacant, destroyed during the first weeks of the war, when helicopters had poured red streams of tracer fire through the windows, either to root out nests of snipers or just to take out the day's frustrations. A few entire floors had gone up in flames, and some windows were now empty and blackened. Whole sections of concrete facing were ripped away and, in some rooms torn open, you could still see the wall hangings and bits of blackened furniture.

Across the street and closer to the river was a no-man's-land of gutted, burned highrises, a landscape of shredded metal and broken glass where some people still scavenged furtively at night, risking lives to search for old door frames, window sashes, broken furniture, anything that might be used for firewood. They crept through the damp and musty blackness, dodging rats and the sweeping beams of the sniperscopes.

Behind the apartment blocks and out of the line of fire was an entire subculture of young people, the strong ones who always found a way to enjoy themselves no matter what the cost. Vlado passed several clusters of chatting teens, some of the older boys in uniform or carrying guns. In one parking lot a basketball game was in progress. Boys dribbled a slick, underinflated ball on a wet court, the ball kicking wildly as it struck the edges of shell dimples. The steel backboard was embossed with an old pattern of shrapnel spray. The boys' jeans and shirts were black from the grime of the ball, their faces and hands as smudged as coal miners'.

The whine of a rocket grenade interrupted the splat and ping of the ball, but only for a moment. Everyone behind the building knew instantly, through some well-practiced inner calculation, that the loudness and tone meant the shell wasn't close enough to do them harm, and life continued after only the briefest hesitation, a collective flinch so slight that a newcomer would never have noticed.

An ill-advised hook shot clanged off the rim. The shell exploded six blocks away. The shortest boy on the court reached on his tiptoes and grabbed the rebound, dirty water flying with the slap of his hands.

After another block Vlado turned right, passing beneath a railroad overpass and climbing a slight hill before turning left toward the entrance of the cigarette factory.

A crowd of nearly a hundred was gathered outside the chain-link gates, bunched tightly but waiting quietly for the daily emergence of the one pound plastic bags of chopped tobacco. They would buy the bags for ten marks apiece, then try to resell them for double the price in the city center to people who didn't have the energy or courage to walk to the plant.

Vlado showed his pass and slipped past three guards toting heavy machine guns. The security here was better armed than outside the presidential building, although these men wore old doubleknit pants and print shirts, with dark caps of napped wool. True to the spirit of the enterprise they worked for, cigarettes burned in the mouths of all three.

Vlado passed more guards at the plant doorway, then moved down a flight of stairs to a vast noisy cellar. Most of the manufacturing had been moved below ground long ago after shells began slamming into the upper floors. Vlado entered a room where ten women lined either side of a long table, stacking cigarettes into packs. The packs themselves had been made from whatever paper was available – old wrappers for toilet paper rolls, soap wrappers, pages from old school textbooks and even used government forms. Vlado wondered vaguely if any of his old arrest reports might be in the high piles. He idly picked up a new pack and began reading a passage from page 283 of a high school physics textbook. Something about Bernoulli's principle.

All around him men wheeled huge green bins of chopped tobacco, heading for the hoppers of machines that were rolling and cutting cigarettes by the thousands. There were always complaints from the factory that supply was down to its last reserves of tobacco, but it looked to Vlado like production was at full tilt. He walked on, watching a conveyor belt carry newly made cigarettes toward the table of women. A man who seemed to be a foreman approached with a frown and a creased brow. They shouted to each other above the din of the machinery.

'Vlado Petric. I am here to see a Mr Kupric.'

The foreman nodded and disappeared around the corner of a large green machine that hummed and banged away. Vlado waited for Kupric to emerge, half expecting someone in a furtive hunch, glancing about nervously. He wondered if he should move toward a darker corner. How did these appointments work, anyway?

A few moments later a man who must have been Kupric strolled around the corner of the machine, preceded far in advance by a grand belly that stretched the limits of a sweaty white T-shirt. He extended his plump right hand in welcome. A large smile spread across his wide face, as if he were meeting a valued client to close a business deal.

So this is our fine and secretive undercover man, Vlado thought.

'Please, follow me.' Kupric shouted into the noise. 'The plant manager has made his office available, where it is quiet and we can enjoy some privacy.'

'And,' he said, his grin widening, 'we can have a few smokes. I work all day in the middle of this, and the only time I can smoke is lunch. Too dangerous. If this place ever burned down the war would be lost in a week.'

It wasn't far from the truth. The factory was one of the great beating hearts of the war effort, every bit as vital as a munitions plant. If most armies are said to travel on their stomachs, the Bosnian forces were crawling painfully on their lungs. Daily cigarette rations kept them smoldering through the nights in cold muddy trenches. The rations were higher for frontline duty, and the soldiers were the only people in the city who got filtered cigarettes. That didn't sound like much of a privilege until you inhaled an unfiltered Drina. The sharp, acrid bite had inspired a cottage industry of handcrafted wooden cigarette holders, which you now saw all over town.

Kupric took Vlado upstairs to the office wing of the building. Leaving the noise, they ducked for a moment into a large meeting room, which looked like it had once been quite splendid, paneled and carpeted. Now the long oak table in the middle of the room was split down the middle, its broken sides covered with fallen plaster and ceiling tiles. Overturned swivel chairs and plaques citing past production achievements were piled together at one end, and the paneling had been torn in long streaks. Overhead, a ragged hole in the ceiling sprouted wires and shredded insulation around its edges.

'From a mortar shell last week,' said a beaming Kupric, who seemed to view the ruined room with pride. 'Fortunately no one was hurt.'

They walked down a hallway to the plant manager's office and seated themselves on his couch by a low coffee table a few feet from a huge oak desk. On the table the manager had arrayed about a dozen sections and shapes of heavy, twisted metal, the choicest surviving chunks from shells that had landed in or around the plant.

Vlado had seen similar displays in offices around the city – at the hospital, at stores, at the courthouse, at the few bureaucracies still up and running. The fascination with these instruments of torment baffled him. He looked for a moment at this assemblage, the conical tops from a few big shells, the jagged sides of smaller rocket grenades.

At Vlado's office, Damir had taken to collecting fragments of spent sniper bullets he'd found on streets and sidewalks. They were torn and tarnished bits of brass. In six months he had amassed 79 – he re-counted them every week or so – and when he was burning off nervous energy he'd sit at his desk tapping the cup up and down to the beat of some tune in his head, occasionally rattling them like a cup of crushed ice.

One saw boys in the street collecting for their own desks and bedrooms, legions of tiny amateur experts who'd learned to identify the range, caliber, and origin of nearly every sort of weapon. They also knew the habits and accuracy of various neighborhood snipers, and if you asked they'd tell you the present likelihood of being fired upon if you stepped into a nearby alley or intersection. They had mapped out lines of fire in their heads the way Mediterranean boys familiarize themselves with local ruins and landmarks, hoping to earn tips from tourists.

Kupric stood for a moment, then plucked something from a wall shelf behind the manager's desk. He returned with his arm outstretched, handing Vlado a small, flat tin of cigarettes. Nicely displayed on the lid was a hand-drawn scene of Sarajevo in its former glory, against an orange backdrop.

'Please, with my compliments, as well as those of the manager,' Kupric said.

By now Vlado was half expecting a welcoming committee to march through the door, unfurling a WELCOME INSPECTOR PETRIC banner while chanting factory slogans.

'Tell me,' Vlado asked, 'are your police appointments always so public?'

Kupric seemed crestfallen. His smile vanished. 'It's not as if people know why I'm talking to you,' he said. 'Or even that you're working for the Interior Ministry. I have the manager's trust. I am a foreman. And when I said I was receiving an important guest from the police he was only too happy to accommodate me. If he had asked for more information I was ready to tell him it was a small matter of the government seeking help in identifying tobacco smugglers, but as it was he never bothered to ask. As I said, he trusts me. And so does your ministry.'

Kupric lit a cigarette, snapping a silver Zippo shut with a rebuking click. 'I would have thought my sort of attitude and ability would be reason for confidence, not ridicule.'

'Perhaps I'm just not familiar with the way these things work,' Vlado said, unsure whether to feel appalled or stupid. He reached into his bag, shuffling through papers until he found a spiral pad and a pen.

'So then, Mr Kupric, if you will bear with my relative inexperience in these matters, I am told you have news of Mr Vitas. Perhaps you could begin with the first time that you heard his name mentioned with anything you considered improper or illegal behavior.'

Kupric's face went long and grave. He said that he'd first heard of Vitas entering the cigarette trade a few months back.

'It was all pretty vague then, something about a ham-handed attempt to stuff Drinas into empty Marlboro cartons. Not much future in that game. One round of sales and then your credibility was burned for good. Unless you were the Interior Ministry police chief. Then maybe you felt like you could make your own rules.'

'And this was when?'

'Two, three months ago. Not so long. The next thing I hear, maybe a few weeks after that, is that he was piecing off a share of the incoming tobacco. We like to complain here about supply, but we had plenty stock-piled from before the war. And no matter how much fighting there is, another load always seems to come in over the hills just in time. The U.N. won't lift a finger for us unless you pay the right people, and even then it's hard. But by truck and by other means, it gets here. Even by donkey cart once.

'So, anyway, this was the supply line Vitas wanted to tap into. As I said, the word on it was vague, but he was supposedly using his people to pry loose some as it came over the mountain.'

'"His people?" Meaning, Interior Ministry police?'

'Who knows? But why not. Easy enough for him to say they were confiscating it for prosecutions in smuggling cases. Easy enough afterward to then make it all disappear.'

'And might I ask where this "word" was coming from?'

'From my sources, of course.'

'Some names would be helpful. Or even a single name.'

Kupric assumed a look of ridicule, as if he was dealing with a rank amateur.

'I am not much good as an undercover man if I blow my sources,' he said, snorting smoke out his nostrils. 'Suffice it to say, these are people who know what they are talking about. These are people who are plugged into the networks, the supply lines, and we all know where those supply lines eventually lead. So obviously they have their reasons for wanting to remain anony-mous, and if we don't indulge them, or if we start throwing around their names in the wrong circles, then they'll be of no use to us at all inside of a week, I can tell you that for certain. Besides, it is their bosses you want. Not them.'

Still, Vlado chafed at the idea.

Kupric continued. 'The longer Vitas stayed in, the more pressure he applied. There are ways this sort of thing is done in this kind of business. One way is to start killing your competitors, frowned upon these days because it attracts the wrong kind of attention. Another way is like with any business, through sweat and hustle. You undercut your competition's prices, move in on their markets with better service and faster delivery.' Another new capitalist who already thinks he knows it all, Vlado thought with amusement. 'Then there's the way Vitas used. He simply began throwing his weight around, and this only invites retaliation, and not the sort that is likely to leave you standing. I think that's why Vitas is dead.'

'You think? Or you know?'

'I know, or know as well as I ever could without having seen the shooting or heard the order.'

'How so?'

'Like I told you, it was the word in the network. One day it seemed to be everywhere: Vitas had pushed too hard, and with too little evidence of having the force to back it up. He was a man with a title and a name, but little else in the way of connections that would help him survive any serious challenge. The only way to deal with that kind of threat was to take out the name and the title. Which meant taking out the man himself. If you make yourself a target in a war zone, sooner or later you're going to be hit. And that's what happened to Vitas, sooner rather than later.'

'Is anything you heard "in the network," as you say, in the way of specifics? Or about the structure of these competing operations that might offer some hints as to who was responsible. Who might have been hurt the most by what he was up to, for instance?'

'Specific as far as who gave the order? None. Nor is it likely that anyone who knows will talk about it, unless he wants the same fate. As for the structure, and who was being hurt, take your pick. Any of a half dozen men in this city had enough power to have ordered it, or even another two dozen from the next rung down, although taking out the chief of the Interior Ministry police probably would come from the top, and you've doubtless seen the intelligence reports on that chain of command.'

He had, in fact – four single-spaced typed sheets that Kasic had tucked into the slim file to brief Vlado on the current state of smuggling in the city. That information squared neatly with Kupric's assessment – a half dozen men, each at the top of a fairly small operation, each with chunks of the markets for every consumer good from gasoline to meat

After a short pause, Kupric said, 'Look, I'm not going to be able to solve your case for you, or point the finger at your man. I'm only telling you what was the common knowledge to be heard during the past two weeks by anyone with ears.'

'Though I suppose you'll want extra compensation for this "common knowledge," if you haven't already gotten it, or whatever it is they parcel off to you from the larger action for these choice pieces of information.'

'Only what is due to me. And nothing that will generate anything more in the way of illegal traffic. I only parcel off, as you put it, the share that would inevitably come my way anyway. Only enough to keep my hand in the game so I can keep my contacts alive.'

'All for the greater good, of course.'

'You act as if you are above all this, with your exemption from the army and your regular pay and your heated office. So tell me, do you have a family?'

'Yes.'

'And they are still here in the city?'

'No,' Vlado said. 'Gone to Germany.'

'Yes, I see,' followed by a silent stare, as if Vlado's answer had closed the case. 'Mine is still here. Four boys and a girl. And my wife, of course. All living in four rooms, although we can't really use the fourth room, the largest, because it faces south across the river and the window is gone and the walls are full of metal. So don't tell me how I should get along in life, or that I am holding back too much, and don't think that you can dictate in any way what I can or can't do.'

For a price I could, Vlado nearly said, though he wasn't at all sure what that price would be, or who would pay it. He only knew he was weary of the justifications for everyone's petty chisel, one game of scramble and hustle after another, and usually for nothing but water, a little extra food and a roof over your head.

6

From the cigarette factory, Vlado recrossed the town toward the city centre, to meet the second of Kasic's sources. He was a butcher, Muhamer Hrnic, who ran a meat counter in a market hall near the outdoor Markale Market. By now it was midafternoon, so the crowds had peaked out. Only a few dozen people were still walking among the stalls and counters inside the dim, drafty hall. This was the best time of year for the half dozen or so butchers who'd set up shop along the long walls of the building. The weather was cold enough to keep their meat from spoiling even though there was no electricity, and the doors and windows of the building were kept open to keep it that way. As customers stooped to peer into the counter windows their breath fogged the glass.

On the counters in the middle of the hall, a few forlorn women in shawls and head scarves tried to peddle the last of their small piles of loose cigarettes and other odds and ends. Others offered orphaned bottles of Sarajevska Piva, the local beer still being brewed, though lately it tasted sourly of corn and old socks.

Nearby at one end of the room were a few card tables selling old sections of garden hose, plumbing joints, clamps, assorted nuts and bolts, tangled lengths of wire, and light bulbs burned to within a few hours of their expiration. It was as if a crew of handymen had dumped out the contents of their toolboxes. Vlado glanced around for Grebo's card table, but he and Mycky had either packed it in for the day or were selling outside this afternoon.

Hrnic's meat counter was at the far end. He was a large man in a white smock streaked with the dried blood of cows, goats, and lambs, darkened into streaks and squirts, then smeared. The smock looked as if it hadn't been washed in weeks. He had a wide face and gray eyes, and close-cropped silvery hair with lank bangs with a few strands drooping toward his eyebrows like untied shoelaces.

His meat looked reasonably fresh. Two sides of what Vlado supposed was lamb were hanging from hooks, suspended over the counter. In the display case there were a few passable pork chops, and arrayed on top were several large boles of deep brown cured meat, the salty ham that went down best with a little bread and a few belts of plum brandy.

The prices never failed to make Vlado gasp, thirty Deutschemarks a pound for the fresh meat, forty and more for the cured ham.

Vlado introduced himself quietly, and Hrnic ordered a teenage girl behind the counter, probably his daughter, into action. She poured hot water from a thermos into a cupful of instant coffee and sugar, then whipped them into a chocolate-colored froth. She brought them over to an empty counter where Hrnic had led Vlado. The butcher then directed his daughter toward the cured meat, holding two fingers apart to indicate the width of how much she should slice. She nimbly wrapped the chunk in white paper and brought it to Vlado.

'For your troubles,' the butcher said.

Everyone was so generous today.

Vlado ignored it for a moment, saying, 'I suppose you know why I am here. You've supplied us with certain information on Esmir Vitas, and I'm looking for any leads or ideas on why he might have been killed and who might be responsible.'

Hrnic followed with a tale similar to what Vlado had heard from Kupric, only this time Vitas was said to be horning in on the meat trade. He was pushing too hard too fast, not going about it the way one had to these days. Then word filtered out that he would soon be dealt with, that he didn't have the muscle to back up his title. It was, of course, common knowledge. Then he was dead.

'Tell me, then, if this word was such common knowledge, don't you suppose a man with the contacts Vitas had would have heard it, too, and would have taken steps to either stop it or fight back? And surely he wouldn't have been foolish enough to meet someone down by the Miljacka alone and after dark.'

'I suppose you would know these things better than me, being from the Interior Ministry's special police,' Hrnic said. He said it with a hint of a sneer, as if Vlado was himself damaged goods by having come from the same ship that until yesterday had such a corrupt captain at the helm.

Vlado took a moment to explain his position, and the ministry's promise of his independence. None of it seemed to inspire anything but further scorn.

'So then you don't even have good ministry contacts,' Hrnic said.

Vlado was feeling pushed toward a dead end. 'No. No ministry contacts to speak of. But we're here to talk about your contacts. Where does your meat come from?'

'Igman,' he said proudly, like a winemaker who had just mentioned his grapes came from Bordeaux.

'Mount Igman? A dangerous place, by all accounts.'

'Yes. We like to say that depending on which way a lamb falls when he is slaughtered he could end up on the platter of one side or another.'

'In fact, any sort of steady supply from such an unsteady source as Igman would seem to indicate a certain degree of cooperation with, what should we call it – unfriendly sources? Tell me, do you agree to this cooperation, or does your source do that? Or maybe it's both of you.'

The smile drained from Hrnic's face. He looked back toward his meat counter, pretending to check on business, although Vlado saw there were no customers at the moment.

'I cannot tell you for sure of course,' Hrnic continued in a lowered voice. 'I only know that my supplier says that Igman is the source. All other arrangements are left to him. I am the last man in a very long chain, so who am I to say where this chain really leads.'

'Unless we decided that for this investigation we should pull in the links of this chain, one by one, which we can do, you know.'

'I was given strict assurances that this would not happen in this case. Strict assurances that my security would be protected,' Hrnic said, his voice rising again, his face reddening.

'Your security,' Vlado said, feeling tired. 'What good is your security when you have information that the chief of the Interior police is about to be killed and you don't bother to share it until he is dead. How valuable can it be to ensure the protection of a source such as that?'

'And I am telling you, I've been assured I will be protected.'

'Assured by who?'

'The Ministry. By the people you don't really work for, because you are so "independent." They told me to cooperate with you, but that I was not to jeopardize either my connections or my operation.'

'Yes, your operation,' Vlado said, and a vision came to mind of a rattling contraption with worn belts and pulleys, wheezing and smoking. He looked over at Hrnic's counter, at its tough husks of cured meat and the stringy lamb, which may have been mutton or even goat for all Vlado knew, and he contemplated the meager profit possibilities at this level of what passed for organized crime.

He sighed, then asked in a weary but pleasant tone, 'You can at least disclose the next link up from you. Your supplier. One name only.'

Hrnic said nothing.

'So this is our fine network of undercover men,' Vlado said. 'Tell me, having met two of you so far today, are all of you so reluctant to ask questions of your sources, so timid about repeating names of anyone except the recently dead? Are you always rewarded for finding out so little so late?'

'The only way to learn things is to stay quiet,' Hrnic said sternly. 'To not ask questions. That's when things begin to spill out, only when they think you couldn't care less.'

'And I guess it's only when they want to grumble about something trivial like the chief of the Interior police being marked for death when they decide to tell you and everyone else about it.'

Hrnic set his mouth in a hard, firm line. Vlado snapped up the white bundle of meat from the counter and dropped it into his zippered briefcase.

'Thanks for the meat,' he said breezily, then strolled away.

He'd walked about thirty feet when the butcher called out.

'Wait,' Hrnic shouted.

Vlado stopped, turning slowly. Perhaps Hrnic was going to ask for the meat back, but Vlado would be damned if he'd return it. There had to be some price for insolence to the police. Besides, he was hungry.

But Hrnic seemed anything but angry. He was grinning, almost wildly, a leering banner of malicious joy.

'You wish to be introduced to the next step up in my "chain of command?" Very well, then. You shall meet him.' He pulled off his grimy apron and tossed it onto a scale. 'Mind the counter,' he snapped to his daughter; then strode past Vlado with the resolve of a man on a mission.

'Follow me,' he said, not turning his head as he passed. 'You'll have your meeting, all right.'

They walked two blocks up a steep hill at a brisk pace, Hrnic panting like an old steam engine that had suddenly found its rhythm after years of disuse. Then they headed down a narrow side street where three young boys kicked a scuffed soccer ball across the cobbles through melting patches of ice. A toothless beggar kneeling in a doorway rose uncertainly to his feet. Seeming to recognize Hrnic, he held out a hand beseechingly.

Hrnic ignored him, striding briskly on without a word until they reached a dented steel doorway half-way up the block. 'Wait here,' he said over his shoulder before disappearing inside.

A few moments later he reappeared, calmer now,

almost smug in the way he looked Vlado squarely in the eye, as if daring him to turn back now, as if he'd had this scene dreamed up from the very beginning.

'He will see you now,' Hrnic announced with the flourish of a concierge.

Vlado followed him through the door, where a raw, elemental stench nearly knocked him to the floor. This must be their slaughterhouse, for the air reeked of fresh blood. It was the smell of life draining away by the drop, of fluids already rotting as they fell, the essence of animal panic lingering in the air like a ghost. This must be what made the animals bleat before they even saw the glint of a blade, or felt the first jab of metal sliding into their flesh.

They climbed two flights of stairs in the dark, the smell growing stronger as they rose. Then Hrnic shoved Vlado through an open doorway, where two bearded men in faded camouflage jackets frisked him roughly.

'Sit behind the desk and turn your chair to the wall,' one ordered gruffly, and when Vlado hesitated the man picked up a Kalashnikov from a chair and poked it in Vlado's side.

'Get moving.'

Vlado sat in a creaking office chair, swiveling himself around to face the wall. What had this place once been? A hole for bureaucrats? The business office of some sweatshop? The whole scene seemed mildly absurd, given what he'd seen so far of the two so-called undercover men. He felt more like an errant schoolboy awaiting punishment than someone in trouble with the mob. He wondered just how far they would choose to push their authority with a policeman. Perhaps they'd be even angrier at Hrnic, for bringing him here at all.

Vlado looked over his shoulder, trying to get a better feel for the room.

'You are not to turn your head unless told to do so,' the man with the gun said. Vlado did as he was told without replying, and for a minute or so everyone was still, obviously waiting for someone to arrive. Vlado didn't know whether Hrnic had left or not, but as the seconds passed he grew fidgety, already impatient with this low-budget attempt at intimidation.

Then, a scuffling of feet as men rose to attention, and the approach of a heavy-booted tread from the hallway. A stern but controlled voice announced, 'So this is our Mr Petric?'

The tone awakened Vlado. This was not the uncertain voice of an amateur. The steps crossed the floor, stopping just behind Vlado.

'And if you please, Mr Petric, you will not turn your head throughout our conversation unless you wish to end up on the heap with the goats and sheep down the hall.'

A gun barrel shoved firmly into Vlado's neck, an uncomfortable prod of cool metal. Vlado could hear a crackle of static from a hand-held phone – a Motorola, everyone called them – the membership badge of any ranking mob functionary. The phones worked no better than any other part of the local phone system. Their value was for status as much as for communication. In a café it was amazing how quickly the service of a sullen waiter improved when a customer pulled a Motorola from his bag.

From the other side of the wall facing Vlado there was suddenly a wild thrashing, a long, high squeal, then the clatter and drumming of hooves before the squeal abruptly turned ragged and guttural, drowning on itself. Gradually it subsided, followed by the noise

111

of a bulky load being heaved upon the floor. Then the muffled scrape and glide of blades easing beneath fur and flesh, or so it sounded to Vlado.

'An unplanned but worthy object lesson,' the voice behind Vlado said. 'Perhaps you will keep it in mind throughout our little chat. I am told that you wished to meet me.' The voice took on a trace of amusement. 'That you might even be eager to ask me a few questions.'

Vlado said nothing.

'Well, do you or don't you?'

'Yes, I do.'

'The questions you can forget. All of them. Because I'll tell you the only answer you need to hear. Especially if you've come to ask about Esmir Vitas. And when I'm finished, your path up the chain of command will be at an end as well, unless you wish to feel more of this,' he shoved the gun barrel a little deeper into Vlado's neck, 'only with more of a bite next time.'

Vlado felt his frailness, his recent loss of weight, as if his spine might bend and break with an ounce more of pressure.

'Vitas was scum, do you understand me? A self-righteous little prick who fancied himself a competitor. But he was unworthy competition. So, untimately, a far worthier competitor killed him. Not me, you understand. Not that I couldn't have managed it, if I'd wanted. Which should tell you how much help you'll get from your ministry if you choose to pursue the question of my identity or my whereabouts any further beyond this meeting. Understood?'

He again pressed forward with the barrel of the gun. Vlado wet his lips to speak, but he was too slow.

'So you understand the way things will work from now on, yes?'

112

'Yes.'

Let's get this over with, he thought. These people had long ago stopped being amusing. Hrnic could have his damn meat back as well. Just deliver him from this stench, this pressure at the base of his neck.

'Then you will be moving on now, with your eyes closed and your hands behind your head until you are out of this building. And if anyone in this room ever sees you on this street again, they will kill you on the spot, then flay you to pieces for the rats. Understood?'

'Understood.'

'Very well.'

The pressure of the gun barrel eased, and Vlado felt his entire body relax. He made a tentative motion to stand, but a strong hand fell immediately upon his right shoulder. The gun barrel shoved back into place, and the voice spoke again.

'Don't be in such a hurry. First you must enjoy a few moments of our hospitality. With our business concluded we can talk as men, as keepers of our families, as fellow patriots. Yes?'

'Yes.'

'We must talk of our wives. Yours, for instance. Jasmina, she is called?'

Vlado didn't like where this was headed, hinting at resources and connections stretching to God-knows-where.

'She is, I understand, working as a clerk for an architect in Berlin, yes? Some kind of designer. And if I am not mistaken, she is technically an illegal employee, working without the benefit of the proper papers from the German government, which I suppose is all right as long as the authorities don't find out.'

It was all true. Vlado had gone looking for a secret portal, but now felt instead as if he had tumbled through a trap door, into a pit where all those goats lay below, gutted and sticky with their own fluids, black with flies. What was it Kasic had said? There would be no turning back. Vlado had been glad at the time, excited. It seemed scant comfort now.

The voice continued: 'Which reminds me, we should let you go soon or you'll be late for this month's phone call. Imagine the unnecessary worry if you failed to call. What would your little daughter think? Sonja, is it?'

Vlado struggled to answer, managing only a dry crackle, barely audible over the static of the Motorola: 'Yes. Sonja.'

'A lovely name. So go and make your call. And keep your eyes closed, please, all the way down the stairs, provided those weak legs of yours can still carry you. Eat your meat when you're home. It will make you stronger. See how even we are doing our part to keep our policemen healthy. Even your friend Mr Hrnic is a patriot? You do see that now, don't you Mr Petric?'

'Yes.'

'Good. Off with you, then.'

The gun barrel raised him upward like a hook, and Vlado clenched his eyes shut, seeing an apartment in Germany with his wife and daughter, with their circle of friends, other Bosnian refugees mostly, some who they knew, some they didn't. He began to see how, even here, the influence of a few unsavory people could extend not only across a line of battle but a border. These were not people he cared to know any better. Not for the moment, anyway.

7

It was at least three blocks before he was fully aware of
his surroundings. Hrnic had gone, presumably back
to the market, off without a further word to tend his
business. Vlado was practically stumbling on the
cobbles, making his way down the hill, somehow
headed in the right direction toward the bridge that
would take him to the Jewish Community Center.

What he needed most right now was a drink, a jolt of
something to stop the wild gyrations of his imagination. He'd heard stories about being shaken down like
that, of course. Heard the ways they found out information and used it against you. The techniques had
always sounded cheap and easy, like card tricks, easy
to master, no more difficult than the way the gypsies
told your fortune after peeking into your wallet. But it
had worked its unsettling magic on him nonetheless.
No matter how hard he tried to convince himself that
the threats were empty, that the show of force had been
illusory, he couldn't escape the sensation that the
stakes of the investigation had suddenly been raised.
The trouble was, he had no idea who had raised them,
or who would decide if he had run afoul of these new,
uncertain rules, by crossing some unseen boundary in
the dark.

Whatever the case, the encounter hadn't lasted nearly as long as Vlado had assumed. He found that he still had a few minutes to spare in making his appointment for the monthly call to Jasmina, although right now that seemed a mixed blessing. As much as he always looked forward to speaking to her, their conversations were invariably full of difficult moments, either from the pain of separation or the distance which seemed greater with every call. And now, when he most needed someone to confide in, to tell of his fears and his dread, he would instead have to keep every hint of fear out of his voice. Everyone who made these calls knew that the line was anything but secure. For all Vlado knew, his tormenters had gotten every bit of their information from his earlier calls. Ham radio calls from any part of town were likely intercepted by the army on both sides, listened to by soldiers in headsets.

Vlado made the calls from the Jewish Community Center, at the old synagogue a few blocks away from police headquarters on the far side of the river. It had become a nerve center of sorts during the siege. Not only was it one of the strongest remaining links to the outside world, it was the only one not directly controlled by the government.

The center's long-distance telephone service was a work of ingenuity. All lines leading out of the city had long since been cut, so a ham radio operator made the connection to the phone network in Zagreb, the capital city of neighboring Croatia, which then patched through calls to anywhere except Serbia or other parts of Bosnia. Serbia was taboo because it was still Croatia's enemy. Bosnia was off limits simply because too many phone lines had been cut. You could call clear around the globe, but you couldn't phone a few miles up the road to a town like Kiseljak or Pale.

Even if there was eavesdropping by the army, the people working in the radio room also couldn't help but hear your call as they kept the connection open. Nor did you have much privacy from the others standing with you in line.

Unless the shelling was heavy, there was always a large daytime crowd at the center. On the first floor you could get a hot lunch of the standard beans, macaroni, rice, and bread. If you were bored you could find a card game, or chess, and there was a welcoming wave of heat from woodstoves and the rub and shuffle of people crowded around small tables.

The center also ran a mail service, sending and receiving by the truckload via the aid convoys that arrived at erratic intervals from the port city of Split on the Adriatic, a ten-hour journey across rough mountain roads that had been carved out of goat paths by British engineers for the U.N. The convoys were often delayed for weeks at a time, either by fighting or by paperwork at the Serb checkpoints at the entrances to the city.

The center also arranged some of the few evacuation convoys that still got out of the city every few months, always crammed full with women, children, and old folks. For men of fighting age, or those who held some technical skill deemed indispensable by the government, the only way out was up over the hills on your own, which required passage through two lines of opposing armies.

Vlado's wife, Jasmina, and his daughter, Sonja, had left in one of the first of these convoys. They had survived shell and shot on the grinding ride out, eventually making their way from Croatia to Germany, well before the Germans decided they'd had enough and clamped down on their refugee and asylum laws.

As the man at the slaughterhouse had known all too well, Jasmina was now working for an architect, although not legally, earning wages and benefits far below the German standard. She and Sonja lived in a crumbling highrise. An old police friend of Vlado's had arranged both the apartment and the job. He was an East German cop who'd survived the background checks after reunification to keep his job, though he was still stuck with his clunky Soviet-made Lada patrol car while his western colleagues worked in VW vans.

Vlado had met him on a trip to Berlin less than a year before the war, during a special training course. Imamovic had bent the rules and the budget to make sure Vlado got to attend, because it was a seminar on handling evidence and searching crime scenes, lessons he'd botched completely the other night as he stumbled around Vitas's body in the dark.

Vlado's memories from the trip were all he had to go on as he tried to imagine Jasmina's new life. Berlin had been in turmoil then, only a few weeks before re-unification. Mostly he recalled the women, so tall, almost spectral, and invariably in black clothes, as coldly grim as winter itself with their severe haircuts, heavy boots, and unsmiling faces. He recalled his rides on the S-Bahn, jostling commuter trains with doors that slid shut with a slam, legions of somber people shuffling on and off at every stop, ignoring the graffiti in their orderly but disheveled surroundings, angry messages in spray paint which demanded, AUSLÄNDER RAUS! Foreigners Out.

His walk to the Jewish Center took only a few minutes, and by the time he arrived he'd mostly calmed himself. The less said about the encounter, the better. He wondered how much he should tell Damir. Perhaps he'd had a similar experience.

There was a crowd in front of the center, faces raised to scan a long list of names of people whose mail had arrived. He elbowed through and headed upstairs to the radio room.

Vlado's monthly phone call was invariably slotted between the same two people – a lovesick young soldier in a ponytail who phoned his girlfriend in Vienna, and a stooped old woman phoning her grandson in Hungary. He always drove up from Belgrade to take her call, crossing the Serbian border into Hungary long enough for their brief chat plus an extended shopping trip for whiskey, gasoline, and cigarettes, which he could resell in Belgrade.

Vlado had come to know the faces of the other regulars, and they usually nodded and chatted while waiting in the hallway, but always without giving up too much of themselves, figuring that they already revealed enough in their phone conversations. Today it seemed especially comforting to see everyone in their places as usual, as if nothing had changed from the last time around.

Vlado had begun to daydream abundantly about Jasmina only a week after she left, and he soon found himself far more mindful of her than when they'd been together, preoccupied with the daily duties of keeping a home and raising a child. Suddenly cut off from those routines and left to face a war on his own, he pictured her often. In idle moments when he least expected it an image of her would stand before him, her long slender legs in black hose, disappearing up into a skirt. The moments crept up on him with a slow building tightness in his chest, and at night he would dream of them astride each other in frantic energy and motion, her face locked in a grimace of pleasure. Always in the aftermath, laying awake on the bed, he would imagine he could hear the slow, measured breathing of their daughter coming from across the hall, asleep in her crib, curled like a fetus beneath a soft yellow blanket.

The lovemaking in these dreams became far more passionate and frequent than it had been during their last year together, and he realized that this was how it should have been before. It had taken the first few weeks of separation to rediscover her as lover, as something more than the wife and mother she'd become. But as the weeks turned into months the dreams faltered, grew fuzzy at the edges. Often as not the face before him on the bed was now borrowed from some woman he'd passed in the street that day, one of the improbably well-groomed women you saw everywhere in the city, in their crisply ironed skirts and dark lipstick, every hair in place.

Two months ago Vlado had clumsily tried to break the cycle by buying a prostitute one night after work. He'd made sure he was the last to leave the office, then walked two blocks to the sandbagged alley outside the side entrance to the French garrison. In the glow of a U.N. security lamp he'd evaluated the prospects – three women standing limp and slack in oversized coats. Two had angled a leg forward, showing long legs in nylons and no hint of where any skirt might begin. The third had tried to smile. Then, belatedly noticing her colleagues, she, too, had slipped a thigh forward from beneath her overcoat.

Vlado had chosen her, as much for her lack of professional polish as anything else. Ever the bad bargainer, he quickly settled on a price of six packs of Marlboros, to be paid from a carton he'd received the week before from a U.N. official. He then took her back to his building and up the stairs to the office, hoping no one had by chance returned.

The place was still empty, and when he flicked the light switch he was relieved to find that the generators were still going. He locked the office door from the inside, then steered her gingerly by the elbow toward a couch along the wall in the office's small waiting area. Neither of them had yet spoken or touched since they'd agreed on the price.

It occurred to him this was probably one of the better locales she'd worked lately. Both the French and the Egyptian soldiers on this side of town preferred to arrange their cut-rate trysts in the back of an armored personnel carrier, their buddies looming out the hatches and doors, chatting and smoking, maybe making a joke or two, and for a moment Vlado thought of her stooped beneath the low armored ceiling, the space musty with old sweat and the smell of metal; sucking off some strange man from a faraway place, then spitting discreetly while he zipped his fatigues and she silently calculated what she might be able to buy with her new packs of cigarettes.

She began to undress, and Vlado followed her lead, both of them fumbling with buttons and zippers, the chill of the room creeping onto them, raising goose bumps. He looked at the pale skin of her face in the blueness of the fluorescent light, and flashed for a moment on what sort of life she must have lived before the war, for it was obvious from her discomfort this hadn't been her profession for long. He pictured her, neat and efficient in nylons and a sensible dress, arriving at an office much like this one, removing the same wool overcoat, then sitting before a typewriter, or opening a file drawer, or perhaps lifting the phone receiver to speak crisply to a subordinate on another floor, illuminated all the while by the same pale, fluorescent glow.

She turned toward him, her face blank, lips shut primly, still unbuttoning and unsnapping.

'Please,' he said in a quiet voice. 'Stop.'

She looked at him, her expression a mixture of relief and worry. After all, she needed those cigarettes.

'Here,' he said hastily. 'Take them.' He handed over not only the six packs agreed upon but the entire carton. 'Take them and go before I change my mind.'

She quickly pulled up her skirt and buttoned her blouse, not fumbling at all now, then walked briskly away, heels clicking toward the stairs as she re-buttoned her overcoat, leaving Vlado to sink back onto the couch, the vision of Jasmina appearing for a moment, then fading, once again indistinct.

His connection to his daughter Sonja had become even more remote. She had been eleven months old when she left, a loyal girl who clung to her father whenever possible, pulling herself to her feet by holding his hand, and crawling rapidly after him each morning as he walked to the bathroom to shave. Now she was two years and eight months. She'd nearly tripled in age since he'd last seen her. She'd learned to walk, talk and count to five.

She chattered now in a blend of German and Serbo-Croatian, and even her voice seemed different the few times he could hear it in the background of his tele-phone calls to Berlin. Although more often lately he didn't hear her at all.

Early on she had come to the phone whenever he called, too shy to make any sound but a giggle, but eager to listen and reluctant to give up the receiver without a piteous wail of indignation. But he'd quickly faded for her, and now she couldn't be dragged close to the phone.

'I don't want to,' he'd heard her say, or simply a stern 'Nein!' her obstinacy crackling through the static from hundreds of miles away. Usually now he didn't bother to ask, although today he felt a special urgency to hear her voice again, to hear the soft, steady breathing across the miles.

A set of photographs had arrived in a recent pack of convoy mail, postmarked October, 1993 – three months late of course, after the long delay of checkpoints and permissions. They'd depicted a robust young stranger, smiling and confident, dressed in a bright warm snow-suit and standing on the raked sand of a Berlin playground. In the background were sturdy wooden swingsets, a fleet of strollers, and other children and their mothers, relaxing on a sunny day without a worry.

It was Vlado's turn to call now, and the radioman glanced at him and repeated the Berlin telephone number into his headset without even having to ask.

After a brief pause he motioned for Vlado to pick up the receiver. Vlado listened to the series of hums and clicks, then heard a phone being picked up. He then waited through that slight, halting delay in trans-mission that always reminded him of boyhood broad-casts of the Soviet cosmonauts, calling in from space.

'Hello,' Jasmina answered. 'How are you?'

'Safe. Quite safe. How about you?'

'I always wonder what I will do if you miss a call, or if you're late. If I'll panic, or what I'll think.'

'No, it's been quiet this week. The war is slowing down. Maybe it's good news.'

He felt himself beginning to deaden, to go numb and cold and dreary as he left the truth behind. Not for the first time he wondered what it must be like for the people who work in the radio room, sitting in on these conversations every day, hearing the index of hope slide off toward the bottom of the register as the months passed without change.

He told Jasmina he almost wished for more fighting to make the days pass faster, then realized as soon as the words left his mouth what a stupid thing it was to say.

'So how are you, then,' he asked, 'and how is the job. And Sonja, how is she.' Against his better judgement he then added, 'I don't suppose that she'd . . .'

'Oh! well, no. I'm sorry. I tried to keep her here as long as I could but she's off at a playground now with a friend. They were in a rush to go swimming. There's a new indoor public pool. There are new lessons for toddlers, and she's very excited.'

In the background Vlado could hear the television. It sounded like the sharp exaggerated noises of a cartoon, the sort that Sonja apparently watched all the time. He felt heat rising behind his face, and glanced around at the others in the room, but they were all facing away from him.

'You'd be so proud of her, Vlado. She is speaking full sentences now. Long thoughts, very complex. She's so smart. And her German is better than mine. You should hear her talking with her friends. Their parents say she even speaks it better than their own children.'

'Wonderful. I'll need a phrasebook to talk with my own daughter.'

Then a pause, followed by either a deep intake of breath or a burst of static.

'Please don't say things to make me feel guilty. It's what we have to do here. You know we would have stayed if it had been up to me. It's hard enough to get along here even knowing the language. We have to assume we could end up here forever.'

'I know. I know. It's all right. And I'm not trying to

make you feel guilty. And you shouldn't. I was just stating a fact. Sometimes I feel she's gone from me forever, even if I could be there tomorrow. And it's depressing, like everything else here.'

'I know. I understand. We shouldn't waste our three minutes arguing.'

She mentioned that some Bosnian friends had spotted a few notorious Serbs in the streets of Berlin, one of them a particularly nasty guard from a detention camp. They'd reported the sightings, given lengthy statements to the police, but no one had seemed very interested. In fact, it was becoming difficult to get any news at all of Sarajevo beyond the daily summary of shelling, perhaps a body count, or a few words about another stalled U.N. convoy.

The radioman motioned Vlado that his time was nearly up.

'Keep yourself safe,' he said. 'Don't trust just everyone. Even the ones from home.'

'You're the one we should worry about,' she said. 'Aren't you the one still living in a war zone.'

'I'm serious,' he said, his voice stern. 'Watch out for yourself and Sonja.' His eyes flicked around the room, but every head was still turned. 'The same people who are dangerous to me can be dangerous to you, even there.'

'OK,' she said haltingly. 'I will.' She sounded puzzled. She, too, knew these calls were likely to be monitored; that if Vlado's safety were somehow unraveling, this might be as specific as he would allow himself to get.

'I love you,' she said.

'And I love you.' And for a change he didn't feel self-conscious, having uttered this before a roomful of grimy, indifferent witnesses.

He offered a meek thank-you to the radioman, then left.

A few moments later he couldn't recall having elbowed through crowds of people down two flights of stairs, or pushing out the front door. He only knew that he suddenly found himself outdoors, shocked by a cold gritty breeze and blinking into the sunlight. He had been wrapped in his family's new world, with its playgrounds, its warm homes, and its crowded, bountiful market. He was always surprised by how deeply he could immerse himself in only a few moments of halting conversation, and by how difficult it was to fight his way back to the surface.

He plunged through the milling crowd gathered at the mail list, gaping about like a man who'd just stumbled from a darkened theater. A glance at his watch. Still plenty of time to make his other stops for the day, back across the river. No need to rush. He strolled a full block at a relaxed gait before noticing that people around him were running, heads bent. He'd moved into an open area, a clearly marked sniper zone, and a busy one as well in recent days. Vlado put his head down and broke into a half-hearted trot for the bridge.

8

Vlado had always found a certain appeal in searching the rooms and apartments of the dead – once the body was removed, of course. It was like entering a time capsule, a privileged look at the snapshot of a life in progress, the point of departure for another unfortunate soul.

It was this oddly pleasant sense of anticipation that kept Vlado going on his way to Vitas's apartment, that kept him from glancing too many times over his shoulder. Although he was still shaken by the encounter at the slaughterhouse, he doubted anyone there had gone to the trouble of following him.

He wondered idly how Damir had fared. He was probably finished by now, while Vlado had yet another stop after this one. He found himself wishing wearily that he'd parceled out more of the day's chores. But perhaps Kasic was right. Vlado had probably best handle most of the work himself. No sense in getting the ministry any more perturbed than it already was, or they might strip him of the case altogether, appearances be damned.

Vitas's apartment was ten minutes away, on the third floor of what had been a nice building in a late-eighteenth-century section of downtown built during the rule of the Austro-Hungarian Empire. After fumbling for a moment with the large key Kasic had given him, Vlado pushed open the heavy wooden door.

Right away he was impressed by the lack of grandeur, the absence of fine things. Vitas had never struck him as the acquisitive sort, or as a connoisseur who might have collected art or furniture, but Vlado had at least expected a mild expression of the vulgarity that commonly afflicts bachelors reaching the top of their field in middle age. Yet here was Vitas's television, no large Western model but a small-screen hunk of brown plastic at least twenty years old. Not that a better set would be good for anything these days.

Vitas's stereo was similarly old, with a broad turntable and a high spindle for stacking albums five at a time. Looking at it you could almost hear the painful clacking, skidding sound of vinyl against vinyl.

The walls were bare except for an old engraving of the city mounted above the couch. No framed certificates or awards from his army days. No photos of family or friends.

There was also no electrical generator, a mild surprise in the apartment of someone with such a high rank. He did have a sturdy new woodstove, and next to it was an ample stack of neatly chopped wood. And the trim copper pipes of well-installed gas lines gleamed from a few corners of the ceiling. Someone had been called in to rig it up, no doubt. And why not? What was the worth of power and privilege if it didn't at least bring a few comforts.

Vlado's second impression was that he wasn't the only other person who'd been here recently. He felt an unmistakable presence of someone recently departed from the room, though he also felt this was silly, because if Kasic's people had been here first – and they probably had, seeing as how Kasic had no mis-givings about searching Vitas's office – then they'd have probably finished here early this morning.

As he strolled around there were small signs of disturbance – partly opened drawers, furniture moved slightly off its old marks in the carpet. The signs stood out because the apartment otherwise seemed to be the home of someone compulsively neat and careful. No dust. No clutter. Vitas had not let things slide just because there was a war on.

Vlado thought of his own place, where pots crusted with beans were only halfheartedly scoured before the next batch went in. Spilled grains of rice were scattered to every corner of the small kitchen floor, and lately he'd never seemed to have the energy or inclination to track them down. His bed hadn't been made in weeks, and the sheets had gone gray from so little washing. True, he had bathed and shaved last night as he'd vowed to himself. But he remembered his towel, sour and stuffed into a corner of the bathroom. Here, fresh towels were folded neatly on shelves in the bathroom, which smelled lightly and pleasantly of soap and after-shave. A candle stood in a small saucer in a hardened puddle of wax.

There were clean sheets on the bed, a bedspread neatly tucked at each corner. In fact, every room except the dining room, which faced north with plastic taped and retaped over the window, seemed in tidy order. This was not the home of a man whose life was at loose ends, nor of anyone who had grown careless.

As Vlado walked toward the kitchen, he heard a stirring of noise from the apartment next door, a thumping sound followed by the crying of a child, someone else's life going on. Then silence again.

Vlado checked the refrigerator. A large block of ice

sat on a shelf, dripping slowly. Some meat was beginning to go bad. There was a half-full bottle of milk. Vlado uncapped it and sniffed. Still fresh. He was tempted to take a swallow. It had been more than a year since he'd had any. He'd never much liked it before but the smell suddenly seemed so beckoning, so full of past associations. But something held him back, whether professionalism or the higher calling of this case or the feeling that he was being tested, examined as he went about his work. If someone else had been here earlier, he might always come back.

Vlado saved for last the large Victorian desk in the corner of Vitas's bedroom, its dark mahogany rich with nooks and pigeonholes. A kerosene lantern hung overhead from a newly installed hook. The ceiling above it was blackened slightly, presumably from many nights of use.

The desk was the only place in the house where there were overt signs of disarray, although it was impossible to say whether they had resulted from a search or from Vitas's own energies.

Vlado went through some papers on top, finding nothing of import. In a few upper cubbyholes were stubs of bills from before the war, along with subscription notices from foreign magazines, still stacked chronologically leading up to the final months, when all such accounts halted. There were a few old letters still tucked in their envelopes, the tops torn open neatly: one from a friend in Vienna, chatty and banal, another from Zagreb, a third from Belgrade, all predating the war and each apparently worthless to Vlado. But he wrote down the names and addresses, all the same.

Nowhere was there any address book, which Vlado found particularly irritating, because there also hadn't been one among the box of possessions at Vitas's office. Kasic himself must have thumbed through it by now. Perhaps later he would receive a sanitized version. All he had in this line was the scribbled name and address that Grebo had found in Vitas's watch pocket.

Among the bits of torn or crumpled paper in the wastebasket by the desk were a few aborted letters to friends, with only a few paragraphs in each, discarded either out of futility with the writing or with the prospect that they might not reach their destinations for months, if at all.

Then one of these false starts caught his eye from the bottom of the pile, not so much for anything it said as for how it was addressed:

'Dear Mother,' it began. There was no date.

So much for his mother being dead, although Kasic had sounded fairly sure. Vlado searched for her address, finding no sign of it on the letter and no envelope on the desk or in the wastebasket. Nor were any clues to be found in the two paragraphs Vitas had written, bland offerings that he was in good health and hoped that she, too, was well.

He looked back through the wastebasket for the other two letters. They were both written on wafer-thin air-mail paper, because even though you sent outgoing mail through departing journalists or via the Jewish Center, someone eventually paid postage, so you tried to keep the weight light.

The note to his mother, however, was on a cream-colored bond, the sort of sturdy writing paper a mother might buy for her son in hopes of receiving some of it back someday. This, too, seemed to be another leftover from Vitas's life before the war, as outdated now as the magazines and bills from an era that already seemed centuries old.

He searched the remaining compartments of the desk. One locking drawer, which Vlado would bet had been forced and sprung, held only old financial records, a few family documents, and a faded photo of an attractive woman standing next to a far younger Esmir Vitas, with nothing written on the back. There seemed to be nothing else of any interest, no names and numbers of butchers or cigarette cutters or whiskey smugglers. If there had been earlier, by now they were stuffed in some file drawer at the Interior Ministry.

By now he could barely see to read anyway. The light had faded to late dusk. As he stood up from the desk the smell of the butcher's gift of meat wafted toward him, making his stomach growl in spite of the apprehension he felt over everything to do with Hrnic. He locked the apartment and started down the stairs, again hearing a child's cry from next door. Once outside, he looked slowly around him but the streets were already empty. Then he trudged toward the river for his final stop of the day.

It was a visit he'd been subconsciously steeling himself for since morning, knowing it would best be delayed until dark. And considering that he had talked to Jasmina only an hour earlier, he felt almost guilty to be making the visit at all, especially because in a small, uncertain way he was looking forward to it.

By the time he reached the Skenderia barracks' darkness the only light was from a small bank of floodlights the French had installed at the perimeter of their compound. Vlado worked his way toward the sandbags stacked at the entrance. Up close you could smell their dampness, an odor like wet cement that conveyed their weight and density. The French had built the walls on a day long ago when the fighting had finally

132

slackened. Vlado had watched from an office window as they piled the bags methodically with a series of solid thunks, a sound that made one realize the very noise a bullet would make when it struck – a muffled *thwack* as the shell made a puckered hole, followed by the hiss of pouring sand.

Just around the corner from the entrance, as Vlado knew from his one previous venture, was the nearest place of business for local prostitutes. By dusk a few had always gathered, like birds flocking at sunset to the bare sheltering trees of a park.

Any earlier and they'd have been too well lit even for the U.N. to tolerate. They'd be ordered off by some sentry dipping his face low into the gathering as much to catch a whiff of perfume as to maintain discretion as he advised them, quite civilly, to please clear off, commander's orders.

But there was no shooing them once darkness fell, not unless the garrison commander wanted a mutiny on his hands, for what other pleasures were there to be taken from this forlorn posting. The French were assigned to abut the frontlines of two sworn enemies, camped along the banks of a river coveted by both while shells and bullets sailed overhead in either direction. Your blue helmet was good for little more than scorn and a guaranteed ticket home if you made it through your six-month tour of duty unscathed. So what did it matter, then, if one bought an occasional woman, or even if a particularly enterprising soldier or two went into a little business for themselves as employers of the local talent. Better to have that sort of distraction than to have too much to drink and perhaps put your fellow soldiers at risk as well.

The spot was exactly where Vlado had made his own ludicrous transaction with the edgy young prostitute –

'the bank teller' was how he thought of her now – and he tensed as he rounded the corner.

He found four women waiting, spaced a few yards apart. A sentry was posted just a bit farther around the bend. You could just make out his rifle barrel and the tips of his boots.

None of the women was smoking. That would have been spending their wages as they worked.

Vlado cleared his throat. Four faces rose to meet his, and he saw her right away, the third one down the line. She wore a red wool dress, still looking a bit prim and businesslike for the profession, although the dress looked rehemmed, or so he would have guessed, about four inches above the knee. The difference from before was that her makeup was heavier, caked and penciled with obvious care but leaving an impression of – what? – certainly not passion, nor willing abandon. Something melancholy, frozen. Yet she was definitely surer of herself than a month earlier, it seemed.

'I'm Inspector Petric,' he said, 'and I need to question the four of you for a moment about a shooting last night.'

'Which one, there were only about a thousand,' replied the nearest woman, the tallest, with long dark hair. She wore a fake fur coat slouched open to reveal a silky black dress. The other two, he noticed, were quite conventionally dressed. Either they were newcomers or they simply didn't care. Or perhaps with a captive clientele like this, there was a certain market for sheer normalcy, the fantasy shopclerk whisked off the street and straight into your armored personnel carrier.

'I'm interested in a single shot fired a little before nine, just before closing time, and probably the loudest one you would have heard all day if you were standing here for long. The victim was standing across the river,

134

a little downstream. Maybe fifty meters from here. Maybe more. And it wasn't a sniper. Whoever shot him was standing right there with him.'

'And you think maybe we climbed up on the bags here for a better look, or to maybe offer a better target,' the first one piped up again, now lighting a Marlboro, showing off her wealth and, in turn, her position among her peers. 'Listen, the last thing that's going to catch my attention is a gunshot. Unless they're shooting at me they're welcome to fire all day.'

'It's not the shot itself I'm interested in. It's the moments just before or after, anything you might have seen or heard right around the time of curfew. The footsteps of someone in a hurry. A car driving on the road by the river, that's rare enough these days. Or any customer you might have turned loose in that direction just before. Anything at all, really, because the streets weren't exactly crawling with witnesses at that hour.'

'Well, sweet one, we're sorry, but there was nothing out of the ordinary to report from here.'

'And you're the spokesman for this business association?'

'For the U.N., in fact.'

She extended her hand, as if for a very British handshake. 'Chief of public affairs, U.N. bureau of personal services,' she said, cackling with a husky wheeze.

Vlado turned toward the others. 'So nothing comes to mind then from last night. Nothing out of the ordinary or even noticeable,' he asked, but the first one was still the only one talking.

'If we told you what came to mind from last night you'd get so excited we'd have to charge you,' she said, while the others shrugged mutely. 'Otherwise, it was nothing but the usual run of lonely faces and insulting offers. Am I right, ladies?'

A series of small nods. Vlado's woman in red stared at the ground. He wanted to take her by the shoulders, force her to look him in the eye, though he couldn't say for sure if it was only because he wanted some answers to his questions. Whatever, it was an obvious dead end as long as the taller woman was in charge. He should have let Damir handle this, as his first instincts had told him. Damir would have had this experienced old crone chatting and sharing cigarettes with him by now, spilling half her life's story along the way.

'Well. If anything does occur to you later, I'm right down the block, fourth floor. Inspector Petric.'

'Don't worry, we know the place,' the first woman's voice called after him as he strolled around the curve of sandbags. 'Some of our best customers work there. Good tippers, too, I hear.'

Her cackle rose high into the darkness, and Vlado flushed in spite of himself.

By the time Vlado reached his apartment a misty cold rain was falling. He was fatigued and hungry. It was his longest workday in months.

Yet he was energized in a way he hadn't been since the beginning of the war. Certainly the case had problems, severe ones. But for all its portents of fear and difficulty, he'd no sooner go back to cases of murdered gypsies and drunks than he would go back to that slaughterhouse, with its stench of blood and panic.

He'd begun the investigation with doubts of his own abilities, and some persisted. Was he in over his head? Perhaps. But who wouldn't be in this landscape, where rules and allegiances could change by the hour.

Far more worrisome than his lack of expertise was

the thrust of the early evidence, such as it was. It seemed too pat, too tailored to his own needs, and those of the Interior Ministry. It might well be a concoction, either for the gain of the informers or for their bosses, who may have been eager to hide something far more complex and lucrative. Even if they were telling the truth, what would it matter. Their stories provided few useful details.

If Vlado was merely interested in disposing of the case in a tidy fashion, as Garovic would doubtless prefer, he felt sure that he need only hand over his and Damir's four 'sources' to Kasic for further questioning. Then, given enough time for more persuasive interrogation or more creative imaginations to bear fruit, Kasic's people would emerge with enough to craft a conclusion.

Someone would be selected from the rough list of mobsters to take the blame. Perhaps the mobsters would even nominate one of their own, seizing a chance to further winnow the competition. The fellows at the slaughterhouse certainly wouldn't be above such a trick.

Then the case would be turned back over to Vlado for its official closing, a fiction that he would sign and offer in triplicate to the appropriate international observers. It would be wrapped in the same soiled bundle with Vitas's bloodied reputation, waved a few times before an uninterested world, then dropped out of sight and forgotten.

Vlado made up his mind that he would not proceed that way, not without being ordered to do so, even if it meant plodding through weeks of dead ends. Besides the possible danger of this approach, the only problem was that he had precious few leads.

But he did have one. Dead end or not, it might take

the better part of a day to check out, if only because of its location.

He pulled from his satchel the crumpled name and address that had been in Vitas's pocket the night of the murder. Then he lit a lazy two-inch flame from the nozzle of the hose leading across his kitchen wall. He strolled to a bookshelf and drew down a battered map of the city, unfolding it on the kitchen table in the flickering light.

'Milan Glavas' was the name on the strip of paper, and the address was indeed in Dobrinja, meaning Vlado would need a car. He traced his finger along the route, crossing the map's creases and small tears. As always with maps, this one took him into the past, into parks and playgrounds with his daughter, into meandering walks of his youth on narrow wooded paths leading up into the hills. He ran his finger down familiar lanes and alleys, crossing snowbanks and green meadows from older, better days, passing the smells of a favorite bakery, the welcoming call of an old friend, now dead.

The world had been so large then, even if the city had been smaller. You could stroll up a mountain to catch a breeze from the northeast knowing that its smell and the way it felt in your lungs would tell you a little bit about every boundary and shoreline it had crossed to reach you – down from the Alps and across Italy, then over the Adriatic and into the dry hills of Dalmatia before finally climbing the green passes and mountains of Bosnia, to this city in the valley.

Nowadays the air only seemed stale and confined, which Vlado knew made no sense. And for the first time in nearly two years he felt the urge to climb upon the roof of his apartment building, to breathe deeply of the mountain air and again heed the call of distant

138

lands. He would inspect his city as it reposed before him in the night, its scars hidden by the darkness. The Serbs should not be the only ones to enjoy the view.

He climbed the ladder slowly, listening for the whistle of a shell that could drive him back down, but the night was quiet. Stepping onto the roof into a scatter of broken glass, he found to his pleasure that the mist had cleared, and somewhere from behind the clouds the moon cast a pale light through the canopy. A staccato message of gunfire called to him from the west, but it was distant, harmless.

He strained his eyes toward the hills to the south, across the far bank of the river, wondering if anyone might be stirring along the battlefronts. Then he turned west, gazing toward the black hump of Zuc, gathered like a sleeping bear. To the north he scanned more ridges, then to the east. And at every vantage point, he knew, were men and weapons that could kill him in an instant if they knew he were out here, looking their way. He wondered what those men must see by day when they looked in this direction, the omnipotence they must feel as they aimed their barrels at buildings and people, seeing unmistakably who stood to die, or what buildings stood to fall, then watching the explosions as their shots soared to their destination.

The image brought to mind some verses from his youth, a poem from one of his advanced English classes. Who had written it? Stevenson, he remembered. Yes, Robert Louis Stevenson, the name that had sounded so funny and foreign to his ears at the time. The poem was 'The Land of Counterpane,' and in having to memorize it some of the verses had stuck with him, had become his favorites because of the way they reminded him of his own boyhood – a child at home in bed with his toys arrayed about him like a tiny empire, of which he was lord and master.

He remembered a line from the middle, something about sending his 'ships in fleets all up and down among the sheets.'

But it was the last verse that captured his fancy most, and which now came to him as he thought of the artillery men in their mountain bunkers, staring down toward his home:

> *I was the giant great and still*
> *That sits upon the pillow-hill,*
> *And sees before him, dale and plain,*
> *The pleasant land of counterpane.*

He looked toward the hills again, and, as at other times, he sensed a subterranean machinery at work, a heave and rumble of forces barely contained by the seams of the horizon. Perhaps if you put your ear to the ground, he fancied, you would even hear it, a throb like a pulse, giving life and order to every terrible action up above.

He yearned to glimpse that machinery, to slip unnoticed between the sliding teeth of its gears and find the men at the controls; to take them unawares and to know. Simply to know.

For all its flaws, Vlado decided, this case was his own best chance to do so, but first he had to believe that entry was possible. He decided it would be, if only because from what little he'd already glimpsed, perhaps the people at the controls weren't always so vigilant. Two years of wartime had left them as dulled and careless as everyone else.

With a final glance toward the far side of the river, Vlado climbed back down the ladder. Then he gently refolded the map, sliced a bit of the cured meat from the butcher's generous offering, and poured a glass of water from a plastic jug. That was dinner, and tonight it seemed like plenty, a feast of the privileged.

Before climbing into bed under a down blanket and three layers of wool, he reached for the stiff plumbing knob that controlled the gas jet. He thought for a moment of painting his soldiers. They sat on the workbench in the corner, untouched for days, going slack and undisciplined on him. He smiled at that thought, then shut off the gas, too weary for anything but sleep. The flame guttered briefly at the tip of the nozzle before disappearing without a sound, back up into the hose toward its source deep in the ground.

Through the wall he could hear his neighbour's radio, playing for the first time in weeks. They must have somehow gotten new batteries. And he drifted toward sleep to the faint, tinny strains of an old folk tune from the Dalmatian coast, a guitar twanging against the static, while a silky layer of cold worked its way up under the blankets.

He fell into a restless dream, where the bright faces of women from the day's streets and walkways came toward him in an anxious and beckoning parade. They smiled, but their makeup was heavy, the colors slightly off. They were too pale and garish, as if they had all been daubed and prettified by the cool, brisk hands of a mortician. But he strolled toward them, nonetheless.

9

Preparing to go to Dobrinja was a bit like outfitting for a wilderness expedition. Vlado had to arrange for cash, hire a car, find gasoline, plan his route in advance, and drive with a reckless precision that would evade shell-holes and torn metal without slowing down enough to invite gunfire. It was not a place for stopping to look at maps, because if Sarajevo had become a sort of hell on earth, Dobrinja was its innermost circle of despair and isolation.

Dobrinja's highrise neighborhoods crouched on a lonely peninsula to the southwest, pinched uncomfortably on three sides by Serb guns and trenches, connected tenuously to the rest of the city by a narrow lane running between abandoned buildings and walls of stacked cars and buses. The route led through checkpoints and security officers, and the reward at the end of the line was a small, hushed community of torn buildings, sandbagged and dug in against the daily tidal surges of artillery.

The safest way to go was by hitching a ride in a U.N. armored car, but that meant going through official channels. There would be forms and waivers to sign, wasting at least a day and drawing unwanted attention as part of the bargain.

Vlado found a car easily enough, his next door neighbor's white VW Golf with two bullet holes in the passenger door. Taped plastic flapped in the rear window. The neighbor wanted no part of driving to Dobrinja, so he handed Vlado the keys and wished him well. He hadn't particularly wanted his car going to Dobrinja, either, until Vlado sweetened the offer of four packs of Drinas with half the remaining meat from the butcher. Judging from his eager acceptance, Vlado probably could have sealed the deal with far less.

Supply and demand, Vlado mused.

Buying the gas wasn't as easy, even though just about anyone could point out the doorways and storefronts where someone sold gasoline. Supply was tight lately, and the first two locations came up empty. The third was two blocks from the city market. Vlado parked on the sidewalk, at a corner where a stubbly-faced man in a wool cap stood behind a folding table covered with paperbacks in the alcove of a shuttered business. Vlado studied the titles – cheap mysteries with yellowed pages and half-naked women on the cover, a repair manual for an '83 Yugo, a travel guide to Greece, a Serbo-Croat translation of Dickens's *Pickwick Papers*.

'Gasoline?' Vlado asked.

'You have money?'

Vlado showed him five crumpled bills totaling to sixty Deutschemarks. He'd gotten them earlier from Garovic, who got cash for special occasions by trudging upstairs to a location only he knew. He invariably went to it hunched and muttering like a worried old troll, reappearing a few minutes later with the bills folded tightly in his right hand.

'Two liters only,' he'd told Vlado. That, plus the puddle already in the tank would barely be enough for the trip.

The man in the cap crossed the street toward the doorway of another abandoned building, unlocking a large padlock on a bent hasp. With some difficulty he shoved open a groaning metal door plastered with scarred posters from prewar circuses and concerts, then disappeared up a dark stairwell.

Vlado shivered, partly from the cold, partly from the eerie resemblance of the whole setup to the storefront slaughterhouse the day before. He looked at the upstairs windows for any sign of light or movement, wondering who might be up there – how many men in makeshift uniforms, lounging with their guns. How many men with Motorolas, smoking at some battered desk before ledgers already filled with black ink. The stacks of petrol cans, reeking of fumes the way the other place had reeked of blood. For all he knew, perhaps even his friend from the slaughterhouse, the one he'd heard but not seen, was up there, paying a visit to another realm of his empire.

A few minutes later a second man emerged from the door, looking around briefly before crossing the street. In one hand he carried a plastic funnel. In the other was a large wine bottle sloshing with an amber liquid. Vlado recognized the label of a wretched wine from Mostar, but the picture was pleasant enough, a pastel drawing of the city's ancient stone bridge. A few months earlier it had been blown into the river by shelling.

As the man moved close Vlado frowned.

'Are you sure that's two liters?'

'Quite sure. See?' he said, pointing to the markings on the label. 'Just as it says.'

'Yes, but the gasoline's not even up to the neck.'

'It's as full as you'll find it anywhere this week,' the man said, breaking into a crooked grin, his breath a cloud of slivovitz and cigarettes.

The gasoline fumes came to Vlado like a tonic, an old smell of nostalgia carrying him briefly to long rides through the countryside, tires thrumming on an empty highway. Hills rolled by, green and unthreatening, then the small thrill of that first blue glimpse of the ocean after the long drive to the coast. You rounded a high curve and broke into a vista of sky and water. Saw the waves marshaling themselves in long, distant rows across an endless sea.

The gas cap closed with a thump.

The man shuffled back across the street, not bothering to glance around this time, relighting his cigarette as he disappeared through the door, leaving his table of books untended. Vlado stole a final glance at the upstairs window, where a pale face appeared momentarily behind the smudged glass. Then, a flick of a curtain, and the face was gone. Vlado climbed into the Golf and swerved it into a U-turn, bound for Dobrinja.

Earlier that morning he and Damir had compared notes from the previous day. Damir's undercover men had been about as productive as Vlado's, meaning he'd gotten little but generalities from them, and their line had been the same: Vitas was horning in on our trade, this time in liquor, and in doing so made himself a marked man.

'They're a load of shit, is what I think,' Damir concluded dismissively. 'Somebody's plants, and damned clumsy ones at that. But whose? And for what purpose? To lead us to something or away from something.'

Vlado mentioned the shakedown at the slaughterhouse, but toned it down considerably, partly out of embarrassment and partly out of the promise he'd made to Kasic to keep most of the facts of the case to himself.

In fact, he felt altogether unsure of how he should proceed with Damir while keeping that promise. Damir would chafe and complain if he felt he was merely serving as a glorified clerk, and justifiably so. Despite their difference in years, Damir was his equal in rank and responsibility. He, too, had earned his chance at a case of substance.

But when they discussed their next moves, Vlado offered only that he was going to pursue a lead in Dobrinja, and already he could sense Damir's dissatisfaction.

Damir volunteered to go back to the whores at Skenderia, and Vlado was only too happy to agree.

'Perhaps I will be a little more comfortable there,' he'd offered with a grin. 'In fact, I know I will. Leave the women to the professionals, Vlado, or at least to the single men.'

It was good weather for Sarajevo driving. Low clouds sagged heavily, leaking cold mist, although there was a worrisome brightening to the west. But even with the poor visibility Vlado accelerated when he hit the wide canyon of Sniper Alley. No other car was in sight, only a few men and women strolling at a leisurely pace, either foolhardy or bereft of hope. He swerved around two shellholes, sensing the gasoline gurgling and draining away at several Deutschemarks per minute. An income that would support an entire family for weeks was disappearing out his exhaust.

He turned left, cutting across rail lines where a few empty tram cars slumped on the tracks as if they'd been dropped from a great distance, full of holes, every window shattered. The government still talked of restarting the trams as a show of spirit and resolve. Brilliant idea, he thought – a moving target on a fixed course for the amusement of the snipers.

Vlado had been to Dobrinja once before since the start of the war, and he vaguely remembered the driver's route, up and over sidewalks, and around army barriers. He headed west, where the high-rises began to thin out, among some of the city's newer suburbs. The Golf lurched across a curb and through the parking lot of an empty mini-mall, thumped onto a sidewalk, and accelerated. Two men on bicycles pedaled out of the way. The car crunched across broken glass then thumped back onto the parking lot. After another half mile in this fashion he turned left up a slight incline and into a parking deck to pass through an army checkpoint, the last stop before Dobrinja. A bored soldier huddled in the protective shadows of the ground floor checked his papers and waved him on.

By all rights, Vlado should have been trembling as he floored the Golf back into the open. A few hundred yards to either side were the advance positions of the Serbs. He would have to run the gauntlet for a quarter mile before easing behind the cover of the high-rise buildings lining the wide street farther on. Yet if anything he felt calmed by his surroundings, and not only because it seemed to be a lazy day where snipers played cards and oiled their rifles, either too bored or too stingy with their ammunition to pay him the honor of their attention. And with a jolt he realized he had begun to fear his own city, as much for the forces within it as for those upon the hills.

Dobrinja, too, was undoubtedly the turf of some smalltime warlord or smuggler, but it was too isolated to feel connected, and that made him secure, or perhaps it was only a sense of release he felt, of escape. The narrow peninsula, with its tight lines of fire, awaited him like a temporary refuge. Anyone choosing to follow would be painfully easy to spot, and as he glanced in the mirror he saw that the road behind him was empty.

As the Golf roared along there was a heavy boom. Vlado flinched, ducking low behind the wheel, but the sound was far off. The clouds had begun to lift.

On either side now were the towers of the Olympic Village, mostly deserted at this end. Whole chunks of brick were missing. Some window openings were black from fires. At others curtains flapped. He felt like an archeologist arriving at the site of a lost temple in the rain forest, some place where a whole civilization had packed up and left, centuries earlier.

He steered the Golf downhill, veering toward curved walls of stacked cars and buses, then he eased onto the main boulevard of Dobrinja amid a warren of apartment buildings and muddy courtyards. Several hundred yards to the left loomed the grassy face of Momillo Hill, its greenness almost luminous in the pale light, lonely and talismanic, like some great ceremonial mound built to plot the whirling of the heavens.

In the most precarious days of the war the hill had been spiked with barrels and turrets, a garden of Serb weaponry that sprouted in the first spring of wartime and seemed as if it would never stop growing. But somehow the locals with their small arms stubbornly drove the Serbs off, gun by gun, and now it was empty, although still a threatening presence. A closer look revealed the faint lines of treadmarks, crisscrossing like the stitchmarks of old wounds.

Every apartment building here was sandbagged at ground level. When the supply of sandbags had run low, people had made their own from old clothes, blankets, curtains, anything that would hold a few shovelfuls of mud. Slowing to double-check his map,

148

Vlado noticed two boys trotting alongside the car, keeping pace. He suddenly realized they were using him for cover to make their way down the street, sheltering behind him as if he were an armored car. He instinctively pressed the accelerator, worrying that his slower speed might draw fire. Then with a pang of guilt he looked in the rear view mirror to see the boys running faster now; not scowling or shaking a fist, just running faster.

Milan Glavas's building was like all the others – tall, scarred and gray, with trenches cutting diagonally across the grounds between buildings to serve as sidewalks. Up against one end of the building was a small, muddy graveyard with rough wooden markers. In Dobrinja you buried the dead where you could.

Rifle shots popped from nearby. Moments earlier a grenade had screamed through the air a few blocks away. Yet the clouds were still reasonably low, and a few children played in a nearby field, kicking a soccer ball through the remains of the slush.

Most of the names on the mailboxes were worn off, and Vlado searched in vain for 'Glavas' until a young woman coming down the stairs asked who he was looking for.

'Do you know a Mr Glavas?'

'Yes. Fourth floor, right rear door.'

Vlado started up.

'Is he expecting you?' she shouted after him.

He looked back, seeing her prim upturned face, her heart-shaped lips with their neat layers of bright lipstick.

'I wouldn't think so. I haven't been able to phone him and I've just come from downtown.'

She seemed impressed, even wistful, merely to think of having been in downtown only moments ago.

'Then knock hard,' she said, 'and be prepared to wait.'

'Is he hard of hearing or just slow on his feet?'

'Both, but only when he wants to be. Mostly he's just old and grouchy and a bit of a bastard sometimes. Or at least he likes us to think he is.'

'Is he likely to be in?'

'He almost always is. Stand outside his door long enough and you'll hear him coughing. It's how we know he's still alive, in there hacking away like a dog who never stops barking. Winter or summer, he never stops. If you live next door it can be like water torture. Sometimes you pray for the shelling to drown him out.'

Vlado smiled. 'I'll offer him some cigarettes. Maybe that will help it.'

'Yes, you do that.' She smiled back. 'And good luck with him.'

Vlado reached the fourth floor and rapped loudly, then stood back looking at the heavy green door. He listened to the sounds moving up and down the stairwell, children racing down a hallway, a shout from somewhere below. There was a smell of old cooking and dampness. Somewhere in the distance a gun began to chatter.

Vlado knocked again. Still no answer but the echo of the door.

Then from within the apartment, as the woman had predicted, he heard a deep rattling cough. It accelerated into a fast series of hacks, dry and croupy, with a sound like sheet metal being torn apart in short wrenching snatches. My God.

He knocked a third time, waited a minute. Then a fourth. Nearly ten minutes passed before Vlado finally heard an approaching shuffle, the slide of slippers across linoleum, then a rattling safety chain, a sound

150

one didn't often hear in the city. One bolt slid back with a crack. Then another, followed by a deep wheezing cough and a wet snuffle. Finally, the click of the knob and a metallic groan as the door swung free.

He was greeted by a shocking face, not for its ravages of age or illness – although those signs were present as well in great wrinkles and splotches – but for its immediate suggestion of a neat, fastidious presence suddenly gone to seed. First there was the man's hair, a thick explosion of whiteness radiating from a face of gray stubble where the signs of aborted shavings could be found in numerous nicks and scratches.

Yet there was still something of the refined old gentleman about him, the way the lines of a magnificent old garden still show through even after weeds have taken over. There was once an elegance at work here, Vlado guessed, once a man who might have kept his nails filed and trimmed, who might have tucked a handkerchief neatly in a breast pocket, and worn pleated trousers perfectly creased. Yet what the man wore now was a navy wool bathrobe over thick wool pants, with a green blanket thrown across it all like a tarpaulin.

There was an essence of old sweat in the air, yet also a light scent of soap and body powder, as if he had just emerged from a steaming bath.

Glavas stood carefully inspecting Vlado a few moments before finally announcing in a deep old croak, slow-roasted by decades of cigarettes, 'To what do I owe the pleasure?'

His open mouth exposed a number of yellow, blunted teeth, bent inward like those of an old skull.

'And for that matter, who in the hell are you, coming all the way out here from town to bother me.'

'Vlado Petric. Police investigator. You are Mr Glavas?'

'Milan Glavas, yes,' he said, and a brief glint of interest flashed in his eyes. He tilted his head slightly upward, as if to take a better look, but said nothing further.

'How did you know I'd come from the city?' Vlado asked.

'Because you don't smell of cabbage,' Glavas said. 'Or of filthy children and their diapers and runny noses. And you aren't coughing like a tubercular case, or look as if you've spent the last twenty months running through mud or cowering in a corner away from your windows. Should I continue? Then, please, as long as you've come all this way at such great risk, step inside.'

They moved to a back room, probably once a guest bedroom but now the living room, judging by the furniture, doubtless chosen for its location away from the busiest lines of fire. A small handmade woodstove sat in one corner, a model fashioned roughly from heavy sheet metal. It looked as if it would crumple if you sat on it, and hardly seemed fit for a strong fire. It was cold, barely blackened.

'My genius neighbor built it,' Glavas said, following Vlado's stare. 'Nearly burned down the apartment first time I tried it. But it worked, in its way. No matter, though. Ran out of wood after three days. And that's after it cost me forty marks. Live and learn.'

Glavas picked up a second wool blanket from the couch and draped it across his back as he sank onto the couch. A half-filled bowl of beans sat on an end table.

'I hope I haven't interrupted your lunch,' Vlado said.

'If only you had. That is a time when I would always welcome an interruption. That and when I have to take a shit on these stinking toilets. I allow myself one flush a week. I just can't bring myself to waste water by

152

pouring it down the john after hauling it up six flights of stairs.'

Vlado glanced around the room. There was a stylish green wing chair in silk upholstery, a thick Oriental rug on the floor, finely woven. He glanced upward and saw two nice pen and ink sketches, elegantly framed, and an oil painting that, even to Vlado's unpracticed eye, looked worth a small fortune.

'Please, Mr Petric, do tell me, although I'm hardly the impatient sort who needs to get straight to the point, what would bring a police investigator to my door.' He leaned forward slightly, as if harboring his own little surprise.

'I'm investigating a murder. The victim had your name and address in his pocket, and I thought he might have visited you recently, perhaps even sometime in the last several days.'

Glavas slowly leaned back, raising his eyebrows. 'Ah. Esmir Vitas, then?'

'Yes. So he was here.'

'Oh yes. Tuesday, I believe it was? Or whatever day it was three days ago. I don't bother to identify the days as such anymore. They are either good or bad, mostly depending on the visibility, and then they're dead and gone. But I remember Vitas all right, yes. My only visitor in months, quite literally. And until you arrived I thought he might be the last one for several months more. When you knocked I assumed you were just another of the bored children with nothing to do but make themselves a nuisance by knocking on an old man's door, then run away laughing as soon as the door opens. Or worse, they don't run away at all. "Please," I tell them, "why don't you run along and play out in the shelling. Call down some artillery on us. Let us watch out our windows while you run for your lives".'

153

He broke into a wheezy chuckle, burbling toward the ledge of a deep cough before somehow bringing himself under control.

'So then,' he continued, now smiling. 'You have decided, perhaps, that I am a suspect in this murder?', saying it as if the prospect pleased him.

'Mostly what I think is that I'd like to ask you some questions. I want to know why Vitas came here, and what, if anything, he wanted to talk about. Were you friends?'

'No. I'd never met him until that day. A Tuesday, did I say? And a horrible Tuesday it was. Grenades zipping around all morning. Man next door was killed, just stood in the courtyard like he was waiting for it. Some people do that, you know, just give up and go out there asking for it. Boy just above here was out on his balcony. Lost an arm. And in the middle of all that there's a knock at the door. Three of them actually, and when I finally open up this Vitas fellow is waiting, filling the doorframe in a dark blue overcoat. I knew he wasn't from around here, too. Clean as a whistle. Not a speck of mud on him.'

'And you hadn't been expecting him?'

'No more than I was expecting you. Phone's dead so he couldn't have called. He'd gotten my name in town and came looking, or so he said. He wanted to talk.'

'About what?'

'A great many things, as it turned out. He was here a few hours. And he got right to the point, as I assume you will.'

'Maybe we could start just by going over your conversation with him, as much of it as you can remember. Even the parts you don't think are particularly interesting, if you don't mind. Because the things that seem meaningless to you might be of great value for me.'

'Yes, I thought you'd say as much. It's exactly what Vitas said,' and with this Glavas burst into a hoarse wheezing laugh that quickly melted into a coughing jag. It took a full minute for the hacking to subside.

'He'd brought a card with him,' Glavas said. 'And he wanted to ask me about it. A 3-by-5 index card with my name and signature on it and a small red circle in the upper-right-hand corner. A card from the inventory files of the National Museum. You're familiar with the place?'

'Yes, right on the river. Saved, just barely.'

'Saved, indeed. By our valiant militia, our thugs in green camouflage. Art lovers, every one, I'm sure. Raging against the philistine Serbs in their enlightened, selfless struggle. But that is another story. So Vitas showed me this card, pulls it out of his coat pocket with a flourish, as if he'd brought me the Hope diamond. Then he looked me straight in the eye, just as you're doing now, and he said, "Can you tell me the significance of this?"

'And I said, "Indeed I can, for hours on end, Mr Vitas, hours on end. Only I'm not sure you'll care to hear the whole story," – which is when he told me what you've just said. Tell him everything, no matter how insignificant. Let him sort out what was important. Just keep talking until nothing was left to tell. Then he offered me a cigarette from a fresh pack. Marlboros, in fact, which I don't suppose you'd happen to have?'

'No. Only Drinas. But I do have a fresh pack.'

Glavas curled a hand out from his coat, waiting as Vlado tore open the flimsy paper. He grabbed the first cigarette greedily, an expression of relief unfolding on his face as Vlado leaned foward with his lighter. Glavas sank back on the couch, sucking in the first draught of smoke just in time to smother a rising cough. A wide grin spread across his face. 'There,' he said. 'Much better. Even with Drinas.'

He inhaled a second time just as deeply while Vlado waited, then exhaled a long, luxurious plume of smoke before resuming, half a beat slower than before.

'So, then, Vitas lit my cigarette, the first of many, so I hope you've brought more than one pack. Then he said, "Well, why don't you just tell me what you know about the card, and when you're finished we'll go back over some of the things I'm interested in." I told him this could literally take hours, because that card had a history going back a half a century, and the fact he was in possession of it told me its history was perhaps still being revised.

'"Oh don't worry about that, Mr Glavas," he said, in a most gentlemanly way. He was like a fine young nephew who'd dropped by for tea. Quite pleasant in his way. Put me completely off guard. "I am a very patient man," he said, "and by the sound of things neither of us will be going anywhere anytime soon." For you see, the shelling was still making quite a ruckus. I was surprised he'd come at all, much less arrived in one piece with such an unflappable air. And you say now he's been murdered. You're certain of that.'

'I'm afraid so. Saw the body myself.'

'Ah, a shame.' Glavas shook his head, tapping his cigarette against the arm of the couch, then brushing away some spilled ash with the quick flicking motions of a fastidious man. He leaned back to savor another slow draw on the cigarette.

'Might I ask how it was done?' Glavas asked. 'The murder, I mean.'

'Shot through the head. Down by the river at night.

Most likely so it would look like he was a sniper victim.'

He seemed to consider this a few moments, then grunted, as having made up his mind to get on with it.

'Well then, so where was I?'

'The index card, the one with the red dot. You said Vitas had one.'

'Yes, it came from what is known as the transfer file, a very important but little-known part of our "cultural heritage," as the art bureaucrats like to call it. I told Mr Vitas that I was very surprised to see that he had the card at all, and he merely smiled and said nothing. So I proceeded to tell him all that I knew of that card, and of hundreds of others like it, and I suppose you'd like a repeat performance, even though you have only Drinas, not Marlboros, and most likely you haven't got any coffee with you, either.'

'Not a grain.' Vlado smiled.

'No. I should think not. And I have no hot water anyway, although I suppose I could have imposed on one of my lovely neighbors by offering a spoonful of Nescafé in exchange. But you have none, so . . .'

Then, with great effort, Glavas took as deep a breath as his wheezing lungs would permit, as if steeling himself for a dive into deep water. He looked down at his hands, as if he might have been holding the very card that Vitas had brought that day. And he began his story.

10

'The card is all about art, you see,' Glavas said. 'Fine works of art.'

Vlado felt a twinge of worry. So would this be the essence of the secret Vitas had died for? Some paintings from the museum? A bit of culture wrenched from a wall?

'Ah,' Glavas said. 'I see that I bore you already. Not even interested enough to take notes.'

Vlado realized with a flush that he had put his pen down.

'Was I that obvious?' he asked. 'I guess I had hoped that it might be something more. More than a few cases of liquor or cigarettes, or a few sides of mutton. And I'm sorry, but a few pictures strike me as an even less inspiring reason for getting yourself killed with a war on. Assuming that that's where this might lead, of course. Meat, at least, you can eat.'

'Yes, meat,' Glavas said. 'That and alcohol and gasoline and cigarettes can make you rich on the black market. Over time. And with a great deal of competition to worry about. But with a mere few pictures, as you put it, you can make yourself wealthy almost overnight. A millionaire, several times over, if you make the right choices. Even with the meager offerings of this town.

'And in the process, you can begin the destruction of an entire culture. Either one of those things alone, Mr Petric, would seem reason enough for killing someone in this climate of looting and genocide, wouldn't you agree? After all, what could be more calming to one's conscience, being able to boast that you were destroying a nation's emotional heritage even as you were lining your own pockets with a fortune to last a lifetime.'

'I guess if you look at it that way, it does seem a little closer to the heart of things.' Vlado pulled his own cigarette from the pack of Drinas that lay between them.

'And in the case of the transfer file, or these cards with the red circle on them,' Glavas said, 'we're not only talking of paintings, but also of manuscripts, sculptures, icons from the churches, both Catholic and Orthodox. Even a few old Jewish relics that the Communists managed to lay their hands on. A few old coins here and there, and some swords, vases, nice old boxes, that sort of thing. And each piece, or at least each piece of art in the "transfer file" has ended up in the museum's inventory files with a little red circle in the upper right corner, and my name on the bottom. And if you care to explore further, you'll find that each of these cards tells its own tale of the way art moves and migrates, comes and goes, hither and yon, depending on the fortunes of war, the greed of bureaucrats, the cunning of politicians, and the whims of fate. Because, make no mistake, Mr Petric, in every tale of war there is always a tale of art on the move, of one culture trying to steal the soul of another, whether in the name of booty or under the gentling guise of "preservation."

'Which is why, in telling you of the transfer file, I must first go back to the spring of 1945, at the wretched end of yet another wretched war. So we'll start there, if you don't mind.'

'Please do.'

Glavas eased forward on the couch, shifting the rough blanket about his shoulders, collecting himself again with another deep breath.

'It was a hell of a lot worse then than now, I will tell you,' he said. 'And that's not just the generational carping of an old man determined to prove he's had it worse than anybody nowadays. I sit here now under a pile of blankets with no heat and maybe two hours a week of running water, and that's on a good day. And by God this is luxury compared to that war. The food now is the same every day, but it is food. The walls now are full of shrapnel, but they are still standing. The enemy shoots at us but he at least stays in the hills. This is a bad game of roulette. That war was one massacre after the other. You want to learn about some real ethnic cleansing? Then go back and read about that meat grinder. Or better still, ask your father, or your uncle.'

Vlado didn't need to ask anyone. He'd heard most such tales in all their gory detail. And while the more glorious tales of heroism tended to be exaggerated – just ask Damir's father, for example – the stories of hardship and horror had if anything been toned down. Croats killing Serbs, Serbs killing Muslims, Communists killing royalists, the Germans killing practically everybody – and for the survivors the old anger and mistrust had never been far from the surface. From their memories had come the embers that now burned so brightly across Bosnia, as if the fire had only gone underground for half a century.

'My village was gone, burned to a cinder, a small place in the east, barely a dozen houses altogether,'

160

Glavs said. 'Wiped out by the Nazis and those nasty Croats in the Ustasha. I'd been a university boy before everything shut down, an art history major with dreams of someday running a state museum, and I'd just won a curator's internship in Belgrade when the fighting started. All that was over then, of course. And the village was gone in about the time it took you to buy your groceries. By the time the soldiers came I'd made it out of town on a farm wagon with four other boys my age. Then we ran from a roadblock and through the woods until I reached here. None of the other three made it. Shot while we ran, though I never once looked back. Just felt them falling around me, going down as if they'd suddenly gotten tired and given up on the spot. Amazing I wasn't hit. For three days I lived on snow and a single heel of bread, and I spent the rest of the war holed up in cellars and back rooms, hiding from what passed for the authorities then.'

Glavas went on for another twenty minutes about those times, his voice rising with a passion as if the events had occurred just last week. Vlado sought a way to steer him back toward the subject at hand, but it was obvious Glavas was going to have his say. A man like this didn't get much in the way of visitors anymore. So let him talk it out, Vlado figured, glancing at his watch. By the sound of it, Glavas was finally nearing the end of World War II.

'By the time you survived something like that you not only had the fear of God worn out of you, you also had the fire of revenge burning in your belly, and you were ready to take this revenge any way you could get it. My chance would come through art. A few months after the war ended I was invited to join the delegation going to Germany to recover the items that had been plundered from the new nation of Yugoslavia during

161

the war. I say delegation, which makes it sound grand, but it was actually just me and one other fellow. If so many museum people hadn't been killed or taken off to the camps, I never would have been chosen. But as it was I was an easy choice for them. My training made me stand out, and when I heard they were looking for help I jumped at the chance. I could extract revenge canvas by canvas. And let me tell you, from the very beginning I had no intention of sticking by anyone's rules. I was full of zeal, ready to claim anything and everything that wasn't tied down, particularly if I suspected it was a piece that really belonged in Germany. My chief worry was how I'd be able to keep my boss from finding out – Pencic, the museum director from Belgrade. And then, of course, I'd also have to deal with the Allied officers in charge of the operation. The Monuments officers, they called themselves. Americans, mostly.

'But Pencic was way ahead of me. When we met to go over our battle plan before leaving he showed me all the documentation we'd be taking. Every available certification and stamp and insurance form for every item we knew to be missing, several thousand items in all. Amazing what had been taken, and the complete thoroughness of it.

'Then he pulled out a stack of blank certification forms. Blanks! And what are these for, I asked, as if I hadn't already guessed. For whatever we might also be able to bring back, he said, and I knew that I had found my master. These were the tools of careful larceny before us, and he had not been content with planning on taking a dozen, or twenty, or even fifty. If he was going to risk fraud and deception, then he was by God going to do it full throttle. He had two hundred blank forms. Two hundred! And we would use these wisely,

162

not for just any claimable piece of trash, and nothing for our own personal gain. We were on a mission for God and country.'

Glavas paused, sighing.

'Have you got another Drina – this one's running low. Thank you.'

Outside a screaming whistle was followed by a huge explosion. The building seemed to tremble. Glavas glanced toward his plastic-covered windows.

'Ah, the skies are clearing. A noisy afternoon ahead, most likely. So, then. We left for Berlin on a Monday in June. In a captured old Fokker, repainted white. My first time in an airplane, and I still remember the marvel of it. We left from here, and it occurred to me how beautiful the city was. Before, even when visiting here as a wide-eyed country boy, I'd always seen Sarajevo as some scar upon the mountains, a great gray gash in the green. But from up there it became a living thing, a long graceful body settled into the valley for a nap after a terrible night without sleep, smoke curling up out of the chimneys. And the river – it was early morning when we took off, in a brilliant sun – the river was like some lovely gold necklace on a very elegant woman. A wonderful moment. Then, up, over the mountains, and onward to Germany.

'Berlin. My God, Berlin. If you want to see the wastage of war you should have seen Berlin. Even after all that had happened I pitied those people. Whole blocks turned to bricks, except now it was becoming neat. Everywhere were these Prussian stacks of bricks, and everywhere these stout women in kerchiefs were making more of them, stacking them higher and higher, passing them in long assembly lines, some of the women actually quite young and pretty, wispy from the lack of food, widowed ghosts roaming the rubble.

163

And if you think women here will do anything for cigarettes, well . . . But what I remember most is the stench. Heaven help you if you ended up downwind of the grand River Spree. It was a giant sewer, and still full of bodies, swollen like dead rats, black and bloated, the size of small whales.'

He paused for a drag on the cigarette. Already Vlado could see why this might take a while, so he nudged Glavas back toward the topic at hand. 'And then you began your search. For the looted art.'

'Yes. We settled in and checked in with the authorities. First with the Russians, over in their occupation zone, which was mostly fruitless. It was all we could do to find anything at all in their zone without them carting it off for Moscow. They were looting the looters, and certainly the way we were thinking we didn't blame them a bit, especially after what they'd gone through. Although by the end of the first week I was as disgusted with them as with the Germans. Strutting around in their boots and great-coats, rolling their tanks over the rubble, checking everyone's papers. Making silly arrests. And helping themselves to half the female population over the age of ten. They really were beasts, although their art people were top notch. Knew exactly what to take first.'

The next twenty minutes were a wandering exploration of the ways and means of the Russian art squads, fascinating but maddeningly distant from the subject at hand. Vlado interrupted a few times, but it was like trying to steer a derailed locomotive. Glavas would leap back on the tracks when he pleased.

'Next came the Western allies,' Glavas said, finally leaving the Russians behind. 'Not much easier to deal with, but at least you weren't worried they were shipping half of what they had back home on the very

164

next boat. And the French would have been just as bad as the Russians if they'd had half a chance. Although don't believe the Brits and the Americans weren't taking things, too. Everybody got something out of it.

'The main collection point for the Americans was in Munich, but in those days there was still plenty of stuff scattered in the countryside, a lot of it out in the middle of nowhere, places where the Germans had stashed things in the last months of the war that still hadn't been collected. We got out our maps and went off with our American guide on one subterranean tour after another, visiting old dungeons, caves and mines, cellars of convents and monasteries, wineries, breweries, castles. Everywhere we went was one magnificent collection after another. I couldn't hold my eyes in my head for days at a time. And slowly we made progress. I had my list and began to tick things off, one by one. They'd crate our items for packing and ship them to a central point for sending back to Yugoslavia.

'And of course along the way we always kept looking out, as Pencic used to say, for "the lost lambs of art," the items wandering unclaimed in empty pastures. It was our job, he said, to welcome them into our flock as if they were family. And so we did.'

Glavas chuckled, smiling.

'I can still recall some of the tales we told, some of the finesse that it took to stake our claims. And I know that sometimes people just flat didn't believe us. But in the end they often had no choice. Quite often these were not curators we were dealing with, anyway, except at the larger collection points. We only had to swindle clerks and low level officers, paper pushers who wouldn't have known the difference between a Botticelli and a Beaujolais. So, in nine exhausting weeks we quite outdid ourselves. By the time we were ready to board our fine little white Fokker back to Sarajevo we had used up one hundred sixty-five of our two hundred blank forms.'

'Weren't you worried you'd be caught?'

'Oh, we knew we'd be caught, eventually anyway. And we were. By the late fifties it was quite apparent what had happened. Our behavior became a well-known minor outrage in some circles of the European art world, not so much for the volume and value of what we took, quite small in the grand scheme of things. What enraged them was the idea that two little people like us had pulled it off with such brazen ease and weren't about to apologize. And of course memories grow old quickly, especially among the great hordes of army clerks who could no longer remember anything about what they'd signed over to us, much less the details of our little fictions and embellishments. But the ones at the top knew we'd made off with the goods.'

'So you had to give everything back?'

'Oh, no. We'd anticipated from the start we'd be found out. The rightful owners, we knew, would eventually become known in some cases. So we took precautions from the beginning that would make it as difficult as possible for these items to be retrieved. And that's where the transfer file comes in.'

'How?'

'We knew we couldn't leave them with our museum collections. Too easy to track down that way. So we immediately began to spread them around. Some pieces went to government ministries, beautiful paintings that would end up hanging behind some gray, grim clerk scribbling on forms all day. The icons went to churches, usually small rural parishes that were more than happy to have them. It was the one bit of government benevolence for religion that Tito ever allowed.

'Some pieces went to a few of the big state-run hotels. But the bulk went to individuals. Party functionaries. Ministry bigwigs. It was the moral equivalent, I suppose, of a millionaire collector hiding pieces in his closet. But it was the best way to display them at all while still ensuring we'd keep them in the country. So once outsiders started asking if they might please have these items back, we could honestly say, "Oh, dear me, these pieces are no longer in our museums, and to track them down would take ages, and, well, we'll certainly get on the job but it can't possibly be a priority, you see." Only we knew all along where everything was.'

'Because it was all recorded in the transfer files.'

'Yes. And I was their lord and master. Even as my duties here at the museum began to broaden, I held on to this role. Partly because I knew more about it than anyone else, but partly because I felt an emotional attachment. I'd rescued them and brought them back.

'But then a funny thing happened. All the Party officials and ministry chieftains who were beneficiaries of our scheme found that they quite liked to have nice artworks in their homes. And of course, their under-lings were all jealous. They wanted art for their houses, too. As the bureaucracy grew, so did the demand. And of course we had nothing left to give them then but our own museum pieces.'

'And did you?'

'But of course. Just because they weren't ministers didn't mean they couldn't make your life miserable if you crossed them. So we complied, and the transfer files began to grow. Museum art began moving, piece by piece.'

He chuckled again.

'I even ended up with a piece, one of the original transfer items, in fact.'

He pointed across the room to the oil painting that had so impressed Vlado when he'd first entered. It was a verdant field of lilies in the light of later afternooon, an impressionist masterpiece.

'It's nineteenth century. Chances are it belonged in a small museum in Stuttgart. "*Tut mir leid*," as the Germans say.'

'Aren't you worried it will be damaged?'

'At first I was. When the war started I put it in the building's cellar in its own locked cabinet. But after a while I couldn't stand the thought of it down there with the mice and the rusting bicycles and the grubby street urchins, with the huddled families too scared to move every time the shelling started. So I went down one night to get it, and a good thing I did. The cellar was ankle deep in water from pipes that had burst in the shelling. The water was only a few inches from destroying it altogether. It was strange. It was exactly how they'd found a lot of the old German sites in cellars and mine shafts. In standing water or encrusted with salt. Blighted with mildew. Some things ruined or half ruined. Others caked in dust or nibbled by mice, or buried alive by cave-ins. They'd shoved paintings between mattresses, draped them with lingerie, blankets, and lace curtains. Amazing what they'd done with some of it. And there was my own precious old canvas, slowly dying as the waters rose. So I brought it up here. If the shells get it, if some sniper puts a hole in it, well, better a quick death than slow torture by moisture and mildew. At least this way I can enjoy it until either it or me is finished. Anyhow, where was I?'

Vlado checked his notebook. 'Art was moving out of

the museums, you said, trickling away a piece at a time.'

'Yes, and strictly by the book. Certainly not just anyone could come in and ask to "borrow" a painting for the rest of their lives. You had to have some connections, or some weight with the party. Some asked but were turned down. I got to help decide who was worthy, which of course meant certain advantages for me. Bartering points. This carpet you see. That chair you're sitting on. One could do quite well in my position while still ensuring that the art was safe, catalogued, and insured and carefully accounted for.

'After a while we even discovered a nice side effect of the practice, apart from our own enrichment of course. We found we were creating room for our own new artists. Most museums will send items off into storage to do that. We, on the other hand, were able to keep our patrons happy by putting art in their homes while also giving our brighter young artists someplace to hang their work. The irony is that as some of them became popular, a few pieces of their work ended up being "loaned out" as well. So, you see, art begets art as it moves and shifts.'

'It sounds like a lot of volume you're talking about.'

'By the late eighties, close to a thousand pieces, I'd say. And as each piece moved somewhere it became a part of my domain. We'd take the card out of the central file, place a red circle in the upper corner of its inventory card, next to my signature, and place it in the transfer file. And even though I was still based here, Belgrade never did get control of it. I think partly because no one really wanted to fool with it once it became too big and unwieldy. Once Pencic died I was the last one left who could really trace the whole thing back to its beginnings. So, I was curator of the world's most scattered collection. The shepherd, if you will, of all our country's wandering lambs.'

'Didn't anyone ever get a little concerned about all this? Having so many pieces – what, more than a thousand, you said? – all over the place like that.'

'What was there to be concerned about? A thousand is a drop in the bucket compared to the national inventory. And it had all happened too gradually to alarm anyone. And let's face it, Mr Petric, how many people except for a few bent old eccentrics really know enough about a museum's inventory to notice if a piece here and there has been removed. So, anyhow, everything progressed smoothly, my empire growing all the while.

'Then the war began brewing. A vague sort of edginess crept in. I slowed down the movement, put a halt to it, in fact. Because if anything we wanted to start putting some of our better museum pieces in more secure locations. Bank vaults, that sort of place. So we shifted our energies. And it was at about this time that I got a visit – here, not at the office – from a most unusual patron, more so even than you or Mr Vitas.'

'And when was this?'

'March of ninety-two. Just before everything went to hell. It was a general, a brigadier in the Yugoslav People's Amy. A General Markovic. He is now somewhere up in the hills near here, I am told. His men shell us every day.'

'A Serb, then.'

'Yes, a Serb. And he had suddenly become very interested in the world of art, and in my scattered little collection in particular. In an official capacity, of course. He said he was representing "government interests." I must say that he wasn't at all the sort of man you would ever bump into in the galleries of the National Museum.'

'What did he want to know?'

'Everything. He'd had a look at the transfer file already, either that or someone had told him about it, and he knew damn well what the red circles meant. He wanted a rundown of every transfer item in the city, a summary on location – how scattered, how easy to find, how resistant owners might be to "protective removal," what our record keeping was like, what the insurance companies knew. And values, he wanted to know what sort of stuff had the best value. Or, as he put it so disingenuously, which items needed immediate attention if we were to save them from the war, if a war indeed began. Did he ask about technique, about the merits of different schools, the value of a landscape as opposed to, say, some abstraction that might signify something larger, something visionary, some totem or talisman? Hell no. It is like I told you, this man was a businessman.'

'Did he ever bother to explain his interest, other than saying he represented the government?'

'Oh, his motives were all very patriotic, of course. He said that he and his superiors feared war would begin soon, so they wanted to get a handle on this very vulnerable portion of our national artistic heritage – the whereabouts, the values, the scope of it all – so that once things got rough he could make sure it was all protected. He said that people at the very highest levels had expressed their concern and put him in charge of protection.'

'Did you believe him?'

'Would you? This big philistine with garlic and slivovitz on his breath? Not for a moment. Not a word of it. If someone had been interested in protection it would have come through official channels, and there would have been visits to the museum, not to my home. There would have been forms to sign in triplicate, memos to circulate and meetings to hold. It would have been more red tape than you'd care to imagine, and it all would have been bungled very nicely, by all the proper channels, so that the art would have been in exactly the most vulnerable location possible at the time the shooting started.

'The general, on the other hand, was interested only in speed, efficiency, and, if you ask me, stealth. Does that sound like an official government operation to you? No, he was a mercenary, a silk-lined old Bolshevik who only wanted to know more about value and marketability. A capitalist in training looking for his big opportunity, the sort of accident that has been waiting to happen to this country since Tito died.'

'Then what did you tell him?'

Glavas sat up straight in his chair, pulling the blanket around his shoulders.

'Everything I knew. Places, values, estimates on how much he might be able to round up and in what period of time. Whatever he asked for, really.'

Vlado was momentarily taken aback. He frowned slightly, prompting an impatient sigh from Glavas.

'Why did you help him?' Vlado asked.

'Why not? Why risk this man's wrath. If I could have a friend in Grbavica with a war coming and the Serbs crouching to spring on the city like a cat, why not. And I am a Serb, Mr Petric.' He leaned forward again, the blanket slipping. 'Not a Serb patriot, or an Orthodox zealot or someone who still laments our glorious losses God knows how many hundreds of years ago on the plains of Kosovo. But still, a Serb, with an identity that I may need someday. That I needed then. And I will not squander the possible value of that identity, Mr Petric, not for you and not for all the goddamned painted canvas in this city. Tell me, Mr Petric, under these circumstances, would you? Toss away your security, I mean, by standing up for principle against some philistine in hopes of keeping a few hundred pieces of art from leaving the country?'

'Is that what you think has happened? That this art has left the country.'

'Has left or is leaving, take your pick. How else would you be able to profit from it. By selling it at the Markale Market, next to the potatoes and the plumbing joints? Prop it up on a card table with the insurance appraisal tacked to the frame? Use your head, Mr Petric. Art may survive in a war zone, but the art "community" that is supposed to protect it usually scampers away on the cowardly feet of foxes. A few diehards always stay to try to hold the old order together, or to try to "protect our heritage," as they put it. But the others get out while they can, using every connection available to them, leaving the rest of us to get ourselves killed. Like your friend Mr Vitas.'

'Is this what Vitas thought as well, that art was leaving the country?'

'He suspected it strongly even before he arrived here, I believe, and once I told him of my chat with the good General Markovic he seemed quite sure of it. Or so I gathered from his questions.'

'What sort of questions?'

'He wanted to know about the current supply, about what might still be in the city from the transfer file. About what might have been moved since the beginning of the war, who had been in charge of moving it, who had been in charge of protecting it, if anyone. And who had been in charge of the records, or had access to them, besides myself. He asked if anyone had been in touch with the insurers, or if anyone from the U.N. had shown an interest. And he wanted to know what sort of market there might be for these items, assuming one could indeed get them out of the city, out of the country. In fact, he wanted to know very many of the same things as General Markovic, except he was obviously a few years behind.'

'You don't think he was involved with the general? Trying to find out if he'd been dealing straight with him, for instance?'

'He could have been, I suppose. When I thought about it later I realized Vitas could have been simply following in the general's footsteps to see if his story rang true. Wondering if he was being cheated by his partner in crime, so to speak. Yes, that occurred to me. It also seemed unusual that the chief of the Interior Ministry police would be doing his own investigation. I'm not in your line of work, of course, but I gather that the chief usually has someone lower down, like yourself, to actually go out in the field and get his feet muddy. Especially if they have to come some place like this. What do you think?'

'I'm not sure what to think. Vitas must have had a reason to handle the investigation himself, if that's what he was doing. Or maybe, like you said, he was trying to check out his partners.'

'No, I decided I didn't really believe that. But he could have been trying to cut himself in on the whole scheme, I suppose, a latecomer who'd gotten wind of the scheme and wanted to make his own killing before the supply was all gone. That could explain his interest, too. Because he also seemed interested in learning how to pick up the trail, how to identify the traces of the items that had already moved, the sort of signs that might be left behind by this kind of activity.'

'And what kind of signs would it leave?'

'Empty spaces mostly. Empty spaces on walls where paintings used to hang.' Glavas broke into a laugh, cackling and wheezing, motioning with his hands for another cigarette. He inhaled deeply, stifling another wheeze, then paused to catch his breath.

'Empty spaces? That's all?'

'No. That's only the most obvious sign. If you wanted to keep the appearance of propriety and cover your tracks, there would have to be new notations on the cards in the transfer files for every item taken. It would be simple enough in a war. "Destroyed, claim applied for," or, "Looted, claim applied for." All with dates since the beginning of the war, in buildings known to have been hit or attacked or seized by the wrong sort of people. That sort of thing. Or if you were simply too lazy and maybe a bit too greedy as well, there was an easier way altogether. You could just destroy the transfer files, then there wouldn't even be any records to doctor. And eleven months ago that's exactly what happened.'

'Destroyed? All of them?'

'Every last card. One freak shell through a window and then a fire. Or so they said at the museum. The fire was miraculously contained in one room.'

'You sound like you think it was deliberate.'

'Look at who was guarding the place. The same thugs who'd saved it. All of a sudden one morning everything in the file is gone, or rather, burned to cinders, yet not a single painting in the museum is damaged. I tried raising a stink, and would still be raising one, but two days later I was sacked.'

'Why?'

'That bastard Murovic, the empty-headed young fool who took over the National Museum three weeks after the war began, right after the director was killed by a mortar shell. He hated all the old hands, and he hated worst of all the ones who knew more than he did, which was two strikes against me right away. Being a Serb didn't exactly mark me for advancement, either. And with the transfer files gone, Murovic had the excuse he needed. I was obsolete without my collection.'

'What's his role been in all this?'

'Murovic? Not much until lately. The museum had been in total confusion anyway since the war began. For two months everyone was more or less in their cellars during the worst of the fighting. Then as they started climbing out, rubbing their eyes and shaking off the dust, that's when people started to think they just might survive this. And then, too late, everyone began to worry about the art.

'But by then Murovic and his young bureaucrats had the jump on me. He'd gotten back in there as soon as he could, staking his claim as acting director and bending the ears of whoever was left at the local offices of the Ministry of Culture. Meanwhile I was still out here in Dobrinja, unable to move. It was another six weeks before I could get into the city, and even then only by riding in a U.N. armored personnel carrier. In those days I stayed in the city a week or so at a time to work, then came back here in those awful rolling coffins. But by the time I'd first made it back into the city Murovic had convinced the ministry that I was a closet Serb zealot who couldn't be trusted, and that furthermore I'd gone senile, wasn't up to the job anymore, especially, as he put it, "in the chaos of wartime."

'I couldn't deny I'd let things slide the last few years,

either. I'd gotten lax, lazy. But my recordkeeping was still clear, and I still had the best institutional memory of the entire ministry. The last person Murovic wanted around was somebody who'd continually be correcting him and second guessing as he took over. But by my way of thinking, I could write down a quarter of the transfer file from memory right now, getting it down to the penny on appraised and insured value, and plenty of the locations, too. All I'd need would be a full week in a clean, quiet room, with good food and an unlimited supply of Marlboros.

'Of course I told this to Murovic, but he just laughed. He found it quaint, wished me well in retirement, told me to stay out of harm's way. He told me the U.N. would sort it all out eventually, and in a far more scientific way. Then he packed me straight off to Dobrinja, and there went my authorization for U.N. escorts into town. He'd exiled me as effectively as if he'd sent me to Elba. So here I am in my confinement, where, I regret to say, I have lost all touch with that insular little world called the art community.'

He paused, sinking back in the chair.

'Another cigarette please,' he said weakly.

Vlado tried to digest all he'd heard as he held out his lighter. Then a puzzle occurred to him. He flipped back through his notes a moment, then asked: 'If the files were destroyed eleven months ago, what was Vitas doing with a card last Tuesday?'

'Ah. That is exactly what I wanted to know. Because it was an original he had, not a copy. My very own handwriting right there on the back. He was very coy about it. Very foxy, yet still the courtly gentleman. He told me it would be better for both of us if I didn't know. He sort of smiled when he said it. I asked if the rest of the files were still around, and he told me something very odd. He said they were in safe hands in unsafe surroundings. Whatever that means.'

'You said he also asked you if anyone besides General Markovic had ever expressed an interest in the file. Other government people, or even U.N. people. Had they?'

'No one to my knowledge. Perhaps you should ask Murovic that.'

'Did either Vitas or Markovic mention other names, other possible contacts?'

'Not one. As I said, Vitas was very careful. His questions told me little, and mostly he just sat and listened, nodding, as if he'd known everything all along. And if he'd ever heard General Markovic's name come up before, then you wouldn't have known it from his reaction. He was as blank as a stone. Not someone I'd want to play cards with.'

Vlado mulled this over for a moment, then offered another cigarette to Glavas.

'So, then,' Vlado said. 'Perhaps you can help me figure out where I might begin. Where I might go from here. If the files are gone, or hidden, then I guess another possibility is in tracking down art that might be leaving. Assuming that pieces were still being taken, or that any have been taken at all, how would one go about getting a painting out of the city without arousing suspicions.'

'Under conditions like these? Use your head, Mr Petric. There has never been a better time. Half the city's evacuated, or dead and buried. Buildings are destroyed or half-wrecked. Even the Nazis didn't have it so easy. At least with them, once the war was over we knew who had it, where to look for it. Under these conditions who's to say where something might end up once it's looted. There will be a thousand suspects to choose from. The Serbs will blame the Muslims, the Muslims will blame the Chetniks, the Croats, too. Everybody will blame everybody, and then you've got the gangsters, Zarko or Enko or any of a dozen hoods in this city alone. And if you don't like your neighbor's looks you can always blame him. I'm a Serb and know my stuff, so maybe someone will even think to blame me. Maybe they already have. Or maybe now someone will pin it all on Vitas. Dead men always have a knack for attracting blame.

'The point is, there are a thousand built in excuses if you want to explain away a lot of missing art, and that gives you all the opportunity in the world for lifting, looting, or "misplacing" any piece you might get your hands on. And that goes double for items from the transfer files, as long as there aren't any records. Who can even say what's been taken if you don't know what existed to begin with? And even if that idiot Murovic ever gets UNESCO on his side, by then anything that turns up missing will be written off as a casualty of war. And whoever took it will be home free.'

'Yes, but actually getting it out of here is a different matter. It's not like you can just crate up a picture and drive it over the mountain in a truck, unless you have a U.N. escort. Even then you might lose it on the way at a checkpoint. The only sure way is by air, and that's strictly U.N.'

'And you think that's an obstacle?'

'Isn't it?'

'Ah, the U.N.'

Glavas cackled, wheezing again, then broke into a splitting cough. By now Vlado was expecting to see his insides begin bubbling out of his mouth in a red-and-gray froth. Glavas lifted a crusted, yellowed

179

handkerchief to his mouth and hawked into it. As he pulled it away a rubbery green thread stretched from his nostrils like a strand of melted cheese from a slice of pizza. Glavas wiped it away with the sleeve of his other arm as he heaved gently with laughter.

'Pardon me, Mr Petric. One thing that I must say pleases me about wartime. No more resting on the need for convention and good manners. It's all too tiring, so I'm free to just be a grotesque old man, and I can blame it all on the Chetniks.'

He laughed again, and for a moment Vlado thought he was about to descend into another gorge of hacking. But the wheeze subsided, and Glavas slumped back in his chair, spent.

'Yes, the U.N.,' he began again, in a softer voice, his face tilted toward the ceiling. 'Our protector against evil. Do you realize, Mr Petric, that if you want to ship in something other than beans and rice and flour that the U.N. won't let you? Not fair, they say. That would be taking sides in the war. Not even medicine. The Serbs would object, they say. Maybe some salt and pepper then? Or perhaps a load of vegetables or two? No, not possible. Against the rules. Yet I firmly believe that if you want badly enough to send something *out* of the city on those empty departing planes, something small and portable and easily loaded into an air cargo bay, then that is entirely possible provided you have the right sums of money. Do I know this officially? Or for certain? No, Mr Petric, I don't. But I feel intuitively from the whisperings I heard around the gallery early in the war, talk of private collectors protecting their choicest pieces by sweet-talking UNESCO underlings and blue-helmeted shipping officers. A few Deutsche-marks here and there. It is all a private matter, a few favors for friends, and then it need never be spoken of again. So, yes, I believe the U.N. is not so great an obstacle.'

'But once you've shipped it, then what? What's the international market for stolen art? Won't someone ask questions about where it's from?'

'Do you have any idea how much stolen art is ever recovered, Mr Petric? Any idea at all?'

'A third? Maybe a quarter?'

'Less than one per cent. And when no one even has a piece of paper to alert the international auction markets, then you're going to shave that figure even closer. All you need is a broker willing to ask as few questions as possible. London, Zurich, New York, any of those three places would probably do. And if there are still worries, there's always some discreet oilman in Texas who'll take it for his basement. Or some rich old German in South America who has half the local constabulary in the hip pocket of his lederhosen. Selling it and keeping it a secret aren't the hard parts unless it's something so notoriously famous that everyone will spot it right away. And nothing from here fits that description. Which isn't to say you can't make a lot of money from it.'

'So how many items are we talking about? You said the transfer files were up past a thousand, but obviously not everything was in Sarajevo.'

'No. But more of it than you'd think. Belgrade and Zagreb never seemed quite as interested as local folks and officials. This always has been a city that prided itself on its tastes, on its private collections. About three hundred or so were here.'

'Then how much money are we talking about? On average.'

'Art isn't something that lends itself to averaging. At least that's what I used to tell people to show off my

181

purity. But I've grown vulgar in my old age, and I'll tell you right now that the worth of the three hundred or so transfer items in the city probably averaged out to about a hundred sixty thousand dollars apiece. Hardly something to get the art people at Scotland Yard excited about. But get your hands on a third of the supply and you've got sixteen million. Not bad for a hard cash economy. And if you're willing to be a little more discriminating you can easily up your average, maybe four hundred thousand apiece for the top one-third. Now you're looking at forty million, or at least twenty million even after you've accounted for the discounting you sometimes have to do when you're selling items of questionable provenance. I can see someone getting killed over that, Mr Petric, can't you?'

So much for meat and cigarettes, Vlado thought. So much for the sad, tawdry underbelly of the city's organized crime. Now death on a small scale began to have a certain logic.

'I'd like you to do a favor for me,' he said to Glavas. 'I can't provide you with either a clean, warm room or good food, and I don't have any Marlboros. But I can leave you a full pack of Drinas if you can start trying to put together what you remember of the local items that were in the transfer files.'

'Under the circumstances, I'd consider that a generous offer.'

'Take the next two days and write down as much as you can remember about the most valuable pieces. Who had them. At what location. Particularly in the city center. Never mind the Grbavica and Ilidza locations. Never mind your piece up on the wall, either. I want to start looking for some of those "empty spaces" you were talking about, the more recently empty the better, and the only way I'll know where to look is with the help of your memory.'

'Consider it done,' Glavas said, flashing some of the old nobility and grace he must have employed during his years in the universe of artists and museums. 'It will be a privilege to feel useful again. I'll begin as soon as you've left.'

Vlado shut his notebook, hunching forward as if ready to stand, then asked, 'Did Vitas say anything about where he was going next. About who else he might be seeing?'

'Nothing, I'm afraid. As I said, he was quite careful about those things. And if someone as careful as him can be killed so easily, then I would think you might want to watch yourself, Mr Petric.'

'The thought has occurred to me. And if you should get any more visitors interested in this subject, Mr Glavas, please let me know.'

'And how am I to do that? How, for that matter, am I to get this list to you once I'm done. The phones here work about once a month. And something tells me you don't want me sending messages out through the police or the U.N.'

'I'll come pick it up. Same time in two days. Though don't be alarmed if I'm late, even if by a day or two.'

'Either way, I won't be going anywhere.'

Vlado stood, stepping toward the door.

'In the meantime, I suppose I should pay a visit to your friend, Mr Murovic. Do you know where to find him?'

'In his new office at the National Bank of Bosnia, down next to the main vault, like Tutankhamen in his tomb. Our Boy King of art, and every bit as naive and easily led. But if you're truly interested in looking for those "empty spaces" right away, Mr Petric, I think I may have a starting place for you.'

Vlado paused with his hand on the doorknob.

'Yes,' he said quietly. 'I'd appreciate that.'

'Try starting with Murovic's head,' Glavas said. 'It's the emptiest space in all of Sarajevo.'

And with that he tumbled into another great outburst of wheezing laughter, which continued as he waved Vlado out the door.

As Vlado started down the steps, the wheezes hardened into a sharp cough, and it was still crashing onward as Vlado emerged from the exit downstairs, where the sound was finally drowned out by the urgent shouts of children and the rattle of gunfire.

11

The drive back from Dobrinja was blessedly un-
eventful, and by the time Vlado dropped off the car the
sun was shining, pouring onto the sugary hillsides
where snow fell earliest and deepest. From down in
the city the distant clusters of rooftops and balsams
resembled miniature Christmas villages, posed for a
photograph. One needed a pair of binoculars to see
where the scene needed retouching – the holes in the
roofs, the burn marks and broken windows. And it
would have taken a particularly powerful model, as
well as some patience, to pick out the gun barrels here
and there, poking from camouflaged burrows.

The Bank of Bosnia, formerly YugoBanka, had been
forced into wartime hibernation by a lack of cash
and the government's need for its deep sturdy vaults.
They'd been built into the hillside forty years earlier,
and it would take a nuclear blast to pry them loose,
much less break them apart. So, that's where the
government stored its most valuable treasures, everything from the rarest museum pieces to records for
property and finance. And it was here, according to
Milan Glavas, that Vlado would find Enver Murovic,
the young new director of the National Museum.

Vlado walked through the entrance into an armed

camp. Five men slung heavily with machine guns immediately rose to greet him, like a legion of bored shop clerks eager to sell him a suit. The place smelled of a year's worth of sweat and cigarettes, and a thick layer of dust coated the empty counters and teller cages.

'Enver Murovic,' Vlado asked uncertainly, and when no one answered he added, 'I'm Inspector Petric . . . representing the Interior Ministry police.'

Still no one answered, but one of the men disappeared out a rear door, while three of the others slowly settled back to their roosts. The fifth strode out the front door, past Vlado without a further look, taking up a post outside, where he probably should have been all along.

Murovic's voice preceded him into the room, a fluttery burst of aggrieved authority, uttered with absolute disdain. Vlado picked it up in midsentence.

'. . . simply can't have these sorts of interruptions in the future without either better identification or a confirmed appointment.'

He emerged from around the corner into the gloom, a tall man, reed thin, dressed all in black except for his glasses, thick frames in bright magenta. His hair was cut neatly, close to the scalp. That, plus his brisk, officious manner, made him strike Vlado as a refined version of Garovic. His style and image were those of an aesthete, yet somehow he still betrayed the careful, grasping soul of a career bureaucrat on the make. Vlado could very easily imagine this fellow shoving old baggage like Glavas out the door. Or down a long flight of stairs.

Abruptly turning Vlado's way, Murovic gave him a slow once-over, his gaze sweeping from top to bottom, then back to the face, a look of appraisal that said, No, this won't do, but we'll be as courteous as protocol requires.

'Yes. I'm Mr Murovic,' he said with a note of impatience.

'Inspector Petric,' Vlado said. 'I'm conducting an investigation on behalf of the Interior Ministry.'

'Identification?'

Vlado showed him his battered police warrant card, explaining, 'I've been temporarily detailed to the Ministry's special police unit. You can telephone Acting Chief Kasic if you've any doubts.'

'No doubts,' he said airily, with the tone of one who'd only been testing, playing a game.

'This way, then. To my office,' he said. He strolled away, glancing over his shoulder to add, 'Before we get down to business perhaps you'd like a short tour. It's quite an impressive little domain, really, and not one that just anybody is privy to. You might as well take advantage of the access while you're here.'

The invitation, plus the appearance of Murovic's office – neat, dusted, wastebasket empty, every thin pile of papers stacked just so – made Vlado smile at the initial show of hurry and impatience. This seemed to be a man with little to do but sit and fidget, waiting to impress whatever visitors might drop by, as long as they weren't 'just anybody.'

They descended a dank stairway, Murovic flicking on lights, then pushing a few buttons on a small key pad to disarm the alarm system. He unlocked the door onto a cellar of caged rooms leading to the main vault.

He unlocked the first caged entrance and waltzed into a chamber crammed with filing cabinets and stacks of huge cloth-bound books. 'Old deeds and property records going back past Tito's day,' Murovic

187

explained. 'Someday they'll sort it all out, but it will be a hell of a mess. I hadn't even known these kinds of things survived the last war, much less the last half century.'

He unlocked a second caged door into a larger chamber. Here, leaning against each other, were frames of all sizes, arranged with a cloth between each.

Murovic sighed.

'These are some of the most valuable items from the museum,' he said. 'Not with the temperature and humidity controls we'd like, of course, and I'd prefer they weren't leaning up against each other like this. But space is limited as you can see. I'm afraid it's the best we can do for now.'

The next room was the main vault, its giant lock shining like the captain's wheel of a ship. Murovic rapped lightly on the door, producing only a muted click against the thick metal.

'And in here,' he said, 'are our most valuable pieces of all. Small treasures that are centuries old. Royal jewelry, the rarest of paintings, an illuminated Jewish Haggadah from the fifteenth century. That alone is worth a few million, and everybody and his brother in the international art community would love to get his hands on it, to protect it until the end of the war, they say. But not a chance. If we let it go now that's the last we'll see of it.

'No one but me and three others are allowed down here most of the time, so consider this your lucky day. You see, there's also a small rollaway bed. And that is where our president sleeps when things get especially bad.'

He offered this with an arch smile, as if their leader had perhaps furnished a love nest in there. He seemed quite thrilled by his proximity to this small whiff of power. Vlado could have laughed. He had grown used to seeing the newly powerful in action as they tried to run this country by the seat of their pants. They were pressed together in this city along with everyone else, their world growing more compact by the day, and under those circumstances the nearness of power only made him feel claustrophobic, as did this vault, this tomb with its treasures.

Glavas had been right. Murovic was a bit of a Tutankhamen down here. All that was missing was the golden headdress and the small, thrusting goatee. If an explosion were to somehow seal him in, perhaps he, too, wouldn't be unearthed for another twenty centuries, left to mummify with his treasures and the bed of his president.

He led Vlado back through the first two rooms, noisily shutting the caged doors behind him, then climbed back upstairs. He then gestured toward an office chair by his desk.

Vlado pulled in a deep breath, feeling a need for fresh, clean air, but receiving only the staleness of a quiet office.

'So,' Murovic said. 'An investigation. What sort?'

'One that may have to do with your transfer files, which I understand have gone missing.'

'I'd hardly put it like that. They're not missing, they're quite gone. Destroyed in a fire.'

'A tank shell, I believe it was?'

'Tank. Grenade. Mortar. What difference does it make. It came in through the window and everything in the room was gone.'

'Through the window?'

'Yes, a freak shot really. I saw the damage for myself the next morning. The guards even showed me some of the shell fragments they'd found. There'd been a big attack the night before. I'd remembered listening to it in bed.'

'And all of the transfer file was gone? Down to the last card? Even in the worst sort of fires you can usually salvage something.'

'Oh, no. All gone. Practically vaporized. I checked personally. There were only three or four drawers to begin with. Nothing but ashes. That was bad enough, but the drawers with the insurance records were destroyed, too. It's a tragedy really. It's the only part of the city's collection that we don't have a handle on yet, so we feel vulnerable for the moment.'

'And you say there were guards?'

'Yes. An entire detail.'

'Army? Police?' Although Vlado already knew the answer.

'Some of Zarko's men, actually.' He said this with his gaze boring straight into Vlado, as if daring him to raise an eyebrow.

'You'd probably call them thugs,' he continued. 'And that's what they are, I suppose. But I'd call them saviors first. Cigarette? They're French. None of those rancid Drinas for me.'

'Because they saved your museum, you mean. Thank you.'

'The museum and everything inside it. We'd spent the three days before the fire moving the best items over here. We'd started with the records as well, the inventories and the insurance appraisals. The transfer files were due to come out the next morning. Another twelve hours and they'd be sitting right downstairs, inside the vault.'

'A freak turn of fortune then.'

'Oh, I realize the odds. And I know what you must be thinking, being a policeman. But these men were quite solicitous, quite willing to take orders from a museum director, vigilant as well. Besides, a handful of men can hardly stop a shell.'

'You weren't at all suspicious? However vigilant, these men were hardly saints.'

'So everyone says, but as far as I'm concerned their behavior was exemplary. If they'd wanted to take advantage of us they could have looted or walked off with any item they chose, on any given night. But they kept themselves clean. Clean as a whistle.'

'But you said yourself that the files alone were valuable, that the transfer items are quite vulnerable as long as the files are missing.'

Murovic practically sneered. 'These men, while courageous, were, how shall I put it, elemental? If they'd been inclined to theft, they would have taken the things that caught their fancy. They never struck me as the type who'd work through some complicated scheme, who might realize the files were a key to something valuable, especially when all those treasures were sitting there right in front of them. It's the mentality of pirates. Why worry about the tricks of bookkeeping when there's a chest of gold to be taken?'

'I was thinking more of their boss. I'm sure Zarko was aware of the value of the right information as much as anyone in this town.'

'Yes, but he's dead now, isn't he.' And for Murovic this obviously closed the possibility of further suspicion.

'Tell me a little bit more about these men, then. What sort of detail did they usually post overnight?'

'Five men, and not just the lowest foot soldiers. Zarko assured me we'd have some of his best people as long as we needed them.'

'His best people. Officers, you mean.'

'His top officer, in fact. On duty every night.'

'His name, if you recall?'

'Halilovic. Lieutenant Neven Halilovic. Perhaps you've heard of him?'

He had. In hearing the name, Vlado felt he was crossing that unseen line in the darkness that had worried him earlier. Halilovic had been Zarko's right-hand man, jailed since the November raid. Or had he, too, been among those killed in the final assault? Or perhaps later, while 'trying to escape,' as with Zarko.

'So he was there when this shell hit?'

'Yes.'

'And were there any casualties among the guard detail?'

'Not as such.'

'No, of course not. Another freak twist of fortune then. And did it occur to anyone afterward, yourself included, Mr Murovic, to perhaps ask an arson investigator to have a brief look around. If only to protect the good name of the vigilant Mr Halilovic.'

'As I said, Mr . . .'

'Petric. Inspector Petric.'

'Inspector Petric. For me there were no doubts. We were in safe hands, hands that had saved virtually everything we had. And being all but on the frontline of a war zone, it didn't seem practical to have an investigator working in and around the building. And quite frankly, it would have been a very tasteless show of bad faith, an embarrassment, considering all that those men had done for us. Perhaps there were no casualties that night, but they'd suffered others before, and quite literally right on our doorstep. I'm aware of their presumed track record, of their smuggling and their black markets. But for us, as I said. Saviors.'

He pulled down on his cigarette for a long, dramatic

drag. Vlado scribbled in his notebook, then Murovic asked, 'By the way, Mr Petric, who put you on to all this? Or do you come by your interest in art naturally?'

'One of your former colleagues, actually. Milan Glavas.'

'Ah, yes. Milan. I might have known. He always was quite taken with conspiracy theories. Always guessing at people's motives, trying to take their measure in an instant. Very much the office politician.'

'Not a very good one, apparently.'

'He told you I sacked him, I suppose. And unfairly, no doubt. He had wanted this job, you know. Museum director. But of course he was simply a few years beyond the energy requirements. And let's face it, Mr Petric, it didn't help that he was a Serb. A good one, maybe. But in light of everything that's happened in the past two years there's not much room for them in high places right now, at least on this side of the city.'

'So you sacked him.'

'Yes. Which embittered him against me forever, no doubt. As if he hadn't already refused to give me credit for knowing much of anything about my business; or about art at all. But if Milan were half as clever as he thinks he would have known that a copy of the entire transfer file exists in Belgrade.'

Murovic said this with a note of triumph, as if producing the answer to a trick question for an especially dense pupil. A flush of self-congratulatory pride bloomed across his face.

'Belgrade?' Vlado said. He had to admit, he'd been taken by surprise. This seemed to explain Vitas's remark to Glavas that the file was – how had he put it? – 'in safe hands in unsafe surroundings.'

'So,' Vlado said, 'Then you do have the files, or at least a copy.'

'Not for another month. As you can imagine, Belgrade hasn't exactly been eager to cooperate with the newly independent Republic of Bosnia-Herzegovina, whose existence it doesn't even recognize, though from what I hear these files are quite a matter of public record to students or art historians. Just about anyone could probably come in off the street, and if we wanted to be backhanded about it there are people we could send in to copy it out by hand and smuggle us the result. Perhaps I was naive, but I wanted to do things above-board. The war won't last forever, and someday we'll need to work with those people again. So I decided to first make a good faith effort through the proper international channels.'

'The U.N.?'

'Yes. UNESCO. Belgrade finally agreed, and on February fifteenth a copy of the documents will be shipped via a UNESCO courier.'

'That's another month. Why the delay?'

'That's when UNESCO's grant takes effect. It's preservation money especially earmarked for Sarajevo. Their man can't so much as requisition a paper-clip, much less book his trains and flights, until the moment the money's officially available. Then he's off for Belgrade. And I must say, it will be a relief. For months we'd been figuring we'd eventually have to do it the hard way, by consulting the old timers, Milan included, to try to piece everything together from snatches of tired old memories.'

'Why not do some of that anyway, at least for a few of the more valuable pieces. There are bound to be some that would spring to mind quite readily. Glavas seems to think he could put together quite a bit of it, if he had the time and inclination, and maybe a little help.'

'Yes, I don't doubt that he does. It sounds like something Milan would claim. A charming man in his own way, really, and full of arcane knowledge, old lore that can be quite engaging when he gets rolling on some story, as long as you have the energy to shut him off. But far less knowledge, I'm afraid, than he'd have us all believe. I think if you were to take him up on his offer you'd come back a few hours later to find him with a few blank sheets of paper and an ashtray full of butts, from your own cigarettes, of course.'

'In fact I have taken him up on his offer. And you're probably right about the ashtray. We'll see about the blank pages. But when UNESCO gets here with the copies, I'd like a look, if you don't mind.'

'Oh, but what's the need? I'm sure with Milan working for you you'll already have everything you need by then.' He burst into laughter, the sort of venomous chuckle best suited for the corners of cocktail parties and small, chic restaurants.

He guided Vlado toward the door.

'Mind the gunfire today,' he admonished. 'Please give Milan my regards. And try not to be too harsh with him when he comes up short.'

He hadn't asked a single question yet about how Glavas was doing, Vlado noted. Not one query about the old man's health or safety out in Dobrinja. War had consumed half the city, but it didn't mean you still couldn't get caught up in all the old pettiness of peacetime.

But Vlado had at least gained two important pieces of information. The transfer files would be back in hand in another month, meaning if artwork was still being smuggled out of the country, the smugglers probably knew they were working against a deadline, and might be inclined to either sloppiness or desperation.

He'd also learned that Neven Halilovic would be worth talking to, provided he was alive and would open his mouth. Kasic would know where to find him. Perhaps Damir would as well, with all the clubs and coffee bars he frequented.

But Goran Filipovic would know, too.

Goran was a friend of Vlado's who had spent the first year of the war as an officer in the Croatian brigade. The unit had been disbanded by nervous government officials once Croat-Muslim fighting began in Mostar and central Bosnia. Its soldiers were dispersed into other units, absorbing the Croat threat into the Muslim majority, although the brigade still defiantly kept a small headquarters on the western edge of downtown, a dingy office in an abandoned pizzeria, with the checkerboard Croatian coat of arms flying on a flag out front.

Goran had seized the opportunity to bow out of the army altogether, citing a shrapnel wound to his right leg. It had left him with a limp that worsened at the approach of any superior officer, and somehow no one had ever questioned whether he was still fit for combat.

He'd then pooled the prewar Deutschemark savings of his in-laws and two old aunts to open a small café in a low-slung, well-protected building in the city center. He timed it perfectly, opening just as people began seeking night life again, realizing they'd either have to begin imitating the rhythms of a normal life or go crazy in their cellars. The café went over so well that he then opened a small cinema in a room across the hallway, stretching a large sheet across the wall at one end for a screen, and rounding up eighty mismatched folding chairs for seating.

Doing any sort of business these days, especially any

successful business, inevitably put one into contact with the people running the rackets and black markets, and Goran had used his vantage point and his army contacts to make himself an informal expert on all the various rivalries and relationships. He'd sniffed out the likelihood of the November raid three days before it occurred, and could tell you on any given week who was up, who was down, and who had better be looking for a way out of the city. Through all this he'd developed a knack for knowing when it was okay to keep gossiping and when it was time to stop asking questions, and he knew better than to ever ask for anything more than his own meager piece of the action, just enough to keep his bar and his theater up and running. It was bad enough owing these people money. The last thing you wanted to owe them was a favor.

Nowadays you could usually find him either tending bar or next door in an office across the hall that adjoined the theater, a cramped place smelling of gasoline and throbbing with the pulse of the two generators that kept his business empire going from inside a small closet. He was almost invariably hunched over a computer keyboard, using special software to type subtitles onto the latest videotape he'd managed to smuggle in via a friendly journalist or aid worker. He now had enough extra titles in stock to print up a small schedule covering the next month of showings, and his efforts at marketing and posting signboards around town had paid off. Except on days of heavy shelling the theater was usually a packed house, even at the princely sum of a D-mark a head.

He and Vlado still drank together every now and then, a few beers rather than plum brandy, just enough to work up a belch or two and make the week's memories shimmer and slide, enough to feel light-headed all the way home, then sink deeply into a yeasty slumber.

Vlado checked first in the café, opening the door onto an atmosphere of smoke and noise so thick it seemed he'd have to shove his way through. He scanned the room, every table full, maybe forty people in all. It was only 4:30, but with a 9 p.m. curfew, night life, such as it was, began with the first sign of dusk. The conversation was loud and boisterous. There wasn't a soul in the place without a cigarette, but Vlado could see only four who'd actually bought a drink – two with beers, two with coffee. The guitars and vocals of an old Yugoslav rock band, No Smoking, blared from giant speakers in each corner. The group had been popular before the war. Now they were disbanded, and the lead singer was in Belgrade. No one here seemed to mind.

Vlado weaved through the tables to the bar, where a young woman stood, looking bored as she searched through a shoebox of cassette tapes for the next selection. He had to shout twice to get her attention.

'Is Goran here?'

'Try next door,' she said. 'In the theater.'

Vlado moved into the hallway, elbowing past four revelers just arriving, then approached another doorway where a man sat at a card table having just sold the last ticket for the evening's first showing.

'Vlado,' the man greeted him, grinning, although Vlado couldn't recall his name. 'You're looking for Goran?'

'Yes. In his office?'

'On the phone. But I'll tell him you're here. Wait inside. You can catch the first few minutes of the movie while I get him. On the house.'

Vlado eased through the door. It was chilly inside, though not so smoky, and apart from the conversation in English blaring occasionally from the movie sound-track it was quiet as a tomb. As his eyes adjusted to the darkness he saw that every seat was filled, a crowd of people still in their heavy coats, the rising vapor of their breath just visible overhead in the wide beam of light from the projector.

From countless other movies and TV shows Vlado could tell right away that this one was set in New York, and by the creeping cadence and low tones of the soundtrack, it was obvious something sinister was afoot, that danger was approaching. But what struck him most about the scene was its neatness and order. Here was a working society with streets uncluttered by shell holes and burned cars. A place with bright lights, glass storefronts. You could walk around the corner and have a beer, a hot meal, a cup of coffee, stay as late as you wanted, and go home to a warm apartment with clean sheets and a light switch on the wall. And all you had to worry about were a few criminals out trying to shoot you. It looked like paradise. Now he realized why these people so willingly gave up a week's pay for two hours of entertainment.

A hand tapped his right shoulder.

'In here,' a voice whispered. 'He can see you now.'

Vlado reluctantly left the streets of New York and walked in to find Goran at the keyboard, muttering, his shirttail hanging through the opening in the back of his folding chair.

He turned, a smile spreading on his broad, unshaven face. 'Vlado. Well, it's about time. For two weeks I can't get you in here for a beer, and now you pick a day when I'm trying to finish with some comedy I'm not even sure I can translate. Too much American hip-hop language and inside jokes. So where've you been?'

'Around.'

'So I've heard. The man about town. Keeping late hours at his apartment all by himself. Exciting life, Vlado.'

Vlado smiled. It was an old and frequent topic between them.

'So what's up, then. Something by the look in your eye tells me you're not here for a movie or a beer.'

'I'm looking for somebody. Neven Halilovic. I can't remember what happened after the raid. Whether he was killed, pardoned into the army, or is still in jail.'

'You can stop looking. Last I heard he was dead. He was put in the army, all right, but never made it past the first month. One of those wild attacks across the Jewish cemetery that never comes to anything but more bodies across the graves. But offhand I don't remember who told me all that, so I can ask around to make sure. Why? You fellows finally getting into corruption cases, or have you joined the special police force without telling me?'

'Only on loan. It's the Vitas investigation. I guess you heard about him.'

'Only this morning.' He shook his head. 'So that's yours, is it?' Goran paused a moment, then nodded slightly. 'Yes. I suppose that would figure. Impress the blue helmets with an independent man. Show that we've really cleaned up our act in all the right places.' He laughed. 'All of which you believe entirely, Vlado, right?'

'As a loyal public servant, I can only wholeheartedly agree.'

'So what's the story on Vitas? Christ, he wasn't up to his neck in the local rat's nest, too, was he?'

He handed Vlado a beer.

'Thanks. I was hoping you might already have formed an educated guess on that yourself. But the Ministry seems to think so. Or at least, Kasic and a few undercover men do.'

'Kasic,' Goran snorted. 'As if he would know.'

'What do you mean?'

'Nothing really. I've just always thought his machinery was a little too well oiled, a case of style over substance, and it's always worked for him. One of those fellows who always manages to put himself in the right place for the next promotion.'

'We can't all sell movies and beer for a living.'

'True. Some of us start painting little French soldiers for our jollies instead.'

Vlado laughed. 'Now you're getting personal. Those are my friends you're making fun of. More mature conversation than I can get from Damir and not always on the make like Grebo. And I don't need to spend a month's salary or a carton of Marlboros to have an evening with them.'

'Now if you could only find a way to paint up one that's about five-foot-five, a redhead with long legs and a low cut blouse, then you could become a business-man, too. And you could charge a hell of a lot more than a month's salary.'

'Maybe if I melted down a whole division. The French over at Skenderia aren't very picky. I could just prop her up on the porch of headquarters next to a price list. I'd have them beating a path of Marlboros to my door.'

'Just make sure you put all the holes in the right places. You can always ask me in case you've forgotten.'

'Another few months and I'll need to.'

'Still that bad, huh?'

Vlado said nothing, just shook his head with a rueful smile.

'What do you hear from Jasmina?' Goran said. It was he who'd had the connections to get her and Sonja on the bus convoy out of town.

'The same. Still settling in. Still learning to speak German. Getting a little bit further from me with every phone call. Sometimes I think I'd be better off in the army. Then maybe at least I could try sneaking out over Igman.'

'That's assuming you even want to leave this place.'

'What, you think I'm starting to enjoy it here?'

'No. You just couldn't bear to leave it behind. You're too scared it might disappear in a cloud of smoke while you're gone, and you'd come back to a big hole in the ground.'

'You know why I stay – as if I had a choice anyway. Leave now and a family of refugees will be living in my house by the time the war's over. And with government approval. I'll be out of a job and, by then, out of money. And probably charged with desertion on top of everything else. Besides, if I can make it through two years of this then I might as well go the distance.'

'For what? The privilege of living here after the war?'

'Why not. It's my home. Yours too. And if it's such a good idea to get away why aren't you sneaking up through the hills?'

'Don't believe I haven't thought about it. But right now I'm making money. Real money. Deutschemarks and dollars. To get out I'd need to spend half of it, and wherever I ended up I'd probably have to spend the rest to keep living while I was looking for work. But if this war ended tomorrow I'd be out of here in a shot. Off to Croatia. Or Slovenia. Anything to get out of this place.'

'That's going to be the time to stay, not leave.'

'You really think so? When's the last time you took a good, slow walk around your neighborhood.'

'Nobody takes slow walks in my neighborhood anymore.'

'You know what I mean, and you don't have to take a slow walk to see what I'm talking about. How many of your old neighbors have either been killed or have packed up and gone.'

Vlado shrugged. 'Maybe a quarter. Maybe more.'

'Two thirds, more likely, and who moved in after they left? Rurals and refugees. Peasants. All with a chip on their shoulder and an ax to grind. Half of the women wearing headscarves and cursing anybody who's not just like them. You're a Catholic with a Muslim wife. Think there's going to be much tolerance for that around here after the war? Take a look at our government if you're interested in postwar demographics. The upwardly mobile will be Muslim and politically active, I don't care how much lip service you hear about a multiethnic society. That died with the first four hundred shells.'

'That's now. When people don't have to fight to live, or stand in line for water, or think their children are going to be blown to bits every time they step out the door, they'll change again.'

'Don't bet on it. And don't think these refugees are ever leaving, either. They've got it too good. They're taking all the best jobs, the best empty apartments. And they stick together. When one gets a job so do all his friends and family. Besides, you're forgetting the way memory works around here. Talked to any old Partisans from the forties who have anything nice to say about the Germans? Or to any old Chetniks who have anything nice to say about Tito? Not to mention the good old fascist Ustasha. This city's dead, Vlado,

203

and so is everyone in it who sticks around after the fact.'

'Maybe. Or maybe I'm just too stubborn to admit it.'

'Not stubborn. Sentimental. You're one of those people who's dug himself deep into his own little bunker and gone to sleep, thinking that if you can just survive the shelling and the sniping then you'll be able to wake up in a few years and the sun will come out, your family will come home, and you'll pick up right where you left off.'

'Not right where I left off. I'm not naive. I know things will be different. I won't be able to speak the same language as my daughter for one thing.'

'That you can fix. That you can repair in a few months, maybe less. But maybe Jasmina had better be wearing a scarf on her head when she comes back. And if you still have any friends over in Grbavica then you better write them a good-bye letter now, 'cause they'll either be moving or they'll be living behind a wall, one running down by the river with a checkpoint at every bridge. If we're lucky we'll be the new Berlin, if we're not we'll be the next Beirut.

'You're one of those poor deluded souls who thinks he's got this figured out, Vlado, who believes that survival is really all there is to it. That as long as you keep your head down, stay off the bottle, and shave every now and then, you'll come through this just as you were, with nothing worse than a few bad memories to trouble you in the blissful years of peace that lie ahead. That's you all over, Vlado, painting your soldiers in the dark and running after your petty criminals.'

'So I should drink, then? Or stop doing my job and join the army? Or maybe whore my way around the city every week or so to let me "live" again. Those are your cures for people like me?'

204

'You should do *anything*, is all I'm saying. Any act of temporary insanity will do. Anything that will convince me you don't really believe you're still the safe, careful man you thought you were at the beginning of this war. Self-control is a virtue, not a religion. Because in a place like this, any move you make – any move – can get you killed, so why not choose a few with some meaning, some passion. Then maybe you won't wake up some morning ten years from now and discover you've buried yourself alive and there's no one left to dig you out.'

As Vlado fumbled for a reply the office door opened from the darkened theater, and the ticket-taker's head popped in. 'Your scene's coming up, Goran.'

'Thanks. Be right there.'

Vlado assumed a quizzical look. 'Your scene? You doing a floor show now?'

'A food scene,' Goran answered sheepishly. 'It's part of the movie, and, well, I never like to miss it. Comes right after the shootout. A huge meal for an American holiday. A bird the size of a hatchback Yugo, glazed and brown. Tureens of hot soup, potatoes, vegetables, pastries. Wine, drinks. It's only a minute or two, but the whole crowd swoons. You can practically hear the drool splattering on the floor. After that who cares about the plot. I've seen it nine times already and I still haven't had enough.'

He rose abruptly to his feet. 'But, listen, I'll run down this Neven tale and get back to you.'

As he moved to the door Vlado remembered something else.

'One other thing,' Vlado said. 'Do you remember hearing anything about Vitas's mother. Where she is. What she's up to?'

Goran stopped, a hand on the doorknob.

205

'Yes, she's dead.'

'Are you sure?'

'As sure as I can be without having seen the body.'

'That's not much assurance, coming from the expert who once said the war would be over in three months. How reliable's your source?'

'Pretty reliable. Vitas told me.'

'When?'

'Must have been about a year ago. He'd come round here doing something a little bit like you are, searching the family tree of one hood or another. I asked after his family and he mumbled something about his late mother. Said she'd died a few months earlier. Old folks die, you know, even when there isn't a war on. Especially when they're bored and lonely, like you. Please, Vlado, don't forget to call next week or I'll come pull you out of your flat myself. And I'll step on some of those little men while I'm there. Now, off to the dining rooms of New York.'

He opened the door to the sound of squealing tires and Hollywood gunshots, which sounded nothing at all like the sharp crack of a sniper rifle. These were soft little pops, the sound of children make believing.

By the time he left Goran's it was probably too late to catch Damir at the office, and chances were the phones would be down as well, which rankled because now he had plenty to discuss. They'd have to remap their strategy now. If Glavas was able to deliver as promised, they'd have scores of leads to check out around the city from the transfer files, looking for lost paintings.

When he reached his apartment he was cold and bone-weary, the first time in weeks he'd felt so tired, a sensation he might even welcome if a hot bath awaited.

Instead there was only a dead phone line. The temperature indoors seemed even colder.

He threw open the oven door and turned the knob for the gas, hearing the weak hiss, then lighting it with a match. He made a mental note to scrounge up some more matches. There were fewer than a dozen left in his box.

A feeble blue ring of flame sprang from the burner. As more families tapped into the pipes the pressure continued to drop, and the supply was prone to frequent interruption, sometimes for days at a time. At this rate it would be twenty minutes before he could boil a pot of water, longer still before he'd actually heat even a corner of the apartment.

He walked to the workbench in the corner of the narrow kitchen, fumbling for a few moments with some half-painted soldiers, but his hands were still too stiff for any detail work.

He sliced a piece of the butcher's meat and chewed slowly, wrapping the rest back in the rough paper, then swigged some water from a plastic milk jug and tore at a stale heel of bread.

He pulled his bed next to the kitchen door, hoping to capture as much of any heat as possible, and decided to leave the oven on all night. It was a risky proposition. If the gas supply was cut the flame would go out, and if the gas were then turned back on, he'd either suffocate or go up in a ball of flame. One or the other event happened about once a week in the city these days, either from a faulty hookup or from a gamble just like this one. It didn't help that the local utility had long ago exhausted its supply of the additive that gave gas its tell-tale warning scent, nor would the Serbs be sharing any of theirs any time soon.

Vlado mulled the facts of the case as he pulled down

an extra blanket from a closet shelf. It was easy enough to figure where the transfer file must have gotten to. Zarko's people, with connections to General Markovic and God-knew-who-else had carted it away. Perhaps they were even running competing operations. But how had Vitas gotten a card? Was he a part of it, too? Or had he turned up a card in his own investigation. Maybe he'd gotten it in the October raid on Zarko's headquarters. Neven Halilovic would know the answers, but he was dead. Everyone who seemed to know anything, in fact, was either dead or on the wrong side of the city. The gallery director, Murovic, would be no further help for at least a month, when the UNESCO grant kicked in. Unless Glavas came through, Vlado would be facing a dead end. And as much as Vlado had taken an instant dislike to Murovic, perhaps he was right about Glavas. Maybe all Vlado would end up with would be an ashtray full of cigarette butts.

But why the stories from the butcher and the cigarette man. And why the show of muscle at his shakedown. They fit with each other but with nothing else. Were they simply opportunists trying to make a few marks, and had Kasic been taken in? Perhaps he, too, was in over his head on this case. The word had always been that Vitas was the brains behind the Interior Ministry, and maybe it was true. Goran had made a worthy point. Kasic had always scored higher marks for style than substance. When all was said and done perhaps he was no sharper than Garovic, just another bureaucrat trying to tread water. The initial reports from the undercover men had seemed like a promising path to a quick finish. He was doubtless under plenty of pressure to wrap this one up in a hurry.

Vlado's teeth chattered as he climbed into bed, stiff and sore. Tonight there was no radio playing next door.

One night of fun and then back to conserving the batteries for more vital purposes. He turned his head on the pillow, peering through the kitchen doorway into the open oven, where the ring of blue flame glowed like the footlights of a darkened theater just before the show danced onto the stage. He drifted off to sleep still waiting for the performance, and soon was dreaming of a woman's face staring at him from a stage, prim and pale, with heart-shaped lips done up a bit too brightly with lipstick. It was a sweet face, but insinuating as well. It was the woman from Glavas's apartment, in fact. Or was it a mask? No, it was a face, but suddenly it turned a shocking white, and now it stared up at him from the bottom of a stairwell, emitting a muffled watery sound that was too garbled to understand. Yet, he felt, she had a message for him, if only she could articulate it. The woman pursed her lips, then pressed a finger to her mouth, either in mischief or in warning, while he backed away uneasily, uncertain whether to smile or to show concern. Instead he merely kept moving, as if guided by remote control, moving farther up a stairway that grew colder with every step.

12

A huge explosion jarred him awake. He opened his eyes to a sunny morning and the tremors of an aftershock, something like the rumbling conclusion of a distant thunderclap. He felt for a moment as if someone had sat on his stomach, and he heard objects dropping to the ground outside.

A wave of cold air stole across him, and he saw why when he sat up and looked across the room. His last intact window had been blown in, and was now a pile of gleaming fragments on the living room floor. Several shards had been driven into the opposite wall. Others protruded in clusters from an old blue armchair, like the quills of a porcupine.

He got up to look for a spare roll of plastic stashed in a kitchen closet, and promptly cut his left foot on a shard by the kitchen door. He looked back at his bed and saw that a few pieces had landed across his blanket, but none with enough strength to pierce it. He checked in the bathroom mirror and plucked two or three slivers from his hair.

That's the way it worked here, he told himself. He'd gotten up in the middle of the night to shut down the gas, prodded awake by some deep, urgent fear of being consumed by either suffocation or explosion. Then an explosion had come along anyway from the outside, as if to remind him that precautions didn't matter. It was all odds and luck, and there was no way to out-maneuver them.

Looking out the gaping window, his hands already numb and his teeth chattering, he surveyed the damage out front as he taped up a sheet of plastic. A neighbor's apartment was torn open. It had been vacant until the week before, when a family of six had moved in, another wandering band of refugees from some small, overrun town in the hills.

From the damage to the roof and to the front it was obvious a shell had slammed directly into an upper corner of the house – nothing of large caliber, probably only a rocket-propelled grenade, but big enough to do the job, wrecking the front room and blowing out every nearby window that had still been intact. With luck the family had been sleeping in the back. Looking through the opening Vlado saw no bodies, and his inclination was not to go looking for any in the cold, especially with more shells possibly on the way.

But he couldn't pull himself from the window. There seemed to be no one up and about. He listened closely, cupping his ear, but there were no moans, no cries for help, only the stillness of an early morning with bright sunshine flashing on a new dusting of snow. A hot metallic smell mixed with the usual sharpness of woodsmoke and burning garbage.

He completed the hasty repair of his window, pressing the final strip of duct tape into place. There would be no more morning inventories of the grave-diggers, and the thought unexpectedly filled him with a sense of relief, the lightness that follows the com-pletion of any long-dreaded chore.

Then, standing back from his work, he thought again

of the family in the next apartment. His window plastic billowed slightly with a fresh breeze, and he shivered. There was still no sound from next door. Someone else would sort it all out later, he told himself. But he decided to take another look, and as he peeled back the new strip of tape there was a voice, a man's, telling someone to stay inside. Vlado rolled away enough plastic to see a disheveled man, his hair and beard full of plaster dust, walking unsteadily through the hole in the front wall into the snow.

'Everyone all right?' Vlado asked. The man turned robotically, and his eyes briefly fixed Vlado with a blank stare. Thin streams of blood oozed from each of his nostrils, but otherwise he seemed in one piece. The man turned back around without a word, and when another minute passed without a reply, Vlado retaped the plastic over the window.

He should put the water on to boil for coffee, he told himself, as he turned toward the kitchen. Should tend to his cleaning, should shave and prepare for work. They would be fine out there, whoever they were. And if not, then the hospital would be far better equipped than he to set them right.

A few days earlier he had seen the two smallest children in the family playing out front, a boy and a girl, cooing and laughing as they tugged at a small raggedy doll. He turned toward his door and walked into the snow.

The man he'd seen earlier was visible through the opening of the apartment's blown-out window. Vlado strolled across the courtyard and over the threshold, and saw that the man was shaking, on the verge of collapse. Vlado grasped him around the shoulders and lowered him into a chair covered with dust and chunks of plaster. A second explosion followed, perhaps a block away, and down a hallway a small child began to wail. Now he could see that there was also a large, ragged hole in the ceiling.

'Come on,' Vlado said sternly. 'Those shots are coming from the north, and there will be more of them. You've got no protection here, now. Bring your family next door with me until this is over.'

The man still didn't speak, but he seemed to stir himself, and he walked unsteadily down the hallway toward where the wail had come from a moment ago. He emerged at the head of a straggling column, with his wife trailing the children. They were all as quiet as the father, the four children staring with wide eyes, the mother seeming only weary, as if she'd finally given up.

'Come. Quickly,' Vlado urged them, more to get their muscles moving than from any fear of imminent danger. Often these 'bombardments' consisted of no more than two or three shells at a time, flung like scattershot toward random points of the city. Then, having made their statement for the hour, the gunners grew bored and went back to their naps or their card games.

But the sooner this bunch was up and about, Vlado figured, the sooner they'd purge the shock from their systems.

He saw with relief that everyone seemed intact, although they had yet to speak a word. They followed Vlado into the snow, not exactly dressed for the weather. He glanced around to make sure that the children were at least wearing shoes.

Once inside his apartment he practically had to shove them into chairs, cutting his right hand as he hastily flicked shards of shattered glass onto the floor from the cushions. He then moved to the kitchen like the anxious host of a dinner party, lighting the burner to heat water for coffee.

'You should probably get yourselves checked out by a doctor,' Vlado shouted from the kitchen, still to no answer. 'The concussions from these explosions can do more damage than you think. You can come away without a scratch and be dead an hour later from internal bleeding.'

'The hospital,' someone finally said. It was the woman. 'Can you tell us how to find it?'

Christ, these really were newcomers if they didn't know that. 'It's on the top of the hill over there,' Vlado motioned toward his covered window to the east. 'Right across the graveyard, and on up the street from there. But I'd wait at least a half hour after the last shell.'

He clattered on with his hospitality, wiping out a pair of dusty and long unused coffee cups, and four small tumblers for the children. He wondered what he might give them for breakfast, figuring bread would have to do. It was probably what they were accustomed to, anyway.

Their silence resumed, and it began to unsettle him. He glanced up quickly, as if to make sure there wasn't a roomful of zombies in his living room, propped in their chairs and going stiff with rigor mortis, and he saw to his relief that the two youngest children had dropped onto the floor, and were playing with something.

When he saw that their toy was one of his metal soldiers, his first impulse was to ask them to put it away. But what better use could there be for them, he told himself. Play with them all you like. The parents, however, remained as silent as stones.

'So, how long have you been in the city,' Vlado asked.

For a moment it seemed no one would answer. Then the father moistened his lips, as if with great effort, and spoke up. 'Four weeks,' he said. He'd stopped shaking and seemed to have collected himself somewhat.

Vlado handed him a hot mug of weak coffee, and another to his wife. 'The children, have they eaten?'

'Yes, some bread,' the mother said. 'We will get more this morning.'

'What was your town?' Vlado asked. 'Where did you come from?'

They named some village Vlado had barely heard of, some dot from one of his maps about forty miles distant, in the middle of a narrow beleaguered supply corridor. They must have had quite a time of it these past few years, and getting here couldn't have been easy, either.

'How did you make it into the city.'

'With another family,' the father said. 'By cart. We came across Igman. Sometimes you can still get through. We were lucky. A family that left only an hour after us lost two sons along the way to snipers.'

'I didn't even know anyone was still trying to get in,' Vlado said. 'I thought it was just people trying to get out.'

'You can't,' the man said. 'At least, not over Igman, not if you're a man. The soldiers in the pass will only let a family in with an able-bodied male. For more soldiers. I keep wondering when they're going to pick me up for that. But it was the only way we got in.'

'Oh, they'll find you soon enough, I'd imagine. But I'd send your wife to the bread-and-water lines by herself from now on, if I were you, even if she can't haul back as much. That's how they get most of them.'

Then, something seemed to dawn on the man. And he looked Vlado full in the eye as he asked, 'And you.

215

How do you stay out? I noticed you our first week here and wondered that. You're young and strong.'

'Strong, no. Young, debatable after two years like this. But you're right, definitely of military age. I serve in the police, though. A detective. Investigating murders.'

The man shook his head, assenting to the reasonableness of Vlado's occupation with the air of one obliging a lunatic. It was hardly the first time Vlado had seen such a response.

'Now, I guess we will have to find a new place to live,' the man said. 'But it shouldn't be hard. There are so many apartments open now, and there will always be more.'

Vlado considered this vast, continual shuffle that had been taking place beneath his nose, an inner circle of migration.

'I am Alijah Konjic,' the man said, as if suddenly remembering his manners. 'My wife is Nela.'

'Vlado Petric.'

'We must leave now, I suppose. Go out to find food and another place to live. And I suppose you are right, that we should see a doctor first.'

They all stood to go without a further word, seeming more composed now, though still reminding him somehow of shellshocked troops being deemed fit for service by doctors under pressure to supply reinforcements.

'Come back if you need anything,' Vlado said, seeing with a pang of disappointment that the small boy had put the toy soldier back where he'd found it. 'And if you need to use my place while you're looking for a new apartment, you are welcome.'

'Thank you, but really, I am sure it won't be difficult. This place was the third empty one we'd seen after we arrived. There really are many to choose from.'

'Do you need extra clothes?' Vlado asked, feeling the desperation of someone whose party has failed, ending too soon. 'Or blankets? I have some spare ones.'

'No. We are fine,' the mother said. But at least she was smiling, and for the moment that seemed like more than enough.

'Children,' she called. 'It is time to move. Please thank Mr Petric.'

And they did so, one after the other, beginning with the oldest and ending with the youngest, as if they were practiced in this routine.

'And like I said,' Vlado added. 'I will be here again tonight if you need me.' But he knew that he would likely never see them again.

He watched them go from his open doorway, the two empty coffee cups still in his hands, and as they trooped away in a narrow line of footprints in the thin layer of snow it dawned on him that they'd been his first visitors since Damir had tipsily barged in on him all those months ago.

Closing the door, he noticed that the room still held their smell, not an unpleasant one, just another few variations on the local mix of smoke and sweat. And as he tidied up from his small duties as a host he felt a small lift, a fullness that had long been vacant.

He mixed his own cup of coffee, making sure to make his own just as weak as the cups he'd stirred for his guests, and as he went through the motions a thought returned to him unbidden from his final moments of sleep. His mind had been sorting, culling, searching through the previous evening's conundrums. But now, with his first sip of coffee, the solution came to him: There would be a way to get a full copy of the transfer file, and he could get it before Murovic, or even

UNESCO. And it would not have to depend on the aging memory of Milan Glavas. But it would require a satellite phone and a fax machine, on a line without a government minder or eavesdropper, and for either of those he'd have to visit the Holiday Inn.

The phones there could be scanned, too, but the odds were far better than with any official phone, especially considering the number of journalists who called in and out at all hours of the day.

He tried again to call Damir, but if the lines had come back on overnight, the explosion had knocked them back off in his neighborhood here. So he pulled on his boots and coat, then headed out the door.

Far across the makeshift field of graves he saw his family of neighbors, heads bobbing, small vapors of breath rising from them as they worked their way up the hill toward the hospital.

The Holiday Inn had become the lodging of choice for visiting journalists and international celebrities, mostly because it was the only choice. Virtually every other hotel of appreciable size had been shuttered or shelled out of existence, and under current conditions no Hiltons or Hyatts would be breaking ground anytime soon. So, on most every night the Holiday Inn had a full house, despite its precarious location three hundred yards from the frontline.

The hotel's garish façade, the color of an egg yolk, looked out across Sniper Alley and the Miljacka River into the blind stares of Grbavica's empty, windowless highrises, where snipers and grenade crews did a brisk business of sighting and shooting, lighting the place up at night with red streams of tracer fire, and the yellow bursts of launched grenades.

The result was that virtually every one of the

hotel's rooms across the front, or south, side was un-inhabitable. The same was true for some on the east side, with gaping shell holes in the walls.

Vlado remembered the hotel fondly from 1984, when it was not only new but the hub of all social life associated with Sarajevo's Winter Olympics. He'd been a single man in his early twenties, partying lustily and late at the overcrowded disco, drinking to the throb of sound and light, then wobbling home, often as not with a girl on his arm from some other part of the world, putting his good English to the best possible use, all of those studies finally paying off.

In those few precious weeks somehow the city had functioned as never before, with miraculously working phones, television signals crisp and clear, and a tram system that sparkled and ran impeccably on schedule. With that had come a certainty that, with Tito already four years in the grave, Sarajevo was about to move forward, beyond communism and beyond Yugoslavia, into some new realm that could only be wildly better and full of opportunity. The world had made its mark, and the mark would never be erased.

Now the hotel disco was dark and closed. The restaurant up front had been moved to a safer location in a rear conference room, chilly and dim, with its own plastic windows. And the only way the world made its mark anymore was with the glare of television lights, or with the white fleets and blue helmets of the U.N. soldiers.

But the hotel kept running, fueled by mob money and connections, as well as the grim determination of its staff to hang on to their jobs. They still managed to serve up three hot meals a day, nearly always with meat. Waiters in stained dinner jackets patrolled with desultory efficiency, quietly setting aside for themselves the unfinished bottles of wine and water so often left on the table by roaring packs of weary journalists. Each afternoon a tanker truck pulled up out back and emptied a full load of water into the hotel's tanks, ensuring another few hours of toothbrushing, cold showers, and flushing toilets. A steady but increasingly expensive supply of gasoline powered enough generators to keep electricity running for part of every day, if erratically, and once in a great many days there was warm water. On such occasions you could almost hear the journalists' groans of pleasure from out on the street.

Thus, the hotel was once again the mandatory destination for any visiting elite, even if the star actors and musicians who occasionally came to town, eager to pick up their Sarajevo merit badge before flying back over the hills, were often of a low or dimming wattage. Sarajevo had become a place where you could boost a sagging career with some quick if risky publicity, not to mention the public relations points earned for 'public service,' or 'solidarity with the people of Bosnia.'

This, at least, was the way Sarajevans had come to see the interlopers. They'd been eager for the attention at first, flattered even, finding a thin silver lining to their predicament. And perhaps the publicity would help. Now they knew better, and saw their flak-jacketed visitors as just that, transients who would climb upon the ruins of their misery for a few brief moments in the world spotlight, then depart once the lights were off. The only impact anyone concerned himself with anymore was the economic ripple of D-marks and Marlboros strewn in their wake.

Vlado approached the building from behind, crossing an open courtyard. The usual lineup of hangers-on gathered near the rear entrance. Little boys stood outside the door asking for handouts. Down-at-the-heels young men chain smoked and showed off their smattering of English, hoping to pick up interpreting and guiding jobs which could pay up to one hundred marks a day, or more if you were lucky enough to latch onto a Japanese television crew.

The talk among the rabble this morning was of a hotel employee who'd been shot in the back by a sniper. He was the attendant of the underground parking garage, lord of the small but expensive fleet of vehicles belonging to the journalists and aid workers staying at the hotel. His job was to make sure none was stolen, siphoned, or vandalized, keeping them locked behind a chain-link entrance throughout the night. Most were armored, but not all, as he'd discovered this morning while moving one behind the hotel to ready it for one of the reporters. A bullet had come in through the rear window, passing through the driver's seat before striking him in the left kidney. A few moments ago he'd been hauled off to the hospital, his shirt and pants soaked in red. The journalist himself was now out back inspecting the vehicle in the lee of the building, flak vest open in front as he peered inside, frowning at the bloodied seat. He then walked to the back, fingering the bullet hole in apparent fascination. Because he worked for one of the wilder London tabloids, perhaps he was already contemplating how a cheap bit of first-person melodrama might be salvaged from the morning's damage: 'It was a bullet with my name on it, but this time someone else took the hit.' Yes, that would do nicely. He'd work on it.

Vlado opened the door to see a guard inside a glass booth, where a droning TV was showing a subtitled American movie on Bosnian television. With the power out as usual across the rest of the city, this was one of the few places you could actually watch the broadcasts of the local network.

The guard stopped him with a stern grunt. Locals were not readily admitted here, especially when they arrived unsolicited to bother the paying customers. Vlado flashed his ID and the guard waved him along with another grunt.

Walking into the hotel's mall-like plaza was like stepping onto the floor of a deep canyon at dusk, dim and chilly, with a hollow echo from every step. Looking up toward the broken skylights eight stories higher one wouldn't have been surprised to see stalactites dripping from the ceiling. Word had it that a French radio journalist had spent his spare hours here sharpening his mountaineering skills by rappelling down the inner walls.

The front desk was surrounded by a jerry-rigged frame of wood and plastic to hold in the warmth from a small space heater. The clerk was mistrustful until Vlado showed his card. He asked for Toby Perkins and was directed to room 434.

He trudged up a darkened stairwell to the fourth floor, then groped along a hallway until he could just make out the numbers on the doors. He knocked.

A voice answered from inside: 'Nigel? Come on in.'

Vlado opened the door to see Toby Perkins, the same pink and well-fed face from the other day, seated at the end of an unmade bed, flipping through a small notebook.

'Well, then, our intrepid detective is it?'

'Inspector Petric, yes. I hope I'm not interrupting.'

'Not at all. A pleasant surprise, in fact. Given that interview a second thought, perhaps? Or maybe my little lecture on social responsibility hit home. No, not that for sure, I suppose. Either way, I was expecting my photographer but you'll do much better. Delivering me a hot tip no doubt.'

There was that cherub's grin again, a face right out of a jolly evening down at the pub. Vlado hesitated at the door.

'Please, please, come in,' Toby said. 'Sit down and tell me what I can do for you. No more coffee, though, I'm afraid.'

The implicit rebuke stung, and Vlado supposed he'd deserved it. But never mind.

'It's a favor I need, actually. Access to a satellite phone, if you have one,' and Vlado had already seen that he did. It sat on a chair by the window, its antenna opened like a white umbrella next to the window, which even here was a sheet of plastic.

'You've come to the right place,' Toby said. ''Was just getting ready to pack it up and maybe head for the airport a day earlier than planned. Getting so slow here lately. My rag was sending someone else in in another week and we figured we could let the place go un-covered for a while. Then ten minutes ago my desk calls and my bloody editor says he wants me here for the interim. Says he thinks things are due to heat up again soon. Calls it his instinct, but that's editors for you. Always seem to know exactly what you don't want to hear. Anyhow, no problem with the phone. Come on in and I'll get it on the uplink for you.'

Vlado dug the phone number out of his bag.

'So then,' Toby continued, 'where are you calling, if you don't mind my asking?'

Vlado hesitated, then figured Toby probably would know by the country code anyway. No sense in trying to keep it a secret.

'Belgrade.'

'Well, then.' Toby's smile melted into a look of

curiosity. 'Not too many Bosnian government employees are in the market for calls to Belgrade these days, I'd imagine. Family?'

'A friend.'

'Yes, well, as long as I'm not participating in anything illegal.' He said it laughing, a knowing twinkle in his eyes. 'I can just punch up the numbers to get you up on the satellite, and you can hit the rest. Country code for Yugo is three-eight-one now, in case you didn't know. Belgrade is still one-one.'

Vlado was about to ask meekly for privacy when Toby said, 'And I'll wait outside, of course, as much as it might be tempting to eavesdrop on a policeman's call to the enemy capital. Besides, even if I could overhear you I don't speak the language, and my interpreter's been out all morning drinking coffee.'

'One other request before you go, if it's all right.'

'Sure.'

'I see you also have a fax machine. If my friend here has something to send me, what number would he use?'

'Well, this is getting interesting, isn't it. Tell me, is this something you might be able to talk to me about? When it's all over, of course. And I'm assuming now this must have something to do with your work, at least peripherally.'

'Yes. Peripherally, as you put it. Perhaps it does. And if you can help me I can certainly promise you no one else will get any of this before you would.'

'An easy promise to make since probably nobody else has asked for it. But sure, I'll go for that arrangement. An exclusive. Fair enough then. Well, here we go . . . Oh, and try not to run on too long, if you don't mind. It's ten marks a minute on my tab.'

Vlado listened to the dial tone come onto the line,

then punched in the numbers, hearing a hissing sound followed by all the old wheezes and clicks one had grown used to in the phone transmissions of the former Yugoslavia. And as he waited for an answer he thought of his friend at the other end, Bogdan Delic. Vlado had known him in university and had stayed in touch off and on until the war began. He was an artist, or at least that's what Bogdan had always called himself, moving from one odd job to another, hectoring galleries to show his work and staying up until all hours with his friends and bottles of homemade brandy.

He was the living denial of the term 'starving artist,' with a wide rolling belly that sagged across his belt, and a big, husky beard that had taken over his jowly face. The last time Vlado had seen him he'd had two loud, grubby children in tow, and a reed-thin wife who never seemed to speak more than two words at a time. It had been vintage Bogdan, muttering and talking about all his old obsessions, as if oblivious to the scurrying children or the beleaguered looking waif of a woman who trailed behind. He'd even managed to ignore the rising wave of Serbian nationalism as it began to catch on in the streets of Belgrade. Well, Vlado thought, we'll see how much of a Serb they've made out of him now.

And suddenly there was his voice at the other end of the line, as gruff and loud as ever. The connection was remarkable.

'Bogdan, it's Vlado Petric. From Sarajevo.'

'Vlado? My God, is it really you? And from Sarajevo? It's like being called by the dead. A call from Sarajevo. Is it as bad as they say?'

'I guess that depends on how bad they're saying it is.'

Bogdan answered with his big belly laugh.

'Same old Vlado. Never gives away his feelings without a joke or a struggle.' It was an observation mildly surprising to Vlado, even a little annoying. But at ten D-marks a minute this was no time to explore it further.

'Belgrade hates you, by the way, not you personally but you as a resident of Sarajevo. And even I am growing a little tired of you. You're all anyone in the world hears about from this war. The whole world feels sorry for you and hates all of us. We have no jobs, no gasoline, inflation that doubles every hour, but it is Sarajevo they weep for on CNN. But now that is off my chest, my friend. For Chrissakes, how are you? How is your family?'

'They're gone.'

There was momentary silence at the other end, and Vlado realized he'd been misunderstood.

'Gone to Germany, I mean. Berlin. Since June ninety-two.'

'Good God. A long time. But they're alive, at least.'

'Yes, alive and growing. Sonja is almost three now.'

Bogdan, with his own children, understood without another word the weight of that remark, and all its ramifications. He knew how quickly children changed at that age, and how quickly they grew apart from someone far away.

'So, listen, Bogdan, I am on a borrowed and very expensive phone and can't spend much time. But what I need is a favor, if you can do it. I don't think it will be risky, but if you decide it is then don't bother.'

Vlado explained what he needed, a copy of information from whatever Belgrade called the transfer files, more particularly those items listed with Sarajevo locations. Bogdan said he'd try. He had friends at the Ministry of Culture who'd find it for him, no questions asked, and the rest would be easy.

'I've been wrangling with some of their people lately anyway. Was finally starting to make a name for myself but now some of them think my work's a little too adventurous. Or subversive is more likely.' He laughed again. 'But I'll tell them I'm trying to compile a list of which of our national treasures might still be in the hands of those dirty mujahedeen in Bosnia, in your incestuous city of heathens and mixed marriages. That ought to get them moving.'

'It's several hundred items, but copy as many as you can, or least the ones with the higher values. And then you can fax it to this number. It's a satellite phone, so it may cost a little. But anything you could do would be a great help.'

'Anything you can tell me about what this is for?'

'A murder investigation. That's really all I can say. Sorry.'

'It's good enough for me, Vlado. I'll do what I can.'

Damir was waiting for him at the office, looking tired and despondent.

'Any luck in Dobrinja?' he asked.

'Maybe,' Vlado said. 'In a few days I hope to have all the leads we could ever ask for. I only hope they don't lead down the same dead end.' Damir waited for more, but that was all he was getting for now. Vlado knew it wasn't fair, but he pressed on. 'What about you? Anything more?'

'All my sources are dry on this one. About all they agree on is that the ministry's undercover men are genuinely shady characters. But maybe that means they're good undercover men. I don't know. The more I've thought about it the more I feel like maybe we're out of our league. Maybe there's a good reason the ministry's been taking these cases all these months, and not us.'

'How about the whores?'

Damir's face brightened. 'There was one I quite fancied,' he said, and Vlado felt a pang of jealousy, wondering if it was 'his,' the 'bank teller,' as he thought of her. Then just as quickly he felt guilty for caring. Some of his mother's Catholicism must have rubbed off after all.

'She calls herself Francesca. A nice blonde, short, a little soft at the edges but in all the right places.' And in spite of himself Vlado relaxed. He thought he remembered the one. By her manner she'd seemed almost as experienced as the one who'd styled herself as the leader.

'Learn anything from her?'

'For our purposes? No. Same problem you had. The bossy one kept opening her mouth. What a bitch. But I'm seeing Francesca some other time, I think. She hasn't been in the business too long to forget that she can still appreciate a man for an evening out. As long as he pays her way, of course.'

Damir was on the verge of further descriptions of this woman's virtues and good sense when Vlado's phone rang. Nice to hear them ringing again at all, he thought.

It was Goran.

'Vlado,' he shouted. He'd been typing when Vlado picked up the receiver, but now the clattering of keys stopped.

'The ghost lives, Vlado. Your man Neven Halilovic, former right hand man of the late lamented Zarko. He's up on Zuc, living in his own little stronghold, if you can call that living. Seems he has managed to put together his own private army up there. Keeps the regular army happy by holding down a key part of the line, and they keep him happy by staying off his back. Though he's not happy at all, by most accounts.

Understandable under the circumstances. Can't think of any other part of the line where there's been more shelling and shooting lately, day in and day out.'

Vlado paused. He was glad to hear Halilovic was alive, but this was hardly where he'd expected to find him. A prison cell would have been much more conducive for a quick and productive interview. But did he want to get to the bottom of this case or not?

'How can I get up there?' he asked.

'Zuc? Are you serious? Even if you went, there's no guarantee you can get past his guards and actually see him. And if that happens he might always decide to hold on to you for a while. He may owe the army but he doesn't owe the police.'

'Are you actually urging me to be cautious, Goran? The man who believes I should live a little bit, even if it means dying? Just tell me how to get up there.'

'It's easy enough, really,' Goran said quietly. 'Replacement units go up every night. Small groups. Mostly the raw recruits, no training and none of their own weapons. They do an overnighter and come back down in the morning just before dawn, turn in their rifles, pick up their pay in cigarettes, and go home to sleep. Boys, for the most part. Kids with pimples and leather jackets and nervous girlfriends who wait up for them.'

'Every night?'

'Tonight even, if you wanted. I was about to say it wouldn't be a good time. The shelling's been heavier this morning. But Orthodox New Year is tomorrow night and you definitely don't want to go then. So, yes, you'd better do it tonight if you're hell-bent and determined to go. You are hell bent and determined, aren't you? Because if you're not you've got no business being up there for even a minute.'

229

'Then consider me hell-bent and determined.'

'Now you've got me wishing I'd never opened my mouth.'

'Exactly what I was hoping.'

'I just wanted you to get out of your house, to have a few beers or something. Are you sure this is worth it?'

'Not really. But the only way I'll find out is to go. Anyway, it's the only way I'll find out anything more than I know already, which is precious little.'

'Well,' Goran said with a sigh, 'I've got a friend you can call to arrange it. They assemble units over near the cigarette factory. I'll call him with your name and number and have him get back to you, if you want.'

Vlado paused a second. Then he took the leap. 'Yes. Go ahead.'

'Okay then,' Goran said. 'But if you come to your senses, call me back and we'll have a beer.'

'Something must be up,' Damir said as soon as Vlado hung up. 'You actually looked excited.'

'Either that or scared to death,' Vlado said, and, after considering once again the implications of where he was going, he decided to level with Damir, at least on this one.

'I'm going up to Zuc tonight. To look for Neven Halilovic.'

'God is great,' Damir muttered. 'I didn't even know he was alive. And he won't be much longer if he's hiding out up there.'

'Runs his own army, apparently. They paroled him to fight.'

'Makes a certain twisted sense, I guess. Which is more than I can say for what you're doing. I guess if anyone knows what goes on in the world of hoods it's

230

someone like him, but what if you get all the way up there and he won't even see you.'

'Possible. Or even if he sees me he might say nothing. But then there's the chance he might be just what we're looking for. Former hoods can always use a friend with the police.'

'That's assuming he's former, not current.'

'Either way he's likely pretty well out of the loop being up there, which would tend to lend him a certain credibility, I'd think, if he does decide to talk.'

'Yes, but Zuc? The reason I kept this lousy job was to stay out of places like that.'

'And I thought all this time you were in it for the comradeship and good training. Or the opportunity to meet interesting new people like Francesca.' Vlado sighed. 'But I know what you're saying. Zuc isn't exactly what we bargained for.'

'So then why don't I go instead. You've got a family. I've got nothing but a few girlfriends who would mourn nothing but the loss of the occasional night on the town. My mother and father can fend for themselves, for all I care anymore. Just lay out the questions for me and I'll ask them, simple as that. It's really no contest, is it?'

'Thanks. But Kasic would have it no other way, I'm afraid. It's my investigation, when you get down to it, and if I'm not going to share much information with you . . .'

'Yes, I'd noticed that.'

'. . . Then I've got no business being so free with the dangers. Which reminds me. I soft-pedaled that shake-down business when I told it to you the other day. Actually they scared me to death, but I'm still not sure how serious they were.'

'Well, it should be good practice for tonight. You'll have plenty of time to be scared to death.'

Damir clapped a hand on Vlado's back, resting it there in the manner of someone comforting the bereaved at the graveside. Then, without a trace of his usual mirth, he said, 'Good luck, Vlado. Up there you'll need all you can get.'

13

What did one take to a war? For it occurred to Vlado that this was where he was going. Off to war. He'd assumed for the past two years he was already living in the middle of one. Yet now that he was contemplating a walk to the trenches of Zuc he realized otherwise. He'd only been working at its fringes, padding about like everyone else in hopes of escaping the notice of the shells and snipers.

Once the ferocity of the first few months of fighting had passed, the bigger guns had refocused most of their attention on the city's edges, on the frontlines of the armies encamped in the snow and the mud. Only occasionally now were there days of heavy firing into the city center. Only now and then did a freak shot fall with deadly accuracy into crowds gathered to play children's games, mourn a burial, shop at a market, or line up for bread or water.

Vlado poked around his house, opening doors and rooms that had been shut for months. He felt strangely unequipped for his journey. A sleeping bag? He didn't have one. A helmet? Ditto. But that was nothing un-usual. Most of the soldiers had little more than their coats and the dark wool caps every man seemed to wear in the winter. A gun? They handed you one at the top of the hill, and you returned it on your way back down.

He opened the door of his daughter's closet, rummaging aimlessly. He picked up a few toys from a small pile on the floor next to the disassembled panels of her crib. He brought a fuzzy red dog to his nose. The synthetic fur was stiff and chilly, smelling faintly of drool and old canned fruit.

He walked into his and Jasmina's bedroom, opened the drawer of a bedside table, and found a half-read book, its jacket stuck in the middle to mark the place where Jasmina had last set it aside. He pictured her sitting up in bed reading it, her every-evening pose, leaning back on a pillow propped against the wall, a small cone of light pooling on the pages of the book, the whiteness of the sheets gathered at her knees, her long brown hair draped across bare shoulders.

He remembered the conversation from one of their last nights together.

'There's a convoy of twenty buses leaving Monday. Goran says he can get you and Sonja on it.'

She dropped the book to her lap, an accomplishment in itself, and looked up, eyes widening. 'And you?'

'You know the rules.'

The rules were, and always had been, that no able-bodied male between the ages of sixteen and sixty could leave the city. They were vital for defense. The unwritten rules were that those who weren't regular army could buy an exception for a going rate equal to three thousand dollars, provided you had the right connections, and even buying your way out came with risks, not the least of which were being either shot in the back or conned out of every penny.

She looked back down for a moment at her book,

staring but not reading, then looked back up, though still holding the book open in her lap.

'All the more reason we shouldn't leave,' she said. 'Why don't we just wait until we can all go?'

But they both knew her defense was bound to crumble, if not on this evening then on some later night. Like everyone, they had assumed at the beginning that the war would be a quick ride into either oblivion or salvation. It would pass like a strong fever, killing or breaking. Instead it had become a long illness that took its toll in slow measures, and they both knew by then that the prognosis wasn't likely to change anytime soon. Those who could get out, did, if they had any brains, even if it meant leaving behind sons and fathers.

'We could wait two years and we still might not be able to all get out at once,' he said.

She closed the book, laid it beside her on the bed, and looked away toward the window, out at the night. She blew out the bedside candle. 'I don't know. Probably not, I guess.'

He waited through a minute of silence, knowing by the rhythm of her breathing that she was fighting to gain control of her emotions, perhaps marshaling her next rebuttal as well.

'I'll stay and hold down the house,' he said, 'make sure it's repaired as it needs it. Keep the roof whole and the windows covered, keep some refugee family from moving in. When it's all over we'll be together again.'

'And where are we supposed to go? Zagreb? And to live where? Karlovac? To live in some tent city with ten thousand other refugees? Germany? So Sonja can be shouted at all her life? Austria? Switzerland? And what will I do? And what does Sonja do without a father?'

'Do you want her to grow up here? With all of this?

Do you want her to get used to this kind of a life, to think it's normal to run from bullets or line up every day with buckets for your water.'

Jasmina pulled the sheets up around her shoulders and turned over, tucking her legs up to think. He moved up against her from behind, curling around her, taking her hand and holding it tightly, and they slowly relaxed into sleep.

Vlado awakened the next morning to shells and shooting, and opened his eyes to see Jasmina dressed and standing before her closet, a suitcase already open on the bed.

Vlado turned away from the bed and opened the drawers of his dresser. Inside were clothes he hadn't worn for ages, having winnowed his wardrobe to a few sturdy shirts and trousers and a single sweater of coarse brown wool. The items in the drawer felt strange to him, as if they were of another era, artifacts in an unsealed tomb. In this room even the motes of dust tumbling through the pale light seemed encoded with the past. He inhaled the staleness, smelled its difference in his lungs, all the old moods and atmospheres shifting and settling inside him. Some inner chemical switch, long untended, briefly fluttered on at the sudden register of these false readings, and he exhaled deeply to collect himself, tears pooling in his eyes. He straightened, blinked once, and swallowed heavily, then began packing a small duffel with some heavy dark clothes, a few old items that he wouldn't mind muddying, and tossed in a blanket for good measure along with a canteen and an old rain jacket.

And that was about all he could do. There was a small flashlight in the house, but no batteries. There were no snacks to scrounge, and his gun, a service revolver locked in a drawer at work, would seem even more useless up there than it did here.

He stripped down to change, smelling the sourness of his unwashed skin. When had he bathed last? Four days ago? Five? He'd sponged himself with a cold washcloth in the dark, lathering up from a thin knife of soap. He'd then felt itchy all the next day.

He turned to see his image in the full-length mirror hanging inside Jasmina's closet door. Staring back was a pale ghostly man, rib bones showing and goosebumps rising, and he was overcome by the sensation of seeing his own corpse, stretched upon a slab.

The chest, now slightly sunken, would be more so, like the broken ground of a frost heave, whitened and deflated; his arm muscles gone flaccid; his eyes vacant, lids swollen, lashes encrusted with mud; hair stiff and standing in every direction. Only the fingernails would be growing, or so the books said, but no longer either pink or clean. He scanned the reflection of his chest, wondering if it would be torn by one of those wounds he'd grown so accustomed to seeing, only uglier, ragged edges caked with dirt, a foul and rusting porthole spilling its slippery contents in a steaming coil. He even knew the smell, its essence of cold and damp soil and of nascent rot after a few days in the elements.

He turned abruptly toward the bed to shake the image, then looked back at the mirror and saw that it remained, the ghost of some future he never wanted to reach, yet would be walking toward in a few hours. Why not just call it off: It's not as if Kasic would mind if he turned over his early results. Then he considered the next day at his desk, feet propped, the under-powered fluorescent tubes humming and throbbing above his head. Garovic in motion toward his desk, a folder in his hand, Damir rattling his jar of shells and

237

talking of his latest conquest. And the siege, lurching onward with its unstoppable mechanical force. No, he would go to Zuc. See what there was to be learned, whether of the war or of this case.

He shut the closet door, swiveling the mirror out of sight, then walked from the room.

So this was the fear of going to war, with its dry metallic taste and its dark play of imagination. He'd read enough about trenches and bunkers and pitched battles to know what he could be getting into by walking up to Zuc. He felt familiar already with the splintered trees, the moonscape of cratered mud, the rats that grew fat and the feet that grew soft and wrinkled within sodden boots. As for the whine and shatter of shellbursts, they, at least, would be nothing new.

He'd overheard the teenage boys in the cafés talking of their weekly one-night stands up on the line. They smiled weakly and forced a few jokes, half out of bravado and half out of cathartic need, their conversations continuing until they eased themselves to an acceptable distance from their deepest fears. At least until next time.

Infantry attacks were rare up there, he knew that as well. Neither side ever gained enough of an advantage to try them often. Both sides were thin along most of the line, and neither could mass enough for an offensive without the other finding out and responding in kind. Defenses were left mostly to mines and artillery, and overnight duty was usually a matter of waiting out the shells while yearning to walk back home. That was the night's reward, a predawn stroll back down into the bowl of the city, with its monotonous comforts of scattershot and siege, its torn plumbing and its weak gas flames, its hard beds rucked against less exposed walls, its slow curl of woodsmoke and steaming piles of garbage, and at night, its inkwell of darkness.

Vlado's rendezvous point was at a brigade headquarters on the west side of the city's center. He arrived just at nightfall. An old woman wrapped in a red shawl squatted on the ground next to a water spigot, peddling a small mountain of cigarettes one by one.

The contingent of men who were to march up to Zuc was to gather in a group of about sixty, then split into six groups of ten that would leave at ten minute intervals, to keep from attracting too much attention from enemy gunners. An unshaven commander told Vlado to follow him in the first group up.

'Just stay quiet and do as I say, that's all I ask. If you get killed all I can promise is we'll bring you back. If you're wounded you'll take whatever treatment you can get up there. You'll get nothing better than what the soldiers get, which isn't always so great. But it's your decision.'

It was clear that none of the arriving soldiers was part of a well-trained unit. They appeared in street clothes and sneakers, as if for a pickup game of basketball, some wearing the same muddy jeans and jackets they'd worn the last time up the hill, not bothering to wash them in the interim.

The commander assigned leaders to the other groups that would follow, then called together the first ten. Three men in their late forties stood by themselves, huddled in the fraternity of age and silence, conserving their energies for getting up the hill and safely through the night.

The younger ones, however, gave way to the school-boy inclination to make light of even the most solemn occasion. They fidgeted and shadow boxed, playing tapes on a large radio shouldered by a tall boy with acne and a black ponytail.

He sorted through a stack of cassette tapes, a cigarette waggling in his mouth as he talked. Another of the younger ones handed him a tape, putting in his request for the walk up the hill.

Another member of this group was busy off to the side, kissing his girlfriend good-bye, he in a caricature of sternness and duty, she in a tearful mime of sorrow.

The slow walk began, and Vlado fell in with the younger ones, partly out of curiosity, partly out of knowing there would be no conversation with the older ones anyway, no way to make the time move any faster. Perhaps that was the difference between knowing you'd have to do this over and over again and knowing, as Vlado did, that this would be a one-time journey.

For a while the only noise was the thump of the bass line from the big radio, still propped on the shoulder of the tall boy, the music jumping as if in time to the movement of his plaid flannel shirttail, which swayed back and forth with every step uphill.

In the darkness they passed people headed down the hill, some saying hello, others carrying water jugs or pulling wagons. Most were going home for the night, although some of the younger ones were headed toward the feeble and expensive offerings of Sarajevo night life.

After a few more blocks the houses began to thin. The higher the group walked, the more damage there seemed to be.

Two of the boys began to kid the third one about his girlfriend. From their conversation it was obvious he'd just met her a few days ago, and after a few minutes of

240

this Vlado piped up to ask how one managed to acquire a new girlfriend so easily while a war was going on.

The three of them looked back, questioning him without saying a word. He told them he was a policeman looking for someone, a witness in a case. Just along for the ride.

'Not much of a ride,' said the boy with the new girlfriend.

The others laughed, as if privy to an old joke.

'So you want to know how to find a girlfriend?' the boy asked.

'Not exactly. I'm married. Just wondering how those things go at your age. From what I can remember it was hard enough taking care of that kind of business when there wasn't a war on.'

'Oh, it's easy. Easier, even. Meeting them, anyway. The hard part's finding time alone with them. Moms and dads are always home now. Always indoors. And it's not like you can go hang out in the park. Your best hope before was to wait until everybody else went to bed. Now there's a curfew and you've got to get home yourself. But there's always a way. She sleeps over at a friend's and you do the same. Or maybe you tell your parents you're off to "the front" again, only you're really off to somewhere else.'

'But easier to meet? That I still don't get.'

'The ones in your building, anyway. These guys here.' He motioned toward his friends in the group. 'None of us knew each other before the war. We hung out with other people, all of us. But now most of my old friends are gone, theirs too. Most left. Some got killed. And in those first few months you remember how it was. Everybody in the basements and the shelters. It was you and everybody else from your building down there, and you weren't going to spend

241

the evening talking to your parents. So you found the other people your age and had a party. A few weeks of that and you've got a new set of friends. A few more weeks and some of the boys and girls are starting to pair off. And when there's a war a month with a girl seems like a year. Everything's more intense. More serious. They start talking about having babies, wanting to leave something of themselves behind.'

A second one joined in: 'And you say, yeah, yeah, let's make a baby, only you're really hoping there won't be a baby, but you're more than willing to keep trying.'

The others laughed.

The first member of the group, the one who'd handed his tape to the boy with the radio, then repeated his request, loudly this time, for his music to be played.

The tall boy with the ponytail answered by ejecting the tape he was playing and popping in another, only it still wasn't the requested one.

'Hey, that's still Aerosmith,' the aggrieved party shouted. 'Fuck Aerosmith.'

'Fuck Guns 'N' Roses,' ponytail shouted.

'He's always that way,' the other boy muttered. 'Plays his own stuff until we're too high up the hill, then puts yours in right when we have to cut the noise.'

'So what's it like up there,' Vlado asked. 'What should I expect?'

'Cold,' one answered. 'Muddy. Lots of mud and lots of Chetniks.'

'Scary?'

'Sometimes. Usually just quiet and boring. That's when you just sit and talk and smoke all night.'

'Can you hear them on the other side?'

'All the time. Sometimes you shout back and forth. They scream something over, we scream something back, then it keeps up until either some officer stops it

242

or it gets nasty. 'Cause when it gets too nasty somebody always starts shooting. Then everybody's mad at whoever was doing the talking to begin with, so you have to watch what you say.'

'Does anyone ever sleep?'

'You're not supposed to, but you're welcome to try. We're never sleepy up there. We don't get sleepy until we're halfway back down the hill. And that's when the asshole with the radio finally starts playing our music.'

They all laughed again.

By then they were out in the open, the road winding along the side of a grassy hill in the dark. When a shell went off now you could see flashes in the sky. They were in farmland now. Each house was a hundred yards or so from the last, places where families used to tend goats and cows and grow long rows of corn, pumpkins, and cabbage. Now the houses were empty, roofs gone, animals too.

They passed a blown-up bus tilted off into a ditch, painted camouflage green. Some sort of army transport that had gone off the tracks. Even in the darkness you could see that the damp fields were pocked with shellholes, as if giant gophers had spent the last few years digging.

From up ahead the screech and snarl of Guns 'N' Roses finally filled the air. A small cheer went up from the four boys nearest Vlado.

Then, following the brief chatter of an automatic weapon from somewhere over the rise, the commander at the head of the column ordered silence.

'Off with the music and off with the talk,' he shouted. 'All cigarettes out until we've reached the top.'

'Fuck you, sir,' the boy with the tape muttered, inhaling fiercely before tossing his cigarette into the ditch.

The tape ejected from the machine with a click that signaled the crossing of some invisible line. A few minutes later they were greeted by a shell, and then a rumble. Then the sky lit up with a riot of red tracer bullets, streaming in a wild search for targets. With the approach of the Orthodox Christian New Year such celebratory firing had been growing more commonplace, and by the next night there would be no stopping it until the wee hours.

They reached a small row of shattered houses, a village high on the hill just before the shank of the ridge, and it was here they halted. An officer greeted their unit, signaling them off to the left. Vlado approached him to announce his title and his destination.

'So, it's Neven you want. You can have him. Down that way, another quarter mile, maybe a little more. I'll get someone to take you.'

Shortly afterward he was joined by yet another teenage boy, in a plaid wool jacket streaked with mud. He seemed glad for the chance to move about.

Boards were stacked and nailed up between the houses, and fortified by mounds of earth. Men squatted behind them or sat on the ground behind the houses, talking in low voices and smoking cigarettes. One boiled water for coffee over a small stove.

Vlado heard chattering in the near distance, followed by laughter, and wondered if it was coming from the other side. Then there was a shout, more laughter, then someone yelling, this time from nearby.

He and the boy moved farther down the line, on a path behind more of the houses, sidestepping broken branches and sinking ankle-deep in mud. The path then curved around the slope of the hill toward more exposed ground, out where there were no homes and trees.

A few moments later there was the whoosh of a shell, a yellow flash, and a crushing blow deep in the pit of Vlado's stomach. There was also a slight heave to the ground, or so it seemed to Vlado as he suddenly found himself in a crouch, his face twisted in fear.

He looked for his escort and saw the boy standing upright, relaxed, inhaling from his cigarette, and regarding Vlado with mild curiosity. 'Relax,' the boy said. 'It wasn't that close.' Vlado would have to recalibrate his definition of *close* if he was to last very long up here.

They finally reached their destination by stepping down into a communications trench leading to a small bunker, where they found a sentry reading a paperback by the light of a kerosene lantern. The boy turned to go without a word as the sentry looked up.

'I wish to see Neven Halilovic,' Vlado announced, as if to a hotel doorman, or the secretary of a business executive.

'General Halilovic usually doesn't see anyone but his own men,' the sentry replied.

General. That was a laugh. Though if you could manage putting together your own army while officially under army arrest then perhaps you'd earned the right to call yourself whatever you wanted.

'Tell him that Inspector Petric of the Interior Ministry would like to speak with him about a case he has some interest in.'

'Doubtful. But I'll pass it along.'

The reply was only five minutes in coming.

'Neven says to fuck off and go back down the hill where you came from.'

Vlado pondered for a moment what to do. It was clear the sentry didn't wish to ask again. Vlado fished in his pockets for a five mark piece he'd scrounged out of a drawer before leaving. The sentry looked at it scornfully, but took it.

'Tell him I wish to discuss the level of art appreciation of the late Esmir Vitas.'

This time it took ten minutes, but when the sentry returned he motioned for Vlado to follow him. They headed down a long, neatly dug trench, stepping deeper into the private war of Neven Halilovic.

14

They walked for a few hundred yards, negotiating a twist and a turn before arriving a few minutes later at a bunker of logs and sod, surrounded by soldiers who lounged amid guns and ammunition boxes. A stovepipe poked from the bunker roof, smoke pouring from it. Then a voice called him inside, where it was warm but smoky, and lit brightly by a kerosene lantern.

And there was Neven, slumped regally in an aluminum lawn chair, its vinyl straps fraying at the edges. He was bearded and looked tired but still carried an edge of ferocity, especially in the bright, round eyes, a deep brown, the pupils almost abnormally large.

He spoke without either rising or offering his hand. 'So. The late Esmir Vitas?'

'Yes. Does that help you or hurt you?'

'Probably neither. But it is something I'd like to know more about. You have the only thing valuable to me anymore. Information.'

He looked at Vlado a moment, as if making up his mind about something, then motioned toward a second tattered lawn chair on the opposite side of a small wooden tea table. 'Please. Have a seat.'

Neven called for an aide, then ordered two coffees as

if in a café, showing off his easy authority as well as the possibilities at his beck and call.

'It is real coffee,' he said. 'Not instant.'

When Vlado said nothing, Neven resumed. 'So, you are here to discuss art and Mr Vitas.'

Vlado decided to lay most of his cards on the table right away, 'More to the point, I'd like to ask you about the transfer files, and how Zarko may have used them. Vitas apparently knew something about the operation, and it seems to have gotten him killed. He may have been participating; he may only have been investigating. I think you can help me decide which.'

'There is very little I can tell you about any of that except to say that I know we had the file cards and that for some reason they were considered very important. But they were either confiscated or destroyed in the raid, so what would they matter now anyway?'

Well, there was something, at least. The files had survived the museum 'fire,' as Vlado suspected, and might still be around. Presumably either the Interior Ministry or the army had them. He wondered again about Vitas's remark, 'in safe hands in unsafe surroundings.'

'Confiscated by who?' Vlado asked.

'You will have to ask the Interior Ministry. You work for them, don't you? I only know we left them behind when we walked out to surrender. Although by then the building had caught fire, so you never know.'

'And then, after spending a few weeks in jail you were pardoned. Into the army, in recognition of your, how did they put it? . . .'

'My invaluable service to my country,' Neven said, smiling for the first time, teeth crooked, a carnivorous smile stained deeply with nicotine. His breath was of onions and fried meat, vapors heavy with grease. Vlado pictured slabs of lamb frying over a cookstove down in the hole of some smoky bunker. His stomach growled as Neven leaned over to stub out a cigarette on the table.

'And that is how I would like to keep my relationship with my country right now,' Neven continued. 'Steady and warm. And I'm not sure I can do that by talking to you about any of this. Maybe all I will do is make them decide that I should have stayed in prison after all.'

'Or maybe they'll decide someone else should be in prison instead.'

'Who?'

'Whoever it is that makes it necessary for you to stay up here surrounded by men with Kalashnikovs, living like this. When you're more comfortable near the Chetnik army than near your own government I'd say you have some enemies you need to take care of, but can't. Maybe some of them are involved with all of this, with this art business. It must have been making more money than anything else Zarko was associated with.'

Neven, who had been affecting something of a bored attitude up to now, looked straight into Vlado's face, his eyes burning with an intense, scornful arrogance. 'Let me tell you how it works up here, Mr Detective, and don't tell me your name again because I don't want to know it, much less remember it. Here I have my own men and the army leaves me alone. They hate the Interior Ministry even more than I do. The only people they hate worse are the military police. Any of these rivalries can get you killed, or, if you know how to use them, they can keep you alive, even make you rich.'

'The word on the streets, in fact, is that you did get killed.'

'Yes. In the Jewish cemetery. It was a helpful story. Even if some people knew it was untrue they decided that it let them off the hook. If people in the city thought I was dead then it was no longer necessary to try to bring me to justice, now or later. And I was in some of those damn fool attacks at the Jewish cemetery, too, early on. That's what convinced me I had to get together my own men and get out of there, even if it meant coming some place like this. So I convinced some soldiers to join with me, in the customary way.'

'You bought them.'

'Of course.'

'And didn't some officers in the regular army have their own ideas about that?'

'They had their ideas, but I had the D-marks, or at least I was willing to spend mine. Why should they waste money trying to outbid me when they could make their own profits on the arrangement?'

'You paid them, too, you mean.'

'At officers' rates, of course. All for the privilege of my own comfortable billet here on Zuc. Remote enough to keep away the prying eyes of the generals, and an important enough part of the line to make myself necessary. One thing I have always been is a good fighter. They know that, and their lines are so thin in places that they're glad to have me.'

The coffee arrived on a small copper tray. The aide poured the thick Turkish brew from an hourglass-shaped pot. Vlado sipped it, and was surprised to find it was even flavored with cardamom, all but impossible to find in the city these days.

'What's to keep you from bolting to the other side. Plenty of others do it.' Indeed, it happened every week, sometimes in units of twenty or more men.

'Let's just say there are even more people on that side for me to fear than over here. They still aren't very

250

happy about what happened two years ago. We made a lot of JNA officers look very bad by holding off their tanks with small arms. And there are always those who are enemies for other reasons.'

'Like General Markovic, for example.'

For the first time Neven seemed mildly impressed. He cocked his head slightly, as if to reassess the potential of the meeting. Then he said slowly, 'Yes. General Markovic, for example.'

'Another admirer of fine art, I'm told.'

'Indeed he is.' He paused for a moment. 'So, you say you may be able to help me. How?'

'Look, we know that art is being taken out of the country, even if the museum doesn't seem to have a clue. If we can tie the operation to Vitas's murder and root it out, I'd imagine we'd end up putting away some of the people who want to see you put away.'

'Like General Markovic? Not likely unless you have a very accurate piece of artillery and some good sources on the other side.'

'No. But we can certainly discredit him.' Vlado ventured out on a limb. 'We have the full backing and support of the international community.'

'The U.N., you mean?'

'And that puts our reach potentially across the river.' He saw by Neven's reaction that the limb had just given way.

'The U.N.,' Neven snorted, smiling crookedly again. 'Who do you think is making it possible for this art to leave the country?'

'That's exactly what we'd like to know.'

'You want to know too much. And all I can possibly do by telling you is to make even more enemies, in more of the wrong places.'

'Look, I'm not asking for everything you know. Just

take it question by question, and when you begin to feel the risk outweighing the benefits, then stop answering. But give yourself a chance.'

And then, Vlado's first and only stroke of providence fell literally to the ground. A shell screamed toward their position from the Serb lines: a high, arching mortar lob from a few hundred yards away. They both sprawled to the ground and were sprayed by a shower of dirt, the earth shaking and grumbling beneath them. When Neven rose his beret was askew, and mud was caked in his stringy bangs. The timbers providing the foundations of his 'office' were bent inward. The coffee tray was overturned. Neven no longer came across as any sort of master, even for this small stretch of the line, and his face momentarily betrayed that he knew it, too. They waited a moment through an answering burst of shellfire and a brief exchange between automatic weapons. Then Neven said, barely audibly, 'What sort of questions.'

Vlado didn't gloat, didn't act as if the dynamic had shifted in the least.

'Let's start with the files. You staged the explosion and the fire at the museum and then stole them, correct?'

'Yes.'

To Vlado's wonderment, Neven then said that the covering artillery barrage had been arranged on their behalf by General Markovic.

'And this was when Zarko joined the operation?'

'It was his first starring role, you might say. Markovic had brought us into it a few days earlier.'

'How did he make the arrangements? There was the slight inconvenience of a war going on at the time, and like you said, Zarko was making Markovic's army look pretty bad.'

'If they could have wiped us out, they would have. Markovic as readily as anybody. But by then it was clear they weren't going to be able to take the bridges, and they weren't going to get to the museum. Once he realized that, he arranged a meeting.'

'How?'

'It was easy enough. You asked for ceasefire negotiations at unit level. That's always the best way to get the blue helmets moving on your behalf to establish an official contact with the other side. So one morning we all got together, Markovic and two of his officers and Zarko, myself and another of ours, along with two of the European Community monitors, those guys in the white uniforms, the ones who look like ice cream men. They always believe that the more they can keep us talking the closer we'll be to peace.'

'You could hardly be seen to discuss smuggling arrangements under those conditions.'

'We didn't, at first. We talked prisoner exchanges, artillery monitoring, sniper moratoriums. All the things neither side had any intention of doing, because no matter how much money we might want to make together, at the bottom of it we still hated them and they hated us. When it came time for the real business Markovic told the E.C. monitors that he and Zarko needed a few moments of privacy, for greater frankness and candor. They gave it to him, of course. So then we set it all up, sitting in a white U.N. APC, right down by the river.'

'And that's where Markovic laid it out for you, and offered to cut you in if you'd help.'

'He told Zarko he wanted the pieces of art from our side of the river. He said that's where the better items were. Said he could handle transportation out of the country if we could get them over the bridge. But first he wanted us to take care of the transfer files. He already had his own copy from somewhere else.'

The Belgrade copy, Vlado figured. If a friend of Vlado's could get a copy, Markovic certainly would have had no problem.

'He wanted the copy in the museum destroyed,' Neven said. 'He gave us a date and said he could provide covering fire. Zarko told him fine as long as he didn't actually hit the building while we were in it. We had a few laughs, a few smokes, a shot of brandy, then we left. The E.C. guys seemed disappointed when we told him we'd accomplished nothing.'

'So. You were to take charge of the museum and find a way to destroy the records. But you kept them instead, didn't you? Then staged a destruction.'

'Zarko wasn't a fool. He figured with his own copy he could run the operation more easily, with more independence. He sold the idea to Markovic as a way of cutting down on logistics, simplifying it so we wouldn't have to risk using couriers or cryptic short-wave messages every time Markovic had a painting he wanted us to pick up. I don't think Markovic ever really got used to the idea, but he kept getting his cut so he lived with it.'

'But first you had to get yourself established at the museum. Move in on the place as its "protectors." Which I suppose was pretty easy with Murovic running the place.'

'He was in love with us. And I mean that literally. Always swooning over the manly fighters in his lobby, bringing us coffee and cakes. I liked to think that he fancied me in particular.' Neven laughed. 'To him we were beyond reproach. We had come to save his fabulous galleries, and in doing so we had saved his job. We were his noble savages, who'd even more nobly resisted the urge to plunder. Zarko was always very strict about that. There was to be no looting of the museum, of even the smallest object, and those were some of the best.'

'Because he wanted the files. And after you had them, then what?'

'From then on only two of us were involved besides Zarko. Alijah Nerevic and me. Alijah was killed on the first day of the police raid in October, standing outside like a fool, thinking it was only the Chetniks shelling while the rest of us ran for cover.'

'Only two of you besides Zarko?'

'It was as many as he could trust. He'd go through the files, find a card he liked, one with a higher value, then send us out to make the pickup.'

'Just like that? A couple of thugs walking into someone's home to take a painting off their wall?'

'It was easier than you'd think. While we were at the museum we helped ourselves to some of Murovic's stationery, so we forged his signature on official permissions for "protective custody," then paid each person a hundred marks for their cooperation and inconvenience. It's amazing how quickly people take the hint. Even if they were suspicious, once you paid them they didn't dare ask any questions of the museum or any other authority. Why risk losing their precious D-marks? Especially when it hadn't really been their painting to begin with.

'But what was funnier was that some people had already figured out the profit possibilities for themselves. At about every fifth stop both the painting and the people who'd been living there were gone. A few others had already crated it and put it in a basement or a closet. They'd go all red in the face and say they'd been doing it for safekeeping. Only one man ever tried to make a stink about us. Yelled at us and threatened to go to the police.'

'And?'

'We took him down to the river and shot him through the head. The next morning the morgue collected him. It was a busy day and they wrote him off as a sniper hit.'

'A familiar technique. That's how Vitas got it.'

Neven didn't seem the least bit surprised.

'Then you just walked through the streets with a painting?' Vlado asked.

'We crated it on the spot. Always took boards, nails and a drop cloth with us. Loaded the crate on a truck, then waited until after dark to make the drop.'

'Where.'

'For a while at a place by the river, near a check-point crossing where supplies came in through a back channel. There were intermediaries cleared for action on both sides who brought in tobacco, meat, liquor. Dangerous work, but they made a lot of money while they lived, and both sides used them for information. They'd take our crate across, or at least until the overhead began to get ridiculous.'

'The overhead?'

'Too many payoffs to too many people. Skimming and siphoning. The operation was leaking like a sieve, and because Markovic was sending everything out over the hills by truck there were more payoffs at every checkpoint, and even then sometimes the freight never reached its destination. So we simplified.'

'How.'

'How else. "Maybe Airlines." It's what the U.N. soldiers call their daily flights because maybe they'll fly, maybe they won't. Guaranteed overnight delivery as long as the Serbs weren't shooting or shelling the airport the next day. And sometimes Markovic could take care of that problem, but not always.'

'So you'd drop off the paintings where?'

'At the U.N.'s freight and shipping depot, near the PTT building on the way to the airport. Right behind U.N. forces headquarters. Especially convenient because it was on our side of the line. We'd drive through the gates waving our U.N. shipping invoice and leave the crate on the rear loading dock, ready for delivery via the first flight out to Frankfurt in the morning.'

'How often?'

'Maybe once a week at first. Zarko didn't want to overdo it, start drawing too much attention. Our U.N. contact was always antsy about it, too. Markovic would push for more deliveries, the U.N. man would push for fewer. Then maybe a month before the raid, we heard Murovic was working to get the list out of Belgrade through UNESCO. So we stepped up the schedule. Three times a week, sometimes even four or five if it was quiet and flights were running every day. We knew it was risky, but once Murovic got the copy of the files we'd be out of business. We talked about killing him, but figured his replacement could only be worse. It might even be someone who'd want to look a bit more deeply into the cause of the fire.'

'Well, he got UNESCO approval all right. But the grant isn't activated until February.'

'So they're probably still doing it, then.'

'How? The raid put you out of business.'

'It did. And that alone should have been enough to get Vitas killed. But he obviously had the clout to make the crackdown stick. What galled Zarko was that he never got advance warning. He'd always bragged he had somebody inside the Ministry, but they must not have been very high up because he never heard a word.

When Zarko was killed afterward, I was sure his source was no good.'

'Wasn't he shot while trying to escape?'

'That's the official version, but there's no way. Zarko had a good lawyer and a lot of D-marks, and too many ways out of town even after getting caught. He never would have risked running. Maybe a well-planned escape from prison, later, during heavy fighting, with plenty of payoffs and inside help. But not a clumsy try at bolting.'

'Why not. Even people like Zarko can get desperate.'

'It *didn't* happen,' Neven shouted furiously.

Vlado gave him a moment to calm down. 'The way you describe it, even Vitas could have been Zarko's contact at Interior. He takes out Zarko, takes the files, increases his own cut, and moves on.'

'Which would also explain why Vitas was killed. More rivalry and more blood. You live by it long enough and you eventually die by it.'

But an insider would have had no need for a briefing from Milan Glavas just last week, Vlado thought. That sounded like an investigator following up a discovery.

'More likely he was killed because he was onto the operation,' Vlado said. 'Which leaves the question of who Markovic must still be working with. Maybe he hired somebody new.'

'There's always somebody willing to take a job like that,' Neven said. 'And once you get an outfit like the U.N. involved these things take on a bureaucratic inertia. You don't stop something like this just by removing one of the principals. You only make it more lucrative for those who're still in the game.'

'So, then, let's look at who was left in business after the raid. There's Markovic, and then there's somebody from the U.N. And who might that be?'

'Somebody at the shipping office. The shipping forms were always signed and stamped in advance. All Zarko had to do was fill in the details. We shipped everything to a Frankfurt contact who, I presume, got a cut for handling the sale, the marketing, whatever. Alijah and I got extra pay for every one we handled, but probably nothing close to what the major players were making. We were just part of the overhead.'

'Let's fill in some names, starting with Frankfurt and the U.N.'

'I don't know any.'

'How couldn't you? They were both right there on the invoice, unless somebody was using a forged signature at this end and an alias at the other.'

Neven frowned, fidgeting and looking at the ground. There was silence for a moment as he stooped to pick up one of the fallen coffee cups.

'Come on,' Vlado said. 'You can't possibly have forgotten.'

'Maybe I never knew them to begin with,' Neven said bitterly, looking straight into Vlado's face. 'Because I can't read. Never learned. Dyslexia, I think they call it now. Except that our progressive schools under Marshal Tito never knew a way around that obstacle. I was a strong boy, so it never really mattered. There were always other uses for me, and people like Zarko were always glad to put me to work. I'd always thought of it as a weakness, then Zarko came along with his loan sharking business and my future was assured. When the war started the future was even rosier. It's why he could always trust me so much. It was my key to promotion. There was nothing I couldn't handle for him, no written message I couldn't deliver without complete guarantee of confidentiality. I was the perfect courier.'

'But Alijah could read.'

'And Alijah was never allowed to hold the papers, or see them. He was only part of the delivery team. So the names, the U.N. shipper and the guy in Frankfurt, I really have no idea. Only Zarko knew.'

'Which leaves me almost back where I started. Unless.'

'Unless?'

'Unless you're still involved. Still running it all from up here, and using me to lay down a false trail.'

Neven smiled, almost wistfully.

'Yes. Up here without the files and without any direct line of communication except the poor dumb boys who come walking up here every day with their loud radios and the likes of you. Besides, if I was still involved you'd be in pretty rough shape right now. Now that I have all the information from you I need, it would be easy to drop you in a muddy hole and forget you, as everyone else soon would. Someday your bones would turn up under the plow of some farmer, or maybe a tourist would find your belt buckle with his metal detector. Do you realize, Mr Detective, how little you know about what makes that place down there run?' He pointed into the valley, to the well of darkness where the city slept. 'It is the same thing that makes this place up here run. Take a look around you at the shitholes and the trenches. This is the future of our wonderful hometown. And if people like me are in charge up here, that should tell you something about the people in charge down there. Do you think any of them will really trust you much longer to complete a fool's errand like this one, Mr Detective? I would say that you are about to become a very lonely man.'

He tossed his Marlboro into the mud and stood to depart.

'And now, Mr Detective, our conversation is finished.'

He turned and walked away, disappearing around a bend in the trench.

15

The boys on the walk up the mountainside had been
right. Overnight visitors to Zuc didn't sleep. They
squirmed and talked, smoked and drank. They cursed
the war, the shells, and the Chetniks. But mostly they
watched and listened, like frightened children tucked
in their beds, attuned to every creak of the floorboards.

Occasionally flocks of red tracer fire streaked crazily
overhead, illuminating a rolling plain of mud. Shellfire
rumbled from the other side of the mountain and
flashed from a distant hill. Luckily most of the action
stayed well down the line.

The biggest surprise to Vlado was the random, aim-
less nature of it all. Even in the ghastliest descriptions he'd read of past wars, there was always the
semblance of a plan. Even the senselessness of World
War I had borne the stamp of some huge, unstoppable
organism of flesh and steel, with a vast network of
communications strung out to all corners of the front.
Bombardments were coordinated, lasting days at a
time, if only to bring on a single frenzied moment of
suicidal assault. Every massive wave of murder was
premeditated.

And here? The war lurched through the dark like a
beast with every limb disabled. Firing was sporadic, as

if by whim. Desultory sniper exchanges quickly turned into heated personal vendettas, then just as quickly subsided. Gun crews worked or didn't work depending on their supply of shells, sleep, and brandy, though most often upon the latter. Command and control were concepts for some other hillside, some other part of the country where the line shifted occasionally, perhaps for some other war altogether. Or perhaps this was the way a war always felt from the inside, as if one were part of a vast portrait that only assumed shape and order when viewed from a distance.

Toward 4 a.m. it began to rain, beginning with a heavy mist that progressed into a steady drizzle of cold, fat drops. Vlado lowered his head, straining his eyes in the dark to watch the water sluice off his sodden cap into a puddle at his feet.

The narrow beam of a penlight swept into his trench, illuminating other men similarly posed. A hand latched onto his right shoulder from behind, jostling him as if he'd dozed off. 'Let's go if you're going.'

It was the officer who'd brought their unit up the hill. They were pulling out.

He climbed out, the soft ground sinking beneath his weight, his joints stiff from hours of standing and sitting in the cold.

They formed up in the grove of splintered trees and began their parade downhill. Vlado was too tired to bother checking who was in front and back of him. They all stared at their own feet. No one spoke. The cookfires that had been burning hours earlier were out now.

It was another twenty minutes before he took stock of the situation, making a mental roll call as he glanced from the front to the rear of the shambling column.

Leading the way were the older men, still grouped by age and attitude. Turning toward the rear he saw to his alarm that two of the teenage boys were carrying a blanket between them, slung heavily like a stretcher. It was obvious someone was in it, dead or wounded. Probably dead, judging by the way the bulge kept bumping the ground.

It was the boy with the ponytail, it turned out, the one with the radio. He'd been hit square in the nose by a chunk of shrapnel, which tore off half his face but left him otherwise untouched. The other boys had turned his body face down into the blanket, hauling him as if he were only napping in a sodden hammock. A corner of his plaid shirttail dangled over the side. His radio was nowhere in sight, either destroyed in the same blast or nimbly confiscated by some veteran of the line.

By the time they reached the bottom of the hill, a dim light was bleeding into the deep gray of the eastern sky, and the rain had stopped. They reached their rendezvous point from the previous evening, and the commander began handing out the day's ration of cigarettes. You got a whole pack for a night at the front. Frontline regulars even got filter tips. The officer thrust a pack toward Vlado, a pleasant surprise until it occurred to him how the pack had suddenly become available. Vlado waved it away. 'Give it to one of his friends instead.'

'What friends?' the officer asked gruffly. 'Everyone hated him. Him and his damn radio.'

Vlado numbly reached out to take the pack, then thought better of it, pulling his hand back.

'Give it to one of them,' he said, motioning toward the others in the unit. 'I'm finished with handouts.'

'Just as well,' the officer said. 'I'll keep it for myself.

Anyone who's tired of taking handouts in this place might as well shoot himself before he starves.'

It was another half hour's walk to home, and it was all Vlado could do to keep putting one foot in front of the other. The conversation with Neven already seemed as if it had taken place days ago, the memory of the scene almost surreal with its flashes of light, the sharp taste of the Turkish coffee. Surely that other world up the hill no longer existed except in Vlado's mind.

He arrived on his doorstep soaked to the bone, and it was times like these when he most wished for a hot shower and a warm bed. Instead he peeled off his clothes and laid them across the bathroom sink, wiping the mud from his body with a damp, sour sponge. He lit two gas flames on the kitchen stove, one to heat a pot of beans he'd left to soak overnight, another to heat water for coffee. The Nescafé was down to the last grains so he used them all, preferring a single strong cup to a pair of weak ones.

A few moments later he sipped down the scalding brew, the brief pain of the heat feeling good in his throat and stomach. Then he pulled on thick dry socks and long underwear, a T-shirt and a sweater, and crawled under his blankets.

He slept until almost noon, waking groggily to the sound of a distant explosion. His stomach was cramped and gassy, and his breath smelled of stale beans and coffee. He tried calling the office to let them know where he was, but the lines were down again. He checked in the mirror, rubbing a hand across stubbly cheeks, but didn't have the heart to drag a cold, dull razor across two days of growth. Outside it was still gray. He swished a glass of water in his mouth, spit into the sink, then pulled a soiled but dry pair of trousers on and shrugged into his overcoat. It was time to walk to the office.

Damir greeted him as if in amazement.

'You're back from the dead!' he shouted, then asked for a complete rundown on the evening. Vlado told him what he'd learned, giving only a few details, mentioning a smuggling operation but nothing about what was being smuggled. Further details could wait until he had the list from Glavas. Otherwise, he still felt bound by his promise to Kasic to hold back what he could. He sagged into a chair, exhaustion catching up to him already.

'Hard to believe the bastard can't read,' Damir said. 'No wonder Zarko trusted him. Once the war's over we'll have to recruit a better class of criminal or else they'll never let us join the European Union.'

'Any further word from anyone?' Vlado asked.

'All quiet. Nothing at all. This morning I was so desperate for something to do I was almost hoping for another murder. No such luck. But this Vitas case – we need new leads, Vlado, or else we're up against a dead end. Whatever trail there was a few days ago is probably cold by now.'

'That's the longest stream of Western detective clichés I've heard out of your mouth since we started working together,' Vlado said.

Damir laughed, but his heart wasn't in it. For a moment Vlado detected a shadow of the bleakness that had washed across Damir's face a few days ago, when he had strolled through the sniper zone.

'What's bothering you?' Vlado asked with concern, although he already had a pretty good idea. 'I figured you at least had your new friend Francesca to help pass the time. Either way your evening couldn't have been as bad as mine.'

'You're holding back on me, Vlado. When you asked me to help out on this investigation I was excited, but I've been completely shut out. I'm nothing but an errand boy. You spend a night with probably the city's most notorious surviving mobster and you sum it up in three minutes of vague chit chat. The other day you spent four hours interviewing some old man in Dobrinja. Four hours! Then you explain it to me in two minutes of broad assurances that soon we'd have a lot of new leads. I'm supposed to take you at your word without even knowing his name or what he does, and then I'm supposed to keep myself happy by talking to whores, which I suppose is all you think I'm good for. Why is it that I think that even when I'm running down these leads I still won't really know what I'm looking for?'

Damir had built a head of steam as he went, nearly shouting by the time he finished. Spent, he eased back in his chair.

'You're right,' Vlado said, 'and I'm sorry.'

He momentarily considered arguing that he was only keeping Damir in the dark for his own protection, because that was indeed a worry. The fewer people who were kicking around this information, the better, for Vlado's security as well, especially given Damir's penchant for café crawling.

Yet, he knew that when push came to shove, Damir could keep his mouth shut as tightly as anyone. Behind the carefree demeanor was a zealous streak of professional ambition that revealed itself from time to time, and Vlado could sense it now in the stubborn set of Damir's jaw, the steadiness of his eyes. This was no merry lad looking for nothing more than an easy good time. Damir wanted to be taken seriously, and was feeling belittled.

Besides, even if spreading the information further was a risk, there was a certain safety in numbers that resulted from keeping Damir better informed. If he knew what to look out for, he'd be more adept at watching Vlado's back, not to mention his own.

'It's Kasic,' Vlado finally said. 'He made me promise. To keep it all close to the chest.'

Damir said nothing. True or not, it was obvious this explanation wasn't sufficient either, and Vlado understood. After two years of watching the Ministry shut them out of the biggest cases in the city, they finally had their piece of the action, but Vlado was keeping it all for himself.

'We'll talk about it later,' Vlado said. 'I promise. And I'll tell you more. As much detail as I can. It's probably time you knew anyway, if I get the leads I'm hoping for from Dobrinja.'

He knew he would have to come up with a way to at least honor the spirit of his pledge to Kasic without further wounding his partner's ego. And, who knows, a better informed Damir might even help turn the tide. But all that would have to wait until early evening. Vlado had gotten a late start and needed to catch up.

But he decided to make the first small offering of information, a morsel to at least convince Damir his heart was in the right place.

'The old man in Dobrinja thinks this is all about art, smuggling it out of the country.'

Damir looked wide eyed, obviously mollified. 'Oh, but I almost forgot,' he said, scrambling to open his notebook. 'Your Nescafé man called this morning.'

It took a moment for Vlado to realize he must have meant Toby, the British journalist.

'He says your package has arrived. And if that means more coffee, then I hope you won't forget your friends.

268

Anyhow, he said you'd better get a move on. Seems he's bursting with curiosity.'

That was the last thing Vlado needed, some reporter asking questions all over town about a copy of the transfer file. He dreaded the idea of another long walk so soon after slogging back from Zuc, but decided he'd better get over to the Holiday Inn.

Toby was in a bright and frisky mood, scrubbed and clean-shaven by the Holiday Inn's private supply of running water.

The thought only made Vlado feel dirtier and more worn out, with an edge of grouchiness. Or maybe it had something to do with where he'd spent the night. He thought for a moment of the teenage boy with a girl-friend, and wondered what he was up to about now. Probably cuddled with her somewhere away from their parents, nuzzled against the warmth of a smooth, womanly neck. Telling her about the boy with the radio, of the way his face had disappeared with a wet, smacking sound and a burst of red mist, or not talking about it at all, but holding it inside, down deep where no one would ever reach it.

'So, you're some sort of art lover, I take it,' Toby said, grinning, waving a stack of fax paper in his right hand.

Vlado could see that the writing was in Cyrillic, alphabet of Serbs and Russians, and wondered how much, if any, Toby was able to decipher. Toby seemed to sense his concern.

'Couldn't resist having my interpreter take a look at it,' Toby said.

God only knew who that was, Vlado thought, remembering the disreputable-looking bunch that hung out by the hotel's rear entrance.

'He says it's nothing but museum stuff, items stored

around here. You doing art thefts now? Or is this something private, something on the side?'

'Please,' Vlado said, feeling too tired to fend off such eager interest. 'You mustn't ask anyone else about this. No one. It is a most sensitive matter, even dangerous.'

Toby's face went solemn and grave.

'No. 'Course not. Don't worry, I know you'll clue me in as soon as you can. In the meantime,' he said, stooping toward his big bag, 'you look like you could use some more of this.'

It was another jar of Nescafé.

I'd rather not, Vlado thought, but his mouth never uttered the words, and his right hand reached for the jar.

He had no illusions about how Toby viewed these transactions. Each donation was a further claim on Vlado's loyalty, a down payment on whatever police secrets might eventually be in the offing. And there had better be some soon, he seemed to be saying, or he'd go off seeking his own interpretations of the facts at hand. For all Vlado knew Toby had made his own copy of the list. Vlado should have known better than to trust a journalist to be a courier of sensitive information. It was like asking an alcoholic to bring you a bottle of wine. But with the scarcity of fax machines and international phone lines he'd had little choice.

'Thank you. It's most generous,' Vlado said.

'Like I said. Comes with the business. Almost routine giving away this stuff by now. And I don't come here half as loaded as some of the blokes you see. Whiskey, cigarettes, sugar, chocolate. Christ, it's all they can do to fly in with a bar of soap and clean underwear and still make the U.N. weight limit. Sarajevo baksheesh.'

Yes, thought Vlado. Another way to keep the wogs talking into the cameras and tape recorders. But as long as Toby was feeling so generous this morning, why not keep him occupied a while longer. Undoubtedly he'd have a car, or access to one, and Vlado needed a ride to Dobrinja to run through the file with Glavas. By the look of it Bogdan had managed to fax details of more than a hundred items.

'Would you be interested in making a little trip over to Dobrinja this afternoon?' he asked Toby. 'We're a little short on official vehicles, and there's someone I need to see. It will only take a few minutes.' Toby thought for a moment, then shrugged. 'Sure. Why not. Not doing anything this afternoon but sitting on my ass, trying to follow up this morning's briefing with a few phone calls, and the lines have been down for an hour. Haven't been to Dobrinja in a while anyway. Always an adventure. And there's nothing doing here until the Serbs let fly with their New Year's bash tomorrow night. The way things are going it's all the fireworks we'll get around here for a while. Christ but it's been bloody slow.'

Vlado wondered if Toby would be talking this way to just anybody in the city, to a grieving mother and child in some gloomy apartment, for instance; so open in his disdain for the war's sluggishness, its lack of media savvy. Somehow he didn't think so. For them he'd have his game face on, uttering sympathetic banalities to coax a few more quotes. But something about Vlado's being a policeman had made Toby drop the pretense, as if he were only hanging out with colleagues. Cops and reporters, Vlado mused, love-hate partners in the weary fraternity of those who'd seen too much.

They made the trip in an armored car, with large blue stickers plastered on either door proclaiming the *Evening Standard* in Gothic lettering. Vlado was impressed by the heaviness and security of the car. The back was stuffed with rattling jerrycans and cardboard boxes filled with food, notebooks, and dirty clothes. He told Toby it was a nice feeling to be bulletproof for a change.

'Grenade-proof, too. Or practically. Some Swedes driving one of these the other day took an RPG round, not a direct hit but damn near. All it did was knock them around a little. Broke a few ribs driving into a ditch but otherwise okay.

'Had a close call myself once. Out front of the Holiday Inn. Colleague didn't shut his door properly, and when I swerved onto the road it flew wide open on the wrong side. Snipers must have been up there saying, "Well, we'll bag us one now," and before I could even turn her around and shut the door three shots were pinging all around us. Didn't think anything more of it until we were filling her up with gas the next day. The petrol tank leaked joyously. A ricochet from the street must've bounded right up into her. Now I can't fill it more than two-thirds. A few inches lower and we'd have gone up in smoke. That was two weeks ago, and I still haven't gotten her fixed. And, Christ, the way they gouge you for repairs around here maybe I never will. For all I know they make a wax mold of your keys while they're at it.

'So anyway,' Toby continued, 'who's this we're going to see?'

'Someone involved with a case.'

Toby waited for more, and when none was forthcoming he smiled, shaking his head slowly, and glanced sideways at Vlado. 'Christ, you do play it close to the chest, don't you. And what sort of case?'

'A murder.'

Toby snorted. 'Just one? Hardly seems worth the effort.'

'That depends on the murder, I guess.'

Toby waited, again hoping for more. But Vlado stared out the side window and lit a cigarette.

Toby began a discourse on his travels around Bosnia. He really had been just about everywhere, it seemed. Central Bosnia, the Posavina corridor near Brcko in the northeast, Banja Luka and Sanski Most in the north, Mostar in the southwest. He'd been to Dobrinja more than once, too, judging by his agility in steering the obstacle course through curbs, sidewalks, and check-points.

He'd even done time in Bihac, a town in Bosnia's far northwest corner holding out much like Sarajevo, only with far less media attention and, as a result, far less international aid.

'Look what they're using for money up there now,' Toby said, fishing his wallet from a rear pocket as he drove. He handed Vlado a wrinkled piece of paper, about 2-by-4 inches. On one side was a small picture of the river that runs through Bihac – Vlado recognized it from a trip years earlier – and the number five was printed in both upper corners. The back side was blank.

'Worse than play money,' Toby said, 'but worth five marks in Bihac. Not even enough D-marks under their mattresses to last them through the war, and none of the government currency, so they had to print these. Looks worse than something from a board game.'

It was odd hearing a field report on the country from this man who came and went like a business commuter, talking about places Vlado had been all his life as if they were district stops on a sales network.

'You've got it lucky here in a way, you know,' Toby

was saying now. 'You're crowded together in this shitty siege, getting picked off one by one. But at least you've kept the bastards out. Once the bad guys get in, no matter who the bad guys happen to be in your neck of the woods, then it's all over. You go to some of these little villages in central Bosnia and find twenty, thirty houses destroyed, not just burned but dynamited. But then you look closer and there are always one or two houses that seem fine. Laundry on the line, windows intact, chickens in the yard, smoke out the chimney. You ask around and find they're the Muslims and everyone else was Croat, or they're Croat and everyone else was Muslim. Now those are the kinds of murder cases a Bosnian detective should be working on. Solve one of them and you'll clean up the whole mess.'

They climbed the stairs to Glavas's house and knocked loudly, but after four tries and five minutes there was still no answer, nor even a cough. Vlado tried the door and it was unlocked, and as he pushed it open he heard footsteps approaching from downstairs.

It was the woman from the time before, the one with heart-shaped lips.

'He's gone,' she said. 'Since yesterday afternoon. Four men in a BMW. A nice dark blue one without a scratch. You don't see many of those around here. Every boy on the block came out to touch it.'

'Were these men armed?'

'Not that I could see. Three of them came up the stairs, went inside, then a few minutes later they left, and he was with them, everybody quiet, hardly saying a word. I haven't seen him since. I thought I heard someone up here last night, but I checked this morning and he was still gone.'

She was obviously worried. So was Vlado.

'Well, let's have a look then.'

The apartment seemed much as before. There was a pile of writing paper and a couple of pencils next to a full ashtray on the nightstand. Pillows were propped against the headboard with the sheets turned back, as if Glavas had been sitting up working when the men came to the door. Nothing was written on a single page. Either Murovic at the museum had been right in his assessment of Glavas, or the men had taken something extra with them.

But the most disturbing absence was up on the living-room wall, where the field of lilies had once bloomed in the fine hand of an Impressionist master. Now it was only an empty space, dustmarks showing the old outline of the frame – exactly what Glavas had told him to look for.

Vlado pulled the ream of fax paper from his bag and thumbed through the pages until he found it: a painting checked out to Glavas, Milan, with a Dobrinja address, since April 1979.

Most recent Reassessment: June 1988. Insured value: $112,000.

'So, is that where one of your paintings was supposed to be?' Toby asked. Vlado had forgotten he was there, had stopped worrying about him because he didn't speak the language. But it must have been easy enough to figure out why Vlado was looking at the list with such concern.

'Yes,' Vlado answered. 'You might say that. Don't worry, you'll be fully briefed on the whole thing. Soon, the way things are looking.'

He turned toward the woman. She was watching from the doorway, as if afraid to step inside.

'These men, were they carrying anything when they left?'

'I don't think so. Unless it was something they'd put in their pockets. Glavas was carrying an overnight bag, or that's what I thought it was anyway.'

'A briefcase, maybe?'

'Maybe. I didn't get a good look at it. I watched them from my front window.'

'And you say you thought you heard someone up here last night?'

'It could've just been some boys on the stairs. I don't know. But yes, it sounded like something. It made me feel better because I thought he must have come back, until I realized this morning that he hadn't.'

'Were the men in uniform?'

She shook her head.

'They were all wearing overcoats. Dark overcoats.'

'How were they dressed otherwise?'

'Neatly. Expensive, if I had to guess.'

'Clothes like you'd wear to an office?'

'More like you'd wear to a nice café.'

Or any other place where mobsters hung out these days, Vlado thought.

He arrived back at the office to find Damir still in an eager and mischievous mood, but he seemed fueled by something headier than the cola and chocolate he must have devoured during the past few hours. As Vlado approached, Damir pointed toward the waiting area by Garovic's office, and Vlado saw, with a sinking feeling, what had made his partner so keyed up.

'You have a visitor,' Damir said. 'A very patient one judging by how long she's been waiting for you.'

She sat on the same couch where Vlado had taken her a few weeks ago, only now she looked prim, knees together, holding a purse in her lap. She looked up, startled to see Vlado headed her way.

'First the Nescafé man, now a visitor from the French barracks,' Damir said. 'It must be your lucky day.'

'Yours, too. While I'm talking to her, maybe you can get ready to start checking some new leads.' He waved the fax from Bogdan.

'What's that?'

'I'll explain when I'm done with her. But if we're lucky, it's the heart of the case.'

She looked different by daylight, or maybe it was just that her makeup was gone. No more rouge, eyeliner, or lipstick, leaving a plain but pleasing face, tired looking but fairly well nourished, more so than the time before, a bit fuller, or perhaps his memory was playing tricks on him.

Vlado approached uncertainly, not knowing quite what to say.

'I believe that this is where we last met in your office,' she said, although thank God not loud enough for Damir to hear. The remark broke some of the tension, and she extended a hand in greeting. 'Perhaps this time the results will be more productive for you.'

'Depends on what you're here for,' Vlado said, regretting the remark immediately.

'I needed to talk to you,' she said, her tone a shade cooler, or perhaps once again it was Vlado's imagination. 'About the shooting. With Maria there the other night I didn't feel comfortable saying anything.'

Maria. That must be the prostitute who'd done all the talking.

'Please,' he said, pointing toward an interrogation room with glass partitions. 'We can talk in here.'

They settled into chairs on opposite sides of a battered wooden table. The aging tubes of a fluorescent

277

light hummed and sputtered overhead. Vlado felt some of his discomfort returning, and moved quickly to fill the silence. 'First things first,' he said, opening a notebook. He scribbled the date at the top and asked, 'Your name, please. For the record.'

'Hodzic, Amira,' she said.

'Address? And phone number, if you have one.'

'For what reason?' she asked, a sudden edge to her voice.

'In case I need to talk to you again,' he said, looking her in the eye. 'Unless of course you'd rather have me come to your place of business to ask any followup questions, in the presence of Maria, who I presume is the one who did all the talking the other night.'

'Yes, she was, and, no, I suppose I wouldn't like that. Number seven-twelve Bosanska Street, apartment thirty-seven. I have no phone.'

Which probably meant she was a refugee, Vlado thought, or else she'd still have the hookup from before the war, whether it was working or not.

'So. The night of the shooting, then. You were there, I presume, outside the barracks.'

'Yes. The usual location.'

'And you heard the gunshot?'

'Yes. Maria was right about one thing, though. There had been shooting off and on for hours. The usual stuff in that area. But this one was different. Louder and closer, and from the near side of the river. Maria thought right away that it must have something to do with her man. Her regular man. Or at least the closest thing she had to a regular man. It turned out that it didn't, of course. Her man was safely off somewhere else. We all heard the next morning who had really been killed. But, well, you seemed interested in knowing any detail, no matter how small, so I thought I at

278

least owed you that, if only because Maria seemed so determined none of us would say a word.'

'Why did she think her man might be out there? Was she expecting him?'

'No. She'd seen him just a few minutes before. He'd come out through the gate.'

'From the barracks?'

'Yes.'

'On foot?'

'No. In a jeep. One of the white U.N. ones. Armored, with thick windows, but we could all see who was driving because we knew him from other times.'

'So he was a soldier, then. Not a civilian employee.'

'Yes, an officer.'

'Rank?'

'A colonel. Or that's what Maria calls him. Her French colonel. Or sometimes she just calls him Sweet Maurice. Or the Little Colonel, like Napoleon.'

'Well, then, a colonel with a regular squeeze waiting at the gate.'

'Yes, I thought you'd want to know, especially when I heard that the man who was killed was someone important.' She glanced toward the table. 'Do you think I could have one of your cigarettes?'

'Please.'

He slid a pack of Drinas across the table. He held out his lighter and watched her inhale, lips tight. When she began speaking again she kept the cigarette clenched in her teeth, making little bursts of smoke with every word. It seemed almost contrived to lend her an air of harshness, but she couldn't quite pull it off. Something in the gesture didn't ring true. Yet she clearly preferred projecting this image to whatever might be the real one, and it occurred to Vlado that there were probably children at home, perhaps a husband in the city or out

279

on some frontline. The pose was for their sake. This was the prostitute speaking, not the mother or the wife. He wondered for a moment what she must be like in that other world.

'So,' he said, 'we have a French colonel driving a U.N. jeep possibly in the area a few minutes or even a few seconds before the shooting,' Vlado said, 'perhaps in a position to have seen or heard something himself.'

'Yes.'

'Can you pin it down a little more? What do you mean by a few minutes. Ten? Five? One or two?'

'One, if I had to guess. It really was quite short, or seemed that way,' she said, with more of the little puffs of smoke bursting from her mouth.

Well, this was something, perhaps. At minimum the colonel would be worth talking to, Vlado thought. If he'd driven in the right direction, perhaps he'd at least noiced Vitas standing on the corner, or anyone else who might have been with him. It was a longshot, but better than any other shot at a witness he had right now, which was no shot at all.

'Is there anything else you remember from those moments right before or after the gunshot? Any other sounds. Someone running. A car driving away, perhaps.'

'I don't know. I'm not sure I would have heard anything else. From the minute we heard the shot Maria was hysterical. It was all we could do to keep her from crawling around the sandbags and running across the bridge to see for herself what had happened. She was screaming for her little Maurice, her Little Colonel. It was close to curfew anyway and we were worried she'd have us all in jail for the night. And frankly, the stories you hear about police and prostitutes . . .'

She stopped short, suddenly embarrasssed.

'What did you finally do?'

'After a few minutes she calmed down. We wanted to walk her home but she refused. Said she was going to his apartment, that he would be there if he was okay, that she'd stay there for the night, so she left. If he wasn't there, she had a key to let herself in, she said. The rest of us – it was only Leila and I that night – we walked home together. She lives in the building next to mine. Neither of us knows where Maria lives, the colonel either. And the next night everything was back to normal. Maria seemed fine. The only time she's acted funny since was when you showed up.'

'This colonel. He was used to having her at his apartment? Is that normal in, well, this business? With U.N. officers, I mean.'

'Is this part of the investigation?'

Was it? Vlado wasn't sure. 'I don't know, frankly. Just a matter of finding every detail I can.'

'You'll have to ask someone who's been at it a little longer than me. I'm new. So is Leila. We started the same week, a little more than a month ago, and from what I hear women come and go from it month to month, except for the ones like Maria who've been doing it for years.'

'So tell me what you know, secondhand or whatever, then, about Maria and this colonel. Maurice, you said. Did she ever say his last name? And that is definitely part of the investigation, 'cause I'd like to talk to him.'

She shook her head.

'From what a few others have told me, it was quite a romance, at least on her part. He'd been posted to Sarajevo a year ago, and picked her up almost right away. A few nights a week. After a while he got himself an apartment. Apparently some of the higher ranking officers do that, and she started staying over at his place two or three days at a time.

'After a while he must have cooled on her. He may even have found someone else he liked better. She ended up back on the beat more and more nights, mooning outside the barracks like a teenager, waiting for him to drive in or out in his jeep. The few times I've seen him drive through he gives her a smile and a wave, that's all. It made me wonder if everything she said about the two of them was true. She's not exactly the most stable person in the world, after all. But she did show us a key she said was to his apartment. And she did seem to know an awful lot about him.'

'Like what?'

'Little details from his apartment. More than what you'd just pick up in a few minutes between the sheets. Knew what his wife's name was. What she and their kids looked like. She'd seen all his pictures from home. Knew what sort of guns he kept. Told us he was an important man with the U.N. Said he was tougher than the others. That if a Chetnik shot at him he'd shoot back, and wouldn't miss. Not like the ones who just take cover and file a report. It sounded to me like he'd talked a lot of manly bullshit to her and she'd believed it.'

'And now I guess we'll find out if he has any powers of observation and memory. Whatever the case, you were right to come in. Sometimes it's the little things that lead to the big ones.'

They went out the door together, and he escorted her to the steps, listening as her heels clicked down to the ground floor, echoing just as sharply as the time before.

He ignored Damir's questioning gaze as he sat back at his desk, but Damir didn't take the hint. 'So,' he chirped. 'Success?'

'Not the sort you have in mind,' Vlado answered.

'But you got a phone number, I hope.'

'Confidential. If you want to reach her you'll have to walk down to Skenderia. Just make sure to take a carton of Marlboros if you want anything more than conversation.' He felt cheapened by the remark the moment he spoke it, though it certainly seemed to be a hit with Damir. 'Besides, don't you have some work to do?'

'That depends. Where are those new leads you were promising.'

'Yes. These.' Vlado pulled the fax from his satchel. 'Here, take a few pages and you can get started right away.'

Damir scanned the Cyrillic writing and his eyes lit up. 'Where the hell is this from? Somewhere we don't belong, that's for sure.'

'Never mind that. Just oil up your rusty Cyrillic and get reading. It's a list of paintings, valuable artworks hanging around town, with their last known addresses. We want to know which ones are still here, which ones are missing. Check them one by one, address by address. If the building's been destroyed, move on to the next one. If the apartment's been destroyed, ask the neighbors what happened, where the occupants went, then follow up. And if the place is occupied but the painting's gone, find out when it was taken, and by who, and the official reason given. Get descriptions of whoever they saw, as much detail as you can. With any luck we'll be on the trail to Vitas's killer within a day.'

Damir glanced down at the papers, eagerness apparent in his features. 'Sooner, if I can help it,' he said. 'I'm on my way.' And he bustled out the door, coattails flying like wings.

*　　　*　　　*

Left on his own, Vlado picked up the phone, and he was pleased to again hear a dial tone. He thumbed through a U.N. directory and dialed the number for the Skenderia barracks. A man's voice answered in English with a heavy French accent.

'Yes, this is Inspector Petric from the civil police. I'm trying to reach one of your colonels, only I'm afraid all I have is a first name.'

'That shouldn't be a problem, the battalion's only got one colonel, and his first name is Alain. Would you like me to connect you?'

Vlado sighed. So much for the delusional ravings of an unstable old prostitute, Vlado thought.

'Never mind, thank you. The colonel I was looking for is named Maurice. I obviously got some bad information.'

'No you didn't. Just the wrong place. You're looking for Colonel Maurice Chevard. He was officially posted here with the battalion last year, but he's assigned to headquarters at the PTT building. Would you like his number?'

'By all means.'

The PTT building housed the headquarters for U.N. forces, a grim, gray fortress on the west side of town along Sniper Alley, near the turnoff for Dobrinja. It was a precarious location, surrounded by sandbags and sprouting scores of satellite dishes and antennae. In better days it had housed the central telephone company and postal service.

Vlado dialed the number.

'Shipping office,' said a voice with a British accent.

Vlado was so taken aback that for a moment he said nothing.

'Hello?' the voice spoke again.

'Yes. Excuse me. I've dialed the wrong number.'

Vlado hung up.

Colonel Chevard worked in the shipping office, which meant he was directly connected to Maybe Airlines, Sarajevo's main lifeline, and the best way in and out of the city for food, soldiers, and, perhaps, valuable works of art. This put the Little Colonel's jeep ride in a new light. Or did it? It really wasn't much of a connection. And he had no idea how many people worked in the shipping office, or how many might have the authorization to make sure a crated piece of art made the next flight out. With the right combination of payoffs almost anyone might be able to do it, he supposed.

Vlado stood up from his desk and paced the room. He lit a cigarette and mulled his options for a few moments, then sat back down, figuring it had been long enough for whoever answered the first time to forget his voice. He again dialed the number at the PTT building.

'Shipping office,' answered the same British voice.

'Yes, I'd like to inquire about the possibility of sending a private parcel out on one of your flights. I normally post them through the Jewish Center's convoys, but this one is a matter of some urgency. Perhaps you could tell me how it might be done.'

'It can't be. Strict policy against it. No exceptions. Sorry.'

And with that he seemed ready to hang up, so Vlado spoke quickly. 'Surely there are exceptions. I'm told these things can be done occasionally, even if rarely.'

'Look, mate, I don't want to get rude with you, but I personally double-check nearly every outgoing manifest, and I can tell you on very solid authority that nothing private, or public either for that matter, ever goes out of here under my approval. My boss would skin me alive if anything ever did, never mind what would happen if the press got hold of it.'

'Might I appeal this. To your boss, perhaps. And I don't believe I got your name, either.'

Vlado had found that, when dealing with the military or other similar hierarchies, requesting someone's name nearly always got you nothing less than a referral to the next rung up in the chain of command. As if by giving you their name they were obligated to send you home a satisfied customer, or else risk having to explain away any sort of official complaint you might lodge. He never understood why they didn't simply refuse to give their name and hang up. Passing the problem on to someone else just seemed to be the accepted way of doing things.

'My name is Maclean, sir. Lieutenant Maclean.'

'Very good lieutenant. And your superior officer.'

'Look, Mr . . .'

'Jusofovic,' he said, saying the first thing that popped into his head – his wife's maiden name.

'Mr Jusofovic. In answer to your original question, there are some rare, quite rare, cases in which we can haul private parcels on our flights, usually only as a special favor to people who have done us special favors in matters of aid operations or supply. And even then it is strictly hush hush, and only as a favor to individuals, and not to the Bosnian government, for obvious reasons of nonpartisanship. If you're asking for that kind of permission, not only can I not handle it, but you'll have to make the request in person to my superior. He's the only one who can say yes, and I can tell you right now that nine times out of ten he says no.'

'And his name?'

'Colonel Chevard, sir, and the earliest he can see

you is next Wednesday. If you don't mind the advice, sir, he can be a bit prickly. If there's any way you can make it seem like it's his idea, you'll stand a better chance. That's the way it works with the French, you know. So, shall I schedule an appointment for you next Wednesday, then? Mr Jusofovic? Are you there? Jesus. All that and the bloody bugger hangs up on me.'

16

Vlado awakened to find it had snowed overnight, then cleared. The sun now shone brightly, and looking out his front door he could see well into the hills with a clarity rare for this time of year.

He felt refreshed, not only from the solid night's sleep, but from a renewed sense of purpose. The disappearance of Glavas had both troubled and energized him. At some point during his slumber he had tried to convince himself that Glavas had impulsively decided to exchange his painting for passage out of the city, that perhaps Vlado's visit had even planted the idea, and that the men who'd escorted him in such orderly fashion – with nothing to hide, apparently, for they'd done it in the middle of the day – had only been starting him on his journey. By the light of day the idea seemed preposterous, but he still clung to the possibility.

Whatever the case, his activities over the past several days had somehow set events in motion that he might now be able to trace if he only knew where to look for the signs. In the weariness of last night such a prospect had seemed hopeless, but this morning, with its rich feel of promise and possibility, it seemed within reach, perhaps only a single flash of insight away.

He broke open the seal on the new jar of Nescafé and treated himself to a luxuriously strong cup. He then sat at his work bench in the kitchen and pulled out the boxful of his unfinished soldiers. It would be a good way to clear his head, to gain some temporary distance from the facts of the case that had crowded his dreams.

He wondered for a moment if Damir had managed to turn up anything yet in his pursuit of missing paintings. The search would probably be more difficult and time consuming than they hoped. Oh, well. He was ready for a full and busy day.

His soldiers, he noted with pleasure, needed very little work before they'd be finished, a matter of a few small but important touches – gold on buttons and belt buckles, silver for the sweeping blades of sabers.

From a shelf he took down an oversize atlas of military history. Published in London, it was one of his most prized possessions. He opened it to a map and full-color drawing from the Battle of Austerlitz. There, at the Czech town of cotton mills and sugar refineries, Napoleon had won his most brilliant victory in 1805, defeating not only the Austrians but the Russians as well. The idea of a long-odds winner appealed to Vlado just now. He was using the drawing of the battle as a model for his Austrian hussars, who'd fared badly that day, routed from the field with huge losses.

He held one aloft with a thin pair of tweezers, into the sunlight that seeped through the dull plastic over the kitchen window, and began daubing gold onto the little man's buttons, taking care not to smudge the bright blue of his tunic. Such pleasing colors. Such dash, with their swords raised in the air, thrust daringly forward. He thought briefly of the muddy men on Zuc, of their faces by the light of cookstoves and penlight. These soldiers had smooth tan faces, and eyes that were dots of blue. He paused for a moment, smelling the paint, sipping his coffee, and letting the thoughts drain from his mind. He absently set the mug down on the book, and when his reverie broke a few moments later he saw he'd left a brown ring of coffee on the battle map, directly across the blue arrow of Napoleon's advance. He plucked a dirty shirt from a pile of clothes at the foot of his bed and wiped clean the fields of Austerlitz, then set the mug on the workbench.

He glanced at his watch, wondering where the last twenty minutes had gone, then gathered his satchel and headed out the door.

Damir's desk was empty, but Garovic was waiting, glancing at his watch with an extra degree of nervousness, his bureaucratic antennae twitching as if he were a cockroach that had just sensed an approaching boot.

'You're to see Kasic this morning, first thing,' he fairly shouted. 'You're running a bit late, aren't you. I tried phoning you at home but the lines were down.'

Vlado had wondered how long it would be before he'd have to make an accounting to Kasic, assuming that was what he wanted.

'Did Kasic say why he wants to see me?'

'A progress report. Here's hoping you have one. For your sake and mine.'

This time there was no waiting in the downstairs lobby. Garovic, ever eager to please, phoned ahead to alert the ministry that Vlado was on his way. He arrived to find a tall man in a dark blue uniform waiting outside the front entrance. He seemed to know Vlado on sight, a bit disconcerting since Vlado had never seen the man in his life. Perhaps it was another small trick by Kasic to impress him. It would have been easy enough to have shown the guard a photo of Vlado a few minutes earlier. But maybe it also meant they'd shown his photo to others, or that this man had watched Vlado on previous occasions.

Kasic was again waiting at the top of the stairs, and once they'd settled themselves into his office he opened with the two words that seemed to preface all his conversations. 'So, then.'

He paused, arranging the papers on his desk. 'Tell me how it's going.'

Vlado had wondered on his way over exactly how he'd answer such a question. Glavas's disappearance had made him wary of just about everyone. And if he could hold out information on his partner for days at a time, then he could hold out on Kasic as well, at least until he was ready to make his final report. Nor did he want Kasic putting his own men onto the trail, behind his back, muddying the waters and drawing further attention to where he was headed. While walking to the ministry he'd formed a general strategy on how to fend off Kasic for now, yet even as he opened his mouth to answer he had not decided exactly what to say.

But Kasic spoke again before Vlado could begin. 'I assume it's going well. Or at least I've decided that it must be, or you would have asked for our help by now.'

So, a challenge right away.

'I may need help yet,' Vlado answered. 'For further interrogation, that sort of thing. But otherwise, yes, I think I'm making progress. Not enough for any arrests yet, but I've developed some theories.' He weighed his next words carefully. 'And they do seem to match with some of your early leads and suspicions.'

Kasic beamed at the news, his gymnasium vitality

shining through his long face, the brown eyes almost fatherly in their softness. Vlado wondered how long the smile would last.

'So, then,' Kasic resumed, 'our undercover men were of some help.'

'For themselves, perhaps. I presume they've both been paid bonuses.'

The smile disappeared.

'As you had said,' Vlado continued, 'they were a little short on specifics. And even in their generalities, well, they were somewhat on the right track. Vitas definitely seems to have gotten himself mixed up in some sort of criminal racket, either from the inside or the outside.'

'The outside?'

'By investigating it. On his own, apparently, without telling anyone else in the department. Either to be in position to cut himself into the smuggling operation or because he didn't trust the rest of the ministry.'

'Meaning me,' Kasic stated, with a trace of indignation.

'Meaning everyone but himself, including you and a few hundred others.'

Kasic paused.

'But as for the other angle from the undercover men, the general angle of meat and cigarettes. Productive?'

'I'm not so sure. It may have been something more lucrative.' This was as far as Vlado wished to go, and he put his strategy into motion. 'Beyond that, I'm afraid I'm not prepared to say anything more just yet. In the interests of the ministry, of course.'

Kasic looked as stunned as Vlado had hoped, though signs of anger quickly began moving across his features.

'Surely you don't consider it to be in the ministry's interest to be left in the dark on this matter. And surely

you have no trouble sharing your findings with me,'
Kasic said, his tone mildly incredulous.

'None whatsoever, if it were merely a matter of trust,'
Vlado said. 'It is more of a matter for your own protection, and for that of the ministry in general.' Kasic
started to interrupt, but Vlado raised a hand and
plunged on. 'Please. Let me finish. Vitas was killed
because of something he found out. Either he was
trying to use the information to his own financial
advantage or against someone else, but either way it
got him killed. That being the case, I see no reason at
this point to jeopardize further senior members of the
ministry or the department in the same way, especially
when, officially, your role in this case is only one of
assistance.'

Then, before Kasic could break in, Vlado played his
one and only bluff. 'But more to the point is the matter
of the independence of this investigation,' Vlado said.
'You should be aware, sir, that certain people in the
U.N. command have made it known to me that they
are watching me closely to see that I maintain my
"objectivity" – their word, not mine – and that I don't
cozy up to the ministry. I wouldn't want to do anything
that would damage the U.N.'s trust in the department,
which, I can tell you on good authority, is quite high at
the moment. I even considered canceling this appointment simply so I wouldn't be seen entering or leaving
the building. But I suppose one visit won't be out of
bounds as long as I don't say too much.'

Vlado wondered for a moment if he'd laid it on too
thick, but Kasic seemed more befuddled than skeptical.
He'd clearly expected a full briefing without resistance.
He opened a desk drawer and pulled out a fresh pack of
Marlboros, this time not offering one to Vlado but
absently lighting one for himself.

'As for your first reason,' Kasic said. 'Your concern for members of the department is misplaced, not to mention unwise. For one thing, the more of us you keep informed – within reason, of course – the more you'll guarantee your own security. The way I see it, working the case alone is what got Vitas killed, whether his motives were good or evil. A lone hunter is always an easier target.

'As for your worries about my safety, don't be ridiculous. Part of my job is knowing how to take care of myself. We're not some bunch of civilians who happened to have witnessed a crime and need protection. We *are* the law, and the more we know, the stronger our position.

'It's your latter point that's the sticky one, I suppose. Although I doubt that even the most exacting official from the U.N. command would interpret your "independence" as precluding an informal debriefing from time to time.'

'I wouldn't be so sure of that,' Vlado said, and decided to stop at that, to let the idea simmer a while longer. As the silence lengthened it was clear he'd put Kasic in a position he hadn't been prepared to defend. How, indeed, could he force Vlado's hand? Even if he suspected Vlado was exaggerating, he couldn't be sure. His only alternative was to shut down Vlado's investigation, and that would play poorly, not only in Sarajevo but probably in Washington, London, and Paris as well. He'd be able to deal with Vlado later, of course, but Vlado could worry about that some other time.

Vlado watched the emotions play out across Kasic's face, and reflected once again that perhaps Kasic was in over his head in this new job. In years of following orders to the letter he'd had few chances to develop the right touch for leadership. Ruthless efficiency was sometimes a poor substitute for agility and flexibility, although sometimes it triumphed anyway from its own brute inertia.

Finally Kasic fell back on his standard opener. 'So, then . . . Obviously you're not budging. And where does that leave us, besides in the dark?'

'It leaves us, I hope, only a few days from getting results.'

'And you'll have names for us then?'

'A few, probably. Or at the very least a general outline of the operation.'

As Kasic digested this he appeared to be engaged in some inner debate. He hesitated a moment, then began haltingly. 'Vlado. It might well . . . It might just behoove you to not rule out internal suspects. Within the ministry, I mean. Or perhaps that's the reason for your hesitation at providing a briefing.'

It was hardly what Vlado had expected, but it was a relief, though he still had to tread lightly. 'Do you have suspicions along these lines?' he asked Kasic.

'Vaguely. Nothing specific. Just talk, really. Old, loose talk within the ministry from weeks ago that, in light of what happened to Vitas, now takes on a different meaning. But nothing I can go into with you, at least, not until I know a few more specifics about what you've come up with.'

Vlado was tempted then and there to tell Kasic all he'd learned. The brown fatherly eyes now seemed more tragic than welcoming. It obviously pained Kasic to admit he might be at the helm of a corrupted ship, and once again he seemed overwhelmed by his new responsibilities.

But the urge passed. For one thing, offering a full briefing now would blow his cover story of U.N.

scrutiny. For another, he still wasn't sure who he could trust. Besides, if he changed his mind he could always contact Kasic tomorrow, or the day after. He did wonder what this 'loose talk' must have been about, although it was clear he wasn't going to get anything further without giving something in return. But there were other ways of getting information from the ministry, and that, too, would require some finesse.

'In the meantime,' Vlado said, 'there is some help you could give me.'

'By all means,' said Kasic, brightening a bit.

'Your files.'

The frown returned.

'Nothing I haven't seen already,' Vlado quickly added. 'Just a few things in Vitas's personnel folder I wanted to double-check, in light of what I've learned since.'

Kasic looked relieved. 'No problem,' he said. 'I've got some business out of the building to attend to, a meeting at the presidency building, so I'll escort you there. Besides, we have a visitor in records right now who I wouldn't mind impressing.' He added the latter archly, as if Vlado knew quite well what he was talking about, though he hadn't a clue.

He led Vlado down a flight of stairs with a hand lightly on Vlado's back, as if shepherding a son to the library with overdue books. They entered the double doors of the records department, its vast file room painted in several peeling layers of industrial green. Recent shelling aimed at the nearby presidential building had begun to knock loose some of the ceiling plaster, and a fine white dust coated the tops of the metal file cabinets, arranged in long, dreary rows.

Facing them across a wide counter was a fidgety-looking clerk who motioned over his shoulder as he leaned toward Kasic, whispering, 'It's Morris from the U.N., sir.'

'Quite all right,' Kasic whispered back. 'I was notified.'

So, Vlado thought, the resident U.N. watchdog was here to poke around, although it was an open secret that in its guise of cooperation the government heavily sanitized anything the U.N. asked to see. Not that the U.N. ever asked for anything particularly recent or relevant, seeming just as out of touch with reality as any other of the world's lumbering bureaucracies. Vlado knew it was the weak point in his cover story, although so far it seemed to be holding.

Kasic placed a hand firmly on Vlado's right shoulder and leaned closer, whispering, 'You'll forgive me for a moment, Vlado, if I use you for a brief object lesson.'

'Captain Morris,' Kasic boomed. 'Visiting us again, I see.'

Morris, stooped over an open file drawer, replied by glancing up from his labors with an unintelligible grunt. But the cool reception didn't deter Kasic.

'This is Inspector Petric, Mr Morris, though perhaps I don't need to introduce you. He's the man called in from the outside to handle the Esmir Vitas investigation, of course. I invited him in for a briefing, and you'll be pleased to know that in no uncertain terms he told me it was none of my business. I grudgingly must agree.'

Morris was staring back now, seeming annoyed and more than a bit puzzled. To Vlado it was plainly apparent he didn't know anything about either Vitas or the investigation, and cared less. He was probably only running an errand for someone else, searching the files for some bit of minutiae to be plugged into a thick report no one would ever read. Kasic seemed not to notice. He was too intent on completing his clumsy bit of theater.

'I hope you don't mind for a moment if he joins you in your browsing.' Kasic then turned grandly toward the clerk and said, 'Whatever files he needs, Krulic,' but by then Morris had bowed back to his work with another grunt. Vlado felt almost embarrassed for this hammy performance, but it had at least served an important purpose, whether Kasic realized it or not.

As Krulic hurried off to retrieve the Vitas personnel file, Kasic leaned low once more to whisper in Vlado's ear, and when he spoke it became clear he'd developed a counterattack to Vlado's strategy. 'Don't forget my offer of help, Vlado. Use our manpower, our expertise. If you feel that our undercover people haven't been completely forthcoming, perhaps we can persuade them to be more accommodating.

'But whatever you do,' he said, his tone carrying a sudden hint of steel, 'don't sit too long on your information. This fellow Morris has been down here three days running. They may be playing chummy with you, but we're not feeling that way with them at all. So if you're worried about tying up every loose end before making any moves, then don't.'

'What are you saying, exactly?'

'That neatness is not a major concern. That speed is everything. That even accuracy, or getting exactly the right man, may not be the most important thing, as long as we get somebody from this city's collection of lowlifes, the faster the better. Better for all of us, Vlado. For the ministry, for the country. And don't forget your own welfare in all this.'

He gripped Vlado's shoulder and smiled, now drilling him with those brown eyes that could look warm and liquid one minute, cold and metallic the next. Was this last comment a job offer or a threat? Vlado wondered.

'Good hunting, then,' Kasic announced to the room. He leaned toward Vlado, whispering, 'But, please, old son, don't stay in the field too long by yourself. It's dangerous out there. Pick your shots soon. Aim wisely.'

Vlado was no longer embarrassed for him. Perhaps he had underestimated Kasic. Krulic returned with the Vitas personnel file, but Vlado knew from previous inspection there'd be nothing helpful inside. What he really wanted to see would take a bit more doing, but with any luck Kasic had unwittingly provided the key. After a few minutes of shuffling through the papers for show, Vlado returned the file and said, 'And now, while you're at it, I'd also like to see the files for the October raid.'

Krulic looked up with a start. 'You'll need approval from upstairs for that one,' he answered immediately. He'd been well trained in saying no, and now that Kasic had left for the day he'd reverted to his natural state as a slothful, chain-smoking civil servant in the best tradition of the Tito era, reluctant to react to anything other than the urge for nicotine, caffeine, or undeserved promotion.

'You heard Kasic,' Vlado said, speaking a bit louder. 'I'm to have access to anything I want. What more approval do you need than the head of the department.'

This time Morris was a more attentive audience, straightening to listen in. Now it was Krulic who was unimpressed. 'Sorry. Permission has to be in writing. It's the rule.'

The rules. Always the last line of defense for entrenched laziness. But Vlado had a final round of artillery.

'Very well. I'll have someone sent out to disturb

Mr Kasic, who has just gone to the presidency for an important meeting. We can have the meeting interrupted and he can be called into the hall, which I'm sure will cause some embarrassment. Then he'll have to come back into the office so he can sign the proper forms, of course, because the rules won't allow him to simply send a note. And he'll no doubt be grateful that you were so diligent in following the rules to the last letter even after he'd made his own wishes so clear only moments before he left.'

It was a direct hit. Krulic held firm for only a moment, then beat a retreat. He slouched off to retrieve the file without another word. Morris ducked back into his drawer, and Vlado allowed himself a small smile of triumph.

Although the Republic of Bosnia and Herzegovina was the world's newest country, and among the smallest, its government had already amassed a pile of records worthy of a nation ten times its size and age. Some were simply left over from the voluminous documentation of Yugoslavia, but in the previous two years local officials had zealously built upon these foundations. They'd fallen back on the old rule of thumb that the more paperwork your department generated, the more important it must be, and after two years of war neither death nor distraction had deterred their zeal.

Likewise, if you were preparing to mount an important law-enforcement operation, one of the final measures of its magnitude would be the volume of its paperwork. For that reason, Vlado had great expectations for the file on the October raid, and as Krulic dropped a thick folder heavily onto the counter he saw that he would not be disappointed.

He took the bundle to a nearby table and settled in

for a long spell of reading. The file told its story in the dry, sterile jargon of police bureaucrats and inter-office memos. But as Vlado made his way through the requisitions, organizational charts, duty lists, assignment orders, mission goals, and sweeping policy statements, he began to acquire a feel not only for the operation, but for the atmosphere that must have existed within the department at the time.

The mood had been grim, a feeling of being under siege by the wild and increasingly bold tactics of the gangs and their warlords. The handiwork of Vitas was apparent in much of the paperwork, and Vlado could sense the way in which he had attempted to shut down all leaks and conduits of information to the outside, so that after a great period of apparent quiet the Ministry would be able to strike with the suddenness of a cat from a dark corner, with all claws bared.

There were forms upon forms, and stacks of signed orders and authorizations, some of which had gone straight from Vitas to the Interior Minister and onward to the President's office.

There were guarantees of cooperation from the local army corps, a pledge of help from the miliary police. Vitas had gone to a great deal of trouble to secure the partnership of others who would share in the blame if things went wrong. Yet he had also taken pains to retain the authority necessary for claiming the lion's share of credit for a success.

With all this activity, of course, it would have been virtually impossible to have kept the brewing operation a secret, no matter how much Vitas clamped down. The gangs had obviously realized they were in for a fight, although according to Neven they'd been surprised by both its ferocity and its timing. Either their sources within the Ministry had failed the gangs by lack of vigilance or had intentionally left the gangs in the dark, for reasons of their own.

It took an hour for Vlado to find the first item he wanted. It was the inventory of property seized from Zarko's headquarters following his surrender.

They'd listed everything, the guns, the currency, the ammo boxes, right down to the bootleg cases of cigarettes, the boxfuls of women's hosiery, and the stacks of pornographic magazines still wrapped in plastic. Zarko's ability to keep his men from tearing open the latter item was the greatest testimony yet to his leadership skills.

Midway through the second page of the single-spaced list Vlado found the first item of interest: *79. Wooden crate, approx 8' X 6' x 2', shipping form attached.*

The next item was further down the same page: *96. Library-style card file, 2 drawers.*

Next to both items were handwritten notations in the margin: *Custody transferred, 10-04-93, see attached.*

Vlado thumbed to the end of the report, where a page of cream-colored bond had been stapled to the back, the same sort he'd found in the waste can of Vitas's apartment. Its message was short: *Items #79 and #96 transferred to personal custody of department head, E. Vitas.* It was signed by Vitas, with no further explanation. The date was a mere two days after the raid. Obviously the items had piqued his interest, and he apparently hadn't felt they'd be safe in ministry custody. And by the time he'd finally gotten around to following up his suspicions, his adversaries had been ready and waiting. At least, that's how Vlado read it. It could also mean Vitas had simply bided his time before trying to capitalize financially on his find.

Vlado reviewed the file materials dealing with the

capture and shooting of Zarko, beginning with a detailed, signed statement of events by the commander of the custody detail. He recalled that at the time there had been a great deal of grumbling in the city over the circumstances of Zarko's death. For one thing, Zarko had still been a hero to many, remembered for his defense of the city. For another, the shooting had carried the unmistakable scent of a summary execution, the sort that had happened in the old days.

The papers showed that the custody detail had included six people, and they'd been assembled with special care more than a week in advance, specifically to handle the assignment that they'd then bungled. Vitas had obviously wanted to get it done right, fearing the very sort of criticism that resulted when Zarko was shot. Vlado reviewed the list of names, recognizing three of the six, including the commander. All were known as reliable, vigilant officers. He didn't recognize the other three, although one seemed oddly familiar. It had been whited-out and retyped, presumably after a typographical error. But there was no reason to assume those three hadn't been selected with just as much care.

According to the commander's report, stamped FOR DEPARTMENTAL USE ONLY, the detail had traveled in a small truck with a canvas opening in the back and armored sides. After picking up Zarko he and his men were to drive straight to the jail. They made one stop at a security checkpoint posted at barricades a block away, shunting past a foreign TV crew, then encountered no further delays until stopping briefly for some children who'd been kicking a soccer ball in the street. At that point, the commander said, the suspect had tried to escape by jumping from the back of the truck. He got only as far as throwing open the rear flaps when he was shot. An attached report by witnesses, however, said that the flaps had never opened, which would mean he'd never actually jumped. No wonder people had been upset. For once the wild rumors of the street seemed to have some validity. There was disagreement as to whose bullet had killed him, the commander said, and his report did not name which of the six men claimed to have opened fire. It was a curious omission, considering that this was strictly an internal report. But someone had undeniably been quick on the trigger.

Neven's words came back to him. Zarko would never have tried to escape, he'd said. Perhaps after three days of fighting he'd snapped, unable to think clearly. But if that was the case, why had he surrendered? Neven was right. It made little sense. And even if he'd bolted, wouldn't he have at least tried to grab a gun first, instead of just jumping out the back? Vlado flipped back to the beginning of the report. Yes, just as he'd thought. Zarko had been handcuffed as well.

Vlado went back to the list of the six-man detail, and the same name as before caught his eye. 'Kemal Stanic.' Where had he heard it before? He asked for the man's personnel file. Krulic sighed loudly, then sluggishly retrieved the file before slumping back in a chair with his newspaper and his cigarettes.

Initially there seemed to be nothing out of the ordinary in the man's background, although perhaps it was a bit odd he'd been a grocer before the war. Age, 35. Nothing odd there.

Not until Vlado saw the names of the man's four children, with the notation 'deceased' next to two of them, did he realize what had seemed familiar about the name. Yes, that was it: Kemal's grocery. There'd been a shootout there a year earlier, when

Zarko himself had been fighting with members of a rival gang. Two children had been killed in the crossfire.

Their father, the grocer, was Kemal Stanic. He'd created a bit of a stir a few days later inside the courthouse, shouting down some judges and attorneys, railing against the city in general and the justice system in particular, for of course in those days no one had made a move to apprehend Zarko. The local newspaper had run something on it, and then it had died away.

Christ, who in his right mind would have put him on a detail to guard Zarko? Vitas, apparently, for his signature appeared on the last page of the assignment list, next to a red, block-lettered stamp, APPROVED.

But Vlado looked again through the Stanic file, and this time the hiring date jumped off the page. He'd joined the force only five days before the raid. Vitas's stamp of approval was dated three days earlier. Two days after the shooting, Stanic was dismissed into the army, but in the space where the terms and status of his separation should have been recorded, there was only the notation, *See attached*. This time there were staple marks at the top-right of the back page, but no attachment. Perhaps Vitas had taken this item as well. He appeared to have been holding all the key cards in the deck when he died. But where had he left them, and who had them now?

Vlado turned back one more time to the list of the custody detail. There again was the name: Kemal Stanic, typed across dried white correction fluid. Was there a typographical error below, or someone else's name? Vlado scratched away at the correction with a fingernail, working slowly, carefully, like an art restorer seeking the original. The name below was longer. The first name began with a B, although Vlado couldn't be sure of the rest. The last name, however, with much of it stretching beyond Stanic's, seemed to be Milutinovic. Vlado asked for one more file.

By now, the U.N. man had gone. So had everyone else except Krulic, who was hunched in a corner, snorting smoke like an enraged but underpowered dragon.

'It's all right,' Vlado said. 'This one will probably do it for the day, and I'll pass along the best of marks on your behavior next time I see Kasic. I need the personnel folder for B. Milutinovic.'

'Boromir or Bosko?' Krulic asked a moment later, a folder in each hand.

'Both.'

Both were reputable officers. Neither contained any mention of a special posting to the custody detail. Vlado wasn't sure that would have been included anyway, unless they were cited later for exceptional work. But an item on Boromir's file caught his eye. A full-year veteran of the Ministry's special police, he'd been cited several times for good work until it had all come crashing down on the last day of September, two days before the raid. If Vitas had put him on the custody team, he'd then lost his services at an in-opportune moment.

The reason for his dismissal: *Illegal conduct. See attached.* This time there was indeed an attachment.

It was a single-spaced investigation report based on the accounts of two undercover operatives, and when Vlado saw their names he felt the skin prickling on the back of his neck. One was a supervisor at the cigarette plant named Kupric. The other was a butcher named Hrnic. Each told a tale of unsavory connections, with the unfortunate Mr Milutinovic linked to the illicit trafficking of meat and cigarettes.

The whole affair had taken a mere two days to initiate and conclude, amazing alacrity under any circumstances, much less amidst the hurly-burly that must have prevailed in the days just before the raid.

Yet, for all the disgrace Milutinovic had suddenly brought down on himself, not only was he not prosecuted, but he'd been given a generous – incredibly generous, under the circumstances – severance payment of five hundred D-marks. No wonder he hadn't made a stink. It was more than he would have made in a year's work. Not that his squawking would have been given much heed in that chaotic time, anyway. In the rush of last-minute details Vitas probably hadn't even known Milutinovic had been bumped off the custody squad, much less replaced by an unstable grocer with a murderous ax to grind. It was tantamount to a death sentence for Zarko. If someone had wanted him out of the way in order to claim a bigger share from the smuggled art, this had done the trick.

Vlado flipped to the disposition report from Milutinovic's disciplinary hearing, and there again was the block red stamp of the word APPROVED. It was dated September 30th.

Below it was the full, bold signature of the man who had orchestrated this entire maneuver, Assistant Chief Juso Kasic.

17

Vlado glanced over his shoulder every few feet on his way home, half expecting to see Kasic, or perhaps the man in the beret who'd greeted him at the ministry, or even the four men in dark overcoats who'd taken Glavas away. Thinking of them he decided on a detour, and he turned toward the small hill on the east side of town that had come to represent so much about the way this war was fought.

Sprawled atop the hill were the buildings of the Kosevo Hospital complex, home to the city's dead, dying, and wounded. This status made the hospital a prominent site on the targeting map of every siege gunner. Although who needed maps when from most vantage points Kosevo was as easy to spot as the highest office tower. For anyone gazing down the long barrel of a howitzer it loomed on its hump of land like a broken medieval fortress, its crowded wards ripe with the promise of being able to finish the work that yesterday's shells had only begun.

The hospital's doctors and administrators – or at least, the ones who hadn't either left or been killed – had duly and painstakingly mapped each of the hundreds of shell impacts. They distributed the maps liberally to journalists, human rights organizations, and visitors of all stripes, another small cry of outrage with its inevitable perverse edge of pride: Look at what we have endured.

Vlado's destination was a low-slung plastered building halfway up the face of the hill. You didn't need directions to it anymore because of the smell that announced from a hundred yards away that this must be the city morgue.

Early in the war the place had been quite literally swamped by death, the chambers of its cellar knee-deep in stacked bodies, maggots, and floodwater from pipes that had burst in the shelling. The director had fled, along with half his staff. It had taken weeks to get another team up and running, and by then the overload was nearly unbearable. The water and most of the maggots had since been mopped away, but the smell from those weeks had never quite disappeared, and some believed it never would.

The smell was even stronger indoors, as Vlado found the moment he opened the door, a stench of rot and putrefaction that nearly doubled him over. He reached for a handkerchief, then stopped, working hard to breathe through his mouth, feeling the rasp of the foul air on his throat. Two men sat behind a dull gray counter at empty desks, smoking cigarettes and reading outdated magazines as if manning the office of an auto garage. Both wore thick, black rubber boots. Stained cotton smocks hung beside heavy rubber gloves behind them on the wall.

'Police Inspector Petric,' Vlado announced, still struggling not to inhale through his nose. Somehow the stench was registering anyway, more as taste than smell.

'I'd like a look at your new arrivals. Particularly anything that might have come in from Dobrinja. Or anyone in the past twenty-four hours who has showed up with a Dobrinja address, no matter where they were found.'

'Got a name?' said one of the men, putting down his magazine.

'Glavas, Milan. Older man. Late sixties, early seventies.'

The man checked a clipboard, flipping back a page, then shook his head as he exhaled smoke.

'No one by that name. But we do have three without I.D.s.'

He opened a rear door and leaned down a stairwell. The reeking smell doubled in intensity. Vlado shifted uncomfortably.

'Mustafa!' the man shouted down the stairs. 'The three no-names, were any from Dobrinja?'

Mustafa came strolling up the stairs in reply, wiping his hands on a filthy rag. His smock, too, was stained brown, only his glistened with fresh additions.

'Yes,' he answered finally. 'Two of them, I think. A man and a woman. Both older. She's still here, funeral tomorrow.'

'And the man?' Vlado asked.

'Buried this morning.'

The clerk turned toward Vlado. 'Sorry, Inspector. Looks like you're too late.'

'I want him dug up.' Vlado said. 'Now.'

'You'll need the family's approval.' Clearly the clerk was ready to go home for the day, and Vlado could hardly blame him.

'Family approval, when you don't even have his name?'

Vlado had him on that one, but the clerk wasn't yet ready to give in.

'Look, we're happy to dig him up for you. We won't

even make you get a judge's order, although technically we could. But it's a bad time of day now. Too much light. It'll be dusk in less than an hour, so why don't you just have a seat and a smoke and wait until dark. You could wait until morning, but the ground will be frozen harder then, so you'd best get out there while the digging's easier.'

Good enough. But he was damned if he'd wait here. 'In an hour, then, but I'll meet your man on the field.'

'Look for him at the fresh mounds. They're the only ones not covered with snow. You know the place?'

'Know it well,' Vlado said.

'Mustafa will be there as well.' Mustafa looked less than happy to hear it. 'In case you make an identification.'

Vlado spent the next hour trying to walk off the smell that clung to his jacket, his pants, his face. He coughed and spat as if it were a bone lodged in his throat, but after a while he couldn't decide whether the smell or merely the thought of it was stronger.

When the appointed time arrived he moved down the hill and across the snowy field, soaking his shoes and socks as he strolled by the rows of rough wooden markers – the narrow slabs for the Muslims mixed with the crosses for the Catholics and the Orthodox Christians. In the gathering darkness he could see that the gravedigger was already at work. The earth was still soft from the morning's labors, so the going was easy, and it was only a few minutes before the shovel struck wood.

A year earlier and the body might not even have merited the luxury of a coffin. Death had come in such a rush that the city had run out of caskets, and most wood had been used for firewood. Now, with casualties slacking off, supply was again meeting demand. The few casketmakers still in business were setting away a nest egg for their future, provided they themselves survived.

Mustafa had also arrived, waiting at the grave with hands on his hips. After a few minutes more the gravedigger cleared the rest of the dirt covering the lid of the coffin. He then dug a small shelf into the mud next to the casket and stepped out, resting on his shovel. Vlado tried to recall the gravedigger's face from all his mornings by the window, but he seemed like all the rest, chiefly recognizable by the slight stoop to his shoulders, the cap slouched on his head, the thin jacket loose across his back.

Mustafa stepped down to the small shelf of mud. He pulled a screwdriver from a coat pocket and pried open the lid, then flicked on a small flashlight. The yellow beam swept onto the face of Milan Glavas.

'Is this your man?' Mustafa asked, looking up at Vlado.

'Yes,' he said. 'Glavas, Milan.'

They'd at least let him change out of his dirty robe and blanket, although his chest was a matted eruption of torn fabric and dried blood. His mouth was ajar, as if it had drooped open in the middle of a nap. His expression seemed almost one of boredom rather than pain or terror. The overall impression was that of someone who'd gone through life dirty and disheveled, and that made Vlado sad. It was not the way Glavas would have wanted to have been buried, that was certain, and for some reason this realization brought tears to Vlado's eyes, as he stared into the grave at the drawn, gray face.

'I remember him from last night,' Mustafa said.

'You examined him?' Vlado asked.

'Yes. He came in late. Later than usual. I was halfway out the door.'

'Cause of death?'

'Shrapnel. Sniper. Who knows? I'm not really trained in those things. Hit by something, though. Whole chest torn open, as you can see for yourself. Death by war. What else is worth saying once you've said that?'

'Who brought him in?'

'Army. From Dobrinja, that's usually the way it works.'

'Did they say where he was found?'

'They never do. It probably wasn't near his home or they'd have been able to make an I.D. They usually ask some neighbors to have a look when they can. He's lucky, though. No-names in Dobrinja usually end up buried in a backyard.'

'Yes. A very lucky man.'

Vlado walked across the graveyard toward home, tired and hungry, the day's information bearing down on him. He was still clearing his throat and spitting from his visit to the morgue, though by now he knew virtually all of the smell must be gone.

Having seen what had become of Glavas, he wondered at his own predicament. Who was he fooling with his persistence, or with his flimsy excuses to Kasic? For that matter, what purpose was he really serving? Even if he cracked the case, who would he report his findings to without feeling he was risking his neck. Kasic was obviously poised to deal with him at a moment's notice. He couldn't count on the U.N. for much help either. To survive two years of war only to die investigating a murder would be the height of absurdity. Why bother?

The last person to walk this path had been Esmir

313

Vitas, and Vlado had seen all too well where that led. If the city's cultural heritage was vanishing, was that so terrible when stacking up against the city's other losses?

Then again, by now the effort to smuggle artwork seemed so much a part of the machinery of the war itself that stopping it would seem to be a calling as high as his work had ever offered.

But another problem remained: How to put his findings to use. If even U.N. channels posed a risk, were there any channels available that would accept the information without then turning it on him as a weapon. As for Kasic, the case against him seemed damning enough, but there was still the possibility he was only the tool of someone else, perhaps even higher in the government. For all Vlado knew the entire ministry was corrupt, now that Vitas was out of the way. There was so much to think about, and so little time or room for doing so.

Even if Vlado wanted to back out of the investigation now, how could he? It was time for him to huddle with Damir, to look for some way out of this mess. He supposed they could report findings tame enough to appease whoever might fear the truth. But would that be enough to protect them, considering what they'd learned? For all Vlado knew, Damir had stumbled onto a home where a painting had been removed, and had set off some unseen alarm with his queries.

Not for the first time it occurred to Vlado how small his world had become. In the last few days he had traversed virtually all of it on foot, and even his most remote destination, Zuc, had been reached in a few hours. There really was no place to run unless one was willing to cross over to the Serb lines at night, and Vlado was surprised to find himself thinking that such a chancy proposition now seemed within reason, or at least an option he could no longer reject out of hand. Even that held extra complications, though. On the other side there would still be the influence of General Markovic to deal with.

The moment he walked through the door, something seemed awry in his apartment. The sloppiness was the same as always. But he felt the same unmistakable sense of disturbance that he'd felt at Vitas's apartment. He walked around slowly, looking for some tangible difference from the way he'd left things. After a few minutes, having found none, he began to calm. It was just his nerves, just an accumulation of the day's facts upon his mind. He would brew a cup of coffee and have a bite to eat, then he would relax. And once his stomach was no longer empty, he would paint his soldiers to clear his head. Perhaps he'd finally finish the platoon.

He picked up the hunk of cured meat from the butcher. There was still enough for a few more meals if he paced himself, though he decided that tonight he owed himself a larger-than-usual slice. He lighted the stove to boil water for coffee.

A few minutes later, the water boiling, he lifted his mug to pour in some Nescafé, and as he did so it left behind a chocolate brown ring on the green fields of Austerlitz, at almost the same place on the page that he'd wiped clean that morning.

Someone had moved the mug.

A coldness stole down his throat to his stomach, and he began a cursory inspection of his painted platoon. They, too, seemed in disarray, brushed closer to the edge of the workbench than he'd left them. In fact, the unit was now a man short. Whoever had searched the place must have knocked one into the piles of newspaper below. Doubtless they'd been in a hurry. Vlado had kept such odd hours recently that they probably figured he might walk in at any moment. But there'd certainly been nothing to find. As always, Vlado had kept all his notes and numbers in his satchel, which he took wherever he went.

Vlado wondered what might have brought this on. Had Kasic's curiosity simply been too much for him? Perhaps Krulic, the clerk from records, had felt a pang of bureaucratic conscience and phoned Kasic to alert him to Vlado's unusual requests. Maybe someone in the morgue had been tipped to watch for anyone inquiring about an old man from Dobrinja. Or maybe Colonel Chevard had gotten wind of the strange request for information on shipping a parcel out of the city. Glavas might have said God knows what before he died, depending on how forceful they'd been with him before finishing him with a shot to the chest.

The more Vlado thought about it, the more he realized how almost anyone he'd talked to during the past few days might have wittingly or unwittingly tipped higher-ups to his progress on the case.

He suddenly felt such an amateur, a complete and utter naif. He was a fisherman set loose upon a reef full of sharks who only now had noticed the rot in the hull of his sinking craft. Far too late he considered the depth of his carelessness as it opened darkly before him.

He'd let Toby, a reporter, see the transfer file, and God knew who Toby might have asked about it. He'd blabbed about Glavas to the gossipy director of the National Art Museum, a man who undoubtedly had his own uses for such information. Then there were his blunt questions to Neven himself, a man looking for a way out of a tight spot, a well-connected man who knew as well as anyone how to use the right sort of information for the right sort of leverage.

Even if Krulic hadn't already phoned Kasic, by tomorrow morning the entire ministry would be aware of exactly which files Vlado had requested. He couldn't have drawn attention to his trail any better than if he'd lit a long line of torches in his wake. He'd barged along as if this were any sort of murder in any sort of city.

So where did that leave him, other than vulnerable? He could tell all to Toby; then Toby would get a nice story. Or perhaps Toby would only ask a lot of embarrassing questions and write no story at all, considering that Vlado still had little actual proof. Either way, Vlado would likely end up with a bullet, and Damir as well. And for a panicky moment he wondered if Damir weren't already dead, stashed in some alley or thrown into the river, having asked one too many sensitive questions, careless if only because Vlado had given him so little to go on.

He could do as Kasic had asked, and turn over the worthless undercover men to the ministry for further questions. But even worthless men working at minor graft have families to support and small mouths to feed, so why sacrifice them? As he stumbled past that thought, his telephone rang.

So, the lines were back up at last. But he was damned if he'd answer it now. With each ring he felt more claustrophobic, as if the air in the room were slowly being consumed by the sound.

He picked up the hunk of meat, stuffing it in his coat pocket, then opened the door. The view was of nothing but mountains, outlined darkly in the pale, washed light of a rising moon that had just broken through the clouds. The graveyard below, out where Glavas and all the others lay beneath their mounds of mud and snow, glowed whitely, with just the hint of a sparkle.

He stepped outside, shutting the door behind him on the ringing telephone, and walked briskly toward the center of town.

Clouds had moved back across the moon by the time he reached the office, and from the look of the sky there would soon be more, further blotting the light on yet another night without electricity. But he was relieved to see that the office generators were up and running, and that everyone on his floor had left for the day. No Garovic to lean over his shoulder. He had just begun to calm his nerves amid the peace and quiet when his phone rang, as if the earlier call had stalked him down the hill.

This time he picked up the receiver.

It was Damir. Hearing the familiar voice sent a wave of relief over him.

'Where the hell have you been, Vlado? I've been trying everywhere.'

'Was that you ringing my house about twenty minutes ago?'

'You mean you were there? Why didn't you pick it up?'

'I don't know. Too skittish. My place had been searched.'

'Mother of God. By who?'

'Kasic's people, if I had to guess.'

'Mother of God,' he said again, in a lower voice this time. 'Vlado, what's going on with this case?'

'That's what I'd like to know. Too many people in high places with their fingerprints on it. You wouldn't believe what I found in some files this afternoon. But it's nothing we should dare discuss over the phone.

Suffice it to say that you should trust no one. The further I go the more I wonder if maybe Garovic was right. Maybe I should've just left this one alone.'

'Well, unfortunately I've got more bad news for you. Some U.N. guy's been trying like hell to reach you all day. From the moment you left to see Kasic he must have called six times. So frantic he was half out of his mind. I told him he could talk to me just as easily, but he insisted that only you would do. He wanted your home number, but I wouldn't give it to him. He wanted your address, too, but well, you know I'm not giving him that.'

'What did he want?'

'He wouldn't say. Wouldn't leave a name or number, either. But I think he really is U.N. Definitely foreign, anyway.'

'French?'

'British, from the accent. And not your Nescafé man. I memorize voices of people that generous.'

'Maybe he'll call here.'

'Maybe. But in the meantime he just called me here a few minutes ago.'

'At home?'

'Yes. How the hell he got the number I'd like to find out, but considering some of the women I know, I think I can guess. I don't like it, Vlado. This Vitas case, we're going to get ourselves killed. Or stuck in a trench somewhere.'

'What did he say?'

'That he had to get hold of you. Had to meet with you. Now, and not tomorrow. I told him there was nothing I could do to arrange it because I didn't know where you were, but the only way I could finally get rid of him was by agreeing to reach you at home tonight. For some reason he still can't seem to get your

319

home number. One of the benefits of your celibacy, I guess.'

'But he wouldn't leave his own number?'

'Said it was too sensitive, that he can't have you calling him when the wrong person might answer, not only at his office but wherever he's living. So all he left was a message. He wants a meeting tonight, with you and you alone. Half an hour after curfew.'

Vlado glanced at his watch.

'Christ, that's in forty minutes. Where?'

'The end of Dakovica Street. Down by the river. He said it's then or never. And Vlado?'

'Yes.'

'He said he's convinced his life is in danger, yours as well. But he wouldn't say why, or from who.'

'And you're sure he was British?'

'As far as I could tell.'

'But not French? You're sure he couldn't have been French?'

'I'd know a French accent right away. My first woman was French, you know, back during the Olympics. I was only fourteen. You think I'd forget French accents after that? I'm just glad this guy reached me and not Garovic. Can you imagine how nuts he would have gone?'

The mere thought of that possibility, of Garovic spluttering and red in the face, paralyzed by the sheer bureaucratic horror of the moment, was enough for some welcome levity. The two of them shared a laugh over the phone.

Damir slipped into a confiding tone. 'Vlado, I know you don't think of me as much of a policeman.'

'That's not true.'

Actually, in some ways it was. Not that Damir wasn't smart, or didn't have the skills. He just always seemed too interested in women, drink, and a good time to ever

320

make a big investigation work. Vlado conceded to himself that perhaps one reason he'd held back had to do with this as well, not just his promise to Kasic, who'd proven unworthy of such loyalty anyway.

'I've just questioned your seriousness at times, that's all. Your commitment. But you're young. You'll outgrow it. And who can learn to be a good investigator with a war on anyway? We're all too busy saving our own skin.'

'Well, one thing I'm serious about, and that's backing up my colleagues. I know you were always closer to Vasic before the war, that the two of you always worked better together. And I understand that. He had a wife, kids, like you. But Vlado, you shouldn't go into this one alone. You don't even know this man's name and you're going to go meet him only a block from where Vitas was killed, by the same person for all we know.'

That had occurred to Vlado, and he was relieved at the offer of a backup.

'Your help would be welcome, but it sounds like two of us might scare him away.'

'So I'll lay low. I'll go early, work from the edges, just like our old boss always taught us back when we had a real boss. He'd be proud of me for a change.'

The reference to Imamovic, their old chief, was somehow calming, as if the old man himself had just whispered a sage word of advice from beyond the grave.

'If I leave now,' Damir continued, 'I'll be able to make it about ten minutes ahead of schedule. I can get the lay of the land before you arrive, and if things look shaky I'll warn you away with a double whistle when I hear you approaching. Consider anything else, silence or otherwise, as an all-clear. As dark as it is tonight, it should be pretty easy to move around without being spotted.'

'Just don't spook him. If he's as nervous as you say he is he'll run at the first sign of being double-teamed. Do you have your gun?'

'Always. You're the one who doesn't think you need to be armed in this city.'

'Well, mine's here in a drawer somewhere.' Vlado again checked his watch. 'We have about thirty-five minutes. You'd better get moving if you're going to make it.' Damir lived on the west side of the city. It would be a haul. Vlado needed only to walk a few blocks. He'd have some time to kill.

'I'll have to hustle,' Damir agreed. 'But I'm younger than you. I'll make it. See you there, then.'

'And Damir?'

'Yes?'

'Thanks. I'll owe you one.'

'One? More like five or six.'

He hung up in mid-laugh.

Vlado set down the receiver. Things were moving too fast. He looked again at his watch. He still hadn't eaten and was famished, though now he had time for some of the meat and a cigarette. Maybe that would tamp down the excitement. Otherwise, everything else – the long walk to and from Zuc, the sleepless night in the trench, and all the day's revelations – might overwhelm him just when he needed a clear head.

He unwrapped the meat from its loose sheath of butcher paper. The smell made him salivate. He'd have to cut off a nice slice for Damir after this evening. Well, let's not go overboard, he thought. Damir seemed pretty well stocked on his own lately.

He reached into his desk for his Swiss Army knife, a coveted souvenir from his prewar trip to Berlin, then remembered he'd loaned it to Damir the week before.

Perhaps this guy from the U.N., if he was indeed U.N., had the goods on Chevard, or even the whole operation. It might even have been the Brit he'd talked to the other day on the phone. Perhaps word of the investigation was spreading to some of the right people as well. Who knew, he told himself, this might pan out yet. But stay careful. And get some food in your stomach.

He tugged at the top drawer of Damir's desk. Locked. No problem. Vlado and his old partner Vasic had long ago discovered a ridiculous flaw of Titoist office furniture, one that not everyone knew, even now. In most offices, one key fit all, desk after desk, drawer after drawer, supervisors' equipment excluded, of course. They hadn't decided if the mistake had been a typical Communist snafu or a devious way to allow Party zealots and snitches to snoop on their coworkers. Whatever the case, Vasic and he had put it to use for many a practical joke until Imamovic found out. He'd requisitioned a whole new set of locks and keys, but, the system being what it was, they'd never arrived.

So, Vlado took his own key and slipped it into Damir's lock. It opened easily.

My God, what a mess. Damir was an even bigger pack rat than he'd suspected. There were coffee-stained napkins, crumpled memos, torn scraps of paper with phone numbers – probably Damir's version of a little black book – cassette tapes of heavy metal music by bands Vlado had never heard of, paperclips, and various other odds and ends. Vlado rifled through the pile, pushing small mounds of crumpled paper aside, wincing in pain as he pricked his thumb on a pushpin.

Then, success. He spied the red handle of the army

323

knife, lying at the bottom toward the back. But as he reached for it something else caught his eye, like the flash of a familiar face in a moving crowd. It was a small blue tunic with tiny gold buttons, handpainted. A tiny Austrian hussar, circa 1805, with his sword, still unpainted, raised boldly to the sky.

Vlado picked up the soldier, holding him aloft in the weak fluorescent light. A victim of Napoleon, now briefly taken captive by Damir. Vlado shut and relocked the drawer, then stuffed the soldier deep in his pocket as he absorbed the implications of his discovery. He tried to come up with an innocent explanation, but there was none. Nor was there time to ask for one, now. He reached into his own desk and pulled his service revolver from a similarly chaotic mess of papers and tapes. Finding its chambers fully loaded, he clicked off the safety and stuffed the gun atop the soldier. The tiny man would now be his backup, he mused darkly.

He grabbed his satchel, slinging the strap across his shoulder. Then he strolled across the office and out the door, leaving the meat unwrapped and uneaten on his desktop, and feeling very lonely indeed.

18

On the way to the rendezvous point Vlado tried to calculate the depth of Damir's betrayal. Perhaps he was only a glorified errand boy who'd conducted the search of Vlado's apartment and done nothing else – it would have worked perfectly, any neighbor who'd seen him would have recognized him as a friend and never have suspected anything unseemly. Maybe he'd filed regular reports on Vlado's comings and goings, his contacts, while little knowing the true role of Kasic. That would explain a few things, he supposed.

And perhaps there really was a frantic U.N. man, who really was trying to reach Vlado with vital information.

Then again, maybe Damir had engineered the whole thing, hoping to bring Vlado to a dark and vulnerable spot after curfew, where anyone killed would be written off as yet another victim of a sniper.

Even if the more benign role was the case, Vlado asked himself if he would have done the same. No, he would never inform on a colleague, not without warning the colleague of the arrangement. But Damir had concluded it was okay. Betrayed by his own father, the embittered Damir had decided he could play that game as well. In Vlado's eyes he was guilty. The only question was one of degree.

If Vlado had the time to consider the matter further, and on a full stomach, he knew he might skip the meeting altogether. But his momentum had reached the point where he felt he had no choice but to plunge along.

The walk was only a few blocks, but Vlado used his extra time for a roundabout approach. Going directly might have put him in place first. He might even have beaten Damir to the spot, a decided advantage. But a Damir who couldn't be trusted might have been telephoning from anywhere a few minutes ago, including the Interior Ministry right down the street. And if Vlado was walking into a setup, everyone would be in place by now anyway, perhaps even expecting him ahead of schedule.

The cloud cover was heavier than ever, blotting the moonlight from the sky, and the curfew had emptied the streets. Sniper fire and artillery had been light that day, as if everyone in the hills were saving their energy and ammunition for tonight's Orthodox New Year. Heavy firing was expected, and the prospect had seemed to clear the bars and cafés early, with everyone heading home to their most secure rooms. Vlado doubted whether even the prostitutes had stuck to their posts as late as usual. If one wanted to plot a meeting with as little chance of witnesses as possible, this was the night to do it.

As he came within a block of the meeting point, he kept to the side of the street, as close as possible to an abandoned office building. He stopped and listened closely. Nothing but the faint gurgling of water, the sound creeping up from the steeply angled stone walls banking the Miljacka River. But there was something else, too, a sound he knew but couldn't identify. It was a ticking sound, slower than a clock. It was the noise a car makes as its engine cools.

He took another few steps, still unable to make out anything ahead. Then a few more, and there it was, a car. No, two cars, facing each other about ten yards apart, only one was easier to spot because it was white. From its silhouette it seemed to be a jeep, and a white jeep could only mean U.N. He supposed that was reassuring, but the second car wasn't. Damir didn't own one.

Vlado waited a few moments, breathing heavily against the pressure building in his chest. He considered turning and walking quietly back toward the city center. Let them make the next move, whoever they were. But where would he stay in the meantime? Where would he work? There was no getting out of this now, and there was certainly no getting out of Sarajevo. He slowly took three more steps, then stopped when a voice broke the silence.

'Vlado. Is that you?'

It was Damir, sounding happy, welcoming. Vlado eased his satchel aside and reached into his pocket, clutching for the gun. A cigarette lighter flicked on, illuminating Damir's face. He was smiling, casual. He might have been sitting on a bar stool waiting for a pal for all the worry apparent on his face.

'He's down here, Vlado. He found me before I found him. Come on down and then I'll move off to a discreet distance so you can talk in private while I keep watch.'

Vlado took another two steps and stopped, now within ten yards of Damir and the edge of the riverbank, but still saying nothing. Damir was squinting into the blackness, trying to find Vlado, and a look of worry began to crease his brow.

'Vlado, it's okay. Nothing can go wrong. I'm here.'

'And that's really the problem with this setup, isn't it,' said Vlado, startled by the sudden loudness of his own voice. 'Especially now that you're collecting my soldiers. Do you get the rest of them once I'm down in the river? Is that part of the deal?'

With that, Damir's smile collapsed. His lighter snapped out, and someone else took the moment in hand. The jeep's headlights flicked on, illuminating Vlado against the building like a man on a stage. He ducked away from the beams, running for the middle of the street. As he did a gunshot crackled. Vlado turned sharply toward the river, darting behind the second car and diving for the verge as another shot sounded.

It was so loud, he thought, so loud. Then he was down on the grass and rolling, well out of the head-lights now, feeling the wet blades brush his face, then rolling again, footsteps clattering quickly toward him, voices shouting. An iron railing brushed against his back, and as he rolled beneath it Damir shouted, 'He's going for the river!'

Free of the railing he was suddenly plunging, his stomach leaping toward his throat. He bounced once, a glancing blow against the stone wall, then fell fifteen feet to the water below. He hit it with a loud splash, shocked first by the cold and then by the stony bottom. The river here was no more than two feet deep, and the impact nearly knocked the wind from him. He spluttered and gasped, hearing shouts and more running. There was another shot, striking in the water somewhere to his right. He dove, but found it hard to stay under in the shallowness. But the current, which had always seemed so lazy from up on the bridges, was already driving him downstream, pressing him toward safety.

The shouting continued, Damir's voice joined by two others, Vlado recognizing neither. Then he realized that for the moment he was safe, rescued by the city's helplessness. The river was an impenetrable gorge of darkness, with neither streetlamps nor city lights to pierce it. Someone had turned the jeep around, but its headlights were useless, leaping out above the river like searchlights aimed to the heavens. Nothing could angle them down to where Vlado paddled.

His problem now was the cold. He kicked for the opposite bank, but his legs were already feeling heavy, his wet clothes sagging around him. His satchel floated ahead of him, the strap chafing at his neck. The gun sagged in his pocket like an anchor, useless by now, and with difficulty he pulled it free and it sank to the bottom. The water tasted gritty, metallic, like a handful of dirty coins.

By now he was some twenty yards downstream. He heard a small splash, followed by cursing and thrashing. His teeth began to chatter. He realized he couldn't stay in the water much longer. There were a few more minutes at the most before he would collapse from hypothermia. Climbing out and clawing up the bank was still too risky, nor was he sure he could make it to one of the spots where iron rungs laddered up the wall. The jeep's headlights were now easing downstream along the road above, the driver probably peering down the bank to see if Vlado had emerged. Whoever was in this bunch probably had the connections to mobilize more men to stake out the north bank for the rest of the night, on one pretext or another, although the New Year's bombardment would complicate matters for them at midnight.

Damir's voice sounded again.

'The spillway! The spillway! Get on the bridge and we'll see him as he comes through!'

Vlado knew exactly what he meant. Every quarter mile down the river were three-foot drops creating a series of small, neat waterfalls that trapped garbage and toy boats at their base. Even in the darkness, a body coming through would show up against the white cascade, an easy target for someone quick on the trigger. Even if the bullets missed, the current might trap him underwater and slowly do the job for them. He kicked again for the opposite bank, legs heavier than before, arms going limp. The current seemed to answer each movement with a force twice as strong. Now he could hear the approaching rush of the spillway, a hiss rising to a roar. He glanced toward the bridge just downstream and saw a figure vaguely silhouetted against the dim sky. A second form appeared, and a beam of light leapt from it and vectored into the river. They had a flashlight.

He surged again for the opposite bank, finally reaching it but feeling only the slime of a wet stone wall, too smooth and steep for a handhold. The current rose around him, the water deepening in the lull before the spillway. The roar of its cascade now drowned out every voice from above, though he could sense the beam of light playing about on the water behind him.

A black, round hole appeared just above him, two feet out of the water. It was one of the storm sewers draining the south side of the city, and with a grunt Vlado was just able to raise his left arm high enough to grab the trailing edge of the pipe as he slid by. His feet slipped into the surge of the spillway, and it took all his strength to pull himself back against the current, though now he had both hands on the pipe. With his final reserve of energy he pulled his head, shoulders and chest into the opening, wondering all the while when he would be spotted and shot. The men on the bridge must be pinning all their hopes on the spillway.

Vlado dragged up his legs and sagged into a shallow stream of water sluicing down the pipe. The air was warmer here, refreshing even, despite its heavy sour smell. The bottom and sides were slippery with algae, but there was ample room to move around. He needed to get away from the opening before the beam found him, so he crawled, wobbly at first, his head bumping lightly against the top. It wasn't so bad, he told himself, although the absolute darkness ahead was ghastly. The only sound was the gurgle of water, echoing from deep into the blackness. But he was out of the river. More important, he was out of sight.

He rested for a few moments, letting his muscles relax even as his teeth continued to chatter. Feeling a bit stronger, a little warmer, he began to blindly crawl ahead. There would be no exiting the way he had come. Eventually someone might realize where he must have gone and decide to come in after him. The tunnel headed uphill, in a direction that could only mean trouble, he knew. The wrong side of the lines was no farther than a hundred yards or so. But for the moment it seemed there was no such thing as a right side of the city. Now all of Sarajevo was off limits for Vlado. He continued his slow, steady crawl.

Stopping briefly to rest, he remembered his cigarette lighter. It was in his pocket, down by the little soldier. Reaching for it he felt the tiny sword, taking care not to break it. He drew out the lighter. The flint was soaked, but after a dozen or so tries it flickered on. The tunnel snaked onward as far as he could see, well beyond the range of the light.

He took stock of himself. His satchel, although wet,

was still zipped shut, perhaps sealed enough to have kept everything inside reasonably dry. He let the light go dead and continued.

He kept crawling for what must have been another half hour, across sticks, a dead rat, and other objects he could only guess at, stopping every few minutes to light his way and catch his breath. Each time the path ahead was nothing but further blackness. He passed a few smaller pipes connecting from either side, but so far each had been too small to allow a detour.

A few moments later he felt something smooth and metallic pass beneath him. It was round, roughly the size of an inverted salad bowl, and almost immediately his face came up against a rough tangle of iron wire smelling strongly of rust. Pulling his face away he felt a sharp snag at his left cheek, followed by the warm ooze of blood, and with a gasp he realized where he must be.

He flicked on the lighter and rolled onto his side, seeing that he had passed across a land mine. By all rights, he should be dead now, but the mine had beaten him to it, overcome by its prolonged exposure to the water. Beyond it was a rusting coil of razor wire, and he spent the next twenty minutes gingerly untangling it and pulling it aside, nicking his hands several times in the process. Slowly he pulled the uncoiled strands past him toward his feet, and when the way was cleared he continued, flicking on his lighter every few minutes to check for further mines. If one side had bothered to mine the tunnel, both sides might have.

But there were no more mines, no more coils of wire. Now he was in enemy territory.

He continued for another half hour, passing another opening on his right. During one stop he heard a vehicle rumbling overhead. Finally he saw a dim shaft of light ahead, reaching it to find a storm grate directly above. There was enough room to rise into a crouch, and he clutched at the iron grid. It was heavy, but movable. He flicked his lighter just below the grating, waiting a full minute for any reaction. When there was none, he forced the grate aside and lifted himself free.

The clouds were breaking, and the moon shone through. Vlado's watch had somehow made it through the evening, which made him wish he'd held on to his gun. It was just after 11 p.m. He had about an hour before the New Year's celebration would illuminate the streets, although here, as on the other side of town, people seemed to have already battened down the hatches in anticipation. In windows here and there he could make out the pale glow from candles, lanterns, or meager gas flames, but mostly there was darkness.

The street was vaguely familiar, though Vlado still didn't know his exact location. But he knew from the heft and heaviness of a black looming hill just ahead that he was far across the river, and well into the Serb neighborhood of Grbavica. And as long as he was here, there was one stop he wanted to make before trying to find his way back. If the wildest of his hunches was correct, he'd find shelter, and perhaps even information.

If he was wrong, there'd be no help at all, only further signs of death, including harbingers of his own.

19

To be caught on this side of the lines would be fatal, and Vlado knew it. Yet he couldn't escape the feeling that he was still very much in his own city, still on familiar streets. It had been more than two years since he'd been in Grbavica, lending a sense of detachment to being there now. As with a young man who returns to a former school or playground, he could recall the innocence of his old walks here, felt their familiarity even now, yet knew the place could never again feel quite the same.

He also felt an odd exhilaration, not unlike what he'd known as a teenager sneaking out of his parents' house after midnight. It was the same sense of sudden liberation, of being on the loose in forbidden territory – wary of the consequences but jazzed by the audacity of finally having slipped behind the looking glass.

He stood above the sewer grate for a full two minutes, trying to get his bearings for the next move, and the grid of streets hazily took shape in his mind like a worn map. He was facing east to west. Which meant he needed to walk one block south, before a right turn back toward the west again. Then three blocks straight and another left toward the south, and there it would be.

He stopped at the first intersection, listening for footsteps, watching for any movement. An automatic weapon chattered from a hill to the east, overeager celebrants literally jumping the gun on midnight, wasting ammunition. Looking up and down the boulevard, buildings loomed up in the dark like slumbering old friends. Here he had chased a ball down a hill with four friends. There he had run errands to a butcher shop that his mother preferred for special occasions, even though the shop had been a full mile from their home. But even in the dark, closer inspection revealed the symptoms of war's terminal illness – the chipping, cratering decay of shot and shrapnel, the white plastic hanging limp in window frames, rainwater puddling on smashed cars, and all those special smells of urban survival – an essence of woodsmoke, burned garbage, and food long past its prime.

To hear the people on his side of the city tell it, Grbavica had it made. And it was true that such items as sugar, coffee, eggs, and meat were easier to come by here, and at lower prices. But as far as the war went, Grbavica was very much in the thick of things, not at all spared from the brunt of fighting as were some of the suburbs held by the Serbs. Here, too, were hand-lettered signs that read, *Beware, Sniper*. Only these were lettered in Cyrillic.

Just up the hill and a few blocks to the east was the edge of the Jewish cemetery, contested ground that had weathered many an assault by the Bosnian army. If an attack ever succeeded it would lay open the neighborhood to firing from three sides. It would become another Dobrinja, with the Serbs pinned against the river. Vlado had watched one of these attacks unfold, as many had on his side of town. They played out on the facing hillside like an outdoor drama in a distant amphitheater, war as a spectator sport. Helmetless men in green darted through tombstones toward a brown slash of mud, which poured smoke and metal back into the cemetery. The rattle of guns echoed across the city while attackers fell to the ground, some to take cover, some to join the assembly of the dead. The bodies of Muslims, Croats, and Serbs fell abundantly atop the buried Jews in a riot of multiethnic promiscuity.

In Grbavica, just as on the other side of the river, U.N. trucks and jeeps rumbled about at all hours, with their cargo of international troops in blue helmets, or with sacks of flour, rice, and beans. That thought momentarily gave Vlado pause, with the idea that Chevard, or whoever had been in the U.N. jeep with Damir a few hours ago, might come looking for him over here. But even the U.N. was easily stymied by the siege boundaries cutting through the city. A crossing would be virtually impossible at night, especially on such short notice. Even at daybreak, some paperwork and smooth talking would be required at any location other than the airport. General Markovic, he supposed, might be able to arrange something in a hurry, but he doubted the smuggling operation would risk a move that would alert so many others – on all sides – to the fact that something extraordinary must be going on.

Twice during the next few minutes he heard the rumble and scrape of trucks grinding their gears uphill, but the sound seemed to be coming from back across the river. It surprised him how close they sounded. He felt as if he had traveled hundreds of miles, yet an unimpeded walk would put him on his own doorstep in less than half an hour.

As he rounded the last corner, he saw the house he was looking for, recognizing it instantly from its gables, its roof line, and, as he drew closer, from the mullioned windows on its upper floors, two of which seemed to have survived. In the dark he could not tell how extensively the place was damaged. Thus, it still seemed an imposing example of the empire architecture left behind by the Austrians in the nineteenth century.

Vlado was pleasantly surprised to see a dim light from behind a second-story window. He knocked at the front door and waited, then tried a second time, still with no answer. He tried the knob and the door was unlocked. He stepped inside, quietly shutting the door behind him.

It was surprisingly warm, though he shivered involuntarily, partly in relief and partly in sudden exhaustion. Unmistakable in the air was the smell of recent cooking. Fried meat, he guessed, and his mouth watered. From around the corner he heard the crackling of a fire, which cast an orange glow across an Oriental rug in the room before him. He also heard the steady ticking of a clock.

From upstairs, a floorboard creaked. He looked up the stairwell and a glow appeared, then brightened, gliding like a foxfire. It was a lantern, and he expected to soon be confronted by the wary face of some refugee, some newcomer sheltering in the home through the war who would have plenty of questions to ask, who might be alarmed enough by Vlado's appearance – for surely by now he looked horrendous – to call for the authorities, or to ask for identity papers.

But instead the face, like the house, was instantly recognizable, even though now it was deeply lined. Her hair had gone white and wispy, tied back now in a bun with a girlish pink ribbon. She wore a long, white flannel dressing gown, much like the ones his own mother used to wear. And for some reason she seemed neither surprised nor alarmed to see him, despite the sight he must have made, not to mention the smell, as he stood there dripping in her doorway. In fact, she seemed almost glad to see him.

'Good evening, Mrs Vitas,' he said.

She paused, as if the voice hadn't been what she'd expected. 'Esmir?' she said. 'Is that you, son?'

Before Vlado could speak she supplied her own answer.

'But of course it's you. You're late, Esmir, and wet. Come in and warm yourself by the fire.' She continued down the steps.

'No. I'm sorry, it's not Esmir. I'm Vlado Petric, an old friend of his.' He added, a bit sheepishly, 'From school days.'

Her expression didn't change. She moved within a foot of him, holding the lantern into his face with one hand while reaching to lightly stroke his brow with the other. She smoothed his wet forelocks back into place. Only then did her vacant smile fade, a look of concern knitting her brow.

'You're right,' she said wearily, as if forced to concede a point in a debate. 'It isn't Esmir. I'm sorry.' As if it had been her fault. 'I had thought not, really. But you have seen him? You have come from him?'

He decided then he would not be the one to bear the bad news. For all he knew she might never learn of her son's death until after the war. Although she had genuinely seemed to expect him to appear, which could either mean that she was deluded and out of touch, or that he indeed had visited from time to time, through whatever channels of influence.

'Yes, I have seen him.'

'And he is fine?'

Once more Vlado had a chance to set her straight,

338

and if he had believed he was dealing with a sound and rational mind he might have found a way to gently let her know. But her demeanor seemed to indicate the opposite. He was also thrown by the home's surreal comforts, its heat and light, its smell of a good meal. Everything, the furnishings as well, suggested a world that had been sealed years ago, well before the war.

As she spoke he registered the same odd sensation he'd felt during his school days, when he'd come by to pick up his knapsack after the field trip to the mountains.

'Yes, he is safe,' Vlado answered.

'He had said he would be.'

'And you see him often?'

'Oh, yes, every month. He would come more often, of course, but he is so busy. He is important, you know, an important man in the city.'

No mention of the war, or of anything else out of the ordinary. Vlado wondered what, if anything, she knew of the goings-on outside her door other than the booms and roars that occasionally shook her home.

'And you have come from him? You are one of his people?' she asked, still connecting everything to the world that revolved around her son. 'He has sent you with firewood? Or food?'

That explained the comforts of the home. So here was how Vitas had exerted his influence. Not for his own enrichment, apparently, considering the sparseness of his apartment, but for his mother. Keeping her supplied from across the river had been a trick, and probably hadn't come cheaply. It explained the unfinished letter to his mother that Vlado had fished out of Vitas's trash can. It also explained the cover story that Vitas had circulated. It would have been far easier to keep the lines of supply open, and secret, if everyone

339

thought she was dead. It could also explain how he might have been able to burrow his way deeper into the maze of the art scheme. Anyone with enough connections to this half of the city to keep a house heated and fed would also have the means of tapping into the smugglers' grapevine. In fact, as Vitas's death had shown, he may have ended up feeling safer on this side of the river than he did on his 'own' side, a feeling Vlado momentarily knew all too well.

That thought gave Vlado an idea, but he knew he'd have to proceed with tact if he was to act on it. It would require some careful lying to a vulnerable old woman, a thought that didn't sit comfortably.

'Yes,' he said, finally answering her question. 'Esmir has sent me. Only this time I have no firewood, no food. I was only to come check on you, and on the house. To see if you needed any repairs.'

'You're wet,' she said, as if noticing for the first time. He was far more than wet. He was muddy and unshaven, stinking of the river and the storm drains. As she steered him by a mirror on their way to the living room he had been shocked by his appearance, and the fact his looks hadn't sent her screaming back up the stairway told him more about her detached state of mind. Everyone but her son, he supposed, ended up cast in the same nondescript mold as far as she was concerned.

'Esmir takes care of me,' she said in a cheery singsong as she seated Vlado on the couch. He cringed as he lowered his soaked pants onto the fine old upholstery, though he also couldn't help but notice the thick dust. The housekeeping was apparently still left to her, with predictable results.

'He tells me it is unsafe for me to go outside of the house. Criminals, shooting and robbing. He says there are a lot of them. So I am not to go into the streets, and he sends everything I need.' All was spoken with a note of motherly pride, as if she might be describing her boy's good manners.

'I'll make some tea for us, then,' she said. 'Esmir always has tea first.' And she rose, gliding toward the kitchen. The ticking clock on the mantle said it was 11:30, and already you could hear the preliminaries racketing into motion, the rattling of machine-gun fire and a few mortar rounds, thumping and soaring. She seemed not to notice, nor did she seem fazed by the idea of a visitor at such a late hour. And with a pang he realized he might well be her last visitor of any sort for quite some time. Forever, even.

Vitas had been dead for less than a week, so there hadn't yet been time for his absence to show up in her supply of firewood or on the shelves of her pantry. But it wouldn't take long, and then what would happen?

When a war swallowed up a city you always heard first and last about the children, it occurred to Vlado, and their tragedy was undeniable; playmates killed by a shellburst as they sledded or played ball; orphans with sad eyes and no apparent future, hardened beyond their years.

Yet the young always had the resilience and energy to keep going, absorbing the blows by the sheer strength of numbers in the great clan of youth. No matter how many of their friends died, there would always be new friends to make. Those who made it through in one piece would always have another life to lead once the shooting stopped.

The old ones, however, ended up like this, or like Glavas, cut off and alone, collapsing from the weight of either fear or neglect, hanging on just long enough to

341

die unremarked, or to waste away until life no longer mattered. One way or another, the war finished them.

There was no way of knowing how long Vitas's mother had been like this, but based on what little Vlado had seen of her in previous years, he figured she'd probably been close to this state before the first shot was fired. Then her youngest son had died – Esmir would have broken the news of that, perhaps – and, if she'd still been clinging to the edge, that would have pushed her across.

At least she still had her house. Even if it was musty and layered with dust, with some plastic on windows here and there, it was mostly intact. And until last week you could say that she still had her chief protector, a son with enough connections to keep her warm and fed.

But now? The rot would begin, and Vlado doubted she'd have the awareness to do anything but slowly succumb to it.

He stood and stepped toward the fireplace, warming his hands, listening to the hissing of the teakettle from the kitchen. He placed another log across the embers, immediately regretting it. The less used now, the better. If she survived the winter perhaps the spring or a ceasefire might finally lure her outdoors, where she'd catch the attention of a neighbor, though he knew he was grasping at straws.

In a few moments the log was burning merrily with loud snaps and pops, smelling of pine resin. Vlado pulled off his wet shoes and propped them against the screen, then peeled off his wet socks and draped them across the top. He stood, arms folded, peering into the flames, into that little world of embers wavering at the bottom, and this was his pose as Mrs Vitas re-entered the room. She was balancing a silver tray loaded with teapot, cups, a sugar bowl – full, to his astonishment – and a pair of small cakes.

'Please,' she said, 'be seated on the couch. It's where Esmir always sits.'

She took an opposite chair, a vacant smile on her face, while Vlado dipped quickly toward the cakes, mouth watering. He stuffed one into his mouth, his tongue snaking out to lap up any straying crumbs, and the sugary flavor burst in his mouth like a drug. He loaded three teaspoons of sugar into the teacup. He would have spooned the rest into his pockets if he'd had half a chance, though he felt shamed by the temptation.

For a moment he had a sensation of descending into temporary insanity. To be confronted with all these comforts so hard on the heels of his harrowing day had pushed him onto an emotional ledge, and for a precarious moment it was all he could do to keep from bursting into tears. He contemplated what had nearly become of him at the river. Now he was here, blocks away, yet practically on another planet.

For the briefest of moment he considered staying. It would probably be easy enough to convince her that Esmir had assigned him to be her live-in caretaker. But he'd be just as powerless to keep the supply lines from drying up. The longer he stayed, in fact, the more quickly her wood, water and food would dwindle. Besides, he had work to do here, and he must do it soon. He blinked back his tears.

'What messages do you bring from my son?' she asked.

'I can only tell you that he is well,' he said, swallowing hard. 'He gives you his best. He speaks of you often.'

It was exactly what she'd wanted to hear, and she smiled broadly. So far, so good.

343

'And he will be coming soon for a visit?'

Vlado looked down at the table. 'Yes,' he answered, barely audible. 'Yes, soon.' He looked back up into her beaming face. Her eyes glittered, but her gaze was slightly off center, just as it had been during his visit to this same room years before, as if she were sneaking a look at something over his shoulder.

'He wanted to come this time,' Vlado said. 'But his work made it impossible. So he said I was to come instead.' He weighed his next words, feeling it was important to phrase them just right. 'He said that I was to check the house thoroughly, to see if anything needed fixing. He said I was to attend to all the business that he usually attends to.'

She seemed to brighten, to change expression, as if his words had unlocked some door. 'Ah,' she said. 'You will want to see his things, then. To check on his things. It is always the first thing he does after tea.'

'Yes. Of course.'

She smiled, seemingly happy to have gotten it right. Then they drank their tea, smiled at each other some more, and it was time. Vlado rose to his feet.

'Where should I begin?' he asked.

'In the cellar, of course,' she said briskly, as if dealing with a dolt. 'It is where all his things are.'

Vlado weaved slightly as he stood. The sugar was just beginning to flare into his bloodstream, crawling like a slow lightning. The basement door was in the kitchen, with a full box of candles and matches on a facing countertop. He lit one and stepped carefully down the steep, narrow steps, shielding the flame with his left hand.

Cobwebs clung to his face, and from below he heard the skittering of mice, perhaps something larger, running for cover at the approach of his candle. This

344

would indeed be a popular place with rodents, he imagined, probably the only house on the block with heating and a full pantry.

And down here in the cellar? He turned one way and saw an old coal furnace, still and cold. Even Vitas and all his connections hadn't been able to provide that precious commodity. Across another wall were old tools, thick with dust and cobwebs, and Vlado began to despair of finding anything at all.

He stepped off in the next direction, and as he reached the far corner the light revealed two items that made his heart soar. Here, at last, were Vitas's 'things,' as his mother had put it. Although Vitas doubtless would have described them as evidence, the sort that one might collect from the captured headquarters of a warlord mobster.

One item was two small, wooden file drawers, the sort one finds in libraries and archives, and it was filled from front to back with index cards. Vlado flipped through a few and saw they were just as Glavas had described them, right down to his initials, scribbled at the bottom of each. There were hundreds, which meant that it must be about complete. This, at last, was the transfer file.

The other item was a wooden crate, about eight feet high, six feet across, and two feet deep, marked with a blue #96 at the top, just as it had been listed on the inventory forms in the ministry's records.

He'd have to hand it to them, they took good care of their art work when they moved it out of the country. Crated to museum specifications no doubt. It probably would have been easy enough to learn just how from an idiot like Murovic.

Vlado wondered idly what sort of painting must be inside, but had neither the time nor the tools to find out. Of greater interest was the blue-and-white invoice sealed beneath a sheet of plastic across the outside.

It was a U.N. shipping form, cleared for transit to Frankfurt, addressed to the care of a Branko Jusic, doubtless their expatriated connection with his own ties to the shadowy edges of the art market, their dealer to the rest of the world. The Frankfurt destination meant it had a place on the American cargo flight that flew first thing every morning, four hours direct from Sarajevo to Frankfurt, local conditions permitting.

At the bottom of the invoice was the authorization signature, and it was no surprise to see that the order had come straight from the top: *Col. Maurice Chevard*, the signature a bit reckless, with a typical French overdose of dash and style. Vlado peeled off the form and placed it on the floor next to the candle.

He flipped again through the file drawers, and as he did so, the Orthodox New Year began. It was midnight. In a few moments the bombardment was proceeding in earnest. He paused for a moment to listen. It must be quite a sight, he thought, the red tracers arching into the night, the shellbursts that looked pretty as long as you didn't bother to consider what happened afterward. He wondered for a moment what Mrs Vitas must be doing upstairs, what she must make of all this. There was no movement on the floorboards, and he imagined her sitting placidly by the fire, its lights dancing in her vacant eyes. He pictured Vitas himself seated on the couch, all those visits with their tea and idle chat, probably mostly about schooldays, with no talk of war or death. Or, more likely, Vitas himself had never come at all, had only sent supplies and these items in the basement via trusted intermediaries. Trusted only because they were well paid.

Vitas himself might have appeared only in the form of a letter, a note on one of those sheets of cream-colored bond. But in his mother's mind, that had been enough, as good as a visit.

Vlado thumbed through the cards, finding that many had been roughly check-marked, perhaps denoting the items that had already been shipped. By rough calculation, totaling the assessed value for each such item, he figured that about eight million dollars worth of art must have been moved by now. Even accounting for the cut rates of the black market in stolen art, it was a lucrative venture, and, from the number of unchecked cards, was still continuing, courtesy of Markovic's own list, probably at a brisker pace than ever considering the approaching UNESCO deadline. He wondered what Murovic would think when he began to find all of his precious pieces missing, if he'd feel at all betrayed by his old pals.

As he looked again at the crate, he pondered the magnitude of what Vitas had accomplished. He must have moved heaven and earth to get these out of the ministry's property room and across the river. He must have known as soon as he'd seen the items at Zarko's headquarters exactly what they signified. For all Vlado knew, that might even have been what precipitated the raid. No wonder Kasic had done all he could to ensure that Zarko would be silenced. It would have solved his problem even as he enlarged his own cut of the profits. He'd then managed to rub out most of the paper trail that connected him to the deed, though he'd trusted too greatly in a small bit of correction fluid.

Vitas's only miscalculation had been concerning his own safety, and now his mother would pay the price as well.

347

Vlado found nothing further in his search of the room. He used rolls of U.N. tape and plastic, left by whoever had covered the broken windows, to bundle up about fifty of the cards from the file box, taking care to include several that had been check-marked and some that hadn't. He also wrapped the invoice, taping both bundles several times to ensure they'd stay waterproof, then stuffed them into his satchel before covering it, too, with tape and plastic.

Then he headed back up the steps, blowing out the candle as he reemerged into the light at the top.

She was still seated on the couch, fully awake. But now she looked at him in a slightly different way, as if plesantly surprised to see anyone at all emerging from her cellar.

'I know you,' she said suddenly. 'You're Vlado. You've forgotten your knapsack. You left it at our place in the mountains last night. Husayn speaks of you often,' she said.

It was the name of Esmir's younger brother, killed a year ago.

'He is a good friend of yours, isn't he?' she said.

'Yes, he is.'

'When you see him, tell him to come home,' she said, in a tone more admonishing than pleading. 'It is time for him to come home.' Her expression became stern, that of a mother scolding her boys as they strolled up toward the front steps, long overdue for dinner.

'Esmir too,' she said. 'It is time for both of my boys to come home.'

'Yes,' Vlado said again, at a loss for any other words. He'd hoped to make his way up to Esmir's old room, to rummage around for some dry clothes, but he saw now it would be best just to leave. He'd make do with what he had.

'I'd better go now, then,' he said, 'if I'm to see your sons.'

'Yes,' she said in a drifting tone. 'We'll look for your knapsack later. But would you like some tea first? Esmir always has tea first.'

'No. I'm afraid I have to go now.'

He edged toward the door, half expecting her to try to stop him, or to implore him to go and find her sons immediately. He feared she would cry. But her expression was as blank as when she'd first laid eyes on him.

'Esmir wanted me to tell you one more thing,' Vlado said. 'He said that it is safer now outside, but only early in the mornings, and that tomorrow morning he would like you to go and see your neighbors, to get in touch with your friends again. To let them know you are all right.'

'Yes,' she said, smiling. 'My friends. Yes. I'll have them over.'

Vlado wasn't certain if such people even existed anymore, except in her own imagination.

'You must ask them for food, or firewood, if you run low,' Vlado said. 'Esmir may not be able to provide any for a while.'

'My son provides all of that. He's an important boy at his school. You know him, don't you?'

'Yes,' Vlado said. 'Yes, I know him.'

He opened the door, glancing quickly in both directions to make sure no one was in the streets. A few shots still spattered in the hills, but the whole block seemed empty. Not a single light was on except in this house. He turned to say good-bye.

'Thank you for everything,' he said, but she seemed not to have heard him.

'Tell them to come soon,' she said, scolding now. 'Tell my boys.'

He backed down the steps and strolled away, heading in the direction he'd come from. He looked back only once, just in time to see her shutting the door, a smile of satisfaction on her face.

20

The only way back was the way he'd come, so Vlado set out for the sewer grate four blocks away, keeping to the edge of the streets and trying to walk lightly, although by now he felt almost invisible, indestructible.

Those feelings vanished a block short of his destination, when a voice called to him from behind.

'Halt! Military police. Please be prepared to show your identification papers. You are in violation of the curfew.'

Heavy shoes clopped toward him, and Vlado turned to see the vague outline of a man far up the block. He hadn't even heard the policeman, and Vlado cursed his carelessness. He debated whether to try to brazen it out, to state indignantly that he, too, was a policeman, then flash his badge in hopes this fellow wouldn't notice the distinctive blue-and-white seal of Bosnia-Herzegovina, or the absence of the double-headed eagle that the Serbs used on all their official papers.

It was too risky, the differences too obvious, and he edged slowly backward. Perhaps in the darkness the policeman wouldn't notice his progress toward the next intersection, ten yards away.

'Halt, I said.'

A flashlight beam swept the street, tunneling a path straight toward Vlado. It was now or never, and he darted for the corner. As he did there was a sudden burst of footsteps and another shout, and then nothing. Either too lazy to run or stopping to shoulder his automatic weapon, Vlado figured.

Vlado had a thirty yard head start and was around the corner, now only half a block from the grate. Getting it open would eat up the difference, though. He'd have to try to shake the policeman first, if the policeman was indeed still in pursuit.

Vlado ducked into a doorway, vaulting the three steps to the door and trying the handle. It was locked. He crouched in a corner, hoping that would be enough to conceal him. The policeman's footsteps clattered around the corner. There was no flashlight now, which probably meant he was holding the gun with both hands. The footsteps stopped, then the light again flicked on, sweeping the streets. It swiveled from left to right, slowly. Then a second time, slower still. The policeman stepped forward, still moving the light, two steps, three, then a fourth, which put him even with Vlado's doorway, no more than ten feet away. The policeman was still breathing hard from his run, the vapors clouding into the night. Vlado thought he could smell slivovitz. Good. The drunker the better. The policeman cursed, snaking the light wildly at windows and doorways. He flicked off the beam, turned, and walked back the way he'd come, muttering something about 'goddamn kids' as he stepped noisily around the corner.

Five minutes later Vlado was prying open the grate of the storm sewer and stepping back into the shallow water. An hour later he'd fought his way back through the razor wire and was staring out the end of the tunnel

352

into the river. Both banks seemed quiet. It wouldn't do to head onto the streets here, though. He dropped back into the river, sliding down the slimy rocks feet first, splashing at the bottom. He began wading downstream, scanning the banks as he moved.

At the first spillway the surge knocked him down as he fell in the three-foot waterfall. The weight of the falls pounded down, but he pulled himself free. Soaked to the bone once again, he trudged through the thigh-deep water. He passed three more spillways before he figured it was safe to climb up the bank.

Safe was a relative term, of course, because he had reached the portion of the river that wound through a narrow no-man's-land between Grbavica and the western side of downtown, a few hundred yards west of the Holiday Inn.

These areas were supposedly mined. But he also knew that people desperate for firewood sometimes crept into them at night, rummaging among shattered doors and window frames in search of anything that would burn. Otherwise, one could generally count on only a few rats for company.

Vlado stepped inside an abandoned building that had been split down the middle like a hickory log, seeming to defy half the laws of physics by standing at all. Sheltered by the walls, he spent the next half hour poking around for wood, striking it rich on the second floor up when he found a splintered window frame dangling from its opening. He wrenched it loose and carefully stepped down the stairwell. He pulled free enough pieces to kindle a small flame with his cigarette lighter, the smoke drifting up through the huge fissure in the building.

He decided to wait there until an hour before first light. Then he would make his move, sprinting back across to his own side of the city. If he hit a mine, then he hit a mine. If he was shot, then he was shot. It was easy to think that way after the evening he had just survived and, as he watched the small flames, he wondered why Kasic hadn't had him killed earlier, and why his investigation had been allowed to get as far as it had. Sure, there would have been some embarrassment if he had died, but nothing that couldn't have been explained away to the U.N. by arresting a few shady characters to take the blame.

Then, the reason occurred to him. Kasic had hoped to use him to find the transfer files, and the rest of the missing evidence. As long as they were unaccounted for, he and the whole operation were vulnerable. Who better than someone under his own thumb to track it down for him. And with Damir reporting most of Vlado's movements, it had almost worked, until Vlado had disappeared into a place where even Damir and Kasic couldn't follow.

The fire had at last begun to warm him. He rubbed his hands above the small flame, wondering how Jasmina and Sonja must be spending their evening, and he began to pace through the debris of the building's first floor.

The room seemed to have once been part of a large apartment. Here and there in the wreckage of crumbled plaster and broken glass were wrinkled old photos jarred loose from their frames. Faces looked up at him, the young and the old, the married and unmarried, with their prewar smiles. He wondered where they all were now, what they'd managed to take with them in the rush to leave this building, and if they would ever return. Or even want to.

As he wandered from room to room, staying clear of the windows in case some vigilant sniper should be watching at this wee, small hour, he imagined himself in Berlin, strolling about Jasmina's darkened flat.

He knew something of the look of the place from photographs, the small but cheerfully painted rooms with a child's crayon drawings in evidence everywhere. He passed through a doorway, picturing a small bed before him, a child's form curled beneath the sheets. He leaned to kiss her brow, a caring father seeing to it that his daughter was safe in the night. He pulled the sheet more snugly around her shoulders, then crossed the hallway, following the scent of Jasmina's perfume, turning back the covers to climb in, then drawing himself close against her back, his stomach fluttery as he felt himself growing stiff against her. He placed a hand on her waist and she stirred, her hair brushing against his cheek as she turned to meet him. He felt the warmth of her lips.

Outside, on a nearby hillside, a New Year's celebrant fired a final reprise from his mortar before turning in for the night. The deep boom startled Vlado, who found himself staring into an empty room, its ceiling torn halfway to the floor in great shards of plaster and batting. He checked his watch and saw that it was nearly 5:30. Soon the sky would begin to brighten, though it was still a few hours before sunrise.

He pulled back the plastic from his satchel and pawed through the contents until he found his notebook, flipping through the pages to locate the correct address. He went over the best route in his head, then crept out the door and around the corner, heading away from the river and out of no-man's-land, angling toward the Holiday Inn.

There was nothing for it now but to run, and he gave it all he had, stepping with as much care as possible through a rubble of bricks, stones, and twisted metal, while wishing he had enough time to check for the little metal boxes with their tripwires, the most common sort of mine found in these places.

On one stride, his trailing foot indeed snagged a wire, and he shouted as he stumbled, a strangled cry of panic, but he kept going. It was probably nothing but the tangle of an old radio, or a fallen telephone line.

He reached Sniper Alley, which for once seemed a symbol of safety, and sprinted across, his footsteps slapping loudly on the pavement, a lonely noise at this hour of the morning. He didn't rest until he'd passed behind the sheltering bulk of the Holiday Inn, then he slowed to a walk, panting to catch his breath. He looked around, but there were no police, nor anyone else. When he reached the next street he turned left, heading west, for the highrise apartment building at 712 Bosanska Street. He climbed three flights of a dim stairway, through a musk of rot and old urine, and arrived at the doorway of apartment 37.

He knocked, and in a few moments Amira Hodzic opened the door, sleep still deep in her face. She wore a heavy cotton robe belted tightly at the waist.

'I need your help,' Vlado said. 'I'm sorry.'

Her face was clear of makeup, her hair tangled, and her eyes tired and bloodshot. Vlado's appearance was doubtless more frightful than when he'd reached Mrs Vitas's house. But she didn't appear alarmed, only weary, and perhaps a trifle put out.

'Why am I not surprised to see you,' she said, then paused on the threshold before opening the door wider and turning inside. 'Come in,' she said over her shoulder. 'I'll make you coffee. You look like you need it. But quietly, please, my children are sleeping.'

She turned to face him again. 'Would you like to wash? I can heat some water.'

'That would be heavenly.' Although it was probably as much a favor for herself as for him. By now he must smell like a sewer rat.

He stood in the tiny bathroom, peeling off his sopping pants, shirt, underwear, and socks. It was chilly in here, but not too bad. And anything was better than staying in those clammy clothes.

A few minutes later, she knocked lightly. 'The pot of water is outside the door.'

He wondered briefly at this display of modesty from the woman who had undressed in front of him for a few packs of cigarettes. Then he forgot everything else as he felt the luxury of the hot water, sponging it across his chest, his legs. He submerged his face in the pot. He held his breath, eyes shut, then pulled out with a gasp, dripping. He almost felt like laughing at the simple joy of it.

A few moments later she tapped at the door again, speaking barely above a whisper in the quiet apartment. 'Here is a towel, and some dry clothes. They're my husband's. A little large, probably, but dry and clean. I've sold most of the rest, so you might as well keep these.'

Dried and dressed, Vlado stepped into the kitchen in his stocking feet to find she had made a breakfast of bread, cheese, and sausage. The gas lines, he could see, had been installed neatly and professionally here. In the corner sat a small woodstove, homemade but far sturdier than the one that had belonged to Glavas. It was burning steadily, an ample pile of chopped logs stacked nearby. He would have liked nothing better than curling up on the floor like a cat to sleep for the rest of the day.

By Sarajevo standards, Amira had established a prosperous lifestyle, Vlado thought. She followed his gaze as it moved from luxury to luxury, seeming to read his mind.

'The fringe benefits of my line of work,' she said. 'It pays better than almost any other job I could have found, even if most of the currency is cigarettes. Appropriate, I guess, that an old farm wife should be relying on a harvest of dried leaves for money.'

'A farm wife. I'd always imagined you worked in an office. A bank, somewhere like that.'

'I'm surprised you'd imagined me as anything at all, other than a temporarily desirable possession. Another commodity on the barter market. Not that I'd have faulted you for it. Without that kind of thinking my children would starve.'

'That's the way I'd have preferred to have thought of you. But somehow I couldn't. I kept thinking of you before the war, in some normal job with normal demands. I couldn't get past that.'

'So that was the problem. I'd assumed you'd had a sudden rush of guilt, thinking of a wife back at home mopping a floor, or wiping a small, runny nose. A baby at her breast and beans on the stove.'

'There was that, too. A wife. But she's in Berlin with my daughter. I haven't seen them in nearly two years. You were my first attempt at, well, anything, since they left.'

'Sorry to have failed you,' she said, her softened tone making it seem almost as if she meant it.

'So your husband?' Vlado asked, tugging at the front of his borrowed shirt. 'He is . . . ?'

'Dead. Killed in the fighting in 'ninety-three. A patriot who died from blind obedience to zeal. He was shot in the chest, but you might just as easily have called it death by intoxication of propaganda. He heard we would have a new nation and needed to defend it,

358

and he took it to heart, never mind running a farm or bringing in a crop or feeding a family. He joined the first week, with no gun and no training. And the bastards put him right up on the frontline where he'd be overrun in the first wave. They never even got his body back, and we'll certainly never get our land or our house back.

'It was all the children and I could do to make our way here on a wagon. Little Hamid wasn't even walking yet. It was a pig wagon. We smelled like pig shit and dirty hay for a week before we had enough water to bathe.'

Vlado thought of Glavas tucked in the hay of his own farm cart, wheels creaking through the same mountains a half century ago.

'What about the rest of your family?'

'We were separated by the fighting. Now they are all in towns near Split on the Dalmatian Coast, living in refugee hotels. My parents and my cousins, a sister, her husband. They've sent a few letters, but that's all. They used up all their hard currency by the end of the first year. It's all they can do to feed themselves, much less help us out. I'm probably doing better than all of them combined.'

'Are you trying to get out?'

'I did for the first year, but we were always too far down the list to get in a convoy. So in the spring I picked dandelions for salad and scrounged for every bit of change or whatever else I could find while we gradually spent every last coin of our savings. When the money was all gone, that's when I first went to the French barracks. I was no good at first. Even you could see that. I was ready to give it up after only a week. Then you came along that night with your free cigarettes. It was enough to keep me going until I had

359

enough nerve to do it right. And now, as you can see, I've become a professional.'

She offered a bitter smile. Vlado was a bit uneasy being cast as the savior of her career.

'Some of the customers even ask for me by name, now. They're disappointed if I'm not there. Although I still don't do just everything. Mostly blow jobs. A year ago I couldn't even have said those words. Blow job. Now it's rote behavior. Blow job. Give me another few months and I'll be doing everything they want, letting them tie me up. Any perverted thing they want.' She paused, sipping her coffee. 'But my children will be fat and warm, and sleep in clean sheets.'

She put the coffee cup down, staring sullenly at the wall. 'A week ago they told us we were finally at the top of the list, that we would have a place on the next convoy of buses to Split. Probably only another month or two. Only now I'm not so sure. If we left now we'd only have enough money to struggle along with my relatives. If I work another year I may have enough to make it all the way to Vienna. I have friends there who will take us in if we can help with the rent.'

She offered more food, including a few slices from a fresh orange. Vlado hadn't eaten one in more than a year. By prewar standards, it was pulpy, a bit on the dry side. But the taste was spectacular. She nearly laughed at the look of rapture on Vlado's face as he bit into a slice.

'Another fringe benefit,' she said, smiling.

'Yes,' he said, feeling embarrassed by his reaction. 'Another successful out-of-towner.' It was a flippant remark, a fragment of his own bitterness breaking loose under the sheer weight of exhaustion, but she was no longer smiling, and her face had gone rigid.

'Don't take it personally,' he said wearily. 'It's just

that people who grew up here feel like they're losing their city as much to the refugees as to the Chetniks.'

'Yes, you great cosmopolitan people who hate no one, except people like me. You have to have somebody to look down on, I suppose. The Chetniks aren't available. They're all in the hills, so you've picked us. You write us off as ignorant peasants and think every woman who wears a scarf on her head is a religious fanatic, and every man who prays in the mosque is mujahedeen. Do you think we really want to be here? That we love your city so much we'll never be able to tear ourselves away from the water lines and these fine rabbit hutches you call apartments, where you sleep in the back so you won't be hit by the shots coming in through the windows?

'What really bothers you is that we seem to be better at surviving than you. We can make a fire, slaughter a goat, plant a vacant lot with vegetables. The triumph of the peasant, and it drives you mad. So much for the wisdom of the streets.'

'If that's all it was we could stand it. It's the attitudes we resent. I'm not saying it was your fault personally, but where do you think this war began? In small towns and villages where people kept alive all the old, narrow grudges for the past fifty years. You were the only ones still worried about finding out who was a Chetnik, who was a Catholic, who was a Muslim.'

'We were the only ones who faced the truth, that's all.'

'And your truth was that a Serb couldn't trust a Croat, or a Muslim trust a Serb, or whoever. Was that your truth?'

'You heard the stories growing up, just like we did. About the bastard Chetniks or the cutthroat Ustasha. You probably had an old uncle just like I did who always warned you after his third drink that it would all happen again someday. But in Sarajevo you just went to the café and had another cigarette. You put it all out of your mind and let your grandparents worry about history. You were good little Titoists who didn't just forget the past, you pretended it never happened. And now you're so shocked and offended that it's happened again, right under your noses, while you were drinking coffee and talking about Western music.

'But isn't it funny how fast you've caught on. Now you're as quick as anyone to call someone by some dirty label. How many times have you said "Chetnik" in the last ten minutes. And who needs Chetniks when you can look down your noses at the entire rest of your country. You act as if you are the only people in the world who are suffering, and that everyone is to blame but yourselves. No wonder even the TV cameras are tired of you.'

Vlado saw that tears had begun running down her cheeks, but her voice was unwavering, unshakable in its low monotone that hammered forward like the drone of a court clerk reading a bill of indictment.

'My husband was just like the rest of you, so committed to tolerance and brotherly love that the first thing he wanted to do was take a gun and go shoot every Chetnik he could find.'

She paused, calming herself, sipping again at her coffee, although by now it had gone cold.

'That was his favorite shirt,' she said, looking up at Vlado. 'It's the only one I haven't been able to part with.' Then her crying broke into a sob. More tears rolled down her cheeks.

'I'm sorry,' he said softly, reaching across the table to touch her face. She stood and walked to the stove, tidying aimlessly. He followed, lightly placing a hand on her shoulder, and she again broke into sobs. She turned toward him, looking into his face as he brushed away her tears, and she pulled him to her tightly, gripping the old shirt.

She leaned her head against his chest and he kissed her hair, with its taste of soap and kitchen smells. Her entire body smelled of a clean, warm bed, sheets rumpled. She raised her face to kiss him, and they clutched at one another. On her cheeks and her neck he tasted the traces of rouge and pancake from the night before. She unbelted her robe, and Vlado slipped his arms inside.

They did not speak. Vlado held her as tightly as he could, and she seemed to gasp. Both were holding on for salvation as much as for desire. Vlado's mind, still jazzed by the hot water and the bite of the orange, now leapt at the feel of warm skin beneath his hands, the body of a woman, someone who still struggled, who was still capable of rage, of life.

A small voice called out from the bedroom doorway, and she stiffened immediately, pulling away gently but with an underlying firmness. The look on her face, like their first time together, seemed a mixture of both relief and disappointment, though of a different nature this time.

In only a few seconds her transition was complete. She was again a mother attending her children, her face a study in careworn tenderness. She deftly re-knotted her robe before turning to face the bedroom door.

'Yes, Mirza.'

'I'm hungry.'

'Then come and have breakfast.'

Mirza, who appeared to be about six, stood looking shyly around the door, as if reluctant to enter as long as this strange man was here. She looked like a miniature Amira, with her slightly upturned nose, and the large brown eyes. Then, behind her, a second small face appeared, a full head shorter, with far different features – blue eyes, blond hair, a broad and jolly face – taken from someone who was lost forever now.

'It's all right, Mirza,' Amira said gently. 'He's a friend. Come and eat. You, too, Hamid.'

She turned back toward Vlado, businesslike but smiling, and said in a lowered voice, 'Do you always have such a way with women? Even when you pay double price, or when I'm willing for free, I'm always putting my clothes back on before anything happens.'

But the corners of her eyes still glimmered with the last of her tears.

Vlado sat with them through breakfast, enjoying the rare luxury of a second cup of coffee. He began to feel restless, despite his weariness, that he should be planning his next move, whatever that might be. But when he mentioned such a possibility, Amira motioned toward the bedroom.

'What you need is sleep,' she said. 'Stay in the back for as long as you like.'

He crawled between the clean sheets, cool but not cold, and pulled a soft thick blanket across his shoulders. Then he curled on his side, sinking easily into a welcome oblivion.

21

Vlado slept for eight hours and awakened with a plan.

He stepped from the bedroom to find Amira on the floor, playing quietly with her children and a set of crayons. A mortar was thumping in the distance somewhere. The small girl had a doll, and the boy tugged at it, crying to hold it. Amira glanced up from her efforts at mediation to say hello, and his presence immediately silenced the children.

'Good morning,' he said. 'Or, good afternoon, I suppose. Thank you for that. It's the best I've slept in months.'

'Laundered sheets and clean clothes work wonders. You should try them sometime.'

Vlado blushed. 'Sorry about the way I looked.'

'I'm still not sure I want to ask where you'd been in those clothes. I've washed them. They're drying outside the window.'

Vlado looked about the room, panicky for a moment.

'Your bag's over by the door,' she said, and he relaxed.

'How long were you planning on staying? I'm assuming you're not exactly welcome at your house right now or you wouldn't have come here.'

'I might as well tell you. There are people looking for

me. People who you wouldn't want to get on the wrong side of. I looked the way I did this morning because I'd been running from them. Swimming, even. I had to cross the river to shake them, and I wasn't exactly welcome over there, either.'

'Does this have anything to do with the shooting from the other night?'

'It has everything to do with it. And that's probably all I should tell you about it, for your own good. If that worries you, I can leave now. With the children, I'd certainly understand.'

She considered that a moment.

'Where would you go?'

'I'd find someplace.'

'You already have. Stay as long as you need. I could use someone to watch the children while I work. I think they're wearing out their welcome with the neighbors. The price of babysitting keeps going up.'

'Actually I might have another place by the end of the day. In the meantime, do you still have any of your husband's tools?'

'We managed to bring a few. I'll get them.' She walked into the bedroom. He heard her rummaging in a closet and in a few minutes she emerged holding a small metal toolbox. Inside were a few screwdrivers, a claw hammer, a crescent wrench, and an assortment of nails and bolts. It wasn't much, but it would do.

'I'd like to borrow a few,' he said.

'Certainly.'

'In fact, there's a chance you may not get them back at all.'

'Fine,' she said without pause. 'They were his. I've no use for them except to sell them, and the market seems glutted right now.' She'd gone back to her businesslike voice when talking about her husband.

'I also need a favor from you.'

'Go ahead.'

'Do you speak any English?' He had scant hope she did, being from a small town. But if that were the case he could send a note, though that would be riskier.

'A little, yes. Pretty good, in fact.'

When Vlado reacted with surprise, she said, 'Some of us did learn something in the provinces besides how to kill each other, you know.'

'Sorry.'

'Who do you need me to talk to?'

'I need to get a message to a British journalist staying at the Holiday Inn. Not by phone, his may be tapped by now. You'd have to tell him in person. I'm not even sure he'll be there, so you may have to wait around, or go back again later. You'll probably have a better chance if you wait until after dark.'

'So I'd be cutting into business hours.'

'Yes. And I've no way to repay you.'

'That's all right. I suppose I owe you one anyway. You're the man who got me started in business.' This time she said it playfully, without the earlier hint of bitterness. He joined in her smile.

'So what's the message, then? And who am I to see?'

'Toby Perkins, room four thirty-four. Tell him to meet me here. He should bring a blanket with him and come in his Land Rover. Tell him to make sure no one follows him. I'll need him to drive me somewhere.'

'And if he asks where?'

'Just tell him I've broken the case, and if this works out then he'll have the story of a lifetime.'

It got him, of course.

Four hours later, with darkness complete, Toby came thumping and wheezing up the steps behind Amira. He

367

entered red-faced, his bulging sack dragging at his feet, but he was clearly excited.

'So, where are we going, Mr Homicide Detective. To solve another one of your individual murders?'

'A lot more than that, I hope. But we'll have to wait until after curfew.'

'Well, aren't we the sly and cagy one these days. Secret faxes to Belgrade. Unofficial trips to Dobrinja. Now you're hiding out in a west side apartment while your office says you're "unavailable for comment" then asks curious questions about when was the last time I saw you and who else has Mr Petric been in touch with, et cetera. They wanted me to come in for a few questions so I gave them the brushoff, told them they'd have to speak to my editor. I get the idea you must be up to something they don't exactly approve of. I like it more all the time.'

So, they were checking everywhere now. Vlado was glad he'd never told Amira's name to Damir, nor was it written anywhere at the office.

'I'll make us some coffee,' Amira said.

'Allow me,' Toby responded, stooping with a grunt to his bag and its seemingly bottomless supply of Nescafé. Out came another jar.

She nodded briskly, as if expecting it all along. Toby seemed a bit taken aback by such a routine reaction to his routine generosity.

They spent the next three hours talking, an odd three-way conversation about life alternating between English and Serbo-Croatian with Vlado interpreting when necessary. At one point, as Toby rattled on about his previous days covering African revolutions, Vlado considered the unlikely combination of events that had brought together this trio. At its root was mostly one form or another of stubbornness – the ethnic stubbornness that had begun the war, the world's stubborn refusal to do anything but nurture along a deadly siege, Vlado's stubborn clinging to a city that had died beneath his feet, Toby's stubborn pursuit of a story, and Amira's stubborn fight for her children's future.

Amira made dinner, half a chicken divided among them, then put her children to bed. Half an hour after the nine o'clock curfew Vlado rose to his feet.

'It's time,' he said.

'Yes, but time for what,' Toby said.

'You'll find out soon enough.'

Vlado turned to Amira. 'The authorities will probably be looking for you on the job. If you can afford it, you had better stay away for a night or two. Once they do catch up to you, be especially wary of my partner, Damir Begovic, or one of his bosses, Juso Kasic. And don't admit to anyone that I was ever in your apartment. Just tell them the story you told me, except leave out anything about ever knowing the colonel's first name, or knowing that he was an officer, or even knowing that he was French. That should satisfy them.'

'And where will you be all this time?' she asked. Toby waited just as eagerly for the answer.

'That depends on how lucky we are.'

At Vlado's direction, they drove the armored Land Rover west down Sniper Alley. Vlado was poised to climb quickly into the back beneath the blanket in case any new checkpoints had been posted. Along the way he reached into his satchel and tore open the plastic taped around the U.N. shipping invoice and scanned the document by the green glow of the dashboard lights, while Toby glanced over in curiosity.

'Where to now?' Toby asked.

'Pull over for a minute. We're almost there. A few hundred yards up on the right.'

'U.N. headquarters?'

'Yes.'

'I thought that's where we might be heading. And who do we ask to see once we're at the gate?'

'No one. We'll be driving around back to the loading dock to see what we might find.'

'And how do you propose for us to get through the main gate, short of ramming it open in a hail of gunfire.'

'With this.'

He held out the invoice as Toby pulled the Rover onto the curb.

'Impressive,' Toby said. 'Looks like it might even be the real thing. But that still leaves you. I've got U.N. press credentials, so no problem. You don't.'

'I'll be in the back, under the blanket. You'll point to the lump I'm making and tell the guard you're making a delivery, as stated on the invoice. Just hope he doesn't ask to inspect the parcel, or notice that the shipping date is a few months old. But you can probably avoid most of the questions by directing his attention right away to Colonel Chevard's signature at the bottom. They should be used to this kind of delivery by now, and in trucks that look a lot shadier than yours. Oh, and tell him you might need a few minutes to do a little hammering, to shore up the crate for shipment. That should give us the time we need.'

Toby sighed, seeming to reconsider the venture as Vlado climbed into the back and pulled the blanket over his head.

'This better be a hell of a story,' he muttered, throwing the car into gear.

*   *   *

It went just as Vlado had predicted. The sentry seemed bored, little interested in anything but Toby's U.N. credentials and Colonel Chevard's signature at the bottom of the invoice.

'Around to your right, sir,' the soldier said. 'Docks are on the far end at the back, behind the sandbags. Take care in your business, though. Sniper was working that side of the building earlier tonight.'

They drove in, Vlado warm beneath the blanket. He felt the Rover stop. He heard Toby pull up the handbrake and say, 'Last stop, everybody out.'

Vlado sat up, relieved to see they were well out of sight of the sentry, and probably out of earshot as well. He was even more relieved to see a large wooden crate standing on the loading dock. The usual invoice was attached to the side, covered in plastic. The crate was roughly the same size as the one in Vitas's mother's basement, though perhaps a little smaller.

'Come on,' he said to Toby. 'Let's see what's inside. The quicker we're finished back here, the better.' He let the better nourished Toby do the prying and pulling with the hammer, while Vlado loosened nails with a screwdriver.

They pulled one side of the crate free, the nails groaning, and Vlado tugged away the bubbled plastic that had been wrapped around the contents.

'Jesus,' Toby explained. 'It's a painting.'

'Worth about one hundred twelve thousand U.S.,' Vlado said.

'How the hell'd you know that so quick?' Toby asked.

'It belonged to Milan Glavas. That's whose apartment we were in the other day.'

'They killed him for it?'

'Partly for that. But mostly for telling the truth.'

371

'So. It's like I thought the other day. An art smuggling operation.' Toby glanced at the names on the invoice. 'And with some very big fish involved, it seems. How much do you figure they've made this way?'

'Millions. Minimum.'

Toby smiled broadly. He slapped Vlado on the back.

'No wonder everyone's looking for you. But don't worry, from now on I'm your personal escort and bodyguard, courtesy of the *Evening Standard*, all expenses gladly paid. So, where to from here? And we should probably round up my photographer on the way. He can get a few snaps of this. The invoice, too.'

'First, we've got to do a little repackaging. Then you're taking the painting with you. The invoice and the crate stay here.'

'"We," you mean.'

'No. You. I want you to take the painting back to Amira's. If she's nervous about keeping it, tell her to burn it. Fine with me.'

'But it's worth over a hundred thousand? Christ. And I should think it's a bloody good piece of evidence as well.'

'So it is. But all the evidence I'll be able to carry is in this bag,' Vlado said, pointing to his satchel.

'And where the hell will you be all this time?'

'Here. Waiting. I'd let you stay with me, but I'm afraid there's only room for one.'

'What the hell are you talking about?'

'I'll be inside this,' Vlado said, patting the side of the crate. 'And when it leaves Sarajevo, so will I. Courtesy of Maybe Airlines. Which is why the painting has to be taken away. To make room for me. This crate's scheduled on the first flight tomorrow morning to Frankfurt. If you're on the flight, too, then you'll be able to snap all the pictures you want once we arrive. I'll even have time for an interview. The rest of the documentation you'll need for your story is in some notebooks and index cards in my bag.'

It was the first time Vlado had ever seen Toby at a loss for words.

'We'd better get to work, then,' he finally said, picking up the hammer again.

It took about fifteen minutes.

Vlado stepped in among the packing material, which Toby then draped around him, making sure he was concealed while still having enough openings for breathing. Toby then propped the wooden side back into place and hammered the crate shut.

'Steady on, fellow, be seeing you in Frankfurt,' Toby muttered into the box, and Vlado heard the Rover drive away.

Vlado was standing, yet the sides offered enough support to let him drift into a fitful vertical sleep, which ended when he awakened to voices around the crate. The packing plastic held most of his body heat, so he'd remained surprisingly warm through the night; it was even a bit stuffy. Vlado then felt motion, listening to the whir and grind of a motor as a forklift moved the crate into a truck bound for the airport.

A few minutes later the brakes squealed as the truck stopped for the usual Serb checkpoint on the way to the airport. Vlado heard the voices of the soldiers, then the opening of the tailgate as they stepped inside. They, too, must have been used to these cargoes by now. There was no request for an inspection. They were more worried about what was coming into the country than what was leaving.

The truck continued on its way, Vlado's second trip across enemy lines in the past thirty hours. At the airport a second forklift carried him on a bumpy ride across what must have been the runway. The crate then settled with a metallic clang inside a space where the noises echoed, as if in a cave. He knew then he was within the belly of the next plane out of Bosnia.

From the sounds around him, he could tell that a few other items were being loaded aboard as well, although outgoing flights were generally lightly packed, having already emptied their payloads of relief supplies for the city. They usually departed Sarajevo with little more than the luggage of the soldiers, journalists, and aid workers who were hitching a ride home. There was room for maybe a dozen passengers, who sat single-file along either side, facing inward, although there were a few small porthole-size windows on both sides if they cared to turn to take in the view.

Vlado heard the passengers boarding. American voices of the flight crew told the arrivals where to place their bags. He wondered if Toby had made it. Sometimes these flights had waiting lists, especially when heavy fighting allowed for fewer flights while increasing the demand for safer transportation. But during the recent days of light fighting, flights had proceeded virtually without interruption, so his chances were probably good.

A second bunch of people clattered aboard, and Vlado heard Toby's voice above the others. 'Hey, wonder what's in that crate,' he asked. 'Smuggled masterworks of art, probably,' a remark that drew a hearty laugh from a colleague.

Jesus, Vlado thought. Don't get cocky yet.

Some of the passengers were moving around, still attending to their bags before settling into their seats, and Vlado suddenly felt a light tap on the side of the crate, followed by the mutter of Toby's voice.

'You're home free. Departure in ten minutes. It's just me, one other hack, and a dozen Belgian soldiers. Bon voyage.'

Vlado listened to the shuffling of feet and the clicking of seatbelts, the strapping into place of a final piece of luggage, and then an American voice shouted to the cockpit that all was ready and secure.

A few moments later the great engines rumbled to life. With some difficulty, Vlado was able to raise an arm, loosening just enough of the packing material to make a small peephole out one side. By craning his neck a bit he could just see out one of the tiny windows. The view now was only of the runway, and as Vlado watched, it began to move. They were taxiing into position for takeoff.

He felt the swivel and tremble of the plane as it rolled across the pocked runway, turning into position for the final run. The plane stopped, and the engines revved to full power, the vibrations loud and violent. There would be no gunshots. No delays. They were right on time, and his heart leapt.

Then, just as the pilot should have been pulling hard on the throttle, the engine eased off, the deafening throbs dropping suddenly to the loud hum of idling. A few moments later the engines stopped altogether, and one of the Americans shouted from the cockpit, 'Sorry fellas. We got a last-minute visitor wants to see us.'

There were shouts, a buzzing of questions from the passengers, and the creaking of the cargo door. A sudden spill of daylight poured through Vlado's peephole, and he worked to close the opening, his elbow straining against the side of the crate.

Footsteps were clanking aboard, several men by the sound of it, with businesslike strides. He heard an unfamiliar voice shouting orders in Serbo-Croatian. 'Sorry to delay your flight, gentlemen,' the voice then said in English. 'But this should only take a few minutes.'

'And who the hell are you,' Toby's colleague shouted impatiently.

'General Dragan Markovic, Bosnian Serb Army.'

Had Vlado not been propped up by the close quarters of the wooden crate, his knees would have buckled. The next announcement was even more disconcerting.

'I believe there is a Toby Perkins on board, a gentleman from the *Evening Standard*?' Markovic said.

Toby must have raised his hand or otherwise made his presence known, because Markovic then said, 'If you don't mind sir, we need to keep you here just a while longer. For a few questions.'

'Sorry,' Toby answered. 'I'll miss my Frankfurt connection to London. I'm staying.'

'Then the plane will be staying, too, sir.'

That threat brought the Belgian soldiers into it, who weren't about to let a British scribbler scrap their departure. It was quickly clear Toby would be leaving the plane. Vlado felt a pang of worry for him, but he'd likely be released in no more than a few hours, none the worse for wear, with another war story for his colleagues. Although Serb snipers enjoyed an occasional potshot at a Western journalist, police detentions were generally conducted on an official level. As long as a Westerner was involved, especially if he was a journalist, they usually resulted in little more than some inconvenience and a burst of sympathetic publicity for the detained correspondent.

But Markovic wasn't satisfied merely with rounding up Toby.

'I'm afraid there's one other order of busines as well. I want the cargo area thoroughly searched. Please proceed men. Pay special attention to the larger pieces.'

The next sounds were those of locks and hasps being thrown open on boxes and footlockers belonging to the Belgians and the crew of Americans. Several Belgians shouted in protest, while one of the American crewmen demanded, 'Where's your search warrant?'

'This is not America, gentlemen,' Markovic coolly replied. 'Nor is it Belgium. This is the Serbian Republic of Bosnia.'

A hand thumped the side of the crate, and Vlado braced for the end. Trying to run from here would be impossible. Even if he made it out the back of the plane and off the airstrip he'd quickly run into gunfire from other quarters of the Serb army dug in around the runway. Whoever had taken hold of the crate began pulling at a board, trying to wrench it free.

Then Markovic spoke up.

'Popovic!' he shouted. 'What do you think you're doing?'

The movement stopped.

'Checking this crate, sir.' He might have been shouting directly in Vlado's ear, the sound was so close.

'Never mind that one,' Markovic said, with the slightest hint of smugness. 'I can personally vouch for its contents.'

The soldier pushed the loose board back into place and moved on to the next item. Five minutes later they were done, and everything was repacked.

'Sorry to have troubled you, gentlemen,' Markovic said, satisfied that his fugitive was nowhere on board and his cargo would soon be on its way to the auction markets of Europe. 'Everything here seems to be in order.'

In perfect order, Vlado thought.

The footsteps thudded off the plane, and the light dimmed as the cargo door cranked into place. A few moments later the engines rumbled back to life, and this time there was no further delay as the plane throttled forward, jolting down the runway until Vlado felt a breathless lift of his stomach as the wheels left the ground. The plane pulled up sharply and quickly curled into a steep bank, aiming for the far hills.

Vlado again pulled back enough of the packing material to look toward the small window without making himself known to the Belgians. Rooftops rushed past below, some blackened and burned, others staved in. Then the plane rolled around the end of the city to begin its run out of the valley.

Someone seemed to be moving just outside the crate, and Vlado experienced a momentary panic. Then he heard laughter, and by craning his neck a bit he could see that the Belgians were already up and out of their seatbelts, snapping Instamatics at each other, celebrating the end of their six-month tour of duty.

Out the window Vlado saw a puff of smoke from somewhere far below, a shell either leaving or landing, then the airfield rolled by, a receding strip of tarmac. The plane banked more sharply, and the silvery ribbon of the Miljacka River gleamed below in the early morning sun, and for a moment he could again taste its coppery brown water.

His last view of the city was out over the burned

highrises to the east and beyond, off toward his own apartment, though his line of sight was blocked by a hill. He could, however, just see the edge of the snowy fields where, judging by the time of day, the grave-diggers would soon be bending to their shovels.

THE END

THE WARLORD'S SON

Dan Fesperman

'The sun did not rise in Peshawar. It seeped – an egg-white smear that brightened the eastern horizon behind a veil of smoke, exhaust and dust. The smoke rose from burning wood, cow dung and old tires, meager flames of commerce for kebab shops and bakers, metal-smiths and brick kilns. The exhaust sputtered from buzzing blue swarms of motor rickshaws, three-wheeled terrors that jolted across potholes, darting between buses like juiced-up golf carts.'

Into this murky chaos of sprawling humanity comes Skelly, a burned-out American war correspondent, now in harness again thanks to a messy divorce and too many children. Post nine-eleven, he's back in the game, in yet another new and extremely hazardous location, dropped from the skies after scarcely as much preparation as one might make for a weekend at the beach.

But first he must find a 'fixer'; someone local yet who speaks English, who's good on the ground, yet can arrange transport; a man who is essential to keeping one alive and safe, yet knows where the action is. And, for every war correspondent in Peshawar, the action is across the border in the mountain strongholds of Afghanistan . . .

Soon Skelly and his fixer, Najeeb, are driving dusty roads north, in the wake of Mahmood Abdul Khan – ex-Mujahadeen, ex-Taliban, currently good friend of the Allied forces. For Skelly has been promised the scoop of a lifetime, the sort that will allow him to write his own ticket back to the States. He and Najeeb are on the trail of the tribal leader whom every American is after, the biggest fish of them all . . .

0 593 05041 x

COMING SOON FROM BANTAM PRESS

THE SMALL BOAT OF GREAT SORROWS

Dan Fesperman

'HUGELY SATISFYING. THIS BOOK HAS ALL THE POWER OF A
GREAT THRILLER, WITH THE HUMANITY AND INTELLIGENCE
OF THE BEST SERIOUS FICTION'
Fergal Keane

Vlado Petric, former detective in war-torn Sarajevo, has left his
beloved homeland to join his wife and daughter in Germany, where
he scratches a meagre living among the dust of former conflicts on
the building sites of the new Berlin.

Returning home one evening, he finds an enigmatic American
investigator waiting for him. Calvin Pine works for the International
War Crimes Tribunal, and he tells Petric that they want him to go to
The Hague. It doesn't take Petric long to accept, especially when Pine
tells him who they are after: one of the men who may be responsible
for the terrible massacre of Sbrebrenica.

What Petric doesn't know is that he is also being used as bait for a
murderer from the previous generation; a man whose activities in the
Second World War make the current generation of killers look like
amateurs.

As Petric travels from modern-day Germany, through the ruins of
Bosnia, to the peaceful hills of southern Italy where bitter,
unresolved tensions still crackle beneath the surface, the stakes
become all too personal. And he soon finds that investigating the
mysteries of the past can be every bit as dangerous as finding his
way through the war zones of the present.

'DAN FESPERMAN HAS WRITTEN THAT RARE THING: A FINE
AND INTELLIGENT NOVEL THAT MAKES YOU THINK, AND
KEEPS YOU TURNING THE PAGES'
Val McDermid

'THOROUGHLY RECOMMENDED . . . HAS THE TANG OF
SOMEONE WRITING WITH CONVICTION, COMPASSION AND,
ABOVE ALL, AN UNDERSTANDING OF THE BALKANS'
Observer

'GRUELLING, EXCITING, EVENTFUL . . . CLEANLY AND CRISPLY
WRITTEN, WITH A VEIN OF SARDONIC ASIDES'
Literary Review

0 552 15023 1

BLACK SWAN

MISSION FLATS

William Landay

Nothing much happens in Versailles, Maine. Until a body is
found in a cabin up by the lake. The dead man turns out to
be from the Boston DA's office, a prosecutor who had been
investigating a series of gang-related murders in that city. Ben
Truman, Chief of Police, heads down to Boston to follow the
few fragile leads he has in the case. Not welcomed by the
police there, he knows he really should get the message and
disappear back to the sticks. Big city crime is way beyond
anything he's ever dealt with before.

But still Truman refuses to let it go. With the help of a retired
cop who knows all the angles, he becomes embroiled in an
investigation which has its roots in a sequence of deaths
which began twenty years previously.

From its violent and shocking opening, through vivid
depictions of battle-scarred inner city Boston, to its intensely
suspenseful conclusion, *Mission Flats* is the most thrilling
literary crime novel in some years – combining intelligence
and thoughtful, precise prose with page-turning action.

'The most promising début since Scott Turow's
Presumed Innocent'
Sunday Times

'Lyrical, keenly observed, and occasionally as dark as a
wrong turn at midnight, *Mission Flats* is a harrowing,
memorable début by a writer to watch'
Stephen White

'*Mission Flats* has action, excellent surprises and a powerful
ending, but it also has strong, well-written characters.
Landay's début novel is a cut above and I'm looking
forward to his next book'
Phillip Margolin

0 552 14944 6

BANGKOK 8

John Burdett

In surreal Bangkok, city of temples and brothels, where Buddhist monks in saffron robes walk the same streets as world-class gangsters, a US marine sergeant is killed inside a locked Mercedes by a maddened python and a swarm of cobras. Two policeman – the only two in the city not on the take – arrive too late. Minutes later, only one is alive.

The cop left standing, Sonchai Jitpleecheep, is a devout Buddhist and swears to avenge the death of his partner and soul brother. To do so he must use the forensic techniques of the modern policing and his own profound understanding of the mystical workings of the spirit world. Both will be vital as he immerses himself in the moneyed underbelly of Bangkok – where desire rules and where he will eventually find the killer, a predator of an even more sinister variety . . .

'Cracking East meets West thriller introducing a half-Thai, half-American cop whose Buddhist beliefs are as important as his forensic skills. Terrific'
Observer

'A fantastic new thriller with an avenging Buddhist cop as its central character'
Mail on Sunday

'Like a modern-day Indiana Jones adventure written by Evelyn Waugh . . . One of this season's cleverest and most stylist entertainments'
Wall Street Journal

'Quirky and highly entertaining . . . Something to enjoy for its sheer bravado'
New York Times

'A thriller as exotic as it is enthralling, and as provocative as it is obscene'
Harpers

'Impeccably researched, this is sometimes poetic, often exotic, and totally hardcore'
Daily Mirror

0 552 77140 6

A SELECTED LIST OF FINE WRITING
AVAILABLE FROM BLACK SWAN AND CORGI BOOKS

THE PRICES SHOWN BELOW WERE CORRECT AT THE TIME OF GOING TO PRESS. HOWEVER
TRANSWORLD PUBLISHERS RESERVE THE RIGHT TO SHOW NEW RETAIL PRICES ON COVERS
WHICH MAY DIFFER FROM THOSE PREVIOUSLY ADVERTISED IN THE TEXT OR ELSEWHERE.

14746	X	**THE MASTER OF RAIN**	*Tom Bradby*	£6.99
14900	4	**THE WHITE RUSSIAN**	*Tom Bradby*	£6.99
15073	8	**ANGELS AND DEMONS**	*Dan Brown*	£6.99
14551	9	**THE DA VINCI CODE**	*Dan Brown*	£6.99
77140	6	**BANKOK 8**	*John Burdett*	£6.99
14578	5	**THE MIRACLE STRAIN**	*Michael Cordy*	£5.99
14882	2	**LUCIFER**	*Michael Cordy*	£6.99
77206	2	**PEACETIME**	*Robert Edric*	£6.99
77142	2	**CRADLE SONG**	*Robert Edric*	£6.99
99935	0	**PEACE LIKE A RIVER**	*Leif Enger*	£6.99
14654	4	**THE HORSE WHISPERER**	*Nicholas Evans*	£6.99
14738	9	**THE SMOKE JUMPER**	*Nicholas Evans*	£6.99
15023	1	**THE SMALL BOAT OF GREAT SORROWS**		
			Dan Fesperman	£6.99
13991	2	**ICON**	*Frederick Forsyth*	£6.99
14923	3	**THE VETERAN**	*Frederick Forsyth*	£6.99
14877	6	**DYING TO TELL**	*Robert Goddard*	£6.99
14878	4	**DAYS WITHOUT NUMBER**	*Robert Goddard*	£6.99
13678	6	**THE EVENING NEWS**	*Arthur Hailey*	£5.99
99796	X	**A WIDOW FOR ONE YEAR**	*John Irving*	£7.99
77109	0	**THE FOURTH HAND**	*John Irving*	£6.99
14901	2	**WALLS OF SILENCE**	*Philip Jolowicz*	£6.99
15021	5	**THE ANALYST**	*John Katzenbach*	£6.99
14970	5	**THE BUSINESS OF DYING**	*Simon Kernick*	£6.99
14584	X	**THE COLD CALLING**	*Will Kingdom*	£5.99
14585	8	**MEAN SPIRIT**	*Will Kingdom*	£5.99
14944	6	**MISSION FLATS**	*William Landay*	£6.99
14966	7	**BLOOD DATA**	*Adam Lury & Simon Gibson*	£6.99
14798	2	**LAST LIGHT**	*Andy McNab*	£6.99
14799	0	**LIBERATION DAY**	*Andy McNab*	£6.99
15043	6	**TRAITOR'S KISS**	*Gerald Seymour*	£6.99
14816	4	**THE UNTOUCHABLE**	*Gerald Seymour*	£6.99

All Transworld titles are available by post from:
Bookpost, PO Box 29, Douglas, Isle of Man IM99 1BQ
Credit cards accepted. Please telephone +44(0)1624 836000, fax +44(0)1624 837033,
Internet http://www.bookpost.co.uk or
e-mail: bookshop@enterprise.net for details.
Free postage and packing in the UK.
Overseas customers allow £2 per book (paperbacks) and £3 per book (hardback).